EXODUS

Steve White &
Shirley Meier

EXODUS

Steve White &
Shirley Meier

EXODUS

Copyright © 2006 by Steve White & Shirley Meier

A Baen Books Original

Baen Publishing Enterprises
P.O. Box 1403
Riverdale, NY 10471
www.baen.com

ISBN 10: 1-4165-2098-8
ISBN 13: 978-1-4165-2098-6

Cover art by Clyde Caldwell

First printing, January 2007

Distributed by Simon & Schuster
1230 Avenue of the Americas
New York, NY 10020

Library of Congress Cataloging-in-Publication Data:

White, Steve, 1946-
  Exodus / Steve White & Shirley Meier.
    p. cm.
  ISBN-13: 978-1-4165-2098-6
  ISBN-10: 1-4165-2098-8
  I. Meier, Shirley. II. Title.

  PS3573.H474777E96 2007
  813'.54—dc22

                    2006029919

Printed in the United States of America

10 9 8 7 6 5 4 3 2 1

Shirley Meier would like to dedicate this one to Jonathan.

And Steve White can only dedicate it to the indispensable Sandy.

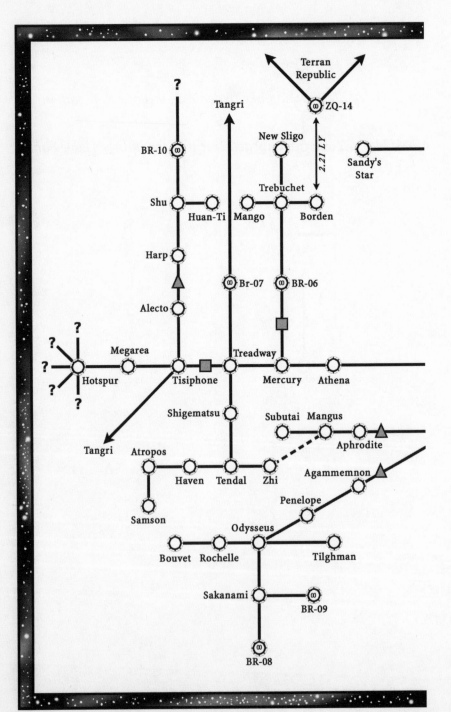

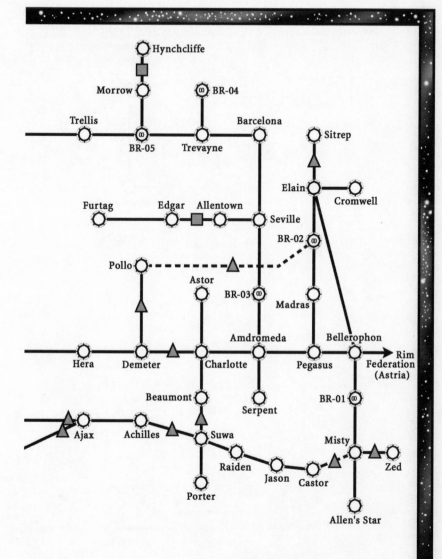

Hynchcliffe

Morrow

Trellis

BR-05

Trevayne

BR-04

Barcelona

Sitrep

Elain

Cromwell

Furtag

Edgar

Allentown

Seville

BR-02

Pollo

Astor

BR-03

Madras

Amdromeda

Bellerophon

Hera

Demeter

Charlotte

Pegasus

Rim
Federation
(Astria)

Serpent

Beaumont

BR-01

Ajax

Achilles

Suwa

Misty

Raiden

Zed

Jason

Castor

Porter

Allen's Star

▲ *Impassible to DT*

■ *Impassible to SMT and DT*

BOOK ONE

BOOK ONE

Prologue

There could be no true night with Sekahmant in the sky.

The sun had set, turning the Auriel Ocean molten in shades of red and orange and *murn*, leaving the giant star unchallenged. Of course, it was only a point source of actinic bluish-*vrel* light—no imaginable object could show a visible disk across even a minor interstellar distance—but that light was of an intensity to banish every other star and trigger the color sensitivity of one's central eye. So Harrok, standing on the terrace of his mountainside villa high above the west coast of Kormat, could clearly see the town below, the coast curving northward in a succession of coves separated by wave-lapped mountains, the mercury-like ocean to the west, and the peaks rising in range upon snowcapped range into the eastern distance.

He could also see this same coast from the tarry deck of a sailing vessel of the Asthians who would, in later centuries, build the town below his villa, for he was *shaxzhu*, and his memories of all his lives was good. But that was a different kind of seeing.

The view had never failed to move him. What a thought in the Mind of Illudor! So much beauty, to be obliterated by that which now only illuminated it! Harrok was no astrophysicist, but he never doubted the truth of the horror that they had revealed with their orbital instruments. After all, educated people had known for generations that the ethereal loveliness of Sekahmant must someday turn destroyer. But so soon?

A rustling sound distracted him as his daughter stepped from the doorway into the Sekahmant-light. Ankaht was the image of her now discarnate mother, tiny and dark, in contrast to Harrok, whose skin was translucent gold—though dulling with age, now—and whose long, thick neck lifted his head to an above-average height. But these were superficial differences. In what really mattered, they were alike, for she, too, was *shaxzhu*. For both parent and child to possess the gift was rare but not unheard of. It lent the father-daughter relationship a sometimes disturbing closeness.

"The decision has been made," she announced without preamble. She had been linked into the global datanet, which Harrok found himself less and less inclined to do these days, when almost all the news was bad. "The nations have granted the new government all the emergency powers it asked for—in effect, dissolved their own existence. (Excitement, tempered by mourning for the old ways.) And the proponents of extended research and development have been overruled. Construction of the first ships will begin with the technology we have now, although further discoveries will be incorporated into later ships if possible. (Deep reservations.)"

Harrok and Ankaht never misinterpreted one another's emotions. The empathetic sense of *selnarm* was extraordinarily strong among all *shaxzhu*, and especially so among those who were also close blood relations.

"Well," he said, "they had little choice. (Resignation.) The last I heard, estimates of the supernova's date had been moved up to two hundred years from now." *No more than three or four incarnations for me,* he thought bleakly, even assuming minimal time spent discarnate.

Not that any such assumption was likely to be justified, given the draconic population control measures that were being proposed. But, again, what choice was there? There was not enough metal in the crust of Ardu to build a fleet of ships that would carry a significant fraction of the present population, or even keep up with its increase. *More time in the dreary less-than-existence of discarnate status for all of us,* he thought.

But it never occurred to him to doubt that the project would succeed, at least in the sense of saving *some* of the Race, nor was his confidence based on the power-urge of politics or the proofs of science or economics. His certitude was a simple philosophical imperative. After all, supernovae also had their existence in the

Mind of Illudor. Could Illudor will His own obliteration? It seemed unlikely. It was also too disturbing a thought to dwell upon—that a Deity might commit suicide—though far less disturbing than the heretical whisper heard more and more of late: that the universe was Illudor's *dream* . . . and that the dream had now turned to nightmare.

He shook off his philosophical musings to listen as Ankaht spoke again.

"I've been asked to join the group that will be planning for the social organization of the ships . . . especially the problem of maintaining cultural continuity for hundreds of years in an environment like that. (Disgust.) We *shaxzhu* will be specially important in maintaining a link with the world we've known. How else will the others even understand there *is* a universe outside those steel walls?" She shuddered. "They want your help, too Father. You probably won't be incarnate when the first ships depart, but your wisdom will be invaluable in the planning stages."

"Of course I'll help in any way I can," Harrok replied. Strong *shaxzhutok* carried obligations as well as privileges and, to be honest, the problems were not without interest. He turned to lead Ankaht inside, then suddenly stopped and loudly clicked the strong, curved claws that tipped his left hand's two primary tentacles. "Oh, yes! I forgot to mention when you arrived this morning; your sister was in a skimmer accident. She's all right, but her new son was killed."

"Oh. (Mild regret.) He was less than half a year old, wasn't he? You don't happen to know who . . .?"

"No. I wasn't there for the birth, and afterwards I couldn't get any sense of who'd picked him. Couldn't have been anyone close."

"I suppose not. Still, it's too bad for whoever he was. I can dimly remember going discarnate in infancy once. What an annoyance! Nothing more frustrating. Anyway, tell Kathmeer I'm glad she's all right. I haven't kept in touch as I should have, but I happen to know that disincarnation would be very inconvenient for her just now. (Grimness.) Inconvenient for everyone, with the birth restrictions we all know are coming."

The reminder of his own earlier thoughts saddened Harrok— sadness which, of course, communicated itself to Ankaht. Silently, father and daughter stepped inside and closed the sliding glass door behind them.

Outside, in an evening filled with wild flixit song and the buzz of second-light insects, Sekahmant continued to glow as if it were an enduring star.

CHAPTER ONE

Rebirth

Prescott City had changed.

No, she reminded herself, for the thousandth time but with undiminished irritation. *Not "Prescott City." Just "Prescott."*

She couldn't remember precisely when, during the past couple of generations, the "City" part had been dropped from popular parlance. But by now the shortened name stood triumphant even in official paperwork and maps. To say "Prescott City" was to declare oneself an incorrigible old fogy. And the Honorable Miriam Ortega—onetime chairperson of the Rim Federation's constitutional convention, subsequently its prime minister for five nonconsecutive terms totaling over forty years, and currently chief justice of its Supreme Judicial Court—was not ready to do that. Even though her one hundred and eleven Standard years arguably gave her every right to.

She shook off the thought. The antigerone treatments to which she was entitled from at least two standpoints—her inarguable contributions to the community, and her residence on a planet the least of whose worries was population pressure—rendered her apparent physiological age a very well-preserved late sixties, and therefore deprived her of whatever excuse senile decay might have provided.

Besides, she told herself, *why shouldn't the name have changed? Everything else has.*

Nowhere was the change more clearly on view than here, at the window of the chief justice's private office on the top floor of Government House.

A hundred and fifty-five years ago—the Standard years that everyone still used, the time it took Old Terra to revolve around Sol—Government House had been built to house the provisional government of this planet of Xanadu, then little more than a raw new military outpost whose civilian workforce had mushroomed to the point of needing such a government . . . but not to the point of needing (or being able to afford) an edifice which would have done credit to some long-established colony world. But Government House had been less a building than a grand gesture—a madly extravagant exercise in what Miriam's mother would have called outrageous *chutzpah.*

Xanadu had been colonized halfway through the Fourth Interstellar War, when humanity and its allies had faced the very real likelihood of something far worse than extermination at the hands of the Bugs: survival not even as slaves, but as meat animals who *knew.* It had been colonized because this system, named Zephrain by its discoverers from the Khanate of Orion, had been only one warp jump away from a teeming Bug "Home Hive" system. Those colonists had known full well that they were living on the front lines of a war whose only outcome could be genocide in one direction or the other. By shaping the planet's native stone into neoclassical monumentality, looming above their prefab "cities," those people (Miriam had often wished she could have known them) had made an eloquent declaration of uncompromising commitment: "This world is ours. We can be killed, but we cannot be moved." In the end they had been neither . . . thanks to the man after whom they had named this city, and whose statue they had raised on a column.

Thus it was that, after the war, Government House had been maintained but never modified. And when a young lawyer named Miriam Ortega had moved here after her mother's death, to be near her father, Sergei Ortega, the local Terran Federation Navy commander, it had still loomed over all it surveyed, crowning its hilltop in a bend of the Alph River, even though the city had grown enough to finally deserve the name.

Now, though, the waves of galactic cosmopolitanism had finally washed over the Rim. Government House lay in the shadows of kilometer-high towers of plasteel and synthetic diamond. Abu'said Field, which had once provided it with an impressive backdrop, had long since yielded to the economics of efficient land use, and a new spaceport served Prescott from what were now the city's outskirts. But the extensive grounds of Government House remained sacrosanct, despite being almost beyond price as real estate, and one could almost imagine that Commodore Prescott looked down with bronze eyes over an unchanged scene from atop his column. . . .

Except that now there was a second column beside it. Miriam's eyes strayed to the statue that crowned that one, and she could no longer put off her reason for being here—this meeting that had nothing to do with the Supreme Judicial Court at all.

Unconsciously, she took out a cigarette and lit it. Cancer, of the lungs and otherwise, had long since been banished into the mists of history for everyone with access to up-to-date biotechnology. But her first inhalation of smoke awakened a scowl on a face that had never been conventionally pretty even in her youth. (Although, the more you looked at it . . .) She angrily stubbed the cigarette out and turned to the two men who had been sitting patiently at the conference table.

"Stupid damned habit," she muttered. "I'm going to quit this summer."

The two men kept straight faces. They'd had a lot of practice at it. They had heard those last six words from Miriam Ortega before each of the last 105 of Xanadu's summers, as it swung around its G5v primary in 0.73 Standard year.

As usual, the small dapper man in academic-style civvies did a better job of concealing his amusement. Admiral Genji Yoshinaka, RFN (ret.), had the pure white hair his one hundred and twenty-eight Standard years warranted, but his skin held the finely wrinkled firmness of one who had started on the antigerone treatments relatively late. His features were of the cast of Old Terra's east Asia, and in fact he was that rarest of birds in the Rim Federation: a native of the mother planet. He had always been a master at keeping those features unreadable, and age had not diminished his subtlety.

The other man could hardly have presented a more striking contrast. Fleet Admiral Sean F. X. Remko, TFN, was still on the active list—although, at one hundred and forty Standard years—he was beginning to think the unthinkable about retirement—and his bear-like frame was clothed in the Rim Federation uniform. That uniform was essentially the black-and-silver of the Terran Federation Navy ... but the TFN of seven and a half Standard decades ago, forgoing the changes in style that had since overtaken the parent service—a sartorial eccentricity fraught with political meaning. Similarly, the beard that had been fashionable among male TFN officers then still adorned a face that reflected more ethnic strains than just the ones his name suggested, for Remko was a product of the melting-pot slums of New Detroit, and his bass voice still held harsh residues of an accent that conferred no great prestige.

"All right," Miriam said with the breezy informality that came naturally to her, and which she could permit herself in this company. She sat down at the head of the table. "I declare the trustees of the person and estate of Fleet Admiral Ian Trevayne in session. Thank you both for coming. If there's no objection, I'd like to dispense with the usual financial report. Instead, I've called this special meeting to discuss the latest medical evaluation I've received from Dr. Mendez and his team."

Instantly, the two men took on a look of focused alertness.

"We haven't seen this evaluation, Miriam," said Yoshinaka carefully. Remko emitted a confirmatory rumble.

"I know, and I'm sorry I haven't had time to make it available to you in advance. But I felt we should meet without delay." She paused with the unconsciously dramatic instinct of a veteran politician. "You see, it appears that we may be able to discharge the trust's primary purpose in five Standard years."

They stared at her with the incredulity of long-deferred and often-disappointed hope.

"Let me review the basic problem," she hurried on, while they were still speechless. "Essentially, it is as Dr. Yuan explained to us before his death fifteen years ago, except that since then, advances in medical technology—about which you can read the details later—have now raised the chances of him surviving the thawing process to about eighty-five percent."

Yoshinaka cleared his throat. "Well, Miriam, this is certainly encouraging news. Thawing him out, as you put it, from the cryogenic bath Dr. Yuan used—without the usual elaborate workup—to preserve his life during the Battle of Zapata has always been half of the problem. But *only* half."

"Right," Remko nodded. "Even if the thawing does succeed, it just brings us back to the reason Dr. Yuan froze him solid in the first place: the battle damage that he took at Zapata!"

"Yes." Yoshinaka nodded, and began to itemize. "Extensive radiation damage, especially to the lower body. Spine severed just below the fifth vertebra. Not to mention the effects of extreme anoxia, concussion . . ." Yoshinaka trailed off miserably as he saw the look on Remko's face, and belatedly remembered what the man under discussion had meant to the burly admiral.

But Remko surprised him. He brought his expression under control and spoke steadily. "That's right. And to all that, you have to add the damage done by the quick-freeze itself. Not that I'm criticizing Dr. Yuan, mind you. It was all he could do. But . . ." He made a baffled gesture.

"Yes," Miriam acknowledged. "Dr. Mendez admits that even today the procedure would be risky in the extreme. Even if he survived it, the chances are that he would suffer permanent impairment—especially in light of the radiation damage, which the freezing did nothing for."

"Well, then, we're back where we started," declared Remko.

"Not altogether. What Dr. Mendez is proposing is that we avoid the risks by not even attempting to salvage this body."

Yoshinaka was the first to grasp it. "Cloning?" he breathed.

"The crucial point," Miriam replied obliquely, "is that Dr. Yuan didn't *entirely* forgo the workup to cryogenic freezing. He couldn't omit it for the brain tissue, given the potential for really irreparable damage. So he did a crash job. And Dr. Mendez has been able to confirm that the brain itself is essentially undamaged."

"Just a moment, Miriam," Yoshinaka interrupted. "I think I see where this is heading. And while I'm certainly no expert, I am aware that selective cloning and force-growing of organs and tissue is almost routine by now. I also have no doubt of the ability of Dr. Mendez's people to graft a 'bridge' into a severed spinal cord, and to make the necessary neural connections. But we're talking about a *lot* of replacements, each one carrying a potential for rejection or other failure. So we're still faced with the mathematics of cumulative risk."

"Actually, Genji, you don't quite see it. We're not talking about a bunch of transplants, but only one: the brain itself. Granted, it's a highly—indeed, uniquely—complex transplant. But Dr. Mendez is confident he and his people can do it."

The two men stared at her. For once, it was Remko who spoke first.

"A . . . a full-body clone?" His voice held a succession of emotions: incredulity rising to horrified realization and then to revulsion.

"Miriam," Yoshinaka said sternly, "we all want this. But you, of all people, should know the law on the subject of human clones: they are legal persons, with all the rights pertaining thereto. In fact, this very legal principle provided the incentive to develop the technology of selective body-part cloning. To use a clone of oneself as a . . . a source of spare parts is as illegal—and, I might add, as morally leprous—as using one's child for such a purpose. And if this is true of chopping organs out of such a clone one by one, it must apply equally to taking the brain out of it and putting another one in!"

"I don't know anything about legalities," Remko growled. "But I do know the admiral wouldn't want to have anything to do with this!" Whenever Remko said *the admiral* in that particular tone of voice, there was no doubt in anyone's mind which admiral he meant. "It's ghoulish! He'd rather be . . . the way he is now." He gestured vaguely toward the city, in the direction of the medical center whose subbasement held an obscenely coffinlike tank, perennially filmed with frost.

"Of course I'm aware of the legal precedents," Miriam said evenly. "With all due modesty, I must claim a better knowledge of them than either of you. And I also know how he would react to what you think I'm suggesting. Actually, I think I can claim a better knowledge of *that* as well."

That silenced them. They had only been Ian Trevayne's friends and comrades in arms. Miriam Ortega had been his lover.

"In fact," she continued, "when Dr. Mendez broached the idea, I raised all the objections you've thought of—and also a few you haven't—in the strongest possible language." Both her listeners knew what *that* could mean in Miriam Ortega's case. "He hastened to assure me that what he was offering was a way around these very difficulties. He believes that by a special application of the techniques used to produce individual organs—a kind of 'reverse engineering'—his team can produce a full body clone *minus* one organ: in this case, the brain.

"The clone would be effectively anencephalic—incapable of any higher brain functions. In effect, it would be born 'brain dead.' Now, for a very long time—I'd have to look it up to tell you just exactly how long, but certainly reaching back to the dawn of the Space Age, before the discovery of warp points—the definition of 'death' has been legally settled. In those days, you see, it had become possible to artificially keep a human body 'alive' by the traditional definition—a heartbeat and a pulse—after the brain function had irrevocably ceased. So the definitions had to change. A brainless clone will be legally dead, and therefore will have no rights. It will be kept in that state while it is brought to maturation—a process which can be accelerated by a factor of four, which is why I mentioned the figure of five years. That's how long it will take to grow the clone to the physiological age of eighteen to twenty, while keeping it exercised with the same techniques used for other forms of long-term life support, to prevent muscular deterioration. At that point, we transplant the brain."

"So," said Yoshinaka slowly, "his fiftyish mind will wake up inside a twenty-year-old body."

"His *own* twenty-year-old body," Miriam said firmly. "That's what makes Dr. Mendez so confident of his ability to perform the transplant."

"But . . . Well, as I said before, I'm no expert. But I seem to recall reading somewhere that if a clone is produced from postembryonic cells—cells taken from an adult, that is—then the clone's cells may 'wear out' faster, resulting in premature aging."

"Oh, yes; that problem has been recognized since the early days of cloning, more than five centuries ago. But today we have the antigerone treatments to counteract it."

"All right. You and Dr. Mendez have obviously thought this through. And just as obviously, you *believe* you have thought through the legal repercussions." Yoshinaka held up a hand as the chief justice started to speak. "Yes, I know. It's your field. But hear me out. I don't doubt you're right in principle. But are you sure your desire for this to happen isn't clouding your judgment about whether this will really stand up to a legal challenge? There may be a revulsion from it on ethical grounds, whatever the law may say. As Sean said earlier, there's something about the whole idea that seems—"

"Ghoulish," Remko repeated, but with less vehemence than before.

"Yes. And you should know, Miriam, that when people want badly enough for the law to produce a certain result, they can usually find a way to make it do so."

"Of course. I know all about the 'court of public opinion.' And I'm *counting* on it!" For the first time, she flashed the expressive smile that had never lost its power to transfigure her face. "Have you forgotten who it is we're talking about? And what he means to the people of the Rim Federation? If you need a reminder, just go to that window over there and look down at the second column out front, beside Prescott's."

They were silent. Of course they hadn't forgotten. How could they?

Eight decades before, in the darkest days of the Terran Federation's terminal civil war, Yoshinaka had been Vice Admiral Ian Trevayne's chief of staff and Remko his flag captain. They had helped him lead his task force through the rebelling Fringe World systems to Zephrain, gateway to the still-loyal Rim systems. There, he had forged a legend as well as a military dynamo that had taken the last resources of the Fringe Worlds' new "Terran Republic" to finally batter to a halt in the bloodbath of Zapata—blood that had included Trevayne's own. But his sacrifice had saved the Rim for the Terran Federation.

The Federation to which it still stoutly insists it belongs, Miriam reflected. *Even while calling itself the "Rim Federation." And while* not *belonging to the Pan-Sentient Union into which the Terran Federation has now amalgamated.*

Go figure, as Mother would have said.

Oh, well, I ought to be grateful that humans insist on complicating their lives into tangles. If they didn't, we lawyers would have to find honest work.

"When the public understands that there's finally a chance to revive him, to have the legend walking among them again," she told her fellow trustees, "they'll be solidly behind it. I doubt if any legal challenges will even be raised. If they are, they won't succeed—even though I will of course have to recuse myself if the question reaches the Supreme Judicial Court."

"You're probably right," Yoshinaka conceded. "So we can't avoid facing the question of whether *we're* behind it. Whatever the law may say, you can't deny that there are ethical issues here. And . . . possibly emotional issues," he added, meeting her eyes unflinchingly.

"I assure you that all of that has occurred to me. And I am compelled to say that if *I* can deal with those 'emotional issues,' the two of you should certainly be able to." They made no attempt to answer the unanswerable. "As for the ethical issues . . . maybe I *have* talked myself into rationalizing them away. But do you really believe we'll ever have a better chance than this? We've waited seventy-five years now, hoping for some 'silver bullet' that will allow him to come back to us unscathed and unaltered, with no messy ambiguities. Well, we're all old enough—and more than old enough!—to know that life almost never works out in such a way as to spare us hard choices. Now life has lived down to expectations . . . and I for one am prepared to make the choice." She took a deep breath. "We three go back too far to need any formal procedure. You know how I stand. But . . ." She raised her right hand. "Well?"

After a moment, Yoshinaka raised his. After a longer moment, so did Remko.

So it was decided. And so the project was put in rotation, and continued for five years.

The sun shone in the crystalline blue sky of Old Terra's Mediterranean Sea, so brilliant that he must squint against it.

But even in that dazzlement, he could make out the chestnut-haired little girl of four, standing on the beach up ahead and waving to him.

"Courtenay!" he called, and began to run toward her.

But then it happened, as it always did.

The Mediterranean sun swelled and bloated into an all-consuming glare into which the little girl vanished—just as she, and her infant sister, Ludmilla, and their mother, Natalya, had vanished into the fusion fires the rebels had ignited over the civilian housing areas of the Jamieson Archipelago on Galloway's World.

He screamed . . .

But all at once, it was gone. And realization came crashing back. He was in the Zapata system, in the midst of the long-awaited battle. The rebels (he would *not* call them the "Terran Republic") had finally turned on his fleet as it advanced along the warp lines to reestablish contact between the Rim and the rest of the still-loyal Federation. Li Han—he had no doubt as to the rebel commander's identity—had already sprung a couple of nasty tactical and technological surprises on him. But he hadn't let self-reproach paralyze him. He had just ordered Sean Remko to take the cruiser screen in and hit the rebel carriers while their fighters were still rearming after a first strike that had drawn more blood than it should have. Then he had sent Genji Yoshinaka on an errand to the flagship's intelligence center, just as the rebels' incoming strategic bombardment missiles had begun to appear on the sensors ... and then the universe had abruptly turned to noise and concussion ...

Yes. He must have lost consciousness ... but surely not for long, as he had no sensation of time having passed.

All these recollections came to him so swiftly that they had flashed through his mind before his eyes opened. Then he saw he was not on the flag bridge of TFNS *Horatio Nelson*.

Other realizations came crowding in. He was lying on his back, and around the periphery of vision—his head seemed to be secured somehow—he could see medical equipment.

So they've taken me to sick bay, he thought. But even as he thought it, he realized something else: there was none of the noise of a warship of space engaged in battle. There wasn't even the barely audible vibratory hum of the drive. *Am I deaf?* he wondered with sudden alarm.

Then people began to enter his field of vision, led by a doctor. He didn't recognize the man—he certainly wasn't Dr. Yuan, *Nelson's* chief medical officer. He was a much younger man ... and he seemed to be in a civilian lab coat.

He opened his mouth to speak, but only a dry rasp came. *Must have been out for a while after all,* he thought. He swallowed painfully, licked his lips, and tried again.

"Doctor," he croaked, "send for Commodore Yoshinaka. It is imperative that I receive an update at once."

As he heard himself speak, it occurred to him that he had just proven he hadn't been deafened. *So where are the sounds I ought to be hearing?* He thrust the thought away. *First things first.* He tried to rise. He found he was completely unable to move. His body was, indeed, secured. And it seemed incredibly weak. And, beyond that, there seemed something ... odd about the way his body felt.

The doctor leaned over him and spoke in an accent he had come to know and love: that of the Xandies, as the people of Xanadu, Zephrain A II, called themselves. And his face held the mixed blood of that world. Only ... as he spoke on, there seemed something just a little bit odd about his speech. Maybe he came from some out-of-the-way part of the planet. And his firmly professional authoritativeness was overlaid with something that seemed almost to transcend respect.

"Admiral Trevayne, please relax. You mustn't try to move. I'm Dr. Jamal Mendez, your attending physician."

"Dr. Yuan—"

"Admiral, Dr. Yuan isn't here. You are not aboard your flagship. Nor are you in the Zapata system. The battle is over. You're in a hospital on Xanadu, in Prescott." Observing closely, Mendez noticed that the dark-brown eyes blinked in puzzlement, as though having heard something that wasn't quite right. He wondered why. "There are a great many things you will have to adjust to. But rest assured, you are perfectly safe."

"How . . . how long was I unconscious?"

Dr. Mendez hesitated, then reached a decision. "It is now the year 2524, Standard Terran reckoning. You have been in a state of cryogenic suspension for just under eighty-one years. The war has been over for very nearly that long. Now, Admiral, I want you to . . . Admiral? *Admiral?* Oh, *damn!* Nurse—the sedative. Quick!"

As he slipped down into the ocean of oblivion, Trevayne held onto one thought with the tightness of a drowning man gripping a piece of driftwood. *We won! We must have won. The fact that I'm alive, and on Xanadu rather than some rebel planet, must mean we won. It must!*

But then he could hold on no longer. Unconsciousness reclaimed him.

When he next opened his eyes, they had moved him into a pleasant pastel-shaded recovery room. It had a window, which evidently faced west. Dust motes drifted through the afternoon sun of Zephrain A. The binary system's secondary component must be at periastron, for he could make out a tiny orange more-than-star-but-less-than-sun in the daylight sky.

Well, so much for any lingering doubts about where I am, he thought dryly.

Other sensations began to register. He now lay in a conventional bed, with no restraints save his own overwhelming weakness. He couldn't sit up, but he could move his arms. In an unconscious, characteristic gesture, he brought his right hand up to rub his beard.

The skin of his jaw was smooth.

Heh! Haven't felt that *in a while. Wonder why they shaved me?* With another unconscious gesture—one of perplexity—he moved his hand to his forehead and ran it backward, to smooth what was left of his hair over his scalp.

His palm encountered a full thatch of short but very thick hair.

For a space, he simply felt that hair.

As a native of chronically overcrowded Old Terra, he hadn't gotten access to the antigerone treatments until middle age. By then, male-pattern baldness had begun to do its work. That could be reversed by genetic retroviruses... but he had never done so, regarding it as just a higher-technology way than toupees for vain middle-aged men to make jackasses of themselves. Instead, he had contented himself with the traditional compensation of growing a beard—which, fortuitously, had been currently fashionable. But now...

For what possible reason would they have done it? he wondered, continuing to feel that inexplicable hair. After a while, the effort of keeping his arm up was too much, and he lowered his hand.

As he did, he noticed the back of that hand. Something seemed odd. The veins didn't look as prominent as he remembered, and the flesh looked firmer, and the knuckles less wrinkled.

He held the hand out so the back was flat. With the thumb and forefinger of his other hand, he pinched the skin covering a knuckle. It snapped instantly back into smoothness.

He lay for a time, thinking very hard.

He was still thinking when the door opened and several people entered, with Dr. Mendez in the lead and other medical people behind him. But they parted to let a woman through: a woman with all the typical indicia of advanced age on long-term antigerone therapy.

But that was the only thing about her that was typical. There was no mistaking that face... that vivid, unique face with its combination of high cheekbones and strongly curved nose and marvelously expressive mouth that now formed the smile that was like no one else's...

"No," he heard himself whisper.

Miriam Ortega walked to the side of the bed and kissed him on the forehead with infinite gentleness.

"Welcome back, Ian," she said softly.

CHAPTER TWO

Bug-Eyed Monsters

Toshi Springer paged through the images she'd just downloaded from the main telescope. "How's that coffee coming, David?"

The other grad student looked up from the antiquated old machine. "A watched pot never drips." He poured their cups and came back to his workstation. "You'll like this. My dad sent it along with the latest inquiry as to how my thesis was coming along."

Her eyebrows rose as she sipped. "This tastes like Hina coffee from Terranova."

Her friend smiled. "It is. Enjoy." In the dim, quiet hours at Philonea University's astronomy labs, when the downloads came in it was sometimes hard to stay alert and coffee was the drug of choice for most students and researchers.

She sipped again, savoring. "He can't be that upset with you if he's sending you good coffee."

David Nanmin smiled, a little twistedly. "He and my mom are still trying to convince me that if I want to 'do' astronomy then I shouldn't still be stuck doing real-time observation and that I'd be *wonderful* in the more lucrative 'warp-line studies.' That's why they send something as luxurious as that coffee, to make a point. My aunt Mai just told me that I'd make more money writing e-greeting cards."

She nodded. "Yup. And they don't realize that not only is every student who can connect the dots crowding warp research fields, you and I and the other telescope geeks just can't—or don't want to—wrap our heads around that particular brand."

Since all travel between star systems was by the warp lines discovered hundreds of years ago and allowing travel time to drop to days or weeks instead of years or centuries, "real sky" astronomy had been relegated to the university equivalent of the study of leeching as a viable medical treatment. The t-geeks would counter that argument with the one that people still needed to study stars that no one had found warp points to yet, among other things. This didn't give them any more status, however, and the tendency of some professors to get vehement about it made some people think of the t-geeks as raving loons.

It was the sort of thing that grad students in the bowels of "Fort Telescope"—as people referred to the building—fulminated on in the wee hours of the morning. Even with telescope platforms in the mid to outer Bellerophon System, people still ended up sitting in the offices in the middle of the night because of computer schedules, giving everyone plenty of time to think among the dusty old holograms of Bellerophon and other star systems surrounding it.

He reached out and held her hand. "You getting a hard time from your folks?"

"Not so bad. The problem is my unit."

"Yeah." His voice took on the fruity tones of a video announcement. "The Few, the Arrogant, the Weekend Warriors of the Reserve... present company excepted, of course. Do any of them even *realize* that if you want to get into Survey, this gives you an edge?"

Behind them, one of the old computers, flat-screen Orion-made, hiccupped and rebooted. Then the next one down the line did the same.

"My commanders understand. They know that you still need this as a solid foundation for Survey navigation. David, you're being a little hard on the guys. I mean Lieutenant McGee and Sergeant De Vega are *not* idiots."

He snorted. "Yes. I admit, that they're fine, and so is Katya, but the rest of them? Just because they haven't seen what a real war looks like doesn't make them experts in anything and it doesn't give them the right to swan around and sneer at you, because you're a t-geek and the best damned navigator they've got."

She just didn't know how much he felt for her. People could look down their noses at him but let them glance sideways at *her* and he wanted to rip their heads off. Her unit wasn't any different from the bulk of the reserves. They were maintained at full strength, not only through Terran space but through all the allied races.

The problem was that the most action that the reserves saw was on the practice range and in the old in-system training ships. Toshi's mother had fought the Tangri in the last war and her father had been chasing those pirates—more likely New Horde—before they married, so she'd grown up in a military family. *More than some of these middle-class idiots who think they're wolves because they have the uniform on.* David himself was a scholarship brat who'd won every award available, but he had the Red Lake quarter burr underlying his "midsea" accent, and an attitude to match.

It was proving to be a more dangerous universe than anyone had thought. Though only the Bugs had proven intractable when it came to negotiation, and since they tended to just devour any meat source without caring whether it could talk, they'd been ruthlessly squashed.

The bigger problem was the races that had the idea that losing the last war was just a fluke. Like the Tangri, for instance. They just could not see anyone else as anything but cattle, and kept trying to prove it. Of course every raid that a New Horde, supposedly a splinter group not controlled by their home world government, made had always been waved away as not a central-world responsibility. The last time, about fifteen years ago, they'd been smacked down pretty thoroughly by Fleet Admiral Remko. All good reasons to have not only the military on its toes but the reserves as well.

Of course, if you had forces at strength and full reserves but very little fighting going on then the soldiers tended to get weird ideas of what war was.

Toshi smiled at David. "They think that each and every one of them is the new incarnation of 'Ian the Great' or a clone of 'Li Han, Terror of the Spaceways.'"

David covered his face with his hand, setting his cup down to wave the other at her. "You watch some of the kitschiest shows."

"And you aren't a fan of *Khan the Merciless*?"

He reeled back in his chair, both hands over his heart. "I'm hit! A palpable hit!"

She laughed, as he'd intended. "That'll show you." She set her empty cup down. "We should get back to this. There's another download coming up soon and we need to get this checked and cleared for the professor, first thing."

"Sure."

They turned back to their workstations just as they both rebooted again. They glanced over at each other. "Both of them going down together?" David said.

"Let me. . . ." Toshi trailed off as she began checking her system. "It seems to have overloaded."

"Mine too. Maybe we have a nova coming in?"

"Or something like it. I'm dropping in more filters." The signal took twenty minutes to get out to the distant telescope arrays; another twenty for the new download to come back.

"Look at this." Toshi indicated the glaringly bright point washing out the upper right-hand quadrant of the screen. "That's not a nova."

David scratched his head. "It's a flare of some kind, but what could cause that?"

She stared at the screen. "Well. I don't recognize it as a natural phenomenon . . . not coming out of Bufo like that."

"To be honest, I don't recognize it as anything I've seen before either."

"Weird idea I have, David."

"Yeah?"

She glanced sideways at him. "Could it be artificial?"

He stared at her. "Artificial?" For a long moment they looked at each other. Then he turned to his workstation. "No. It couldn't be. It's the wrong frequency for that nutbar hobbyist with his model rockets who was ruining all the downloads a few years ago. Besides, the police shut him down as a danger to in-system traffic. See?" He pointed out the comparison screens he'd pulled up. She started pulling up the last series on her own screen. "There's no obvious motion showing between the two arrays, so it has to be outside the system, whatever it is."

She looked up at David. "It's no frequency *we* would use." He turned away from his workstation, to stare at her as she continued. "It's too steady to be a weapon flare—there's no maneuvers scheduled for another three weeks."

"Why don't I bring up the spectrogram? Maybe that will tell us what it is. It could be a minor flare-up out of Bufo, there's always something happening in that nebula."

"If it's in the nebula it can't be artificial."

"Well, nothing could deal with the radiation."

"Right. But it's a hell of a lot further out than in-system, because it's on both downloads." She tried another couple of tests. "There's a parallax though, that puts the flare about . . . half a light year or so out."

They stared at the spectrum on her screen. "Toshi. That's . . . what the hell *is* that?"

She exhaled softly. "It's a drive flare."

"A what?" he asked with an uncomprehending look. Then the puzzlement cleared from his face, to be replaced by incredulity. "You mean . . . are you saying . . . a *reaction* drive?"

"Yes," she said softly.

"The hell it is," he said flatly. "Nobody's ever . . . And besides, it's not the same spectrum. There," he said as she pulled up another spectrogram. "It's not the same at all."

"Yes, it is." She pulled the pattern all the way to the violet end of the scale where it matched the downloaded image perfectly. "It's blue-shifted."

"Do we wake the professor?"

She clutched the edge of the desk. "Get him out of bed! If it's blue-shifted that means whatever it is, is coming here!"

"Professor! Professor Gerard! Question! Professor!" The media hounds swarmed the old lecture hall, bringing more excitement to the university than since the North Tower burned down. They were ranked in the first rows of the seats, rising away from the dais with its ranked dignitaries for the press conference. The seats reserved for the military were empty as the reporters tried to get the jump on their competitors by starting things early. "Professor, is it true that another alien species has been disco—" "Professor Gerard, can you comment on—" "Chancellor—" "Professor Duane, your colleague believes—"

The chancellor, who had been trying to get some quiet, turned up the gain on her microphone until the feedback squeal cut through the avalanche of questions. Into the ringing silence after she'd cut it back, she said. "Thank you. Thank you, genteels." Her eye skimmed over the newsies, where it was caught by the folded tight ears and pained expressions on the faces of the sole Orion news crew in the room. Least Claw Showaath'sekakhu-jahr, and her team were all mavericks as far as Orion was concerned.

It had taken the intervention of the Khan himself to get her into the journalism training at all and that had been on Yowl, the first Alliance jointly settled world, hardly a prestigious school. The journalist was shorter than most females, her pelt a glossy, aristocratic sable with striking bright tawny gold flashes from her nose up either side of her head. She was the only surviving child of Great Claw Meerheeowa'rehfrak, and when she'd decided that professional curiosity was a virtue her father had publicly supported her. Of course, the human media had been fascinated with her and at least one pundit speculated that an Orion journalist—if she hadn't been so visible—would make an excellent spy for the Khanate. But that very visibility was, in part, her safety from those kinds of charges.

She, like her home planet, was outré enough that they often fixed the attention of the Terran media, especially since the Federation had an eye to promoting its own success stories.

Her crew were brown or golden-pelted, her camera-male a brindle, whose harness proclaimed his status as considerably higher than a simple minion. He tended to hover. *Bodyguard,* Toshi thought from where she stood next to David, behind the professors, the chancellor and the board of directors. Showaath and her crew were the only aliens in the hall, next to the mechanical feeds. The infection of human journalism was slow to spread.

It had been complete coincidence that she was even on Bellerophon, at the shipyards, covering the Orion deal for a new class of merchant ship and the emergency refit of an Orion carrier, when this had come up.

Toshi and David stood behind the dignitaries, him in his gray suit with the worn elbows, her in her full dress blacks—she'd had to run over to the apartment to grab them when the press conference was called. It had already been made very clear since last night that she was no longer a reservist. Everyone was already being called into active duty. It wasn't as though anyone *expected* the new aliens to be hostile, but it was certainly better to be prepared.

It bothered her that they both had to be there. The next downloads were coming in and that would give them more data. She checked the link in her ear—nothing useful yet. She didn't want to be standing here while suits discussed what to do with . . . Her thoughts ground to a halt as the door opened and the Fleet Admiral Waldeck himself and his staff entered and took places on the dais. *He always did know how to make an entrance.* The crowd of journalists murmured into their mics or directed bumble-cams higher, but showed admirable restraint, for once. That could have been because of Waldeck's presence. Even though he was all of 132, he still carried himself ramrod straight. Some of these very newsies used the term "martinet" when referring to him, but only the most extreme. Despite his white hair he was fit, though he carried the Waldeck beefiness.

"He hath a hungry look," David leaned over to whisper in her ear.

"Yes. 'But he is not lean and I fear him not,'" she misquoted back at him. "Shut up, someone might pick us up." She hid her smile behind her hand, before brushing it away over her chin as if scratching an itch. A staffer leaned over and handed Waldeck something and she just caught the discreet glance at Showaath. *Nose plugs for his allergy.* If she tried to get an in-depth story he didn't want to be sneezing all over her. Of course his antipathy for Orions was known if not, as he would put it, "bandied about" and Showaath was surely aware of it as well.

"Genteels," the chancellor said again, using the latest, squeakiest new, fashionable term for a group of mixed beings. "Thank you for being here on such short notice."

Professor Duane looked like hell, but then so did they all. It had been two days of intense analysis, calling in Professor Gerard and his students before they were sure enough of the data to inform the university. It had meant that no one went home and everyone even grudged the time for brief ablutions in the change-rooms off the gym. That and eating a lot of takeout. All other projects the telescope arrays had been booked for had been dropped and every extrasystemic platform had been brought to bear on the distant drive flares.

The chancellor had called Waldeck the same hour, not only getting through, but getting him out of bed, once she'd reassured herself that her particular set of weirdoes hadn't just gone off half-cocked.

"Thank you for coming. First of all, I would like to formally announce that, two days ago, Professor Duane's team detected a photon drive flare coming out of the Bufo Nebula." She held up her hand as the hubbub threatened to begin again. Toshi suppressed a smile to herself at hearing herself and David referred to as a "team." *Makes us sound more legitimate and better funded.* "We are certain that the flares—and I use the plural quite deliberately, are decelerating a number of sublight ships. How many, we cannot yet estimate."

"They are approximately point zero five light years away and, from the observations, appear to be three months away at the rate they are decelerating. At this point I will turn the floor over to Fleet Admiral Waldeck."

"Thank you, Chancellor Davenport."

". . . we will be calling in the fleet as a precautionary measure."

"Damned straight you will." First Space Lord Li Han of the Terran Republic Navy was not in the habit of addressing her media console in such tones. She rose from the chair by the window more abruptly than she'd intended. Like so many abrupt motions these days, it had a disagreeable way of reminding her of her 123 Standard years, even more than the pure white hair she saw in her mirror. It could have been worse, though. Here on Bowditch, the moon of Beaufort that served as the Terran Republic's capital, the gravity was only 0.5 standard Terran G—considerably less than half that of her native Hangchow. Her enjoyment of the sensation worried her, even though she knew it shouldn't. As far back as she could remember, people had been warning her that she was in chronic danger of becoming a bore on the subject of her own imagined inadequacies and unworthiness.

She dismissed the thought and considered Cyrus Waldeck instead. If she knew the Rim Federation Navy admiral, he would do everything necessary to make sure that people felt safe and not inclined to do anything rash.

"Query? Action required?" The unit's dulcet tones were reminiscent of an ancient entertainment program.

"Yes, unit off." It shut itself off, cutting off Waldeck's description of his intentions regarding the new aliens.

Li didn't indulge in the practice of naming the control system in her office, though her secretary did address it so. Peeves? Jeeves? Something like that. It seemed an immoderation.

She was not in the habit of saying "Why now?" or "Why me?" either. Things would happen as they would and she had no intention of applying a petty desire to inconvenience her to an insensate universe, though if she remembered correctly her grandfather on New Tibet had insisted that if anything the universe was actually working toward a benevolence of some kind.

She allowed herself a grin at the recollection. With advancing age, she found herself remembering him more and more, in a kind of rediscovery. Her family on Hangchow hadn't exactly emphasized that element of her ancestry—not too surprising, considering the history of Chinese-Tibetan relations on Old Terra, at least as far back as the eighth century when the Tibetan Empire (every dog has his day, as the saying goes) had cut Tang Dynasty China off from its central Asian provinces and the horses and horsemen that went with them, and set its decline in motion.

The thought of horses brought her back to her earlier glum reflections, for no reason other than a nickname—a stupid nickname, inasmuch as the Tangri didn't really resemble horses in the least. Be that as it might, the Horse Heads were at it again and they weren't going to stop no matter what. And then there was the "ReNurturers" lobby group. They'd formed as a response to the faction arguing the necessity of wiping out the Horse Heads completely. "The Tangri Problem," they called it. It was something that Li herself had considered and was still considering with less and less reluctance. It was the old capital-punishment argument. *That* particular murderer isn't going to kill anyone else. How could she, in good conscience weigh the continuing deaths of her own—and she had to consider all Allied species her own on some level—against the genocide of another species?

It was the thought of genocide that made the ReNurturers' argument compelling. Foster Tangri young to other races. Have them raised outside their own culture. Retain everything possible of their culture but excise the rabid xenophobia. That raised a whole nest of other problems. For example, who would ever agree to parent such children in the first place? And on and on.

Wouldn't it be less paternalistic to just apply the Final Solution to the whole mess? It was a resolution less dangerous to Terrans in the long run. She *hated* pirates with a vengeance and the source of that piracy was the New Hordes. Li tried hard not to hate, but in this case found it impossible. It was vileness. It was evil. If someone—and she didn't care what shape that someone had—if someone was prepared to hurt you, to kill you or your children, your family, then they'd stepped outside of the definition of sentient and placed themselves in the realm of monster. They'd made the choice to become monsters and thus had lost the argument that they did not deserve the treatment meted out to fiends.

And now there was a whole new problem landing on her desk out of Bellerophon dragging everyone's attention away.

Her eyes strayed to the night sky outside the window and sought the great purplish-blue globe of Beaufort—the birthplace of Fiona MacTaggart, whose murder had ignited the Fringe Revolution. She spared the always-inspiring sight a moment's reflection, then sat down at her desk, manually pulling up the files she'd been studying.

No doubt about it, it's a colossus. A beautiful colossus, if you're into that kind of firepower. Of course the purists and Orions would make the arguments for smaller ships, preferably fighters. And of course the disadvantages of reaction drives were too obvious for discussion. In terms of sheer speed and strength, however . . .

It could be necessary that they have something on the same order of size the next time the Horse Heads came boiling out of their space. She massaged her temples. *And we'll have to see how many of these ships we need if the new aliens prove hostile.*

Genji Yoshinaka had put this moment off as long as possible.

It hadn't been hard to delay the inevitable. First, there had been the long period of physical therapy. Dr. Mendez and his team had knitted Ian Trevayne's new body and his brain together with consummate skill. Indeed, their work had been beyond criticism. But fine-tuning those links into the smoothly functioning gestalt of old had taken time. Overlapping with that had been an intensive reeducation covering eight Standard decades of history and all the social and technological changes that implied even in this era when lengthened life spans had moderated the pace of change. So there had been little or no opportunity for sightseeing.

But the inevitable cannot be delayed forever, which is why it is called the inevitable. Now Trevayne stood on the grounds of

Government House, staring aghast at the statue-crowned column flanking Andrew Prescott's, while Yoshinaka shriveled with embarrassment.

"I *tried* to talk them out of it," he finally wailed, breaking the silence.

Trevayne didn't hear him. He was in a temporary state of shock, seeing nothing but the pedestal of the column, with its carved inscription in quotation marks. Finally, he turned to Yoshinaka with an *et tu, Brute?* look.

"You actually let them—"

"I *told* them you never said that!" Yoshinaka protested. "But they wouldn't listen. Somehow, everyone had become firmly convinced that at the Second Battle of Zephrain, when the Republicans—the *rebels*, I meant to say—were first detected entering this system, you sent it out as a signal to the fleet. I told them over and over that they were confusing you with Admiral Togo, at the Battle of Tsushima."

"Lord Nelson, at the Battle of Trafalgar," Trevayne corrected automatically. "Togo stole it from him."

"All right, all right! I'm not going to get into *that* old argument again. And—" a flash of uncharacteristic acerbity "—it's your own fault, you know, for naming your flagship after your hero Horatio Nelson. Somebody must have looked him up in history, and unearthed that signal to the fleet, and associated it with you, and . . . well, one thing just led to another."

Trevayne didn't argue, for he had turned back to the column with its inscribed "quotation." He shook his head slowly.

"'Terra expects that every man will do his duty,'" he recited numbly. "So *that's* what I'm remembered for nowadays!" He shook his head again. "Bloody hell!"

"Not just for that," said Yoshinaka with renewed gentleness, smiling inwardly at those last two words, so quintessentially Trevayne. At that moment, there was no question in his mind, on any level, as to who this man really was.

Such certainty didn't always come easily.

Granted, the long-legged, six-foot-three body that held Ian Trevayne's mind was recognizably his—as it must have appeared when he had been in the Academy. His clean-shaven face was less weathered than the fifty-odd-year-old version Yoshinaka remembered so well. But by now he had spent enough time outside for the rays of Zephrain A to have brought out some color, in collaboration with the genes bequeathed by a late-twentieth-century Jamaican immigrant to England. His dark coloring was the only visible sign of that legacy, for his features were those of northwestern Europe—but they hadn't settled into harshness, nor his voice into roughness. And of course he had all his brown-black hair.

And yet he didn't *move* like a youth of twenty. Oh, there was none of the advancing stiffness of middle age. But neither was there any of the residual awkwardness of postadolescence. Once the brain had meshed its gears with the body, the reflexes taught by five decades of experience had taken control of those supple young muscles and joints. The effect was subtle, but odd. So was the fact that the clear, youthful voice spoke as an experienced and mature man speaks. Likewise, the young face was set in lines that were not young—the lines of a man who knows who he is, in a way no young man can know.

Also, there was the matter of clothes. In his capacity as governor-general of the Rim, an office to which he had appointed himself after creating it, Trevayne had always indulged his flair for understatedly elegant civilian attire—one of the many unexpected facets of his personality. But now, his fashion sense hopelessly adrift after eight decades of dizzying change in styles, he had put himself in the hands of a tailor. The tailor had been unable to mentally edit out his legendary patron's youthful appearance, and Trevayne now unwittingly projected a look that, while hardly "flashy," was certainly not in keeping with his old sartorial persona.

It all added to the difficulty of knowing just how to react to him. The absence of his beard didn't help either.

Trevayne himself was thinking of that beard at that moment, and he unconsciously rubbed his smooth jaw as he gazed up at the bronze statue surmounting the column. He knew everyone had been expecting him to grow it back. He hadn't, for two reasons. One was apprehension that it would probably come out as the thin, patchy horror that was all most college boys could achieve. The other was that during his long cryogenic sleep beards had passed into the realm of the old-fashioned, verging on archaic. People who had known him in his previous life found it surprising that that concerned him—but on a certain level it did. Cultivating an image of crusty conservatism was one thing, but he'd be damned and roasting in hell before he'd appear *quaint*.

He shook himself. "Well, it can't be helped now, can it? There's nothing more futile than trying to correct legend. After a while, one comes to the realization that the windmill is winning. Let's go and—"

"Admiral!"

"Sean!" Trevayne turned with a smile toward the broad steps leading up to Government House's colonnaded façade, between the two projecting wings. Sean Remko, trailed by a bevy of staffers, was descending. He advanced with a smile of his own, as the staffers hung back with a mixture of awe and curiosity, not unmixed with a sense of incongruity at the deference with which Fleet Admiral Remko, something of a legend himself at a hundred and forty-five Standard years, addressed a man who looked like a college student with expensive tastes in clothes.

But then, they had never clawed their way up out of the New Detroit slums by sheer guts and ability, and finally met a commanding officer who genuinely didn't give a damn how they talked . . .

"I've been meaning to come see you, Admiral," he rumbled. Trevayne made no demur at the title; he really *was* a fleet admiral, carried on the Rim Federation's inactive list for the last eighty years by special act of Parliament. "But there's a crisis on, and—"

"Think nothing of it, Sean. Unlike some of us, you're still on the active list, and your duties have to come first. Besides, I haven't exactly been very accessible myself lately. So much to learn—"

"And so much money to decide how to spend!" Remko grinned in his now almost all-white beard. (Age had not diminished his lifelong indifference to fashion.)

Trevayne winced with something resembling embarrassment. As a member of one of the Terran Federation Navy's centuries-old "dynasties" of career officers, he had always been financially upper middle class—comfortable but not wealthy. But the same act of Parliament which had kept his quick-frozen self on a full tax-exempt pension had also made his life support the charge of a grateful Rim government. So for eighty years he had had no expenses and an income which his trustees had invested very wisely. Not the least of the surprises awaiting him had been the fact that he, individually, was a major economic force in the Rim Federation.

Of course, the Rim Federation itself had been an even greater surprise. . . .

"Yes," he heard himself saying. "And so many changes. So many *political* changes . . ."

Remko understood, with the perceptiveness that no one ever expected. But then the inarticulateness that everyone *did* expect closed over him as always.

"Well, you know . . ." He gave a vague gesture that somehow encompassed the Rim systems, connected to the Terran Federation only by a single warp chain running through the Republic, now open only by grace of the treaty that had ended the rebellion, despite the heroic best efforts of Ian Trevayne to blast it open. "I suppose . . . well, it sort of had to be this way. Especially what with . . . well, you know, the Pan-Sentient Union."

"Yes, I suppose so," Trevayne replied absently. It was strange. The proposed amalgamation of the Terran Federation with the Khanate of Orion had been the proximate cause of the Fringe Worlds' secession, and formation of the "Terran Republic." So arguably the Pan-Sentient Union of today was what he, Trevayne, had been fighting for all along.

So, he asked himself, not for the first time, *why don't I feel like it was?*

Of course, I'm evidently not the only one who feels that way. His lips quirked upward at the thought of the Rim Federation, which considered itself part of the Terran Federation—complete with a figurehead governor-general appointed from Terra—but *not* part of the Pan-Sentient Union to which the Terran Federation belonged. *It would take a lawyer to figure that one out*, he thought.

A lawyer like Miriam . . .

He shied away from the thought.

"Yes," he said briskly. "In some ways, the Terran Republic had been the *least* difficult thing for me to accept." He smiled at Yoshinaka. "I know, Genji-san: you've been valiantly trying to remember to call them 'the rebels' out of deference to my feelings. But that isn't necessary anymore. I can't waste this . . . second life that's been granted to me, fighting a war that ended eighty years ago. And, to be honest, I was always able to understand the Fringe Worlds' grievances." He gave another smile, at the sight of his two old subordinates' expressions. "Oh, of course I could never publicly admit that I did, in those days. In fact, I couldn't even admit it to myself. Not after . . ." He could go no further, and he no longer saw his listeners. They understood. They knew he was seeing the wife and daughters who had died at the rebels' hands . . . and, worse, the son who had died at his own hands after joining the rebellion.

They wondered if he had accepted the existence of the Terran Republic as fully as he claimed. He himself wondered the same thing.

"So, Sean," he said, changing the subject to everyone's relief, "what brings you to Government House? I believe you mentioned a 'crisis.'"

"That might have been a little too strong. But . . . I know you've had a lot on your mind, so you may not have heard about the sighting in the Bellerophon System."

"Actually, I have. I've tried to keep abreast of current events while catching up on eighty years of old news. I haven't always succeeded, mind you. But this was hard to miss. A fleet of *sublight* interstellar ships . . .!"

"Yes," Yoshinaka chimed in. "Using photon drives, according to the scientific consensus. That's a first, even though it's been a theoretical possibility for some time."

Trevayne nodded. The photon-drive concept involved the conversion of mass to propulsive energy with near-total efficiency. The process was not controllable enough to be used as a power source that would revolutionize the economy, but it was the ultimate reaction drive. Only . . . nobody had used reaction drives since the invention of inertia-canceling drive fields which, in addition to their sundry advantages in the areas of maneuverability and survivability, required energy but no reaction mass. Granted, such reactionless drives had a upper limit on the velocity they could attain: 11.7 percent c for a long time, later increased incrementally, and now upped to about 50 percent c under certain circumstances by the new "phased gravitic drive" he had been avidly reading about. It was called the "Desai Drive," he had been delighted to read, recalling his old subordinate Sonja Desai—a brilliant woman, if not exactly a "people person."

Reaction drives—loosely, "rockets"—could in theory accelerate up to the very edge of Einstein's Wall, given enough time and reaction mass. But that was their sole advantage. And when the warp points that made interstellar travel practical were separated by merely interplanetary distances, who needed that kind of velocity?

The answer, it now appeared, was: someone who didn't know about warp points but had a compelling reason for wanting to cross interstellar space.

"Then you may have also heard," Remko continued, "that we're sending a task force to Bellerophon. Just a precautionary measure, of course, and just to make sure there's an impressive Rim Federation presence there when whoever-it-is arrives, so there'll be no doubt about who Bellerophon belongs to. For the same reason they want me, as senior officer of the Rim Navy, to command it." Remko's embarrassment had built up visibly, and now it spilled over as he blurted, "They ought to have put *you* in command, Admiral! I mean . . . after all . . . ."

"Oh, rot, Sean! I'm not even on active duty. And I'm still desperately trying to catch up on eighty years of advances in military technology. And besides . . ." Trevayne gestured eloquently at the midshipman's body he wore.

"Your legal age is a hundred and thirty-one Standard years, Admiral," Yoshinaka pointed out mischievously.

"And you used to accuse *me* of having a strange sense of humor!" Trevayne snorted. "But all nonsense aside, Sean, I envy you. You'll be present at our first contact with a newly discovered race."

"Right. And," Remko added in his invincibly prosaic way, "it'll be good to see Cyrus Waldeck again. He's in command at Bellerophon, you see, and I'll be assuming command from him when I . . . Admiral, are you all right?"

"Quite all right, Sean," Trevayne gasped as he brought his coughing fit under control. "Ah . . . did I understand you to say, 'Cyrus Waldeck'?"

"Sure. You remember him, don't you? Well, after the war, he went back to the Federation . . . the *Terran* Federation, I mean. But now he's on detached duty with the Rim Navy. Confidentially, he told me he likes it out here better than in the Pan-Sentient Union, with all those Orion officers. He never could quite get used to them . . . and besides, he's allergic to their fur."

"Yes," Trevayne deadpanned, "I can see how that might impose a certain social handicap. And yes, of course I remember him. He was your flag captain at Zapata." Only a short while ago, in Trevayne's memory. "But now I gather he . . . has no problems about serving here in the Rim, under you?"

"Oh, no." Remko looked mildly puzzled. "He really likes the people out here; I think he looks on them as a bunch of Fringers who stayed loyal to the Federation. And as for us..." Remko chuckled and unconsciously paraphrased a pre-space Terran politician. "He may be a Corporate Worlder, but he's *our* Corporate Worlder!"

"I see," said Trevayne as those fresh—to him—memories came crowding back in.

Cyrus Waldeck belonged to a family of magnates whose insensate greed had played a leading role in driving the Fringe Worlds into desperate rebellion. Trevayne had recognized his competence, but had indulged in just a little unworthy chuckling at the thought of him serving under someone with Sean Remko's background. And, as he had hoped, they had succeeded in turning their mutual loathing outward, turning on the rebels the hatred that Navy discipline had prevented them from releasing any other way.

I always thought personal issues were more stubborn than political ones, he thought bleakly. *But evidently even loathing and hatred can be worn away by the slow erosion of eight decades.... Decades that never existed for me. I can only stare at what seem to be sudden changes in the landscape.*

"Well, Sean," he said aloud, "I'm glad the whole business has worked out so well for both of you. And don't mind me. It seems everyone I used to know is either dead or changed. Only to be expected, of course." His eyes strayed to Government House, but only for a moment. His face cleared and he extended his hand. "Good luck, Sean. And give Cyrus my best."

CHAPTER THREE

"They're all insane."

The roar of explosions filled the command deck of the *Hurusankham* until the communications officer unfroze and told the computer to cut off the sound, the mental equivalent of a lunge for an off switch. The appalled silence in the control center that followed was a stark contrast to the sheer violence of the images flooding the main screens. Ankaht stood back and controlled herself with an effort. (Shock, calm through will.) The captain, Nefarat, of the First Wave Flagship, sat without motion, even in his lesser tentacles. (Calculation/aggression.) The low-level belligerent response was so much a part of him that it almost didn't bear commenting on, but she wondered at the Council choosing him as captain. It was less puzzling when one considered that he and the senior admiral were very alike, both well respected *Destoshaz*, the warriors. "Senior Admiral to the bridge," he said quietly, his words passed on from the command nexus in his control niche.

The lighting was brighter and bluer than human eyes would have found comfortable, and the predominantly yellow light flaring and blasting from the screens looked washed out.

Communications Officer Yegire (Distress, fear.), who had never expected to encounter alien communications, had her hands up over her face as if she could shut out the hideous images flooding in from the planets they had hoped to make a new Ardu (Comfort embodied.) A new home. She had been cycling through to contact the *Buvastash* when *that* excrescence had exploded on the screens, freezing everyone in their places.

The commander second had his emotions well in claw but his skin tone was chalky yellow-flecked red. All of the control crew were so frozen that even the under-flow of emotion, the *selnarm,* was dampened, the equivalent of an emotional whisper.

On the screen, tiny ships flew over the planet below and ugly clouds marked where nuclear strikes bloomed, clustered in horrible precision. The ships fought each other and larger vessels, and monsters stood and spoke and waved what looked like normal arms save they lacked tentacles and some lacked claws. The digits were disgustingly stiff. Almost all of them had fleshy appendages upon their heads that tended not to move much, and not one of the monstrosities blowing each other up seemed to have more than two eyes.

Some were the varying browns and beiges of diseased skin; some were completely coated with fur. There seemed to be a scattering of patches of fur on various places on most of these monsters. The ones coated with fur like yihrt had fangs as long as that extinct predator, others were birdlike with what looked like proper feathers, like gigantic flixits. A full cluster of odd things sat around a desk? A table?

The door hissed open quietly, the only announcement that the senior admiral had arrived. Torhok relieved the captain from the command niche with his (Assumption of command.) and the (Acknowledgement, relief to a superior.) response. He was medium size for *Destoshaz,* compact and solid as a shield generator, his skin smooth gold. And his attitude always set Ankaht's tentacles into a knot. He did little *matsokah,* or "training of the soul," and his *sulhaji* was not the "true seeing" or "true vision" that she perceived. All in all, there was no good *narmata* between them. She set her mouth grinders together firmly and clamped down on her emotion. It was no time to spread ill will and discord through the *selnarm.*

"Yegire," (Firm support.) Admiral Torhok spoke more gently than his usual harsh style as he sat down in the command niche, trying to bring his communications officer out of her shock. "What are these things saying? Are they communicating at all?"

"Sir, there is only noise. (Distress dampened, emphatic.) There is nothing on the *selnarm* frequency. They're like machines, sir."

"Illudor's Nightmares." The admiral didn't look around as someone whispered it (Revulsion, sinking despair.), but his attention snapped like a thunderclap, enough to make Ankaht flinch back. (ATTENTION.) "We are not first-borns. We have countless lives behind us and we will act accordingly!" (Implacability.) "We are, by Illudor's will, Dispersed by Sekahmant and as reflections of the Mind of Illudor, we Remember." He turned his chair slowly. "I am assuming that the other ships of the fleet have been picking that up"—he nodded at the screens where two things with various colors of fur on their heads sat behind a barrier of some kind, making yapping noises at each other—"and that panic will be spreading" (Calm, controlled will to defend.) Yegire, set up a conference in one hour with all ships captains and their councils that we may consult and act in *narmata* under Illudor's eye."

(Relief and relinquishment of control.) flowed from most of the bridge. Ankaht, as eldest Sleeper-Wakened, let only a trickle of (Reserve.) out as part of the narmata. She disliked the way the latest ship generation resigned their self-control to the officers, often without thinking. It was a diminishment of the race, a lessening of potential *holodah* for every individual as far as she was concerned and it made her uncomfortable to be in the flow of the ship generations. Their *narmata* were limited and harsh in a way that grated on her nerves.

"Yes, Senior Admiral. Within the hour."

He turned his attention to Ankaht. "Eldest, if you would gather your fellows and give us the benefit of your (Suppressed resentment.) knowledge?" Though he was known by other *shaxzhu* as a Warrior commander, he himself had no memories of past wars and commands held. *If, by Illudor, there was no one else but "Us," then why choose a War Leader as senior admiral of the First Fleet? But now, obviously, there is more than "Us." And someone must have had a thought that perhaps we would find something that required an aggressive response.*

She was better at reducing her unintended emotions than he was, even though biologically they were of an age. Her *shaxzhutok* and planetary experience gave her an advantage that he could not even begin to swim. (Soothing deference.) "Of course, Senior Admiral."

✧   ✧   ✧

A full ship's day later, the awakened sleepers all sat quietly in the darkened gathering room, swimming in their *narmata*. They had been in hibernation as generations had borne incarnation inside the ships, growing more and more distant from their *shaxzhu* of the planet born. They were also aware of the pressure of the disincarnate, waiting for the race to expand onto a planetary surface once more. On the flagship, though there were only 452 *shaxzhu*, it was still easier for smaller clusters to meet before bringing the consensus together in the full cluster that would gather shortly.

Ankaht had set the light in the gathering room to just past sunset and before Sekahmant-rise, the dimness lending itself to calm reflection. She sat in the cluster of deliberation with the others of her immediate collect, their tentacled fingers interlaced to better facilitate *narmata*. For all that the room was a perfect miniature copy of any gathering room at home, she was acutely conscious of the differences that made it clear they were not home and never would be again.

The artworks that represented *sulhaji*, there to remind everyone that *holodah* was ultimately attainable for every individual, on the planet would have been more that just holograms, meant to be touched and *shotan* if the discussion grew too heated. It was an acceptable way to break cluster when emotions ran high, to contemplate an artwork. Here, if someone needed to let *narmata* settle both in themselves and the group, they could only look at the works and not touch. There was no weight to them, no heft more than the weight of a photon, and she missed it.

The hiss and sigh of ventilation and the faint smell that was like nothing but the most sealed of environments was a constant low-level irritation that she had to brace herself against, and the minute vibration in the air, even in a ship this size, marked the monstrous faint thunder of the drive. She pitied the first generation who'd had to raise children knowing nothing but this, and praised their disincarnate selves. They would surely be the first in line to be born when the new-planet generations began. Unless these aliens stopped them from settling.

The newly awakened had been spending more of their waking hours in each other's company rather than with the ship generations, despite their best attempts. Both Ankaht and Thutmus, a *Shaxa zhu* with many lives in common with her, had counseled that they were there to connect the old *narmata* with the new, but they'd all found the new generations very hard to be with, save two. Neferek and Silar, both of the tall, bright variant, found the Shiplings more comfortable than their peers out of sleep. Their presence was a simmering thread of discord in *narmata*, the sharpness of spoiled fermentation in a sweet soup.

Ankaht reminded herself of this firmly, sending tendrils of (Openness, acceptance.) in their direction, as fully capable of controlling her dislike of them as she was of the senior admiral. She was fairly sure that none of those who upset her knew that they did. *It is my duty to the race to ensure* narmata. *It is our survival and the future incarnation of those who wait and our hope of* holodah. She drew comfort from the other-flow of contact, the solid clench of tentacles on either side of her. Thutmus was as dark as she was, calm enough even in the face of this disaster that his central eye was closed.

Hathrok, on her other side, was as bright as soul as he was cool and Ankaht was happy that she had them both.

"Clearly, we are not the only Reflection of Illudor," Thutmus said quietly. (Reasonable reflection.) "We have had the obvious held under our eyes." He clicked his claws decisively, without disengaging the cluster.

"Not so!" Neferek closed even her central eye. (Rejection, rejection, negation.) "We have no proof that these things are even intelligent!" (Betrayal, rejection, anger.)

The *narmata* in the room was clearly against her, but she continued swimming against it. "They are not. Perhaps there were People once and these are their semi-intelligent pets? (Hope?) We've been watching these things for days now and there is no sign of conscious *selnarm*! Nothing but meaningless noise, like a flixit!" There was a tiny wave of grief for lost pets, for there had been deemed no room for even things as small as flixits. Ankaht felt a small pang of loss for the song hers had sung.

It was not as if the animals of home were lost, after all, they just could not be alive and awake in the ships. They existed only as viable embryos frozen in the gene banks in each ship waiting for the New Home. In the few weeks she'd been awake, Ankaht had had far too many dreams of being frozen in the banks, but awake and not able to let anyone know she was conscious, no one able to hear her distress for some reason. As reasonable as all dreams were, of course, unless they were *shaxzhu* memories coming back. Before the recollection of her dreams could spread by *selnarm* and contaminate *narmata*, she shook herself mentally. (Agreement one, Uncertainty twelve, Disagreement twenty.)

"Clearly they are intelligent or they could not create new technology... that is obvious from some of the images. We think that we are beginning to recognize extra-*selnarm* indicators like the gestures. Perhaps their *selnarm* is olfactory or on another frequency," Ankaht said firmly. "Illudor's Mind is bigger than we credited." (Wonder, joy, fear, apprehension.)

"These things kill each other in their thousands," Silar said. (Closed to reason, obdurate.) "They clearly do not communicate properly. And it is clear that they arbitrarily choose a species to disincarnate, groups against groups. Illudor would not think of such hideous creatures." (Fanaticism.)

"That is yet to be determined." (Reason in the face of ignorance.) Hathrok, as impulsive as ever, snapped. "It is kind of you to let us know the Mind of Illudor since you obviously have a personal connection!" (Cont—)

(—Calm.) Ankaht cut in. "We cannot bicker amongst ourselves." (Reasonable judgment, continuing.)

Neferek shut down her flow of *selnarm* to a trickle. (Offended, slighted.) "You cannot deny that these creatures have killed at least two entire races from what we've seen and seem to repeat the story of how they did it many times, casting it out into the universe. They smashed planets together to destroy a race."

(Silent terror.)

(Stillness before a predator.)

(Defensive rage.) The room was filled with the click and rustle of claws against each other and that of their neighbors. The cluster looked like an anemone of defensive claws as the ancient reflexes seized them.

"Yes." (Uncertainty.) Ankaht said pulling her hands down gently, bringing the defensive ring down with them. "But we may simply be misunderstanding them. We do not want a repeat of the mob action that happened in the time of Harrok the All Encompassing. Several of us were there and couldn't stop it."

A suppressed shudder as she reminded them of that life, that atrocity. It had all been a manipulation by the First of Warriors, a time of fire and blood when many were sent disincarnate for all the wrong reasons.

(Openness, Curiosity tempered with caution.) "We cannot assume anything."

(Agreement 30, reserve 2, disagreement 2.)

Senior Admiral Torhok was sick of listening to his advisors tell him that he should be more cautious, less aggressive. These things were a clear danger to the race. They killed and seemed to celebrate it. Part of the noise in the transmissions was music if one could call it that, and there was enough congruity that one could almost pick up *selnarm* from it. It seemed to glorify the planet smashing. The genocide.

He didn't take his hands out of the palm rests of his niche, only clicking his main claws gently against the buttons to show his restraint. He'd been in that recess far more than anyone had thought he'd be, since everyone had thought that Illudor would, of course, have thought of a suitable new home for the race who reflected Him, having just driven them out of Home.

The First Wave was his responsibility, every one of the twenty-six ships. And all the subsequent Waves right up until the radiation and shock wave had killed the last Wave that had failed to outrun the stellar explosion. They would have had to be up close to the speed of light to have a chance of the shielding working and they hadn't had time. It had been dust almost more than the radiation, moving at near light speed and in high concentrations that had killed the last three million who had tried to flee.

There were some disincarnate who would undoubtedly remember the Crippling, when the planet itself evaporated and the last ships were caught and overwhelmed by the expanding star. The *selnarm* had transmitted the shock wave of the dying, giving them all nightmare proof that the frequency of that sense lay beyond the speed of light. *Selnarm*ing another death was often uncomfortable, but not particularly shocking. Often enough, one would be tired of a lengthy life and the death would come as a minor relief. In this case it was the enormous amount of death felt that sent the entire remaining race reeling for weeks. The Sleepers were spared that and the ingrained memory of that, when the race as a whole became a defensive cluster and it was his job to see that that cluster survived.

It had been the scientists of that generation who had gotten the bugs out of transmitting *selnarm* between ships without requiring massive trauma. And it allowed communication that was faster than light.

He tapped with his fore-claw, which brought up the latest analysis on his command screen. *At least whatever happens to us, all the rest will* selnarm. *They might not know details but they will be prepared for whatever happens.*

These monsters—he refused to think of them in any other way—obviously had some way of traveling between stars that wasn't Myrtakian space. Either that or they could create ships out of nothing, which seemed even unlikelier. This was also an explanation for the sheer number of physical types—different species apparently. All of whom showed no signs of *selnarm*, and displayed consistently violent, genocidal behaviors. In his thought, that made things easy. They were all monsters and threats to the race.

The soft chime at Sean's desk caught him just as he was tabbing up his pants. It chimed again as he cleaned his hands and he called, "Remko here," over his shoulder.

"Sir, we're coming up on sensor range of the alien fleet."

"I'll be on the bridge in a moment."

"Yessir."

As he straightened his tunic, his mouth twitched at an irrelevant thought. *None of the vid heroes ever seem to get caught in the head.* That was more the thought of his younger self, and a sure sign of the stress he was under, the stress they were all under. The fleet was heading out to intercept and that meant far more time in regular space than anyone was used to. It was one thing to spend hours or days between warp points but quite another to be heading out into the immensity, the vastness that was Newtonian space, to contact a new alien race. Which was another whole can of worms.

The effect was also doing so in force. Every tin can that was armed and could be called spaceworthy was part of what the media were calling the "Greeting Fleet." There were a full dozen SMTS, fifteen DDs, a handful of antique battlecruisers and even the Orion CV, that Showaath had been reporting on had been rushed back into space. A solid group of politicians were screaming that sending out a fleet armed to the teeth was hardly a gesture of goodwill and fellowship. One small faction was even promoting sending a single drone broadcasting, "We come in Peace," and other arrant nonsense in all the sentient languages currently known.

Thank God that people with more military sense quashed that idea, Sean thought. *We've been fighting interstellar wars for hundreds of years and people want to go out to meet someone who could be a carnivore—wearing a steak suit with a sprig of parsley in the lapel.* He came onto the flag bridge moving briskly, but not rushing; no need to make anyone nervous by looking harried. He moved to take the command chair from Captain Gilford. The *Haida* was a missile-heavy SMT, meant to stand off and pound an enemy from long outside the range of known energy weapons. In the fleet he also had *Williamsburg, Nunavut,* and *Dallas* all designed to wait out the missile exchanges and close to energy range, if necessary. All of which, he hoped, would be unnecessary. But no one knew what they'd be facing.

It was all different somehow; having someone coming at you from directions that you couldn't predict, like having the whole sky suddenly becoming a closed warp point. These aliens were approaching space travel a whole different way, which pointed to a whole different attitude from everyone else. They were willing to plow through regular space over thousands of years to travel between stars, and could come from *anywhere*—which the journalists seemed to have mercifully stayed away from. *Thank God. The last thing we need is all twenty three million souls on Bellerophon imagining another Bug invasion coming from unpredictable directions.* As he settled into the chair, he made a mental note to himself to spend more time training because the short jaunt had left his heart rate up. *Not good, even if I am almost halfway through my second hundred. Of course, I have other reasons than mere exercise to elevate my pulse.*

"Admiral on the bridge."

"At ease. What do we have, Nora?"

Nora Thompson, a lieutenant new enough that she nearly squeaked, adjusted the image on her screen minutely. "We're just at the edge of the range, Sir. I'll have it clearer in a moment. . . ." He settled back into the command chair as she tinkered with her sensors. ". . . Ah. Here, Sir." For all her youth, she was one of the best, practically making her sensors purr.

"I have Admiral Waldeck for you, sir," Jorge Miezaki, his com officer, spoke quietly.

"Good, pipe him through."

"Yessir."

Waldeck was on his own flag bridge aboard the *Antietam*, another of the missile-heavy supermonitors that the Rim favored, and Sean could almost imagine the patrician form intent on the information finally coming clear in the tank.

"Admiral Remko, are you getting this?" Waldeck's voice was clipped, blunt to the point of rudeness, as usual. For an instant Sean was transported back to when Cyrus was his flag captain and while still doing everything brilliantly, managing the Waldeck sneer down his nose at the Rim accents around him. He shifted one shoulder minutely, the ghost of a shrug, as he thrust that ancient feeling of irritation that the Corporate World drawl still sometimes brought up.

The image Lieutenant Thompson was calling up sprang up in the tank and everyone stared, though they tried to focus on their own duty stations. Where the usual display showed various colored points of light, with the distances between them vastly reduced to allow showing the whole thing in one image, this time the alien ships showed appreciable disks. "Magnifying," Thompson said quietly. She brought up one of the alien ships.

"Yes. Yes, Cyrus, I'm seeing them." Sean's voice was an atypical monotone as he gazed at the image, realizing what he was looking at. It was almost worse when Thompson brought up a schematic of an SMT to give the proper scale.

"Jah love us." The whisper came from Ensign Perry over at fire control. Privately Sean agreed with her. It was a monster.

"Smallest ship, Sir, is twelve kilometers long." Thompson's voice shook as she read out the figures. "Twelve kilometers."

"Sean." Waldeck's voice stumbled only slightly before he continued. "Admiral." He was shocked enough that he was retreating to formality and Sean was just as glad. He was having a hard enough time keeping his own face impassive.

"Yes, Cyrus." He took a breath and pulled himself back in iron control.

"I do not believe this is a social call, not with twenty-six ships this size. Unless these aliens are giants and they need ships that size—which is extremely unlikely—there are thousands of aliens on them."

"I agree. A bit much for just a hello, but we can't assume they're going to arrive guns blazing."

"I must however advise extreme caution, Sean. The largest is . . . over four hundred billion tons."

Sean's lips pursed in a soundless whistle. *I hope to God they aren't here to start another war.* "It's your job to be cautious, Cyrus. I hope you're wrong." He turned to his communications officer. "Mr. Miezaki, anything on any channel?"

Jorge looked up and shook his head, pressing one finger against the skin on the implant over his left temple in a gesture as old as earspeakers. "No, Sir. Nothing on any frequency and the computer is monitoring ranges both above and below everyone's normal hearing."

Sean nodded. "Thank you, Jorge, let me know the moment anything comes through. In the meantime, start hailing them—"

"Sir! The aliens are launching smaller ships! Fighters?" Thompson's voice rose in a slight question because the ships being launched were so big. "Multiple launches. I've got seventy-five birds already, sir. They're the size . . ." She paused for a second. "They're SD sized, sir, and they're reactionless-drive."

"Ms. Marcus, all ships, we need to be stopped relative to them." *They have no choice but to come to us, they are in full deceleration and can't cut their drives. I have to deal with those parasite ships since they can maneuver against us.*

The vast ships came on in the same stately deceleration, unwavering in their arrow-straight course for Bellerophon, while the smaller ships darted toward the Contact Fleet, like water bugs skittering away from a ponderous turtle.

"Multiple launches, sir! Smaller ships, about the size of battlecruisers."

Sean snapped out his orders, after the barest hesitation, that no one noticed but him. "Cyrus, pull all ships back, we don't want to look unnecessarily aggressive. Least Claw Zteeffwiit'gahrnak, ready to launch your fighters if we need them, on my command."

"Acknowledged," the translator took all the emotion out the Orion commander's response but it was just as crisp as Cyrus's, and the Contact Fleet slowed and flattened into a loose wall.

"The alien ships are slowing, Senior Admiral. They're spreading out."

Torhok, as little as he felt it, sent (Reassurance.) "It could be the beginning of an attack formation."

Ankaht protested from her observer's station. (Negation.) "Admiral, if I may... that's an assumption. They are not attacking."

(Anger.) "Yet, Elder. They may be slowing, but they are still coming on."

"Senior Admiral, a communication."

The alien on the screen was a wide individual, wearing what the People believed to be a cloth covering associated with the genocidal creatures that had control of the armed ships. The creatures that they had seen destroy races. It spoke and Torhok looked to Senior Communications Technician Nerfiht, who shook his head and shrugged (Distress, nausea, fear.) "No *selnarm*. Nothing but the noise."

"Admiral," Ankaht said quietly. (Calm reason, peaceful harmony.) "They are talking to us, not just shooting."

(Suppressed contempt.) "I understand that they are attempting communications, Elder. It is, however, my job to protect the People. We are the first hope. Nothing will stop me from getting them to their New Home. I am *Destoshaz* and this is my *narmata*. *Shaxzhu* or not, if you continue to obstruct my *sulhaj* I will assume that you are challenging *matsokah*. (Building rage.) I would be loathe (Suppressed lie.) to lose you in this life, but would manage."

"They are indeed communicating, but it could just as easily be a warn-off." His flow of *selnarm* shut down almost entirely as his rage and fear grew. "That could be an attack formation!"

"Junior Admiral, the squadron is awaiting orders." (Fear.)

"Then let them. We await orders from Senior Admiral Torhok." Junior Admiral Vakelnar let his anger at his captain flow. The squadron was his responsibility but the larger responsibility were the Home Ships behind them. He was young for his rank, and his *shaxzhu* said he was young in soul, as most *Destoshaz* were and he was horribly afraid for all the people behind him. His ship, the *Hurusankham*, where his raising circle was, where his *selnarm* partner prepared for her ship launch, were horribly vulnerable and his tender, *Rahrahmpaht* and her consorts were a thin shield against machinelike monsters.

His tentacles curled into a tight knot on the armrests of his niche as he waited for word from Torhok, waited to defend the race. He was clenching his grinders, blinking all his eyes more than needed. His *selnarm* poured loud, combining with the rest of his bridge crews'. (Fear, rage, anxiety, nausea.) Even as the People focused on their duties, the air seethed with their fear and confusion, the clicking of claws angry and unconscious, unnoticed. The air stank of fight-rage and defensiveness.

"Entering extreme sensor range, Junior Admiral."

"Put it up." He and his partner had just spawned in anticipation of Home and the children were in the raising circle on the Home Ship. It didn't matter that he didn't know his children, that wasn't his job. It was his job to protect them and all the others new or old spawned. He swallowed as the alien ship appeared on-screen—a killer ship from the broadcasts, he recognized it and had studied what it could do.

"Admiral! Scanning intensity has decreased dramatically! We're being hit with multiple energy signatures!" He froze for a terrified instant before exceeding his orders.

"That's targeting scan! Launch missiles! Fire!"

CHAPTER FOUR

"They've fired on us!"

There is an unfortunate principle in human hierarchies, particularly military ones, that people are promoted not just to their limit of competence but of necessity just past it. Military strategists write endlessly about disastrous decisions made by officers, both junior and senior and yet, unlike the Orions, have no real solutions to this problem.

Whether it is a decision based on lack of knowledge, say of monsoon wind patterns leaving an army slogging unsupplied through the most deadly desert in the known world, orders that sent light cavalry into the teeth of heavy cannon, or a miscommunication that plunged battlecruisers into combat with superdreadnoughts, humans tend not to summarily execute the officer in question, preferring to wait for courts-martial years later. Sometimes—though not often enough from the enlisted point of view, given that officers like these tend to lead from the rear—the engagement itself does humanity the favor.

For twenty-two days the *Montana* had been his. Captain James Hajii leaned forward, sweat beading his forehead and upper lip.

Those *things,* whatever they were, were not going to take her away from him. His ship versus unknown monsters out of deep space. His beautiful ship.

"They're firing on us, sir!"

"I can see that!"

"Captain, our point-defense—" The huge salvo from the alien SDs was massive enough to swamp the defenses of *Montana* and her sisters. Captain Hajii, though he had been an exemplary junior officer, was less certain about his own ability as captain and knew that it showed. He feared his new-minted position even as he'd accepted it in the rush to get allied forces out to meet the new aliens. *Alien threat* is what he'd thought, though everyone was careful not to say any such thing.

He'd been tense as wire and had ordered the active sensors as much to reassure himself that he was doing something . . .anything, as to gather information. He seized the arms of his chair to brace himself. The point defenses of the *Montana* and her sisters, *Novalis* and *Temuchin*'s were good for a battle group that hadn't fought together before. With all the skill of their training over the days to interception they swatted alien missiles out of space but the massive salvo couldn't all be stopped.

The *Montana* staggered, as one, then two and three alien missiles, too many for her point defense to handle, overloaded and tore through her screens, blasting James Hajii's crew. Alarms screamed and blast doors slammed shut. The ship lurched, a sickening feeling when everyone's life depended on unchanging stability, wrenching and twisting her into ugliness.

He bit his lip and held his silence for a long moment, feeling the fear twisting in his gut. *Montana* reeled as another missile found its way into her vitals and threw people jolting against their shock-frames. "Return fire!"

In his ear, he could hear Admiral Waldeck, "Captain Hajii! Cease fire! That's a direct order!"

"Sir!" Thompson's voice cut across the flag bridge. "The *Montana*'s bringing up active scanners!" Sean turned to stare at the tank even as he heard Cyrus's order along the command-link.

"*Montana*! Shut down! Captain Hajii, passives until further notice!"

"Aliens launching missiles, sir."

"Defensive fire only, Cyrus!" Sean snapped. "Fall back, Defensive formation—Abel 2." Even as his orders rang out to pull his ships back, the *Montana*, followed by *Novalis* and the *Temuchin* carried the fight to the aliens.

"Hits on the *Montana*, sir. She's firing—sir, they're firing back."

"Pull back, all units, disengage!" Sean could feel the whole engagement slipping out of his hands in a way that no one could have anticipated. They might still cool things down, make contact. It was possible.

The attempted peaceful contact unraveled like wet paper.

"Support Junior Admiral Vakelnar," Torhok snapped and the defense squadrons from *Ahknemakseht* and *Rahmehk* launched missiles. *Thank Illudor that the "Others" heresy had us building "obstacle removal" missiles or we'd have nothing with which to defend ourselves against these . . .genocidal ghouls.*

Ankaht closed all three eyes to shut out what was happening, clamping down hard on her (Rage, dismay, outrage.), though her *selnarm* was lost in the reaction of the *Destoshaz*. *This is all incorrect*, she thought before being caught up in the flow of *selnarm* of the whole First Fleet, in defense of the Race.

"Pull back! Pull back from those sublight monsters!" Sean leaned forward and realized his mistake as all of the alien fleet attacked. The Behemoths opened fire as well and he'd have to consider them targets, though their salvos weren't anywhere near the weight of fire from the SDs. Individually they didn't seem to have much, given their size, but when they added their fire the total amount of ordnance was staggering.

"Sir, those missiles . . ." The scan-tech's voice only faltered a moment. ". . . approximately thirty-four hundred, Sir . . . I'll have more accurate numbers . . .ah, thirty-four hundred three hundred eighteen, Sir."

If there was one thing that Sean Remko was not, it was incompetent. Certain people never find their limits, not in a single life, anyway. "Belay that last order. Engage. All units engage." If he wanted to save anyone out of this mess, they'd have to fight them to a . . . not a standstill. The sublight ships would keep coming whether they were in one piece or not.

Hostile. He had to think not only of all the people in his fleet, but all of Bellerophon, the twenty-three million people on that planet and the rest of the arm behind. The Behemoths wouldn't be able to transit warp points, but the tenders were small enough to. Even if they hadn't figured warp technology, whatever they were, they weren't stupid.

All this had only taken a moment's thought, his orders continued smoothly. "Least Claw, launch your fighters, pick your targets."

"Acknowledged, Shaaann Remmmko, they will feel our fangs." Even the flattening effect of the translator couldn't mask the Orion's fight-rage.

"Sir, the missiles seem to be SBMs but they're not as heavy—not as light as an HBM, though."

The weight of the missiles wasn't the problem; it was their sheer number. A second and a third launch equal to the first roared out from the alien ships. Eye-searing radiation bloomed silently in space as the alien missiles were destroyed, or clawed and raged and died against the Contact Fleet's screens. But as efficient as those defenses and screens were, they couldn't stop all those missiles, and icons in Sean's tank began to flare out.

"Sir, we've lost *Etla.* Sir . . . Sir, one of the alien battleships just rammed."

He turned from the tank to stare. "They what?"

"Rammed, Sir."

Waldeck's voice crackled across the command link. "Sean, we can't concentrate on the SDs. The bulk of those missiles are coming from those Behemoths."

"Yes. Target this one, Cyrus." The icon in the tank began flashing. "Help Zteeffwiit and Captain MacDonald. We'll cover you on that side. We'll stop them. We have to. Cy, I'll even throw my dirty socks at them if that's all I have."

"That, my friend, may actually win the day. Acknowledged." There was no hint of what Waldeck was feeling in the dry-as-dust tone, but Sean knew him well enough that he could hear the unspoken *Be careful.* "Helm . . ." He paused a moment, realizing what was about to happen. "Take us in."

Ankaht watched in silent horror (Desperation.) as fire blossomed all around the Home Ships and her claws clenched and spread. She wasn't *Destoshaz* and found it nearly impossible to separate herself from the *selnarm*. Torhok snapped orders quietly as the screen flared and darkened, struggling to compensate for the violence happening all around them in space. She felt that they were suddenly falling into a fiery pit that had sprung open before them and could only watch as the battleship *Maatsehnk* sacrificed herself to destroy one of the monster's ships. Their *selnarm* thread of absolute dedication to the survival of the race—to the survival of God— made their deaths bearable. They died too quickly to transmit more than a flash of pain and that, one that the entire Race was used to. Teaching on that was universal. It was fear of that pain that slowed one's transition into the state of death and retarded attainment of *holodah*.

"All ships, all ships." Torhok's voice was harsh as a whip-crack. "Home Ships, energy batteries, open fire!" The massive generation ship's batteries sprang to life as well as their missiles as the alien ships came into range. Originally meant to defend against unknown threats or Oort objects in the target system, against Sean's fleet they flared to life with deadly effect.

Only one or two of Ankaht's lives had been *Destoshaz* and she found it very hard to access those memories. She closed her eyes and submerged into the *selnarm* necessary, keeping a kernel of reservation locked tight against the emotional surges of the Shiplings, the *Destoshaz* who had never known anything but space, vacuum, and constant threat. It took all of her training to maintain her individual thought. She struggled to access her tactical and strategic memories, aided by swimming in the *selnarm* of all the others because she had to do something, but forced into the role of the passive observer.

The alien ships, bigger than the tenders, smaller than the Home Ships, swatted missiles away from themselves like a swarm of blood-flies. They were moving into a different configuration that she could see was offensive. *In response?* Ankaht seethed at her own sensations. (Helplessness, fear, outrage.) *This . . .* finally one of her *Destoshaz* lives gave up its memories to her. *This was probably all a miscommunication, like the siege and burning of Tel Mirmarnan.* It felt like that disastrous sack of a city after the war was already over but neither side on the field knew. It felt the same. *This is all wrong.*

The alien ships were moving into a split wall that targeted the two nearest the Home Ships, effectively using their sheer bulk to block energy fire from the majority of the fleet. That kind of tactic obviously didn't work with missiles but it reduced their effectiveness.

Are they so confident? They are so few against the First Fleet. They cannot hope to stop us.

"Sir, we've lost *Novi Berkley.*" Thompson's voice was calm, though what they'd just seen had startled the bridge into silence again. The alien ship had closed to energy range and though *Berkley* had fought back with her primary beams, cutting into the alien hull like a sword into a charging bull, even dead on its feet, with its heart pierced, the bull can still kill you.

"They rammed. They didn't even try to . . . try to . . . they just rammed. Sir, *Temuchin* is reporting fusion—"

"I see it, Nora." Sean sat back in his chair, making the restraints whine. They worked on the same principle as the compensators but being such small units they didn't adapt well to sudden motion.

"Ensign Perry, given that we don't know their design, pick your targets—but I would suggest, here." His light pen indicated an area on the schematic he'd just opened. It was near the collar of the enormous engines and the eye-searing light of the deceleration flare. Eye-searing despite the best filters, and the largest numbers of question marks from his analysts like—*fuel?*—scribbled in the margin of the flimsy. That particular note still sat on his desk in his ready cabin.

"Captain, pass along the suggestion."

"Aye, Sir."

The ensign didn't look away from her screens, acknowledging automatically as her eye skimmed over the unfamiliar design. *How can he be so calm?* They were heading into the thick of it and her fingers hammered down harder on the keys than absolutely necessary. Her body knew it was going into a fight and adrenaline overrode the knowledge of required force. Even the most highly trained, on some level, are when fighting, the equivalent of a primate with a rock. But Sean had been fighting for most of his life and his calm was iron clad. Only he knew how hard it was for him to appear so cool.

As good as the human defense was, *Dame Margaret* and her sisters were taking damage as they closed. An alien primary sliced through the flag bridge, and amidst the shrieking alarms human cries mingled and Lieutenant Thompson silently fell sideways onto the floor, flooding it with blood as it sliced up through her torso and neck.

That was when Judith Perry fired primaries and the Contact Fleet found out a crucial bit of information about the aliens' fuel source.

The Arduans had not hauled a source of fuel with them, nor dealt with cumbersome "cumulative" drives. Deep in layers and layers of shielding and controls, using up 98 percent of the energy it produced just to control it, was a pinhole-sized black hole, a drive source that was never meant to withstand true combat. Even at their most "prepared for everything" thinking, the designers of the evacuation ships could not imagine facing intelligent species in combat, so this hardware that had worked well for almost fourteen hundred years failed. In the *Ankseksumarnat* some of the controls on the electron-sized hole vanished and it simply evaporated.

It was the sun blinking. One hundred seconds of a star's output compressed into one. The fourteen-kilometer ship just—disappeared along with half a dozen of her own defenders. Remko, the *Dame Margaret,* and her crew vanished mid-thought, along with twelve of her sisters. In that one second one hundred thousand beings died.

Nefrexhat, the sister ship to *Ankseksumarnat,* was just barely three light seconds away and lasted two full seconds, just long enough for her engineers to start to react before she blinked out as well, taking all eighty thousand Arduans aboard quite suddenly into the between life, as well as five of her own SDs.

(Shock, fear, rage, Rage, Rage, Rage.) The wave of *selnarm* rolled through the First Fleet turning the remaining Home Ships into the deadliest of reactions. Torhok, as senior admiral, threw his guidance into the surge. His officers, as green as they were, were also able to amplify his direction.

Ponderously their formation began to broaden and deepen as the enormous ships widened the light seconds between them so that they would no longer be a danger to each other, their parasite ships that remained became a webwork, the instinctive defensive cluster, in space, became almost a flattened sphere, somewhat like a red blood cell.

Torhok pulled himself further out of the *beserkergang* gestalt that the First Fleet had become and turned to Ankaht with a snarl. "*Shaxzhu*. Do you honestly think that *this* is all a misunderstanding? A *mistake*? They've proven how bloodthirsty they are. These vermin would grind half the universe against the other half to slaughter it. Our new Home is covered with ravening animals who would send the whole Universe into its next life. I will defend the Race and I will hear *nothing* from you that is not sensible. No more pacifistic nonsense in the place of advice!" Without waiting for her response he turned back to the battle that had turned into an interstellar equivalent of a brass knuckles brawl.

The Arduans had to batter the RFN back to missile range since their big ships were so very vulnerable, but even as they fought to do so, *Telalamrhat* and *Buvastash* both blinked into miniature suns.

Torhok leaned forward, folding his tentacle clusters together. "All junior ships. Announce targets before you destroy them. We have the numbers of the small ships. Save the Fleet and you are assured a quick rebirth. We will celebrate you in your next life, *Destoshaz*."

"Pull back." Waldeck's voice was even, as always, but his hands on the arms of the chair were white-knuckled. *Dammit, Sean.* His initial shock of grief at losing his friend and all the people in those ships could only be expressed to himself in that inappropriate and inadequate thought. "Missiles rage, ah, range." No one even twitched at the Freudian slip.

The RFN didn't have the forces to be able to take out the Behemoths at energy-weapon range and he wasn't about to order anyone into what was blatantly a suicide mission. And he'd mourn later. His job now was to make sure that these things didn't make it to Bellerophon and her state-of-the-art shipyards. *We will all have the luxury of mourning, later. I swear.*

"Sir, we've lost thirty-eight percent of the Fleet." Flag Captain Hodgson's voice was barely audible.

Then there was a totally unmilitary exclamation from Lieutenant Pearson. "Oh, shit, Sir."

"What is it, Lieutenant?"—barely out of Waldeck's mouth before he saw for himself.

"Sir . . ."

The aliens were kamikazeing. All the little ships, and something inside him winced at calling something the size of an SD "little," targeted and went after the RFN's supermonitors, completely unheeding of their own survival. He snapped, "All units, evasive action! Zteeffwiit, MacDonald, get your people out of range," even as ships not designed for close-quarter maneuvers were forced into them in an effort to save themselves.

The SMs writhed out of range of their attackers, brutally flushing their racks to keep the aliens off. Even in a battlefield light seconds across it was too close for these kinds of explosions. The aliens were not perfect in their coordination, targeting multiply redundant attacks on some ships while leaving others, like *Williamsburg*, *Antietam*, and *Vicksburg*, completely untouched.

For twenty-two days, four hours, two point zero seven seconds, the *Montana* had been Captain James Hajii's beautiful ship. And then she was an expanding ball of searing wreckage mixed with the remnants of the alien ship. Captain Hajji never knew that the *Montana's* last missile flight had chewed a hole in the screens of the *Turankaton*, one of the largest of the Home Ships, and destabilized her drive.

When the sixth alien Behemoth blew up, along with the kamikaze attacks of the smaller parasite ships, it crippled any hope that Cyrus might have had to actually destroy the rest of what he was now thinking of as an invasion fleet. In that last stupendous explosion, there came a pause in the battle, a hiccup in the flow that any good commander seizes control of the moment it becomes apparent. In some cases it is a shift in advantage.

"All units, disengage. Disengage. Everyone pull back."

The alien commander was also pulling his parasite ships back to their big ships, and the two sides pulled apart, Cyrus retreating faster than the alien heavies. In this instance neither commander had the weight to follow up on the enemy's retreat, neither could seize the advantage.

"Analysis! I need all the information I can get!" Waldeck's aristocratic accent was harsh over the flood of damage reports.

Lieutenant Pearson cleared his throat before announcing, "Sir, we've lost forty-eight percent of the Contact Fleet. So far."

"The closest warp point and its defenses is Pegasus but they aren't heading anywhere near those coordinates," Commander Lawrence Nickle offered from his station.

Waldeck nodded thoughtfully as he stared at the tank. The four warp points were scattered almost equidistant along the ecliptic of the system, but the battle that had just happened was above them all, and the fourth warp point, Astria, was "below" the whole system slightly.

The reinforcements from further down the line wouldn't be able to get here in time to help them, vid heroes notwithstanding. They wouldn't be here for months. The planetary forts . . . only defended the yards themselves. They wouldn't be worth a tinker's damn trying to defend the planet itself.

"Nothing from the aliens, Sir."

"Thank you, Ensign."

The forts at the warp points could not be moved. They were equipped with station-keeping ability and that was about it. What was left of the fleet could, perhaps, defend the inner system if they pulled back all the way.

The mining in the major asteroid belt had been shut down days ago as a just-in-case, and he frowned, realizing that even if the last ships in the yards had been anywhere near completion they would have also been destroyed or hidden. *How does one hide something that big? In plain sight. One turns a hull into an unpowered "asteroid" and hopes to find it again.*

But. But. The big ships could obviously not transit warp, but the parasite ships were small enough. *They could just spread down the arm while we were holed up here defending the planet.* He unbent enough to pinch the bridge of his nose while he was thinking. A whanging headache was starting up behind his eyes. It was something he could only relieve in the privacy of his own cabin, if he had the time to grieve. No one would see him lose control. Not even now. So he ignored it, composing his features.

"We can defend the planet. Or we can hold Astria." His gut twisted in time to the pounding in his head but he'd never been one to let his emotions get the better of him. Better that he feel it physically. "We know that other forces are on the way; if we're lucky it will be as little as three months away. We cannot let these aliens through." It was a bitter, vile thought. He could not defend the twenty-three million citizens on Bellerophon. The ringing silence from his officers marked their own reactions as they worked it through and came to the same conclusions.

"All units. Retreat to Astria. Repeat, all units retreat to Astria."

"Sir, *Graf Spee* reported that she will not be capable of matching speed, but is taking on survivors from *Yasuyoshi Maru* and *Indefatigable*. With repairs she might make it to the yard."

"Acknowledged. Tell Captain Sedore to do what she can and join us at Astria. If not . . ." He paused for a long moment. "She is to leave the ship with the yard dogs and aid the planetary population as she sees fit. Her contact will be Commander Elizabeth Van Felsen at the Fleet Base."

"Senior Admiral." Torhok put down his drinking vessel with a carefully controlled click. *Finally.* The *selnarm* was full of the seething frustration of being held back and the willingness to change state, rage and fear offered freely to the *Destoshaz* commanders. It was a sweet and wild outpouring into his senses, echoing his own ecstatic urge to fight, to smash the danger, and he savored it like a fine meal. He was ready. He'd been ready days ago, but had ordered his officers to rest and care for themselves before the next—and last—push.

It hadn't taken as long as it could have. When the aliens had begun retreating to a point away from the inner planets it had only made it clear that it was one of these "transfer" points that apparently led to other habitable solar systems. Even though the Arduans didn't have that technology, they were already working trying to reverse engineer it beginning with clues offered by the broadcasts.

The Home Ships hadn't changed their deceleration, except for *Kungankseht*. Her damage was bad enough that even though they hadn't lost control of the fuel, they were required to divert enough power to that end that they hadn't been able to decelerate at the same rate. They'd overshoot the target and would have to work their way back unless things were settled enough here that another ship would be able to assist, later.

The lesser commander proffered a pad with the numbers blinking steadily downward. "We are within twelve transfers of clearing the noncombatants from *Hurusankham*. *Alamirinehk* will be cleared of all non-*Destoshaz* in five more and *Kirru* will be ready in one."

"Excellent. Then we will make this system safe for us all, Huremheb."

"Yes, Sir!"

"Here they come." Lieutenant Commander Huang's voice was soft as she called it and Waldeck nodded. The human forces had dropped back to the cover of the forts and minefields at the warp point. Even with fully 53 percent of the original fleet gone, there was a good chance that they'd be able to hold the point. The aliens had followed, ponderously in the case of the Behemoths, while their fighter SDs had harassed the human fleet as they fell back.

"They're accelerating, sir, coming in at five point four eight Gs." It was an oddness to speak of acceleration, which with modern human drives was a nonexistent measurement. But the Behemoths did not have the reactionless drives their smaller ships had.

"It seems that that is the best speed they have," Huang said.

"Yes, Commander." Waldeck wanted very badly to rub his face but restrained himself. "Our ships are much faster and tougher. If we're lucky, the Big Mothers will not be able to avoid the mines."

Waldeck's ships were already engaging the Behemoths, hoping to stop them more than three light seconds out from the forts. If he managed to destroy those monsters they'd take out the forts even as they died. If the RFN did enough damage to make them leave the point open, that was enough.

Least Claw Zteeffwiit and his battered carrier had retreated, as ordered, to the BR-01 warp point to support Vice Admiral Erica Krishmahnta who commanded the forces trapped on the other side of it, ready to head down the line with every bit of information that had been gleaned from the last battle and whatever could be understood from here.

At least that's one Tabby I could make see sense. The Orion's beloved fighters were all but useless against the Behemoths and could only engage the battleships and there seemed to be few of those. Whatever these aliens thought, they certainly built big.

He'd sent Captain Kirby-Hypher and her *Eldorado* through Andromeda with all the information for the forces there.

"No attempt to communicate at all?" Waldeck turned to his com tech, who shook her head.

"Nothing, sir. There doesn't even seem to be a lot of intership chatter. I've even tried the Bug frequencies and there's nothing there."

"Keep trying, Ms. Brooker."

"Yes, Sir."

Over the days they'd had for preparation as the aliens slowly changed course and came after them, the tension had strung tighter and tighter, like a violin bow arching itself the wrong way. The relief to be doing something other than repairs and trying to recoup losses was palpable. The frantic scrambling aftermath of the battle had butchered morale as well as ships and crews. Now, they had a chance to hit back, when Fleet Admiral Waldeck leaned forward slightly and said, "Engage."

Temuchin and *Novalis*, now part of Flag Captain Anderson's group, were the first to falter in coordination and a dozen alien missiles out of the hundreds roaring down on them slammed home.

Waldeck cursed to himself as he saw the alien parasites refusing to engage his supermonitors but skittering around his formation to attack the forts directly. Kamikaze again. There seemed to be no attempt to save their own lives at all. No lifeboats. *Fort Maenad* expanded into a blazing boil of energy as two SDs rammed home.

Williamsburg and her sisters pounded at a Behemoth as Waldeck began to realize that he couldn't hold the point after all. The aliens were avoiding the minefields, targeting the immobile forts with a complete disregard for their own lives. Against that he didn't have the firepower.

"Retreat. All units, retreat." The words were bitter in his mouth but he had to get what was left of the fleet out of an untenable situation.

"Commander, I'm forced to retreat."

A strange voice answered him. "Commander Stokes here, sir. The LC's dead. Get everyone left out. We'll cover your a—backs."

"And surrender after, if you can."

"Yes, Sir."

The pounding that the *Williamsburg* was taking was enough to start shaking things around him. "Drone message to Van Felsen. We are being forced to retreat. Offer no resistance to the aliens, Elizabeth. Surrender, and that's a direct order."

"On the tick, Sir."

"Thank you, Lieutenant."

The RFN forces were falling back, one after the other making transit under the cover of the others, and just as the last units were pushing through, *Ozymandias* struck a final lucky blow. Her primary beams sliced into and through one of the aliens' mobile moons.

That Behemoth actually seemed to stagger as the governors on the pinhole singularity in her belly vaporized, and under the fading glare of that blast, *Williamsburg* managed to limp through the warp point, barely able to make transit, leaving the system undefended. The humans and their allies had destroyed eight of the most enormous ships they'd ever seen, unknowingly killing almost four million of the aliens for whom they had no name.

We lost fifty-eight percent of our force and took out eight percent of theirs, Waldeck thought. *A Pyrrhic defeat.*

CHAPTER FIVE

"We can't let her get away with this."

In the vast distance between stars, the enormous ships of the Second Fleet diminished to less than atomic significance, lost against the infinite black. Amunsit, senior admiral for the Second Fleet when it left Ardu, flexed her claws in the darkness. She had always liked the unrelieved black of outside and formatted her walls to show nothing but that restful black while she meditated.

Second Fleet had, in effect left on the heels of the first. Their improved drives and shielding, with the entire world focused on building better ships faster, had enabled them to certainly gain Tau. Indeed, if they had been aiming at the same target star it was entirely possible that they could almost have overtaken First Fleet.

But of course it made no sense to choose the same destination and Amunsit, as senior admiral, raised in a culture focused on nothing but the flight from destruction, had chosen a target that suited her. It was one of a dozen choices with variations in distance under fifty light years and Second Fleet had set out under her purposeful tentacle cluster. *I remember leaving orbit, the planet below an ochre and muddy blue ball. The* shaxzhu *insisted it was never that color before, describing clear skies and water. They said that the ruthless*

*stripping of the biosphere had made it that ugly mess. All the more
pleasant to live in orbit, aboard the ships we made.*

Against all established protocols, she had been senior admiral
then, before she'd altered the political basis for the Council and had
herself put into sleep like the *shaxzhu*. But unlike them, she was
periodically wakened to take her proper place as senior again. She,
not the few *shaxzhu* they had left, would be the stability of the Fleet.
For those who could not bear the weight of the interstellar void,
there were the *holodah'kri*, all loyal to Illudor of course, and her.

This was her fourth awakening and one of the younger admirals
had protested her automatic assumption of senior position. *Actually
it is a good sign that Veelahnt challenged me. It shows that the*
Anaht'doh Kainat *haven't grown weak and complacent. It will also
give me a chance to remind everyone that I know what I'm doing. That
I'm strong.*

She loved this peaceful time before day cycle began, when the
darkness of sleeping minds almost approached the deep outside the
skin of the ship. It was a cleansing time, but a self-indulgence she
only allowed herself occasionally.

From the old stories told by *shaxzhu*, the people had no real
understanding of the vast deep between stars. The displays onboard
made it clear how planet dwellers could get it so wrong. The holo-
tank displays were severely out of scale—focusing inappropriately on
the tiny specks of dirt circling the stars. Any display that fittingly
showed the vast distances between mere planets would have to be
more than two leagues long.

She shook her head at that thought and unfolded herself from the
niche, stretching her arms and legs and back carefully. *It was such
typical* shaxzhu *nonsense, ignoring the real space, to focus on planets.*
There was a kink in her lower limb that she paused to work out
before she headed out, leaving her cabin comfortingly dark.

Time to go kill Veelahnt.

"Veelahnt, this is nonsense. We grew up with the knowledge that
the senior admiral was coming back. You have to withdraw your
challenge." (Distress.) Her cluster partner Pahtmuran showed actual
physical discomfort. He was tall and golden and if there was
anything he was usually good at it was *selnarm* expression. She sent
(Determination. Reassurance.).

"Yes, but where are our *shaxzhu*? Amunsit never allowed them to be revived. Who is to keep us in touch with who and what we are? Even when we find another Home, without them will we ever have our souls back? How is she damaging the existence of Illudor by decreeing that she be the only memory of Home that we have? We can't let her get away with this." (Disgust. Outrage.) Veelahnt sat calmly as she argued with him, central eye closed. "Besides, it is past time for such arguments. The time for the duel is here. I would appreciate support rather than fear," she chided him gently. (Love. Irritation.)

(Shame. Acquiescence.) "Of course." (Love. Respect.)

The entire fleet's attention was on the duel. It had been loudly proclaimed and was the latest nine-day wonder in the monotony of travel. The *maatkah* circle was the focus of every transmission. The machine referee differed from ancient tradition and the only two figures in the room were the combatants.

Both females radiated purpose, both tall, golden-phase *Destoshaz*, kneeling opposite each other in the harsh lighting. The *selnarm* struggle had raged for far longer than anyone expected, with parenting clusters turning up the filters high to protect the watching youngsters.

(Implacable will.)

(Active opposition.)

(Perfect Conviction.)

(Conviction.) As she felt her lesser *selnarm* thrust bounce, Veelahnt finally moved. She seized the two *skeerba*, one in each hand, leaped upward into (Flying Will), claws flashing, met by Amunsit in mid-air. One set of *skeerba* locked with another, two fanged jaws closing one on the other. The sound of grating tooth on tooth. The *skeerba* flashed free.

(Flying Will) ran into (Razor Wing) and they tumbled, breaking apart, both bleeding. Amunsit's forehead bled down her face, gory as all head wounds, Veelahnt unable to raise one arm. This match might see the winner tended by the medics, if not sent to the afterlife, too damaged to easily continue.

They stood, panting, then Veelahnt circled into (Wind Considers) and Amunsit turned slowly (Darkness Beckons).

(Shadow Dancer) fell into Amunsit's darkness. She leaned away from Veelahnt, turned on one foot. She moved in a way that no one had ever seen in *maatkah* before, a blur of motion where she'd been. (Space Is) Veelahnt froze, pinned on Amunsit's outstretched left hand, the *skeerba* driven into her chest so hard that Amunsit's own claws were sunk into the chest wall.

A sucking noise as the senior admiral pulled her hand free, coated to the elbow in Veelahnt's blood, releasing a spray of fluid. Veelahnt fell in the crumpled, emptied way of the newly shed body, the *maatkah* circle floor already soaking up the shed blood.

Amunsit turned to the cameras, bloody claws and weapons raised. "I am Senior. Do any challenge?" (Blood-Glee. Determination.)

In the ringing silence as everyone muffled their emotional outflow, she waited out the traditional time. The machine chimed. "Duel complete. No new challenges."

(Submission.) From the Fleet.

Amunsit placed her *skeerba* on the victor's patch on the wall, where they would stay, their image broadcast continuously on one channel, until she returned to clean them, and left to tidy herself up. (Satisfaction.) Only barbarians had to make the point of meeting the staff covered in a challenger's blood.

The vast hibernation chambers on the *Ptahtoranknefer* were visible to everyone who cared to look, mostly clusters of school-aged, being shepherded through by their teachers and mentors.

One could only see the outsides of the chambers of course. No one wished to be on display like a frozen piece of protein in the food synthesizers. Everyone knew the *shaxzhu* were here. Their consciences. They were in the first ranks.

Unlike the First Fleet, a larger proportion of passengers were sleepers, rather than breeding generations. A decision that Amunsit approved of. There were many more people under proper care and control that way. It was safer to be hibernating. But she never acknowledged to herself whether it was safer for them or for her.

She stood in the main gallery, on the care floor rather than the observation gallery, clusters of sleepers ranged around her like the comb of a hive, the cool hum of machinery making the image stronger. In the late-night cycle there was almost no one there, save a service tech off in the distance, checking the systems, a slow, careful rotation of maintenance so that no moment of inattention or neglect should threaten the race. The light was Sekahmant high, Sun down, all surfaces reflecting the white/*murn* light and stark black. She found it chill and calming. *Selnarm* was minimal, only the techs awake and the very distant service crews like the sleeping pulse of the ship.

Her hibernation space was off to the left, darkened now because it was empty, waiting for her to finish her work this cycle, making sure that her vision for the Race would continue on its well-ordered track. Cool, *murn* light enveloped her and she whispered her assurances to ears that could not hear. "You will be safe. As safe as I can make you. You are Illudor's dreams and I am the guardian at his gate."

It is my sacred trust and it is one I will not fail. "I will see you safe."

She could feel the darkness around the Second Fleet, enclosing and protecting it like the walls of a hibernation pod. Culture frozen in place until it drifted down into a life-supporting atmosphere. "I will see you safe."

Her words clicked and rustled against the cool, silent pods as brittle as insect wings, falling back to her ears like shards of crystal snow. (Certainty. Fanatical will.)

CHAPTER SIX

"What do you mean, 'We're surrendering?'"

The noise in the briefing room was incredible. Not only were the black uniformed Marines physically present making themselves heard, those on duty and present on the monitors were also shouting, trying to speak. Those in the room were on their feet. No matter what exactly they were saying it was a uniform "No!" against Cyrus Waldeck's last orders. In fact it was a "Hell no!"

Elizabeth Van Felsen sat quietly and listened to the wave of anger and fear wash through the room for a long moment. It was not only almost impossible to stop the reaction in these soldiers; it was also inadvisable *not* to let it happen. She had her teeth set behind her calm face, a throwback to the Northern European type with white-blond hair and surprisingly almond-shaped blue eyes. There was also a heavyset, muscular form under her trim RFN uniform that tended to short rather than rangy. She'd been within a couple of millimeters of being too short to be a Marine. Her cousin Ulla always said that if she weren't training like a maniac, she'd look like round little great-great-great grandmother Anzehla swathed in widow's black. Whereupon Elizabeth would always try to thump cousin Ulla and not succeed because Ulla was a gold medalist on the dojo floor and no slouch herself.

The noise was building to an explosive level when she reached forward one hand and briefly pushed the "panic button" that set off the base alarms. As the raucous tone cut through the hubbub she leaned forward and turned it off, leaning on her forearms. Into the sudden silence she said quietly, "Now that you have that all out of your systems, ladies and gentlemen, may I remind you that you happen to be Marines?" The silence took on a weight as her words marched on inexorably. Quietly. With deadly calm.

"As Marines you will obey orders given by a superior officer even if you don't like them." Her amplified voice was getting slowly louder as she spoke. "And you people will bloody well bust your asses to follow said orders!" She gazed over the rows of faces, her eye picking out NCO Wiese's impassive face here and Lieutenant Cheung's black glower there. "Or are we talking mutiny in the face of the enemy, here?"

The Marines on their feet sat down. Some abruptly, like Captain Peters, or more controlled like Corporals Wismer and Li. As commander, she knew them all, and ran her eyes over them regulars and reservists alike, the bulk of the reservists the presence on the monitors. Lieutenant Alessandro McGee particularly was having a difficult time controlling his feelings about being told to surrender.

"As Marines we will keep our faith, as we swore, but ..." She stopped and held their attention, focusing them with that single word that could make all the difference. "But, we are not going to follow them stupidly. Is that clear?"

There was some coughing and clearing of throats as people nodded and a rumble of "Clear, Sir" rolled through the room. Van Felsen tapped the red dragon on her collar and allowed a tiny smile to appear on her face. "Sergeant Danilenko, if you've got a pack of Vile Wolves circling the house and barn do you just go charging out by your lonesome with a rifle blazing in each hand?" Igor Illyich Danilenko, whose family was homesteading on Madras, smiled dryly.

"Only if dying young you would be. Unless vid heroes like Awesome Man and his Tabby sidekick you are, with invulnerable purple tights."

There was a rasping chuckle at the image of the cartoon hero and his Orion companion who had muscles on his muscles, rueful as the men and women in the room began to realize that they were no longer in a stand-up war but a guerrilla war.

"Now, ladies and gentlemen, we have only got a few hours before the aliens actually manage to get here so there are going to be some massive changes. All the reservists and one half of you people were never here and never in the military at all. You will disappear into the population and your job is to be available for whatever we need to do. We will be establishing ways to make contact and get orders, without being terribly obvious about it."

She sighed, quietly enough that the pickup didn't catch it. "The fleet withdrew. We don't have support. Commander Wu and the strike fighters are out of contact and though we're trying to reestablish the connection it's slow going. Acrocotinth Base is refusing to respond."

There was a collective inhalation at that particular piece of news and she had no doubt that the rumor mill would be buzzing with the argument that she and Wu had had just before this briefing. The one where he'd hung up on her.

Van Felsen, though she was furious with him and felt betrayed, she knew that he was only doing what she herself ached to do. But her job was to see that she and all of her Marine detachments along with the Peaceforcers obeyed orders.

"We only have maybe forty-eight hours before the aliens get here, Sir." Commander Wu nodded slowly, then more decisively. "Well, we'll do what we have to." He looked down the briefing room table at his officers and behind them, on the wall, his satellite image of the planetary surface. It was the planet he loved, the six island continents, each with its entourage of islands, down to the last rocky shoal and frilly bit of coastline. The sensi-artist had incorporated the acid/iodine smell of the ocean and the faint cry of gulls in the distance into the piece. Some people thought it was inappropriate for a briefing room but he thought that it focused people on what was important, Bellerophon itself, and its people.

He knew that he was disobeying orders but could not see himself as a mutineer. *Don't give commands that you know cannot be obeyed. They won't be.* His officers' faces showed their mixed emotions, their need to fight an enemy who had killed so many of their own with the sinking sensation of failure to obey direct orders, but they were obeying him. That made it doable. It would be on his head, the way it should be. Acrocotinth would go down fighting.

"We'll do what we can, people."

"Carrying unfamiliar warriors and not refitted enough to fight, our gallant ship, ordered into retreat by the Human planetary defense commander transits to make contact with Vice Admiral Erica Krishmahnta. We will continue recording, even as we lose contact with Kaazyorzza News. Sending, from the front of the new war at Bellerophon, this is the Least Claw Showaath'sekakhu-jahr."

"Cut."

Zheelanak lowered his camera as the ready light went off. "I repeat my admonishment, Showaath." The word he used for admonishment would have translated into Terran as "claw strike across the nose."

"Oh, I know. We should have covered the war from the other side of the warp point. No, my *theernowlus*"—she used the word that meant personal risk-taking necessary for honor—"says we'd be cut off from information then, Zheelanak, and our duty is here."

He growled as he packed up his equipment, and cast a glance where the *Celmithyr'theaarnouw* had vanished. "We agreed that the rest of the crew would do better there, but I've noticed which side of the warp point you are on." She preened her face whiskers, smoothing the pale lightning flashes of fur, narrowing her eyes.

He found himself unconsciously reacting to her as a female and turned away, annoyed with himself. It was a quality that carried through the media and made her very popular with Orion males who watched her news broadcasts.

"Personally," she continued, "Knowing your father, I'm surprised that you aren't trying to get hold of a fighter to go out and engage the enemy personally. It would be the highest honor."

He jerked his chin at her with his chuckle, the closed-lip smile of a fanged species. "And I'm not surprised, knowing *your* father, that you are going to go underground with the Humans, rather than risking yourself in a fight."

She ducked her head to attend to packing up her own microphones. With the rest of the crew gone, they had minimal equipment . . . all of which could be easily concealed.

"There are those at home who would think we are both *theermish* for not fighting," she said, unable to keep the reflexive growl out of her tone. He hissed at the word and turned abruptly to face her.

"You are not a risk-shirker or coward. You do not send others out to fight for you." He spat at the thought, his fur bristled out around his harness. "Stop that. We are establishing the honor of the journalist. To knowledge. To truth."

She hissed softly in response to his vehemence, suddenly glad to see that he wasn't automatically being protective because of hormones. "To the truth."

He nodded and picked up his case. "My father once explained the difference between true honor and mere reputation."

Showaath laughed. "Mine as well. He said that if your own honor was satisfied, then everything else was *chofaki* shit."

"Sounds like him. Let's go, Least Claw."

"Of course, Cub of the Khan."

"Minor Cluster Commander, we are coming up on maneuvering point one."

"Thank you, First Tentacle SenAnkaht." The young *Destoshaz* visibly colored with nervousness as Daihd acknowledged. Everyone was off color with encountering these creatures and now they were coming up on the planet that would be First Fleet's New Home and it seemed that the surface was teeming with them.

What should have been New Homecoming for the Dispersal was tainted with this, though a surprising number of the *Destoshaz* were beginning to see it as Illudor's way of validating the *Anaht'doh Kainat*, the Star Wanderers. Daihd wasn't sure of what she felt, personally. She was as shocked as the rest of the Fleet at all of it, but she set her mind to do her duty.

The bigger ships were coming around from that spot in space where the aliens had disappeared, after clearing away the fortresses that had guarded it. It took time for the biggest to change direction at all, and none of the scientists wanted to shut off the drives that had worked so well for almost fifteen hundred years without some assurance that they could start them again if necessary. Thus it was that Daihd had suddenly inherited command of Mobile Squadron from the unfortunate Junior Admiral Vakelnar.

"Small craft rising from the surface, position *ranteen* by eighty-six." There was no moon for this planet, with the orbit-grazing asteroids in inconvenient period for any kind of base, which would make this easier.

She clasped tentacles and tapped her main claws together. "Let them come to us, Primes Trumanhk and Ilrasenk."

"Acknowledged." Her two division primes responded almost as one and she felt satisfaction that they worked together so well. The five tenders vastly outnumbered the small fighters rising to meet them and she wasn't terribly worried about what they could do. No matter how many Arduans they would inconvenience with what one of her year-mates had called "a temporary case of death," these creatures would not stop the settlement of New Home—or New Ardu, given that people were still arguing over which would be more appropriate, even after fourteen hundred years.

Lieutenant William Chong tapped the implant over his left ear as he pulled the strike fighter's nose up steeply, juddering just on the edge of stalling as they howled through the fading grab of the atmosphere. He'd been meaning to have the com link looked at, since it was sending annoying, barely audible, bursts of static at random intervals, but now it looked like he just wouldn't have time.

The planet-based fighters were heavier than the carrier birds, given that the support crews were also heavier. The squadrons weren't designed to go into high-Bellerophon orbit but they were heading out past the Roche limit where a moon could exist, if the planet had had one. The aliens were coming and it looked like they were all that opposed them. Chong didn't think about what his orders from Commander Wu meant. He knew. So did everyone in every one of the fighters climbing out of the atmosphere.

For a second he let himself see and feel the heart-stopping blue that the border of the planet, the periphery of the atmosphere was; the shining gleam of the leading edge of sunlight and spangled stars of cities and towns in the night behind it; the towns that he was going to defend if . . . until . . . he died trying. Then he turned his attention outward into the dark into the night where the aliens would come. "Bogart Squadron," he said as the last of his group cleared atmosphere. "Clear."

"Lamar Squadron, clear." He tapped the com unit again and the transmissions came in clearly for once. "Brando Squadron, clear."

The other squadrons cleared cleanly, except for Streep and Zerephi, both of whom had fighters in them that should have been down for maintenance and were lagging. Not that it mattered. As long as they could actually get out to four hundred thousand kilometers and fight when they got there. It would play merry hell with their groups' coordination, but that was better than them not being there at all.

They formed up and headed out to intercept the aliens before they could reach orbit. It took a few hours before they all cleared the last of the shipyards and it gave Chong a chill to see how empty the usual approaches were. The private hulls had left and corporations had pulled out every vessel they'd had in Bellerophon space. There had been an enormous, but mercifully short political battle to get evacuees onboard. There were only a few thousand of those because you could only pack so many private ships to the bulkheads. Anything that could make the warp had. But this space was empty enough now that there was no need for traffic control.

Lieutenant Chong shook off the mood. There were millions still to defend and hostiles on the horizon. He wasn't descended from the humans who believed in Valhalla, but his ancestry was Japanese as well as Chinese. He had bushido in their genes.

"Missiles! Incoming! Incoming!" Chong narrowed green-gold eyes and he heard, over static, Cappelli and Onehawk yell something decidedly nonregulation, but didn't reprimand them, as they engaged. *See you in hell, you bastards.*

The sound of the vid in the next room kept pulling Jennifer Pietchkov out of her latest attempt at "Flight." She knew that she couldn't work effectively, not now, but it was better than sitting, waiting, flipping through the various shows, knowing that a hostile alien force was approaching the planet; knowing what she did from Alessandro, who was pacing back and forth in the other room, his steps moving from tile to carpet and back again. He'd raged at first when he'd been evacuated from the asteroid mines where his company had based him, and if he'd raged then he'd been white-hot when ordered to "surrender," by Commander Van Felsen. Now his anger was icy, contained in his 180-centimeter frame, clutched tight in his broad hands.

He was a rare redhead, a throwback to his forbearers on a small island on old Earth. Jennifer had always teased him and called him her Abyssinian tiger, all red sand, chocolate stripes and a need to flex his claws. His fellows in the Reserves just called him "Tank."

—ffering theories about the amount of energies contained in the "quantum foam" of empty space. This energy is visualized most readily to a layman by picturing the spontaneous creation and immediate destruction of pairs of particles and antiparticles. This occurs in what would otherwise appear to be all of ordinary vacuum, and since the sum amount of matter and energy involved remains a constant null, it has no direct effect on our perceptions. Thus, the universe is not overwhelmed by the titanic forces erupting from the distance between nothing and nothing.

Some theorists tell of possible means by which the parity rate of particle creation and annihilation could be altered. This excess of either particle would result in a net outflow of energy and matter from what would otherwise seem to be originating from an empty volume of space. Many of these theorists, eager to cling to the basic philosophical prospects of conservation of mass and energy, describe this resultant energy flow condition as a "pinhole" in the fabric of space-time as we know it.

The amount of energy involved is significant: a single cubic centimeter of vacuum contains, in some estimates, more than enough energy to rival the output of a small star. Others claim this estimate is low by a mere factor of thirty-six decimal places. Some amusing wagers have been attached by leading cosmologists should any empirical testing be allowed.

A much smaller pinhole would still create incredible power, but as the energy was radiated into our universe, it would most likely take the form of hard radiation, and extend into creating exotic particles that have not existed in our universe since the primordial monobloc degenerated into the Big Bang. Such particles could range from simple neutrinos to macroparticles massive enough to collapse into quantum black holes, with masses ranging from billions of tons to those of a small asteroid. An adroit physicist—or her competent grad-student assistant—would perhaps promote a more efficient harnessing of the energies from such a pinhole by "throttling" the dimensions of the "opening" of the pinhole into our universe, perhaps to the scale of a few Planck radii, and further discriminate which particles could be permitted to escape out into our own universe.

Sacrificing most of the energy into such a filtering mechanism—and then shielding said physicist and possibly even the grad student from the outflow - would still leave one with an abundant amount of energy. It would be more than enough to propel even the most gargantuan of vessels to the very edge of Einsteinian space. It would be reasonable to surmise that since these visitors have been decelerating with these drives spewing their output in our direction for what would be some time now, and our detection equipment has not noticed an excess of exotic particles in the local solar system's environment, one could assume if this is thei—

"'Sandro, would you please turn that thing off? All we're getting is these university types blathering about stuff that's not important anymore." She put her 'caster down on the work table, sat down with her head in her hands, running her fingers up into her tight, glossy brown ringlets. She was, like most of humanity, a café au lait color and had the sharp-edged features of what had once been Uzbekistan. Those fingers were calloused with use of power chisels, scrapers, and sensi-caster. She'd kept working, even when it had become clear that the alien contact had gone terribly wrong; it was her way of dealing with her feelings, to the point that her insulated cabinets all around the room were full. She'd even had to leave a couple of statues out with insul-blankets tied around them and they still leaked if you got too close.

The fear was almost palpable. Or maybe it was just her own. The unknown, coupled with the knowledge of hostility was enough to ruin everyone's sleep.

. . . hand, if one can "tune" the pinhole to emit specific particles, a spray of positrons and antineutrons could be emitted from the exhaust of such an engine. Alas, while it sounds effective, I would be loath to spray such materials out into the path I was decelerating into. Since they did not do this as a means of defense, I can assume either they cannot, or that I should be on somewhat stronger antipsychotic medication. . . . I would be loath to take such a delicate mechanism into a combat environment, especially one where the dominant energies it would produce are needed to restrain the very forces harnessed. I would certainly not wish to be near one such engine if it malfunctioned.

We must not assume too much or too little of our visitors. All of their vessels function under the same laws of physics we dwell in. Their smaller vessels seem to function using technology similar in design to our own, if not in scale. None of the "tenders" seem to use the more flamboyant drive of the larger vessels. Perhaps there is an economy of scale in the support mecha—

With a snap, Alessandro finally cut off the droning voice of the university fathead, before coming into the room and enveloping her with a hug. "You're right, ma sweet."

He buried his face in her neck as she clung to him, for a moment just resting in each other's strength, breathing together, as if they could hold off the anxiety with sheer will.

"You're reverting to your accent, love," she said, finally as she raised her head. "I knew that Ruari Mac Ruari would get you one day." Jen managed to startle a laugh out of him. His arms tightened as he did.

"You think?" he said quietly. "If there's anyone we're going to need it's that character." The persona he'd created, of an eighteenth-century Scottish highwayman for a group he'd belonged to in university, had been a joke between them, since that had been how they'd met, Jennifer being Bess, an English innkeeper's daughter. It had been years since they'd played at being historical figures but Jen always had to smile because 'Sandro reverted to Ruari's accent when he was severely stressed.

"I know it's hard to wait." She put one hand on his cheek, feeling the bristle of whiskers. Even if he depilated twice a day, his beard always seemed to be just ahead of it all the time. "You'll manage. Your commander's a sneaky one."

"Ya. I just . . ." He shrugged, lifting her right onto his lap. "I suppose I'll learn patience."

"You'll have to." They both glanced upward as though they could see through the ceiling and miles of atmosphere and space to see what was happening off-planet, then away. "Why don't I make us some coffee," she said. *Though I'm going to let mine get cold again.* "Then you can help me position the holo generator for the Thai Gallery's new piece."

She could feel the effort he put into relaxing his muscles, making himself stand down. "Sure and I'll help you, lass." He lifted her off him and set her gently down on the cough, easy as thistledown though she wasn't a small woman. Jen sighed and bit her lip. She loved the man dearly but he wasn't the sort of partner you'd call into the bathroom to watch you pee on the little plastic strip. This was just the lousiest time to tell him she was pregnant. Hell, it was the lousiest time to *be* pregnant.

Lieutenant Chong ignored the shrieking alarms and redlining gauges. He was close enough inside this monster's shields that he could see, even as he focused on his last missile target. *My last missile. Everyone's last missiles.* Out of the corner of his eye he could see, by eye, the fireball as the last of squadron Streep plowed into the alien SD, gouging a glowing hole in the hull. *We can't do enough damage. We . . .*

He whipped his fighter around in a maneuver that he shouldn't have tried, as the energy emplacement sheared through his port side. *Hull breach.* His suit air kicked in and he blinked watering eyes, shaking his head, trying to keep his target clear. *Missile away.* Somehow he pulled the limping fighter out of the chaff, and his drive cut out.

Then, astonishingly, there was silence. He was still alive. His gauges were still red or amber. His drive was dead. That wasn't supposed to happen. Generally any kind of engagement was all or nothing. He hadn't expected to survive that last run. He had no ammunition left. His primary was nonfunctioning. And they hadn't killed him. Was anyone else left? He tapped the implant . . . got only silence. He wasn't aware that there were tears on his face.

Was there something else he could throw at them? Anything? Only his unvoiced curses. He could only sit and watch as they shrank from enormous to merely huge as they bypassed him, then they were small against the darkness and smaller until they vanished, heading into a lower orbit. "Squadron, respond. Respond." They hadn't blown him out of the sky, but they hadn't stopped to pick him up, either.

Nothing. He rerouted power feeds, sent the repair protocols running. The memory metals and transpolymer filaments made it possible that he might be able to get some kind of power. His hands moved on the controls lightly. One of his gauges flickered from red to yellow and then another. His engine readouts bounced from zero to max and back before coming up to five percent power. He couldn't catch up to those . . . He struggled to control his emotional reaction. The aliens. He would not allow himself to hate.

His first duty was to see if he could even get home at all, then he'd report and see if he could continue the fight, somehow. He touched the sleeve pocket where he kept Jeannie's pic. It hurt, having hope, even the little he had now. But it was better than being dead.

Daihd flexed her claws absently working the kinks out as she watched the screens. (Concentration.) The bridge of the *Nasanhkorat* would have looked very strange to human eyes. Not only was the light wrong, but all of the stations were set in a ring that mimicked their clusters, with open space around the outside. It had, of necessity, expanded past the tight ring that physical defense required, but retained the ancient quality. This was one of the older tenders. Daihd would have preferred the new designs that incorporated the vertical as well. She didn't maintain minimum gravity in the ship the way some did, but did drop it considerably in all her training, and now, combat. She'd be a fool not to take advantage of something that reduced fatigue and raised reaction times.

The *shaxzhu* might nag about maintaining gravity at "normal" levels to facilitate the transition to planetary life, but they hadn't even had a good argument for that until four hundred years ago when it became clear that the target system had nongas giant planets for Arduans to settle on. Up until that point they might have had to create space stations around the star. Daihd herself wasn't sure if she even *wanted* to become a planet dweller.

"I have a fix, Cluster Commander. That island, there." (Excitement, willingness.)

"They are broadcasting something, Cluster Commander. Audio only, again." (Fear, disgust.)

"Put it in the files, perhaps we'll figure it out sometime. Prepare to bombard that island." (Satisfaction, completion.) "I want kinetic strikes because we don't want to dirty up our nice new home now, do we? There was a ripple of amusement around the control circle. "Then we need to try to communicate with these things. After the strike, respond to that broadcast. I will speak to it and see if it can understand language."

The handful of missiles slid out of their launch tubes. Against the darkness and vacuum silence, their launch flares sparked like small stars, winked out, blinked on twice more as their courses were corrected, went out as they fell noiselessly toward the planet. They entered the atmosphere under power, their tracks lighting up white, like magnesium flares. The shock wave didn't roll across the sky until long seconds later.

Alessandro had turned on the vid again and stood in front of it, clenching and unclenching his hands. "Jen." His voice was flat.

She came out of the workshop and stood as well. The BRR news satellite showed the missiles hitting the upper atmosphere, red glows brightening to eye-hurting brilliance. The news cams were in the wrong position to show people what happened, but an independent feed on a sailing craft gave them the images.

"—Jeez, Hal, can't we get any more speed out of this bitch? . . . Oh, shit, there go the aircraft. They cut it fine— . . . could the engine help? No, dammit. Oh. Hell. Here it comes."

The picture, tipping up and down with the movement of the ship shifted from the aircraft evacuating the fighter base to the streaks of light across the sky, blocked for a second by the edge of sail. They seemed to become dimmer as they hurtled deeper into the atmosphere. The camera lost their track, picked up the old, old thunder of their initial entry. It focused on the shimmer that was Acrocotinth in the distance and for a moment nothing happened, the peculiar ringing hush before disaster: seeing the first motion in an avalanche, understanding that the volcano is belching a pyroclastic flow of superheated gas and rock that can outrun a car.

Alessandro put his arm around Jen and held her tight as they, like everyone else on the planet, watched. There was a multiple blink like a string of firecrackers going off at one's feet, only a thousand kilometers away, that overwhelmed the capacity of the screen; it blanked white for a moment. An expanding ball of dust rose, its core glowing as the air caught fire, towering up into the sky as the dome of expansion was pinched in by the inrush of air. The shock wave hit the boat, a confusion of images, a wild swinging of the camera, spume and a sail in tattered flames tilting upward to gray-green and white; then nothing.

In the tank before Van Felsen's desk there was finally an image, with a voice that the translators sputtered and struggled with for long moments. The thing in the image was bald and bright gold, had three eyes—one larger and centered above two smaller ones and what seemed to be masses of tentacles on the ends of its arms. Its expression blank, it clicked two claws on one "hand" together and said, "### #### stop ### #### fighting."

CHAPTER SEVEN

"It's a war, all right."

Waterside was one of the oldest residential districts in Prescott, sprawling along the Alph estuary downriver from Government House and ending at a seawall overlooking the harbor. In fact, it dated back to the city's early days as a city, as distinguished from a military installation's residential annex. Typically early colonial, the houses made extensive use of native materials and nestled among old native trees. Less typically, they embodied a distinctive local style which architecture critics of an antiquarian bent called "Neo-Tudor" although no one else on Xanadu understood the reference.

Miriam Ortega remembered Waterside from the time of the Fringe Revolution. She had been living in a small rented house that, like its neighbors, had settled into a kind of shabby/picturesque upper-middle-class ambience. There, she had received word of her father's death in the First Battle of Zephrain. And there, a short time later, the already almost legendary Admiral Trevayne had rung her doorbell—a courtesy call which had developed into something very unexpected. . . .

She thrust away the thought and concentrated on the view through her ground car's window. Subsequently, the district had been rediscovered and the old houses restored and extended. But, pricey though Waterside had become, Ian Trevayne could have afforded something far more pretentious—a suite in the high-technology wonderlands of the sky-spearing towers, or a large and equally cutting-edge estate out in the hinterlands. But when a riverfront house not far from the seawall had gone on the market, he had told his agent to buy the place.

Parking the ground car, Miriam passed through the gate in the low stone wall that enclosed the small front garden and rang for admittance. The door swung open as the security system recognized her as one with automatic access. She stepped into a dim hallway, beyond which sliding glass doors opened onto a terrace overlooking the estuary. It was a warm early summer afternoon, and the doors were open. Miriam stepped through onto the terrace, which commanded a superb view. To the right, beyond the headland, the ocean stretched to the horizon. To the left, upriver, the towers of central Prescott could be glimpsed in the hazy distance. Directly across the estuary, at the water's edge, homes not unlike this one peered out from foliage in which Terran oak and hickory mingled with native featherleaf.

And, silhouetted against the riverscape, a tall young-seeming man stood at the balustrade, hands clasped behind his back, staring fixedly out across the water.

"Hello, Ian," Miriam said quietly.

He turned, startled. "Oh, uh, Miriam," he stammered.

"The robot let me in," she offered by way of explanation.

"Naturally." He nodded.

Silence stretched.

"Nice place you've got here," she said, making conversation. "I still remember this area. Do you think my old house is still standing?"

"Yes, it is," Trevayne said . . . and immediately realized just how promptly he'd said it. "Uh, that is, I just happened to pass it on one of my walks around the area. Of course, it's been renovated quite a bit since we . . ."

"Yes, of course."

Again, silence closed over them.

It was the first time they had confronted each other without any third parties present to cushion the awkwardness. She thought she understood that awkwardness better than he did—or, at least, she ought to with the advantage of age.

No pair of old lovers in human history had ever faced a situation remotely like theirs. Trevayne's memories of that love were fresh— only a few months old. Those memories included a Miriam Ortega in her thirties, almost fifteen years his junior. But he had awakened to find her in antigerone-mitigated old age, their love overlaid in her memory by eight unshared decades of recollections and experiences of which he had no part, including . . .

"How are your sons?" he asked, to fill the silence. "And their families?"

"Oh, they're well enough. Aaron has accepted a professorship on Aotearoa now, which is where his daughter and her husband are. I keep telling him I hope his grandchildren don't pick up the accent they have there!"

"The one you always say—or always *used* to say—reminded you of mine," he said accusingly.

She looked blank for a perceptible and hurtful moment before recalling the old mock bone of contention, then laughed. "Ramon is still here on Xanadu—a senior partner in his law firm. He has three children, and I've almost lost count of how many grandchildren!"

"Yes," Trevayne said softly. He reflected on her sons—both far older now in duration-of-consciousness terms than he was—and her grandchildren, whose bodies were physiologically older than his. He also reflected on their father. *Who would ever have dreamed it? Miriam and . . .*

"Joaquin Sandoval." Realizing he had murmured the name of the young fighter jock who had been his operations officer out loud, he hastily added, "I was sorry to hear about his death."

Miriam nodded. "Even after he made captain, and even with the prosthetic leg he had after Zapata, he could never resist taking crazy risks. But I knew that, or should have known it, when I . . . when we . . ." Her voice trailed off. But her eyes continued to meet Trevayne's, level and unapologetic.

"Of course," said Trevayne, nodding. The two words covered a great many things.

After a moment, Miriam spoke with an attempt at briskness. "Ian, the governor-general asked me to come and see you. Have you heard the news?"

"Oh, yes." All at once, the melancholy she had interrupted was back. "I was just now thinking about Sean."

"His loss was a terrible blow to us all. I know how you must feel."

"I'm not sure you do." The words might have been brusque, but his voice was not. He was talking as much to himself as to her. "To you he lived a long, full life, even as such things are measured nowadays. As you're mourning him, you can remind yourself of eight decades that, for me, simply didn't happen. As far as my consciousness is concerned, he was cut off in his prime." *As our love was cut off in its prime,* he didn't add.

Looking in her eyes, he knew he hadn't had to add it.

"Ian . . ." she tried to begin.

"I know," he said, nodding slowly.

And there was nothing more to be said. Standing only a few feet apart, they gazed at each other across a chasm unique in human experience. When she spoke again, it was as if that cryptic exchange had never taken place.

"It's not just the loss of Sean, Ian. It's . . . well, the government is still in shock over what's happened. The sheer *size* of these ships is terrifying."

"That's not what the government ought to find terrifying. This is the first time in history that the human race has encountered hostile aliens who came to us through normal space. Are you aware of what a shock it was when closed warp points first came to light?"

"Well, yes," she said, puzzled at the seeming irrelevancy. "It was centuries ago, and I've never been a history buff like you, but I do know it came as a surprise that here were warp points which, for whatever reason—and as far as I know it's still not fully understood—simply couldn't be detected until somebody actually came through them."

"Precisely. Before that, the universe of interstellar travel had seemed an orderly and relatively safe one. You simply went through one warp point and emerged into a new system, which you then surveyed for other warp points. And so on. But then it turned out that nasty surprises could appear out of nowhere. That was bad enough, even though closed warp points proved to be relatively rare. But now . . ." Trevayne swept his arm around in a gesture that encompassed the cloud-fleeced blue firmament above. "Now the entire sky has, in effect, become one vast closed warp point! If these aliens crossed normal space to Bellerophon, they can cross it to *anywhere,* given enough time."

"But Ian, surely *no* civilization limited to a single system could launch more than one expedition like this! My god, those ships—!"

"That may be true. But have you considered that this may not be an 'expedition' in the usual sense of the word? Maybe it's an ... exodus."

Miriam Ortega stared at the youth's body that contained the man who had, long ago, won her love. And she began to remember why.

Trevayne turned away and leaned on the balustrade, staring out at things far beyond the river. "Slower-than-light interstellar ships—'generation ships' was the term—were common in both fiction and scientific speculation before the discovery of warp points. But there were always problems with the concept—ethical ones, to begin with. Presumably the initial crew would be volunteers; but what about their children, and all the unborn generations? By what right could *they* be consigned to such an unnatural existence without their consent? And then there was the impossible political economics of the thing. What society would be willing to make such a staggering investment in a project which couldn't possibly show any return within the lifetimes of the taxpayers' many-times-great grandchildren, if ever?" He turned around to face her, and his eyes were somber beyond their apparent years. "No. Such a thing could only be justified by the direst necessity: species survival itself."

"So you think they're running from something," Miriam breathed. "But what? An invasion?" A chill went through her at the thought of an enemy able to send the race that could build those incredible ships fleeing for its life.

"I hardly think so. That wouldn't have allowed them time to prepare a fleet like this."

"That's a relief. But in that case ... what?"

"Haven't the foggiest. A nearby supernova ought to do it."

"Whose light wouldn't necessarily have reached us yet." She nodded, recalling the paradoxes of the warp network.

"Precisely. But the point is that they might well have launched more than one survival fleet. In fact, I should think they would have. There's an old saying about not putting all one's eggs in one basket."

Miriam took a deep breath. "This is certainly food for thought. You may well be right. If this really is a species with its back to the wall, it may account for something that's been worrying the government almost as much as the size of those ships: the apparent disregard of these beings for their own lives. In fact, that's caused something close to panic."

"I can well imagine. In my time, seemingly suicidal tactics meant one thing to most people: the Arachnids. And I doubt if that's changed much now. The Bug War was an experience burned permanently into the human psyche." Trevayne shook his head. "But I can't believe that the galaxy could hold more than one race like that at a time. And there's more behind that feeling than just an instinctive recoiling from horror. The scientific consensus holds that a technologically advanced hive consciousness was a freak of chance."

"I hope this is one of the times the scientific consensus is right." A shudder ran through Miriam. She reached inside her briefcase and withdrew a sheaf of hard copy. "This is an intelligence analysis of their tactics. There was the usual bureaucratic horseshit about 'security,' but getting around it was no trouble after I reminded the governor-general that it was *you* we were talking about!" Her nasty grin faded quickly. "It also includes our total losses. It's been withheld from the media. For once, I agree."

Trevayne skipped ahead to that part. He immediately wished he hadn't. He was afraid he was going to be sick.

"It gets worse," said Miriam grimly. She took out her personal pocket computer and set it on the balustrade. It was one of the late models that would accept verbal commands. She spoke a few words and a holographic display screen came to life in midair. It showed a warp-line chart of the usual sort, which bore absolutely no relation to the actual three-dimensional locations of the stars in the real space. It looked more like a very old-fashioned circuit diagram. Trevayne examined it. It showed the Bellerophon Arm.

"As you know," Miriam began, "I'm the most unmilitary person you'd ever hope to meet—"

"Yes, I remember," smiled Trevayne, who had always found her candid avowals of ignorance refreshing, even while recalling Shakespeare's *"the lady doth protest too much, methinks."*

"—but even I can see the strategic implications of what has happened. By taking the Bellerophon system, they've cut off the entire Arm—like chopping a tree at the base. Furthermore, Bellerophon is—or was—the only major Fleet Base in the Arm. The naval people tell me that we have no great strength in the rest of the Arm—"

"No need for it," Trevayne interjected.

"—so the local systems can't hope to resist these beings when they figure out about warp points and start working their way up the warp chain."

"Which they will," Trevayne stated unequivocally. "I gather they've observed warp transits. And anyone capable of normal-space interstellar flight can surely work out the implications. Our own ancestors weren't even close to such a technological level back in the twenty-first century when the *Hermes* blundered through Sol's one warp point on its way from Europa Station to Neptune." He shook his head slowly, contemplating the sheer improbability of the accident that had made humanity a player on the interstellar stage.

After a few moments, Miriam broke the silence. "Ian, as I told you, the governor-general asked me to come. He probably thought I should be the one to talk to you because of . . . well, you know . . ."

"Yes, you did mention that." Trevayne rescued her with a getting-down-to-business tone. "And I've just been indulging in speculation—'farting at the wrong end,' as Sean always said. I do appreciate being given access to this information you've brought. But I'm not clear on *why* I'm being given access to it. Or on what it is the governor-general wants of me."

"No, you wouldn't know, would you? You've been so busy familiarizing yourself with the present-day world and keeping up with the big news stories that you haven't had a chance to get out and . . . Well, Ian, the fact of the matter is that the people of the Rim Federation have been looking for something—or someone—to turn to in this crisis. And they're starting to look at you."

At first he simply stared at her, stunned beyond the possibility of a response.

"There is, I think, almost a mythic quality to what they're feeling," she continued. "Something deep in the human psyche: the hero who will return when his people need him. Like King Arthur, or Holger the Dane." She smiled at Trevayne's evident surprise. "Yeah, I've actually read up on those Old Terran legends, to help me understand the way public opinion has started to fixate on you. Only, unlike those guys, you really *have* returned! The people see the founding father of the Rim Federation walking among them again."

"But I never wanted for there to *be* a 'Rim Federation!' All I was trying to do was hold the Rim for the legitimate Terran Federation government."

"That's been lost sight of for a long time. But yes, I suppose there is a certain irony in the way the people of the Rim look on you now."

"'A certain irony'? It's absurd—as absurd as that bloody statue you let them put up. 'Founding father' indeed! You're the Rim Federation's founding mother."

"I'm too modest for false modesty." She grinned. "But the times require a warrior hero. Like it or not, you're it. People have even been comparing you to Howard Anderson."

"*What?* But . . . but . . . !" Trevayne was inarticulate in the face of what was, to him, a form of blasphemy. Howard Anderson, the legend who had led the young Terran Federation's navy through the fires of the first two interstellar wars, then guided the Federation through the third as its president, and later . . .

"Well," said Miriam with her old mischievousness, "you *are* chronologically almost as old as Anderson was when he came out of retirement for the Theban War. And you're the most senior officer in the Rim Federation Navy."

Trevayne brought himself under control and took a deep breath. "Miriam, on the large assumption that this isn't an overelaborate joke, let me try to enumerate the objections. First of all, I'm not even on the active list."

"That's easily remedied."

"All right. That just leads to the second problem. My 'seniority' has been accumulated while doing nothing but getting well and truly freezer-burned! Bloody hell, Sean Remko had an active career twice as long as my entire conscious life span! So has Cyrus Waldeck. There must be other officers with almost as much experience as that. How do you suppose they'd feel about having some relic out of an historical novel placed over them? And you can be sure my current apparent age wouldn't help a bit!"

"I can see how some people might feel resentment," Miriam admitted.

"Then consider this: they'd be *right* to feel it. I'm still hopelessly out of date on modern technology. All the mythic resonance in the galaxy isn't going to matter to them. What they're going to be asking is whether I know what I'm doing well enough to keep them alive. No, if I went back on the active list now, I wouldn't be anything except . . ." Trevayne's face went blank with sudden realization—and instantly hardened into a glare. "I wouldn't be anything except what the governor-general and the prime minister and their advisors *want* me to be: a kind of mascot, to be trotted out on demand to hearten the troops!"

"Oh, Ian, I really don't think that's fair . . ." Miriam's voice trailed off miserably, and her eyes slid away from his coldly angry ones. Normally, she had a working politician's ability to deny anything with a straight face. But not to this man. Nor did it help that she had tried to warn the fatheads in the cabinet that they'd forgotten whom they were dealing with . . . and then, momentarily and inexcusably, forgotten it herself.

"Ask yourself this, Ian," she started over, all useless denials tacitly shelved. "If there's *any* contribution you can make to the defense of the Rim, even as a living symbol, do you have the right to withhold it? You may not have foreseen the Rim Federation, and you probably wouldn't have approved of it if you had foreseen it. But it exists now. And it's the same Rim you fought to defend. And now it's in peril again."

"Miriam, I've come to accept the existence of the Rim Federation. And yes, I'm willing to do my duty. But my duty is *not* to serve as a talking head to rally public support for the government. If I resume active duty, it will not be as a public relations ploy. It will have to be genuine or not at all. And . . . I'm not ready for that yet. I need more time to bring myself up to speed. Bloody hell, I've practically had to go back to the Academy!"

"I understand that, Ian. How about this: I'll ask the Admiralty to assign a special liaison officer to you—someone who's a technical expert but also a good communicator. We'll turn it into a crash course. And you alone will be the judge of when you're ready. Fair enough?"

"Fair enough." He nodded.

"Good. I'll take that word back to the governor-general." She gathered up her things and started to leave, then paused. "Only, don't make it too long. The Admiralty is starting to plan a counteroffensive already, and we want you to be ready by the time the fleet is."

"That latter could take a while, from what I've been reading," Trevayne remarked dubiously.

"Yes. That's why we've been screaming for help from the Pan-Sentient Union—through its Terran Federation component of course. In fact . . ." Miriam looked thoughtful. "I'd have to consult the astronomers. But considering what you were saying earlier about other 'survival fleets,' it's possible the Terran Republic could become involved." Her trademark grin flashed as she observed his expression. "If they do, you could end up renewing acquaintances with another old friend, if that's the word: First Space Lord Li Han!"

The supermonitor slid through space, the light of a nearby sun glinting off its flanks and bringing out the intricate complexity that contrasted with its more-than-mountainous mass.

Trevayne, however, could discern telltale patterns in that complexity, and he recognized this as a specialized missile ship, configured to hurl the heaviest possible salvos of heavy bombardment missiles, hopefully consuming any possible enemy in a holocaust of antimatter annihilation long before he could close to energy-weapon range.

I bloody well ought to recognize it, he reflected. He himself, after fighting his way through the Fringe Revolution to Zephrain, had ordered the first SMTs put into production and supervised the development of the HBM to arm them. So he gazed with a kind of paternal pride on the awesome killing machine, the backbone of the Rim Federation Navy's battle line, as it made its stately way through space.

Of course, the columns of multicolored words and numbers that hung in space off to the side somewhat spoiled the effect. . . .

So did the familiar voice of his liaison officer. "They considered naming it the *Trevayne* class. But they decided that only dead people can have ship classes named after them."

"Good of them not to insist that I meet the qualifications," said Trevayne dryly. He focused his mind and thought a command. The illimitable space through which the supermonitor had moved—and in which he himself had seemed to float like a disembodied god—vanished, leaving the bare walls of the training room.

Trevayne could have turned off the hologram manually. But he needed to practice with the direct neural interfacing that had merely been a theoretical possibility in his earlier life, as it had been for four centuries before his birth. Even now, it was still new technology. And only a small fraction of 1 percent of the human race (and even fewer Orions) possessed the talent for true mind-link, making computers extensions of themselves even though those computers were as far from genuine sentience as they had been eighty years before.

Trevayne had been secretly relieved to hear that last part. And he was not among the tiny talented minority. But he could, with the mental discipline that had always been part of his makeup, give simple commands.

The liaison officer gave a nod of approval. Lieutenant Commander Andreas Hagen was normally attached to the Rim Federation Navy's Bureau of Ships, but had recently been seconded from BuShips to the faculty at Prescott Academy, the Rim's naval academy. There, he had come to the attention of Genji Yoshinaka, who had mentioned his name to Miriam Ortega. Thus it was that he'd been seconded again, and his initial reaction had been ambivalent: awe at the thought of the living legend he was being asked to nursemaid, tempered by the patronizing attitude inherent in the nursemaid relationship. The fact that the living legend looked like one of his students at the Academy only added to his confusion.

But by now his feelings had settled into a kind of equilibrium: solid respect, untroubled by any mythic residues but occasionally jolted out of complacency by surprise at how readily a figure out of history books caught on to things.

He gave another nod. "You've mastered the concentration techniques remarkably well."

Trevayne waved the praise aside. The technology was something he could cope with but which didn't really engage his interest. To his way of thinking, it was a matter for specialists. He needed to know the capabilities of the system, but not the details of how it worked—details which Hagen would be only too appallingly willing to impart, given an opening. So he changed the subject.

"I've gathered that these predominantly missile-armed ships make up two-thirds of the Rim's inventory of supermonitors."

"Yes," Hagen affirmed, dispensing with the formality of "Sir" as Trevayne had asked him to. "The other third are almost equally specialized beam-weapon ships, intended to deal with anything that gets through the long-range missile envelope. But the main reliance is on HBMs. I've always told my students that the doctrine goes back to *you*."

"And now it's being put to the test," said Trevayne, not altogether comfortable with the responsibility. "But I've also gathered that other navies have other design philosophies for their supermonitors."

"Oh, yes. The Terran Republic favors generalist designs with mixed armament, able to engage at any range. The Pan-Sentient

Union uses what they call the 'carrier/main combatant' concept: something like the Republic's, but sacrificing most of the HBM armament in order to pack in as many fighters as possible, for long-range strikes. This, despite the inherent design inefficiencies involved in incorporating fighter launchers into a ship that isn't a purpose-built carrier."

"That's the Orion influence in the PSU," Trevayne chuckled. "They've loved the fighter since the moment it appeared, because it lets them get out and risk their pelts in individual combat as the code of *theernowlus* tells them it befits a warrior to do. A Tabby who's a cog in a large organization with millions of tons of capital ship wrapped around it doesn't feel like a warrior at all."

"I'm sure there's an element of that behind it. But there's also a rational argument: it enables them to deploy so many fighters that they may be able to mount an effective attack against a modern first-rank fleet. That's also the reason for the disappearance of the lighter carriers that existed in your day." (Hagen had learned that this turn of phrase didn't give offense.) "The largest fighter strike you can send out is none too big."

"You know, for me that's been one of the most difficult concepts to adjust to: the decline of the fighter as a deep-space weapon. It's had quite a long run since the Rigelians introduced it."

"Almost three hundred years." Hagen nodded. "But several factors have caught up with it. One is improved screen technology. You remember, of course, the original designs introduced by the Terran Republic."

"Vividly," said Trevayne with a wince. The new energy screens, which automatically reset when they overloaded, instead of simply collapsing in a heap of fused circuits like the older "shields," had been one of the unpleasant surprises Li Han had sprung on him at the Battle of Zapata, mere minutes before the great discontinuity in his life. "And now I understand their generators have been miniaturized by a factor of two."

"Right. But even more importantly, they'll now stop energy emissions in all wavelengths, including x-ray. So ships are a lot more resistant to most fighter weapon packages than they used to be. At the same time, shipboard defensive weaponry has improved. Modern point defense installations can engage up to six fighters at a time, thanks to computer advances. And anti-fighter missiles are effective at much longer ranges—especially the capital AFHAWK mated with strategic bombardment missiles. They can engage fighters at a range of up to thirty light-seconds! And any fighters that get through all this face a storm of powered flechettes—some of them from the new space superiority fighters."

"Ah, yes. That. Another development from a reb— from a *Terran Republic* innovation." Trevayne looked thoughtful. "Naturally, the mere existence of the space superiority fighter requires that anti-shipping fighter strikes have their *own* space superiority fighters as an escort. And those take up launcher capacity. So, aside from its inherent ability to destroy strikefighters, the space superiority fighter has degraded the strikefighter's effectiveness simply by reducing the number of them any given carrier may operate." Trevayne paused, and gazed into Hagen's openmouthed countenance. "Am I not correct?" he inquired mildly.

"Uh . . . yes, Sir," Hagen managed. It was a point he had been about to make, in carefully elementary terms. "And finally, there's the proven impossibility of scaling phased gravitic propulsion down to fighter size—which means that in deep space the fighter has lost its speed advantage."

"Ah, yes: the Desai Drive." Trevayne still had difficulty imagining a velocity half that of light, achieved instantaneously in the usual manner of reactionless drives. The mention of his old subordinate's invention reminded Trevayne that he had sent her a greeting via the courier drones that plied the warp lines through the Terran Republic between the Rim Federation and the Pan-Sentient Union.

"The drive has its drawbacks," Hagen cautioned. "It's not at all maneuverable, and due to gravitational harmonics it won't function at all within a massive body's 'Desai Limit'—roughly two light-minutes from a typical habitable planet, and twenty light-minutes from the kind of stars such planets orbit. So fighters still have a role in planetary defense. And they have some new capabilities for playing that role—notably the FIDATS system." (Hagen stopped himself short of reeling off the full "Fighter Information, Data, and Tactical System." Trevayne would already know what the acronym stood for.) "It permits larger command nets, so larger squadrons are practical."

"Yes," Trevayne mused. "A great deal has changed. But not everything. Ship-to-ship armament is fundamentally as I remember it. The missiles are essentially unchanged."

"The warheads they carry have undergone some development in response to improved ECM and point defense," Hagen argued. "The idea has been to enable them to inflict damage from a greater distance. The laser torpedo for instance—it only has to get within hetlaser range of the target. And the very old shaped-charge concept has been revived in the form of a mag bottle that channels blast effects into a stream of highly radioactive plasma."

"Yes, yes... but the missiles that carry them are essentially unchanged. The same is true of the traditional shipboard energy weapons. They have a higher output-to-mass ratio, due to the general advances in energy storage, but that's a difference of degree rather than kind. The same can be said of the variations on the primary beam that have come in since the new screens reduced the laser's effectiveness." Trevayne smiled wryly. "Of course, there's this new 'energy torpedo,' but I'm not sure whether to think of it as a beam weapon or a nonmaterial missile."

"There's also something else." Hagen hesitated, then seemed to reach a decision. "It's still under development, and highly classified, but I've been told that you have an unlimited clearance and an across-the-board need to know. It's a spinoff from the Desai Drive that turns the drive itself into a weapon whose power is directly proportional to the drive's power. It involves a kind of unidirectional twisting of space. Theoretical ranges go up to twenty-five light-seconds. Like all beam weapons, the damage it inflicts drops off with range. But if there's any truth to the figures in the classified message traffic—to which I'll see that you have access—a capital ship with one of these things will be *really* scary, especially at the shorter ranges."

"I *definitely* want to see those data." Trevayne took on his thoughtful look again. "This can only further accentuate the trend toward larger ships, and away from fighters—which, as you've pointed out, can't mount the Desai Drive." Once again, he was reminded of Sonja Desai. And it occurred to him that he hadn't gotten a reply from her, although there had been time. He wondered why.

CHAPTER EIGHT

Arming

The image floating over the desk sensors was a thing of beauty as it rotated slowly in place. It didn't seem very different from a normal supermonitor, until the view expanded and included an SM—the TRN *Alligator*—in the field of view. Then the size of the ship snapped into perspective and you could see how much larger it was, in orbit around Seuss, one of the Beaufort system's gas giants. It gleamed silvery, hard to see against the misty blue and cream bands of atmosphere, but shone stark as the camera rotated to show the ship against star-spangled blackness.

Li Han's office was well lit, but wasn't quite as tidy as usual, with Li Magda's brief-pad and half-empty cup of tea on the small table next the window, along with a stack of flimsies. The owner of that office allowed herself a small internal sigh as she looked around and wondered that even after all her years, her daughter could still make a room messy with very little "stuff," then she shook herself and turned back to the ship they were evaluating.

As they watched the recording again, the massive "devastator" type ship moving through the test, Li Magda—Mags to her friends, but never in front of her mother—wondered at how calm Li Han looked. She seemed almost indifferent to what this class of ship could do, but that serenity had fooled a lot of people. Li Han almost seemed not to watch, her hands slowly folding yet another in a long succession of paper cranes but both of the Magdas—Rear Admiral Li Magda, TRN, and Fleet Admiral Magda Petrovna Windrider, TRN (ret.)—knew that her attention was riveted on the performance of the test ship.

Li Han set the bright red crane, no bigger than the end of one of her fingers, gently on the desk. "Point six seven percent larger, you say?"

Magda nodded. "Yes, around two million tonnes. Which means that she can carry a lot more, just in terms of magazine capacity. There's room for ECM and stealth ECM."

Mags was nodding, already itching to try one of the new ships. "But I did notice," she said, "even though it's fast, as you said, it's not nearly as maneuverable."

"There are always some tradeoffs." Magda shrugged and leaned back again, crossing her legs. "We'd all like infinite hull capacity, infinite speed, the ability to turn on a half credit with change and go anywhere." Mags snorted.

Li Han pulled a flimsy out of the stack, straightening the remainder of the pile. "It's very nice. Very good. And I did notice you included the 'go anywhere' part."

Magda sighed. "Yes. It will have to be used in systems where the warp points can handle them. For all others . . . well, that's what we still have smaller ships for. And you know that timing is often more important than size." She set her cup down. "But we know we'll need the firepower if the Tangri keep up the pressure. I'll recommend we stack this beauty with laser and shaped-charge warheads." With that she nodded to Li Magda who had long been a proponent of the laser torpedoes, as well as gee beams, as major components in the modern fleet.

Shaped-charge warheads were either nukes or antimatter charges in front of a mag bottle generator. That generator was the key to the whole idea. Just before detonation, it projected a venturi-shaped magnetic field to channel and focus the blast effect even as it was destroyed.

"I shall say, Magda," Li Han said, as she turned another piece of origami paper, white this time, on the desk with the tips of her fingers, considering. "Sienfeld Starship has out-done itself." She looked up and smiled slightly. The room brightened slowly as

Beaufort rose, the cool planet glow competing with the yellowish lights in the office. "But then, you knew that."

"As the First Space Lord says," Mags chimed in as she stood and stretched. "Sienfeld does good work and though I'd much rather be off on my own doing 'tedious Survey stuff,' as a certain mother of mine has been heard to say, I'm looking forward to putting that ship through its paces myself." She struck a dramatic pose. "The TRN commands! Who are we mortals to disobey?"

Li Han looked over at Magda and sighed. "Please excuse the excess. The daughter was ever under the tutelage of her esteemed father and doting godparents and has picked up unfortunate habits."

They all three smiled at the old joke. "Ma," Mags said and caught Li Han's raised eyebrow. "Mother."

"Yes, daughter."

Mags nodded at the tiny crane on the desk and the half-formed one in Li Han's hands. "I never asked . . . when did you start folding cranes?"

Li Han ran a careful thumbnail along a crease before pausing and looking up. "About eighty years ago, when I was a POW."

That had been when she had been forced to surrender to Ian Trevayne. Her voice and face were serene and time had eased the ancient sting of that defeat. After all, they had won.

"Yes," she continued and took up the slow, careful folding again. "One hundred eighteen years ago, my grandmother taught me . . . and my mother approved because she thought I did not have enough 'ladylike' qualities." She set the new-made crane down next to its brother. "I refused to fold for years."

They had been allowed more access to hard copy than to electronic, and the first crane she'd folded had been a larger gray one, in the middle of the night when she hadn't been able to sleep. "Then it became important."

Li Magda nodded, as her mother's careful voice continued. Magda's silent presence was somehow reassuring as part of the past she hadn't thought to question was made real for her. "I folded the first thousand during that time." She took up her tea and looked from her daughter to her friend and colleague. "Of course I folded a thousand for you and a thousand for your brother." That had been when she had thought she would never have children.

She and Robert Tomanaga had decided to attempt it, having her ovaries removed and the ova scanned for genetic damage before

having them fertilized and reimplanted in her own womb. Though it
had taken an enormous amount of trouble, though thankfully less
pain due to modern surgical techniques, it had worked not just once,
but twice. "Since then, I have lost count."

A moment of stillness in the room, the image of the new DT
floating silently in Beaufort's light, before Windrider began leafing
through flimsies. "We need to settle—" The chime of the com cut off
what she was about to say.

"Yes?" Li Han answered.

"First Lord," the secretary's voice came through, crisp and
efficient. "I have a priority flash for you. From the RFN."

"Thank you. Send it to my desk." Both of the others had security
clearance necessary, so Li Han called it up directly, replacing the
image of the DT with the Message Start icon with the flashing
symbol that indicated it was a multiple send.

Cyrus Waldeck's bulldog features snapped into view and Mags
was shocked at how haggard he looked. It was impossible that he
could have lost weight in the short time since she'd seen his image
last, but it looked as though he had. His eyes seemed hollow, in a
face that for the first time she could remember, looked old.

"President, President Emeritus, First Space Lord." He paused as if
the simple salutation were almost too much, then plowed on
resolutely as he always had; facing each problem head down, full on.
"We have been forced to concede the Bellerophon System. Our
losses are, I regret to say, are fifty-eight percent."

"Oh shit." That was Magda. Li Han nodded and Mags said
nothing but started pacing as the message continued.

"I have withdrawn, to Astria, and will hold the line as best I can.
Recording of the battle is attached."

Mags sat down and the three of them watched in deadly silence,
as the Battle of Bellerophon unfolded in front of them. Halfway
through Li Magda turned to her own brief-pad and called up a
three-dimensional depiction of the Bellerophon Arm.

At the Message End icon, she spoke up. "They've cut off a huge
chunk of the Rim Federation."

Han nodded and pulled up the same map on her desk where they
could see it more clearly. "We are talking about an invasion force
that we've only knocked down by 31 percent and they hold the
system. They have what is left of the shipyards, and they've shown

that even though they do not –yet—use warp points, they are aware of their existence and their importance to us."

Magda fanned her hand through the display. "All this . . . we're talking about the isolation of over four billion beings."

At that point, Li Magda's brief-pad beeped. "I hate to say it, but I have a bad idea, here."

The other two just looked at her, waiting. They knew each other so well that they didn't need to throw out a great many questions.

"We've gotten all the information from the astronomers. Their best guess is that the aliens are from the Bufo Nebula area . . . if not further, but Bufo is still the most likely. Why do we think that the aliens sent out only one fleet? Look."

She pulled up a star chart that no one could immediately understand. It wasn't a nice, orderly warp tree, with lines connecting neatly one to the next, but a convoluted wad of light as orderly as a tangled ball of wool.

"If I take away the warp connections . . ." She had to fight her machine for a moment or two to make it do just that. "This is real space. I'm just not used to thinking this way, but look." She highlighted Rim Federation territory, weirdly smeared through and around Republic Zones and Ophiuchi space and . . . it was too confusing to follow. But the blinking stars were obvious.

"There are a number of Rim Federation stars in the forty-light-year radius from that nebula. Now if I were planning to evacuate a system from a . . . what did they call it? A 'novalike incident' or a flare, I'd pick target stars wherever I could . . . and the most likely are all clustered in that direction, along the spiral arm." The globe of space that she had outlined began a slow blink. "We can't assume that this is the only fleet."

"Can you highlight all human and allied stars inside that target area?" Li Han leaned forward on both elbows, her cheek resting on her laced-together fingers, intent as a cat at a mousehole.

"I'm not sure my brief-pad has enough memory," Li Magda said.

"My desk unit certainly does." Li Han sat back and let her daughter struggle to make the tank spit out the odd images, her eyes still on the display. Then she punched in numbers on her desk pad, pulling up identifiers on this reconfigured star map, along with actual light-year distances, again having some trouble doing so.

"Got it!" She stood up as the desk tank image settled into its new configuration. "I've marked all our stars in blue, green, or gold." The three of them took in the chaotic mess of stars and considered the implications.

An Orion star hung between three RFN star systems; the PSU flung in a wild spray of stars along the spiral; the TFN was scattered, ironically through an area of space that was interspersed with Tangri, Rigelian, and Ophiuchi star systems, with Sol itself off to one side in an area of the galaxy surprisingly barren. It was a way of looking at space that no one but the old-fashioned astronomers ever used anymore.

"There are some of our systems in the same target area," Magda pointed out quietly. "The best-case scenario is that they only have the one invasion . . . but worst case—" She stared at the display over Han's desk. "We could have as many as a dozen of these alien fleets bearing down on not only the RFN, but us too."

They stared at it a long moment, trying to resolve the image into something they could recognize. It was difficult to think of space as actually being structured this way, rather than a neat grid of warp connections.

"You see," Han said and pointed to Bellerophon before her finger shifted to indicate a nearby star system, about six light-years away. It was affiliated with the PSU, a small G1/K2. She accepted the data from her daughter that extrapolated possible flights from the nebula. For a long moment the three studied the scrambled star map before Li Han clapped her hands together decisively. "I need to cut this meeting short, Li Magda, Magda. Seinfeld has its approvals; my secretary will forward all the information and signatures."

"Of course." The other two women were already gathering their things. "I hope we're wrong," Li Magda said quietly. "But we do have to plan as though we're not."

"That's for sure." Magda was clipped as she sealed her brief. She stopped as Li Magda impulsively hugged her godmother, hugging her back hard. "Impulsive child," she said with a slightly distracted grin. "Just as your mother says."

Mags straightened her collar as she scooped up her own flimsies. "Unfortunately not a child and not nearly as impulsive as I was twenty years ago."

"Ladies." Li Han nodded at her daughter and best friend, reaching for the intercom switch. "I will call you both tonight.—David, call the second and third space lords for an emergency meeting."

"Yes, First Lord."

CHAPTER NINE

"Just keep your heads down."

"—tay calm. Refugees from Melantho have just been settled into auditoriums and sports stadiums in the cities of Icarius, Asphodel, and Hallack. Governor Mackenzie and Commander Van Felsen are relieved that casualties, so far, are light and urge all civilians not to resist the aliens. We turn to our cams on-site across Melantho, so far the only city the aliens have claimed in its entirety across the continents of Ithaca, Sisyphus, and Sparta. . . ."

Jennifer started as the door chimed, got up, and opened it to let Corporal Wismer in. "Hello, Jonathan," she said absently, glancing past him to see if anyone else was around.

The street, with its quaint old row houses, looked very odd, almost deserted in the bright, hazy light of late afternoon that brought out the sweet scent of the Heliobarbus trees all along the boulevard. People would have been out at this time of day, just after supper. Everyone was staying in, except for Mrs. Jarvis who insisted on her routine and was out gardening. Her Terra Originalis roses took precedence even over alien invasion. It wasn't as if bricks and mortar would save anyone should the aliens decide to flatten a block but people felt safer. In the distance she could hear the odd sound that marked an alien small ship overflying the city.

Jen closed the door behind the young corporal who set down his case just inside. "Can I offer you a cup of coffee, Jon?"

"No thank you, Ma'am. I'll just find my way downstairs." *To relieve Diane.* Corporal Narejko, that was. Jen liked the young man's old-fashioned Neopent manners, but having a surveillance team in the basement wasn't the world's most pleasant of things. She sighed and went into the kitchen to run a pot of coffee anyway. The surveillance team would want some, she was sure. Aside from making coffee she officially ignored the people coming and going into their basement, and like half the planet waited to see what the aliens' next move would be.

She sighed again and headed out to load "Summer Day" into the truck. It was a commission she'd gotten for a local garden café and you did your best to keep on as though everything was normal, as normal as you could with one of the hastily organized teams working out of her and 'Sandro's basement.

She hadn't figured out a way to tell Alessandro yet, and it just never seemed like a good time to bring it up. She'd have to tell him soon. Her morning sickness was getting worse and now that he wasn't out in the asteroid belt half the time he'd notice soon. She settled into the cab but instead of starting the vehicle, she sat in the peculiar closed silence and put her head down on the steering wheel. *I can't sit here all day.* For all that she was more tired than expected, she couldn't just crawl into bed and wait for 'Sandro to come home, or for the aliens to decide that they didn't like the look of their block and reduce it to slag. At her touch on the pad the old truck hummed into life and rolled out of the alley on its parking wheels before lifting gently onto its ground effect. She'd stay at street level. It was only prudent.

The minor command center was one of a dozen on the planet and Van Felsen and the remaining Marines had abandoned the main base. This center was in the middle of a cluster of lakes on Sisyphus, chosen purely on sheer luck. The aliens seemed to favor the barren seacoasts and rain forest regions of the planet.

Outside, she knew, at this latitude the season was autumn and the rolling hills were just past the fiery display of leaves, leaving them rolling gray and flashed with bright yellow of Fell Larches. The lakes were already cold and dark under deep blue skies. Van Felsen was deeply affected by cold, even though she knew it was mostly psychological, and deep in lower levels of the base where this conference room was, she knew it was as perfectly climate controlled as a ship in space, but she still crossed her arms and tucked her hands casually into her armpits as she called the half a dozen people to order.

Around the table were mostly junior officers, excepting herself and Captain Falco who headed up the communications team. Lieutenants Heide, Adams, and Kovyazin and Ensign Montaño were what she had. Lieutenant Heide, a weedy man with thinning mousy hair and a scholar's stoop, called up the initial analysis over the table and stood to present his findings.

"Commander, we've all seen the aliens and this is our analysis of the variations in the species." Images of the dark variants and the gold variants flashed into view. "In all of the images there is no significant change of expression and we cannot tell if the color changes of the tegument are related to emotional changes of any kind, since we don't have enough information to correlate. Captain Falco's teams has not been able to make the translators any more consistent and it is providing a significant problem in my data analysis."

Considerably more problems than with your data. Van Felsen squelched the thought and refrained from even quirking an eyebrow at Falco. Heide was the best they had. The man was a cold fish who lacked empathy and he didn't even realize that that was why his promotions had come so slowly, and why he hadn't been one of the higher-ranking officers they'd lost on Acrocotinth. Falco didn't respond but she could see the muscles of his jaw clench from here. They were all under strain, trying to cope with the invasion and keep any more people from being killed. *And fight back, once we have enough information.*

"Thus, we are reduced to grunting and waving of hands."

"And shooting people, Lieutenant," Van Felsen commented dryly. "I will remind everyone that when the aliens speak, they speak once and the translator does the best it can. Then if you do not comply they shoot you. Even if you happen to be three years old."

There was a clenching, a rage barely contained all around the table; that went right over the lieutenant's head. He merely looked confused and vaguely insulted that he'd been interrupted and then went on with all the grace and tact of a bull Aurochs in an art gallery. "Commander, I am forced to speculate that these aliens are like the Arachnids. We never did achieve communication with them."

Everyone else around the table reacted to that, a slight tensing, a struggle to keep a face straight instead of breaking into a fight grimace, the clenching of teeth. Van Felsen had the gut reaction herself and could see the quiver in her people all around the table at the mention of the Bugs. It didn't matter if they had combat experience or not. It was a reaction to the most horrible alien people had ever encountered, horrible in all the ancient hind-brain, atavistic ways: totally silent, hairy, multilegged, bulging bodies, swift moving, and the perfect size to prefer sucking people's children dry.

The idea of their existence still gave people howling nightmares and the mildest response was nausea at this too-casual connection. Lieutenant Heide, charmer that he was, missed it completely.

"Commander, that is what I have for you."

"Thank you, Lieutenant." With relief she watched him sit down and turned to the peach-faced youngster down the table to her left. "Ensign, if you please."

Ensign Nicholas Montaño was surprisingly calm to be presenting, but just by the number of times he'd checked his notes before this briefing had started, she knew how nervous he really was. Of course, when this crisis was over he'd have just as tough an audience when he finished his thesis and defended his doctorate in xenopsychology. A lot of the reservists had been university students.

As he stood, Heide just had to open his inept mouth one more time. "We never did establish any kind of communications with the Arachnids."

She could just have punched him herself as the feeling of horror and despair curdled in the room. The man's effect on morale was disastrous. Van Felsen cleared her throat. "We'll trust that this is not the case this time, Lieutenant. The Bugs seem to have been an anomaly, thank goodness. I'm sure we'll eventually be able to talk to these aliens." She nodded at Ensign Montaño, who had been patiently standing, waiting for her to squelch Heide yet again. He swallowed, his Adam's apple bobbing in his throat, before beginning.

"They've settled approximately three point five million beings on planet already, with housing and infrastructure." He brought up the map, showing the alien settlements in yellow, the human cities and towns in blue. Fortunately there was very little green overlap since the aliens tended to favor the smaller islands and coastlines away from human cities.

"Infrastructure? Already?" That was Lieutenant Adams down the table. In days the alien cities had burgeoned along coastlines all over the planet.

"Yes, Lieutenant." Montaño paused to run a hand through his thick brown hair. "They have not yet noticed our stealthed cameras—"

"—or haven't bothered to respond to them," Falco put in.

"Or that, Sir, yes. It appears that they have broken up their big ships and have used them both as smaller ships and raw materials for their cities, somewhat like a connective toy being pulled apart into components."

"They're here to stay."

"Yessir, I would say so." The ensign hesitated before continuing. "Melantho is the only city that they've just taken over entirely and almost all casualties happened there. Aside from . . ." His voice trailed off.

He stopped and adjusted the light pen lying on the desk in front of him, obviously reluctant to continue, then looked up. "The aliens are very efficient in the removal of severely injured and dead." He stopped to swallow again. "They don't appear to have medics for more than minor injuries. Anyone badly injured seems to be treated as already dead. Something that the translator has not yet managed is said, the injured one is shot and incinerated. They are treating our injured in the same way."

He paused and there was silence in the room before Lieutenant Adams broke the stillness by shoving up from the table and turning away. "Excuse me, Sir." He was shaking.

Commander Van Felsen, sick at the confirmation of rumors that even she had heard nodded at the ensign. He cleared his throat, tugging at his collar slightly. "They get someone to clear up the—debris." Even the aliens' pin-sized incendiary devices didn't incinerate a body completely. When the three-year-old and his mother had been shot, and the father for trying to stop the incineration of the bodies, it had triggered a riot that had caused the aliens to retreat to their tenders and create what analysts tended to call "a salutary example." The whole town had been wiped off the map. *Fifteen hundred civilians gone, just like that.* Things had gotten tenser after that, but the aliens had proceeded to build their own cities and landed their own people with no further atrocities.

"They are like machines, sir. Their language has zero inflection. Their color changes, as Lieutenant Heide said, outside of the context of anything said."

"We'll take that under advisement, Ensign."

"Yes, Sir. That's all." He sat down and Van Felsen waited for Lieutenant Adams to get control of himself.

She took a sip of her water as he sat down and smiled at them. "I have some good news. Falco, the Orion news team has offered their services. Since they have military rank, however honorary, they consider themselves under command and I'll take every expert in alien thought and language I can get. I understand that Showaarth'sekakhu-jahr—" She paused to cough as her abused vocal cords protested as she made her best attempt at the Orion name. "—has an advanced degree in xeno-psychology herself, Orion style."

Falco, looking as though he wanted to say something along the lines of "Oh shit, hurrah" nodded and schooled his expression. As far as she knew he didn't belong to one of the violently anti-Orion faiths so he'd be all right working with them.

"And one of the strikefighters made it back."

"All right!" Montaño subsided back into his chair abruptly as sudden smiles were suppressed all around the table.

"Although the expression was unorthodox, Ensign, the sentiment is appreciated," Van Felsen said quietly. "Unfortunately it is a wreck and quite impossible to fix. We, however, do not treat our people the way these tentacled horrors do and Lieutenant Chong will be back on the duty roster soon. I'm sure when this is all over some idealistic monument sculptor will have him standing heroically gazing skyward next to his wreck, but he was a bit more bashed up than that."

She shut down the faintly cascading "wait-mode" display over the desk. "Thank you, gentlemen. Carry on. Unless something of note comes up we will continue these briefings. Dismissed."

Ankaht gently closed the lid on the memory box and it sealed itself with a faint hiss of vacuum as she laid it in the hole and began burying it. It was a good place for such a cairn. Her first for this new home. (Quiet grief, acceptance.) All the old memories buried on

Ardu would have no one left alive to find them, even if they were buried deep enough to escape Sekahmant. The Voices of Illudor were still debating whether planets had soul and were reborn.

She stood up and wiggled her tentacles to clear them of dirt, dragging claws over each other to clear the soil off them. The clay was white on this rise of land overlooking the cliffs and the sea beyond, and much more inclined to stick than that of the last place she'd buried a memory. But it would be a few lives before she was inclined to come back to this place and even if the purple- and *vrel*-colored sea below wore away the pink sand beach and the granite cliff, it wouldn't reach this spot. The sun was warm on her neck and she stretched, gloating in the sheer luxury of uncontrolled space. As *shaxzhu* she had less trouble adjusting to being on planet. *Trouble, ha. I am positively luxuriating in it. Especially since, by necessity, my office space is unfortunately ugly.* She sat down in the grass, closed her eyes, feeling the wind on her face. *Wonderful.* (Deep contentment, thread of worry.) She thought of the beach near her father-in-this-life's villa and was suddenly smitten with intense homesickness. A cloud passed over the sun and she did miss the fiery pinprick of light that had destroyed everything they knew. The light truly was dimmer and some colors would be forever wrong but that was a tiny price to pay for being out of the ship. This gravity could not be easily modified by anyone. She fisted up one of her hands and pounded on the dirt with it, just to feel it, just to *shotan* and absorb it all. It was home, it was real. (Happiness.)

Then her gaze moved away from the pristine sand to the roughed in new city of Punt and her *narmata* soured. Over thirteen hundred years there had been refinements and modifications made to allow the swift dismantling and creation of new homes from the ships they'd arrived in, but the Dispersal had changed over the generations of traveling and careful plans for spacious homes on the new planet had been scrapped when the settlers refused to live so far apart from each other. They had left a few of the individual homes as built and cobbled houses together in clusters of tentacles that to Ankaht's eyes looked odd and ugly. All of the public garden spaces had been cleared. None of the shiplings wanted any private gardens other than smooth-paved spaces because no one but the hydroponics engineers wanted to deal with the problems of real plants growing in dirt. Dirt. Everyone but those who remembered clearly complained constantly of dirt.

Insects were a huge problem and the younglings tended to either flee the fliers and crawlers of this world, or try to stamp them out of existence. Even though everyone had trained for planet surface with holographic simulations there were things that were just too controlled. Everyone was complaining of the blowing dust. And wind. It had rained four times since they'd begun Punt and there was an outcry that no one had warned them it would.

The weather satellites would only predict general weather patterns once they were functioning and had enough data to predict patterns on this world, with no moon and only solar tides. The sodium in the water, the stinging sea things, the odd textures and smells. It was all cause for complaint, disturbance in the *narmata,* the emotional storms of *selnarm.*

The admiral had his claws full with trying to deal with, or defend against, the *griarfeksh.* They were absolutely terrifying in their resemblance to real people but with no ability to communicate.

She shaded her eyes to look across the bay where the *griarfeksh* city lay. It was attractive in a way that she hadn't expected, graceful and fragrant boulevards and buildings of the pink granite, tucked into the opposite cliff like a leafworm scarf, but she shook her head and looked away. No matter how elaborate a structure could be built by a zifrik colony, it didn't make them people.

With the *Anaht'doh Kainat* having so much trouble with the planet surface, it had fallen to her and all the clusters of *shaxzhu* to ease the transition onto the planet. But as time went on there were increasing numbers of individuals and even whole clusters who were showing signs of *xen-narmatum,* mental illness that could infect the healthy through the *selnarm* so they had to be identified and removed from the main population before everyone was affected through the give and flow. No one had seen such illnesses in centuries before the Dispersal and everyone had assumed that the tendency had just been selected out. After all clusters and macroclusters affected with the illness tended to destroy themselves. Now it had all landed in her claws.

There was a flying creature circling far above and she watched it, her central eye shut against the sunlight. *How do I break it to the esteemed admiral that a whole ship has recently decided that they will not come down? They insist that we need orbital colonies and they refuse to set foot here. Daihd passed the word on to me after the fighting stopped and made it clear that enormous numbers of the young ones consider it a dueling matter. Sometimes I think all* Destoshaz *are* xen-narmatum.

She got up and picked up her digging tool, slinging it into the unit on her belt before walking down to her flyer. She'd already stretched the time she could reasonably allot to a *sohkata* exercise. It was time to get back to her ugly little office space.

"Illudor's claws and tentacles, Torhok, you can't just let them keep running around all over the planet like that!"

The senior admiral didn't pause in his slow stretching as his best friend and senior cluster commander ranted, flooding the exercise room with (Rage, fear, passion to convince.). It was just the way he was and one of the ways he tended to warm up for *maatkah* sparring. He was deadly when it came to jolting his opponent off balance by lightning strikes of *selnarm* in addition to the mock *skeerba*, or "claw-knives." The *skeerba* was a band with three teeth that projected up like an additional set of claws; there were only one or two authentic old *skeerba* "teeth" that they had brought for examples. It was unlikely that anyone would want to re-create that particular predator on the new world, except perhaps in animal keeping clusters. But that was still to be debated. In the meantime the traditional *skeerba* wasn't even carved of bone any longer but was a high-density razor-sharp plastic.

The exercise room was the common one on the *Hurusankham* in orbit around New Ardu, empty at this hour, with the massive reduction of personnel onboard. It was a large enough cubic that it was almost as good as having a *maatkah* training circle. It had no corners and all the equipment folded away into the niches, the illumination turned to maximum, like High Light on Old Ardu, washing out the pale blue walls and floor pads.

Torhok needed this workout more than he needed sleep at the moment and he ignored Iakkut's rage as he fitted a sheath over his claws. The brain would note any contact and call points. It was an ancient conceit that painted the edges of the sheaths with dye to mark skin. (Concentration, concentration of purpose, focus.) He kept up his *selnarm* to shield himself, to distance himself, from the *narmata* between them.

"You know they're vermin! They fight like animals—defend themselves as if they are never going to be reborn."

"Enough, Iakkut. We should be glad that whatever they are, they are providing enormous quantities of highly refined material for us, already in orbit." He stepped up to the edge of the circle marked in the matting, flexing his tentacles to settle the claw sheaths before he took up the *skeerba*.

"That hardly makes up for blowing up half of our fabricating facilities!" Iakkut was a hybrid form, dark skinned but tall, and a formidable *Destoshaz*. Even as he spoke he was stepping up to his side of the circle. They both paused a long moment before kneeling, each setting the *skeerba* on the mat in front of their knees. Into the silence, the mechanical brain chimed once.

Neither of them moved but they strained against one another in the traditional *selnarm* opening, each trying to force the other onto the defensive. A *maatkah* match between two masters sometimes never moved to the physical level at all, other than a twitch of inner eyelid or a clenching of grinders.

Torhok strained (Victory.) against Iakkut's (Win), shifted to (Will.) and he retreated to (Resistance.).

(Will, force, focus, I will this.)

(Resistance, stubborn, stolid, granite.)

(Water.)

Iakkut snatched up the *skeerba* and rolled into the circle in a fluid motion that used Torhok's *selnarm* flow to make it even stronger, intending to trap the other's weapon against the floor before he could seize it, but it was already in Torhok's fisted cluster and Iakkut was forced to avoid claw strike and tumbled into (Wave Rising) to make it to his feet, but he was still retreating. Torhok spun in a standing somersault and blocked him finishing but he slid into (Cliff Face) and Torhok bounced, landing hard.

(Wall Falling) from Iakkut would have ended it but (Earth Shaking) threw him off and the admiral bound his legs and landed on his chest holding a *skeerba* to his neck, two of the three teeth pricking skin.

The machine chimed.

"Good!" Iakkut sent. (Pleasant, pleased, surprised.) "But I'll beat you best four out of six."

"Not since we were in our birth cluster, oaf." (Relief of tension, clarity.) Torhok let his friend up and they shook out their tentacle clusters before kneeling to begin again.

At the end of six they were both wet from exertion and considerably calmer of mind. "Thank you for your input." Torhok's voice was somewhat overridden by the dryer as they stood under the jets of warm air.

"You're welcome. I'll owe you dinner any time you please." (Humor, amusement.)

Torhok paused to look (Twitch of amusement.). "Unless you find more practice time you won't ever have to suffer my choice of menu."

"It's not that, my friend." Iakkut shut the box with the *skeerbah* in it. "You are more convinced of the creatures' monstrosity than I am and it gives you an edge. (Revulsion, rage.) I should know better than to mention them before sparring you."

While Iakkut talked Torhok just stood, listening, leaning on the wall. "Old friend. I think you are right. And I know that we've just driven them off for now. I fully intend to make this planet safe for Illudor's children, if I have to rip open space where they disappeared with my bare claws and follow them. (Implacability.) So you don't need to push me."

"Yes, Senior Admiral! (Amusement, relief.) I'll push my cluster engineers instead of you, agreed?"

(Wall of granite.)

CHAPTER TEN

Fighting Back

Astria was that rarity, a type-F main-sequence star that wasn't too young to have birthed a life-bearing planet. That life had, to be sure, only evolved to the level of green scum floating on the seas when the humans had arrived. But it had been enough to release free oxygen and produce an ozone layer which—together with genetically engineered night-black skin—had protected the colonists from their new sun's ultraviolet-lavish light.

Now that light glinted off the flanks of the latest reinforcements as they arrived under Cyrus Waldeck's cold but satisfied gaze.

As much as he had come to love the Rim Federation Navy since being seconded to it, that service's gradual drift away from the TFN's traditional orderly system of naming ship classes had been an affront to his equally orderly mind. Ironically, the first such convention to go had been the most recent one: Ian Trevayne's practice of naming his new supermonitors after wet-navy heroes of Old Terra's history. It seemed nobody else in the Rim had known those heroes' names.

But Waldeck had tried, with a patience and tact that had finally come to him at some point between his eighth and eleventh decades, to steer them back onto the straight and narrow. He had finally had some success with the supermonitor class that was the latest, cutting-edge expression of the RFN philosophy of optimized missile ships. They were the pride of the TFN, and Waldeck now had six of them—not a full datalinked battlegroup by the standards of today's computer technology, but with the four remaining "slots" filled with escort cruisers to provide extra point-defense fire. He watched the last of them to arrive as they ghosted past the viewscreen of his new flagship, the original member of the class: RFNS *Zephrain*. All of them, at his urging, had been named after systems of the Rim. Ian Trevayne, he reflected, would have been proud of him.

The thought awoke the ambivalence he had felt since hearing of his old commander's unique rebirth. Back in the days of the rebellion (his newfound enlightenment had its limits, and the name "Fringe Revolution" was one of them) he had resented Trevayne with an intensity he now had difficulty remembering or understanding. It hadn't troubled him for a long time—for what had once been thought of as normal human lifetime, in fact. But now he wondered how he would react the first time he encountered the disconcertingly youthful-seeming figure Sean Remko had described to him.

He dismissed the thought and turned away from the viewscreen to face his staff. There had been a major shakeup since he had transferred his flag to *Zephrain*—it was effectively a new staff. They sat with respectful patience around the sunken holo tank that showed the Bellerophon System. Behind them, on a higher tier, sat the holographic images of the subordinate flag officers who, in their own flagships, gazed on displays mirroring this one. As he watched, Rear Admiral Rachel Dumont, aboard the ship whose arrival he had just observed, flickered into ghostly existence.

In the old days, holo-projection equipment had been too bulky for this kind of shipboard use. Awkward flat-screen dodges had been the nearest thing to such virtual conferences. Most often, attendance had been in person. Waldeck was grateful for the improvement in technology... especially in the case of Seventeenth Least Fang of the Khan Zhaairnow'ailaaioun.

After a couple of ill-advised attempts, the Pan-Sentient Union Navy had given up trying to impose a uniform rank structure on its component elements. Thus, Zhaairnow was a least fang and not a vice admiral (just as Waldeck was a fleet admiral and not a great fang) and wore the bejeweled traditional rank insignia of the Khanate on the harness that did not conceal most of his russet pelt.

He had arrived a few Standard days ago with the task group the PSUN had rushed to Astria—fast ships, most of them Orion, including half a dozen assault carriers, nine fleet carriers, twelve battlecruisers, and an array of more than thirty lesser cruisers. Waldeck had been glad to see them. He had even been glad to see Zhaairnow, with whom he'd served before. But he was also glad he didn't have to risk the embarrassment of an allergy attack.

He would have been even gladder to have the heavier PSUN elements that were making their relatively slow way to Astria. But . . .

"Well, ladies and gentlemen," he began, using the accepted formulation. He despised the address "genteels," fashionable now among self-proclaimed intellectuals. He found it effete and precious.

In any case, nonhumans' earpiece translators rendered it as whatever was appropriate . . . and anyway, Zhaairnow was the only nonhuman present. "I'm sure you all join me in welcoming Admiral Dumont." An affirmative rumble arose. "Rachel, your task group's arrival brings our order of battle up to the figures that have now been downloaded to all the flagships. For your benefit, I will note that we have now attained and slightly exceeded the minimum strength level to put our plan for a counteroffensive into operation, as determined by the staff." Waldeck glanced at Commander Nathan Koleszar, the operations officer, for confirmation.

Everyone could see the order-of-battle display: fifteen supermonitors, twelve monitors (considered obsolescent for a war of movement nowadays, but not without their uses for a warp-point assault), twenty-two superdreadnoughts, thirteen assault carriers, seventeen fleet carriers, over fifty battlecruisers, and scores of lesser cruisers, not to mention all the noncombatant support vessels. It was—the thought seemed almost disrespectful—a more powerful force than Ian Trevayne had led into Operation Reunion, even considered in terms of mere numbers and tonnage without factoring in eight decades of advancement in the technology of killing.

And yet . . .

Koleszar cleared his throat. "Yes, Sir. The task force is now in sufficient strength to reenter the Bellerophon System with an acceptable probability of success, according to our theoretical projections."

"Then, Commander, is there any reason why we can't go ahead and schedule execution of the plan?" prompted Waldeck. The ops officer's words had had the sound of cautious, grudging admission.

"No, Sir. Except . . . well, I'm somewhat concerned with the lack of intelligence our recon drones have been able to provide."

Waldeck made no immediate reply, for he himself was privately more than "somewhat" concerned.

The recon drone had revolutionized space warfare—or at least its most deadly aspect, assaults through defended warp points. (Ian Trevayne had once called the warp network "one long series of Surigao Straits," a wet-navy historical reference that had caused Genji Yoshinaka to wince.) The prospect of materializing into the midst of the enemy's defenses had been especially daunting when there had been no way to know in advance what those defenses were. The unmanned recon drones had changed that. Only . . . they weren't changing it nearly enough in the present instance.

"Well," he said with self-conscious briskness, "it must be assumed that the enemy have taken all possible steps to patrol the warp point. They have, after all, had nearly three Standard months to do so. And there has always been a high attrition rate among the drones on transit, even of a pre-surveyed warp point like this one. Furthermore, the 'saturation' approach we've been using may, in retrospect, have been self-defeating. Remember, drones which make multiple simultaneous warp transits are as subject to interpenetration as anything else that does so. The enemy can scarcely fail to observe the resulting detonation, which vitiates the stealth capability of the second-generation drones we've been using. I think these factors, taken together probably accounts for the failure of the drones to report back in adequate numbers."

"Still, Sir," Koleszar persisted, "I'd like to know more about what's waiting for us. Minefields, in particular. Our own mines at the warp point would give them the idea, even if they weren't capable of thinking of it themselves, which I'm sure they are."

"That's true, Nathan," said Captain Julia Monetti, the chief of staff. "But they're reckoning without the AMBAMM. We ourselves didn't even factor it in when we emplaced those minefields."

Everyone nodded. The Anti-Mine Ballistic Anti-Matter Missile was a new system of which great things were expected. Essentially an unmanned frigate-sized ship built around an immense antimatter warhead, it could wipe out mines in wholesale lots by the sheer, brute violence of its radiation-sleeting detonation.

Rachel Dumont spoke up hesitantly, because she was a new arrival and because it was her nature. Waldeck had met her before, and remembered her as a reliable voice of caution. "Admiral, I've familiarized myself with the reports of the Battle of Bellerophon, and—meaning no offense to Commander Koleszar and his people— I can't help wondering if our established criteria for estimating acceptable force levels are applicable in this case." Her formality wavered. "My God, the *size* of those things!"

A snarl that the earpieces did not translate erupted from Zhaairnow. "Size! What does that matter to a warrior? Those interstellar ships with their reaction drives—!"

"Well, yes." Dumont stood her ground, earning Waldeck's respect. "They used photon drives for their interstellar ships because, unlike reactionless drives, they have no theoretical velocity limitation short of that of light, although the capabilities of their radiation and particle shields probably impose practical limits short of that. And therefore they simply can't maneuver, in any sense we'd recognize. But their parasite warships—*parasite* warships, for God's sake! They carry superdreadnoughts the way we carry pinnaces!"

"So?" Zhaairnow stroked his luxuriant whiskers in a gesture of contempt. "Those superdreadnought-sized ships are slow. It is clear from tactical analysis of the Battle of Bellerophon that they lack the Desai Drive. So they are just as vulnerable to fighters as the capital ships of half a century ago—fat grazing animals at the mercy of a pack of blood-mad *zegets!*" He used the term referring to a rather terrifying predator from the Orion home planet.

Waldeck ordered himself not to smile. He understood how the intense felinoid felt. With the eclipse of the strikefighter as a weapon of decision, the Orions had grown increasingly morose. But now they were faced with an enemy who lacked the innovations that had caused that eclipse, and it was as though they were charging back into the good old days.

Cyrus paused a moment thinking of the confrontation in his office a couple of hours ago that he was sure most of his staff had heard. He'd had to lean across his desk, nose to nose with Zhaairnow, who had actually forgotten himself enough to dig a gouge into the desktop. "I should not have to repeat myself, Least Fang!"

Waldeck was intensely grateful that his eyes hadn't started watering as he glared into the Orion's snarl. He was used to staring down bared fangs even if he didn't like doing it. They were as long as his fingers. His own lips pulled back in what wasn't a smile either.

"You and your command will deploy when and where *I* command, however much you want to charge in the forefront, claws swinging!"

Zhaairnow visibly controlled himself, lips tugging down to hide his teeth but his howl still made the translator squeal in feedback. "It would make more sense—"

Cyrus cut him off with a flat sweep of both hands. "No. It does not make sense. Only if you want to get yourselves all killed in the name of honor. Enough, Least Fang!"

It had taken a long, long moment for Zhaairnow to respond but Orions had learned in two bitter wars with humanity that tactics beat personal combat most of the time. He straightened stiffly, his pelt still ruffed at the neck and along his arms, stinking of fight musk.

Well, at the time I was sweating a bit as well. Cyrus thought.

"Of course, Fleet Admiral." He'd done the formal claw-flash that was the Orion's salute to a superior but hadn't waited to be dismissed, growling. Apparently his enraged sulk didn't extend to that kind of insulting formality. And doors in a warship didn't slam worth a damn.

Cyrus pulled his attention back to his officers.

Koleszar's concern about the lack of data from the recon drones had more validity than Waldeck cared to publicly admit. Sending carriers (which required time for their electromagnetic catapults to stabilize before they could launch fighters following a transit) was always a risky proposition, and Waldeck wasn't about to do it in his present state of ignorance of what lurked on the other side of the warp point. A mix of missile-armed supermonitors and beam weapon–armed monitors would lead the way into the unknown.

"Sir," said Koleszar, breaking into Waldeck's thoughts, "I agree with Admiral Dumont's reservations about the parameters we've been using. With respect, I suggest that we wait for more reinforcements before committing ourselves to an attack."

Zhaairnow looked like he was about to explode, but he kept his voice level. "Is it not true, Commander, that any delay will give the enemy more time to strengthen their defenses?"

"Undeniably, Least Fang. But I point out that they have only the resources they have brought with them, and those they have seized in the Bellerophon System, to draw on. We, on the other hand, have the Pan-Sentient Union behind us. Why not wait for the heavier, slower-moving units we know are now on their way? Coming by the same route your own task group used, through Republican space . . ." Koleszar trailed miserably to a halt, for the mention of the Terran Republic had reminded him of the real reason his suggestion was impractical.

Politics, Waldeck thought disgustedly.

Zhaairnow's dash to Astria had been possible because the Republic had allowed passage through its warp connections. But the word had arrived that their help might also take more tangible form. Actual TRN reinforcements were already under discussion, and the Rim Federation government was in no position to refuse out of hand. But neither did it want to be in the debt of what a few of the older and more reactionary types still called the "rebels." It was an open secret that Waldeck had been under unremitting pressure to retake Bellerophon using only the Rim's immediately available heavy elements (the last of which had now arrived with Dumont) and the PSUN reinforcements Zhaairnow had already brought.

"Your suggestion will be given due consideration, Commander," Waldeck deadpanned, knowing (as everyone else knew) that it wouldn't be. "But in the meantime, in anticipation of the final decision, we will proceed to make detailed contingency plans using the original timetable, activated as of now with Admiral Dumont's arrival. Let us now turn our attention to it."

The Arduan briefing room was dim to allow maximum harmony in *narmata*, given that the room was filled, in three dimensions under the microgravity. It replicated true conditions in space—if one's drives were out, or if a vacation from gravity was desired—and the cluster commanders and secondary cluster commanders "sat" with their lower limbs crossed, knees tucked under the seat straps.

Iakkut sat next to the empty space that would shortly . . . ah, here he was. Torhok was on-planet. With all the troubles settling people he deemed it necessary, however much he hated it.

The senior cluster commander ignored Ankaht's image after his acknowledging nod. The *shaxzhu* annoyed him even more sometimes than the vile creatures infesting their new planet.

"People, (Satisfaction, fight-willingness, stress.)" Torhok began. "I will begin by informing you that our research clusters have developed a way of unmasking the small ships of the enemy and of their information gathering devices. Paired force-field generators disrupt the force screen pattern that hides them. Our enemy will continue to attempt to hide, I am sure, and we will easily spot them."

(Wave of satisfaction.)

"We cannot surmise, however, how fast they will respond to this situation so we will be able to take advantage of this fact only once— in the battle which I have no doubt is coming." Torhok was unable to contain the slight sour tinge to his emotions as he spoke, since it had been Ankaht and her cluster who had pointed out this fact. *The shaxzhu—all of them—just no longer understand who we are. They were supposed to be guides and now all they can do is get in the* Destoshaz' *way.*

"So far, all reports show that we have destroyed every one of the information-gathering machines sent through this 'twisted' area in space where the enemy disappeared." (Intense need to fight— consensus.) (Satisfaction—consensus.) "Senior Cluster Com- mander." Torhok turned to his second and he sent a flicker of (Attention, direction.) toward his juniors who had compiled the reports. Humans would have found the stillness in the room unnerving, the lack of motion or expression, and the side channels that hominids would gather information from almost entirely missing.

"We have fortified the area with our own mines and then buoy- mounted energy weapons." He laced his tentacles together. (Anticipation.)

"Senior Cluster Commander?" asked Third Cluster Commander Nefret. (Curiosity.)

"Yes, Nefret?"

The young *Destoshaz* deepened in color slightly under the scrutiny of the command cluster. "Sir, if there is one such passage in this space allowing the enemy to flee, might there be others we haven't found yet? And what is stopping them from coming through those others that we have found?"

"We actually have only theories about why all the focus seems to be at this twist point and once the Home Ships have been disassembled to take up in-system patrol, those other points will be reinforced."

"Yessir." (Willingness.)

Iakkut paused a moment before continuing. "Commanders, it seems that we have an advantage in that our computers work together faster and more seamlessly and with all examples we have examined it is obvious why; the lack of any capacity for *selnarm* communication in any of their machines." (Repugnance.) "Senior Admiral."

(Acknowledgement.)

"Cluster Commanders. There is a battle coming. We know this because of the madness of these creatures that they will attack. They have, however, left us copious quantities of raw materials in orbit, already refined for our use. The Home Ships will become our new fleet once the settlements are complete and their conversions are finished. And if we are not ready right this moment, we will be soon. Continue working like this and New Ardu shall surely be defended." (Pride, fierce will.)

(Acknowledgement, anticipation.)

"Incoming!"

The cry from the sensor station had barely ceased echoing through RFNS *Aotearoa*'s flag bridge when the supermonitor reeled from the latest wave of missile strikes, slamming Rachel Dumont against her crash couch. Black wings of unconsciousness beat against the edges of her mind. She angrily shook her head to ward them off, if only for a little while . . . which was probably all she had left.

"Comm!" she shouted as soon as the hellish noise had died down, ignoring the damage figures on the board and the latest Code Omega from one of her ships. "Is that drone programmed?"

"Almost, Admiral."

"Get it off ASAP! Admiral Waldeck has to know that these beings have a way of canceling our cloaking fields."

It was, she thought, the only possible explanation for the nightmare she had led her task group into. And that knowledge was one thing they might possibly salvage from the wreck.

They had commenced the counteroffensive in the orthodox manner, with a massive SBMHAWK bombardment. The carrier pods that could make warp transit and spew forth a load of strategic bombardment missiles had been around for centuries, and it was hard to recall how revolutionary they had once been, now that they preceded any warp-point assault like the "artillery preparation" of half a millennium ago. Waldeck had demanded lavish resupply of them before he would even consider a counteroffensive, and he had expended them lavishly, in waves interspersed with the new

AMBAMMs and immediately followed by recon probes to report back on the robot assault's effect. The last had been strangely unavailing. But no one had doubted that little could be left on the warp point's far side, and the assault waves had gone in.

What they had gone into had been Hell.

The minefields had been only the beginning—minefields of far greater density than anyone had dreamed the AMBAMMs could have left in existence. Even more of a shock had been what lurked beyond those mines: fields—no, clouds—of laser buoys. The concept of the robot energy weapons was nothing new, but humanity and its friends (and other acquaintances) had always found the lower-maintenance homing mines more cost-effective. Expecting the new enemy to think likewise, they had programmed the AMBAMMs to sweep mines from the space immediately surrounding the warp point . . . and even in that they'd had no great success, as it now turned out. The buoys had been left practically unscathed, and the energy weapon-armed monitors that accompanied Dumont's missile ships had sailed into a blowtorch.

And then there were the superdreadnoughts, firing missile salvos from further out, safe from her energy-weapon ships, which should have eviscerated them at what passed for knife range in space combat but which had never gotten past the laser buoys. Hasty intelligence analysis of those ships, referring back to the data from First Bellerophon, had been ambiguous. It appeared that the mysterious enemy had repaired some of the damage from that battle. But at the same time, there were indications of fresh damage, suggesting that the SBMHAWKs—which had been programmed to seek targets in the SD-mass range—had been more successful than the AMBAMMs. Which in turn suggested . . .

"The superior speed of the SBMHAWKs seems to have done more good than the AMBAMMs' stealth fields," Dumont heard her intelligence officer muttering from his nearby station, recording for the drone as she'd ordered him to do, without being bashful about indulging in theory and sheer speculation. "Come to think of it, the recon drones' stealth fields also weren't much help. We're evidently dealing with some means of nullifying stealth fields."

Dumont stopped listening, for she was concentrating on the next incoming wave of missiles. Those missiles were little if any bigger than an old-fashioned standard missile—which accounted for the staggering numbers of them per salvo—but they were coming from

SBM ranges. And now they were coming in from beyond the shell of superdreadnoughts, from the final shell of this nightmarish defense.

Generation ships. Eight of them, the largest twenty kilometers long. Zhaairnow had been right: they couldn't maneuver, as maneuvering was understood in the era of reactionless, inertia-canceling drives. But they didn't need to maneuver. They just sat out there at extreme missile range and poured in an inexhaustible stream of missiles. Dumont could at least fire back with her supermonitors' HBMs, whose great antimatter warheads blasted out chunks the size of light cruisers. But those monsters could absorb so much damage it was almost pointless.

"Drone away, Admiral!" the comm officer called out.

"Good," Dumont breathed, in a voice that could not be heard over the alarms as the latest missile salvo from the generation ships—better coordinated than before, she noted—sleeted in.

Datalinked point-defense installations stopped whole waves of those missiles, causing the space outside *Aotearoa*'s energy shields to erupt in one vast, blinding, stroboscopic glare. Then those shields overloaded and collapsed, and the glare and the din of tearing metal were all there was in Dumont's universe just before it all went out.

First Defensive Cluster Commander Anubhat sealed her helmet, bracing herself against the wild gravity fluctuation before the backups kicked in. The air circulation had cut out in the last salvo of small agile missiles from the enemy when a number of them had gotten past Prime Ahniram's cluster.

"Commander!" (Wild elation, fear.) From Junior Prime Fehnakk. "Environmentals off-line. We have hull breaches in areas Two, Five, and potentials in the Aft quarter. Repair teams on the way!"

"Good. Keep me updated." (Calm.) She turned to Prime Ahniram. "Ahn, analysis?"

(Concentration, flare of elation.) "They've caused a fair amount of damage to our superdreadnoughts, Cluster Commander, but our systems are beginning to pick them off. The missiles in question are a smaller, more agile type but the computers are adjusting and unless they are lucky they won't be able to get much more damage on any of our ships, at this point."

"Excellent. Damage we can live with as long as we win."

✧ ✧ ✧

By the time the first few Omega drones arrived with their tidings of death, Cyrus Waldeck knew his options were limited in what history was going to remember as the Second Battle of Bellerophon.

To be precise, the most he could hope for was to prevent it from being as great a disaster as the first one.

"Admiral," he heard Captain Monetti say, "Fang Zhaairnow is begging—I mean, requesting permission to take his assault carriers through."

"Negative!" Waldeck snapped. "They're far more fragile than the supermonitors that are already dying. They'd never last long enough to launch their fighters." He turned to face Monetti, wearing an expression from which the chief of staff shrank. "What matters now is the preservation of a fleet in being. Abort the offensive at once. I'll have no further useless sacrifice."

"Yes, Admiral." Monetti hastily began to send out the orders that halted the assault waves still moving toward the warp point.

Waldeck stared for a long time at the board that displayed the latest Code Omegas, including the one that told him Rachel Dumont would not be returning from Bellerophon. Then he turned a very controlled face to his staff. "Well, Commander Koleszar, I suppose this hasn't been entirely for nothing. We at least have some valuable information."

"Yes, Sir," said Koleszar cautiously. "The data will have to be analyzed by Intelligence, but I think we can draw some conclusions. Their missile drives, for example. And the fact that they evidently have some kind of . . . stealth scrambler, I suppose you'd call it."

"Indeed. So this hasn't been entirely for nothing, has it?" said Waldeck absently, unaware that he was repeating himself. Then he turned and left the flag bridge, walking very slowly and carefully, like an old man.

CHAPTER ELEVEN

A Long Bloody War

The pale fall sun seemed as cold and washed out as the veiled gray sky over Prescott. Even though the sun shone a thin, driven mist of snow whirled from the sea into the faces of those gathered at the Cenotaph. It was cold enough that many of the millions watching or attending their own services shivered in their uniforms but it could have been worse this Memorial Day. This time of year it could have been a driving, freezing rain.

The wind had no chance to tear apart the sound from the massed ranks of pipers before the Cenotaph, the rough column of native stone, its base clad in polished pieces cut from nickel/iron asteroids. The pipers themselves wore faded plaids in memory of the fallen, in battles won and lost hundreds of years before humanity ever left the home planet. As the pipes had traveled to regiments in the New World, so had they been part of the spread of humanity to the stars and under alien skies played the ancient laments to honor the dead. Fifty side drums, a dozen bass drums, and three hundred pipes thundered to a final flourish that made the silence after much deeper. It was a silence that stretched long as the wind tore at the sprigs of red sea heather on every coat, or hat, before a single pipe began "Flowers of the Forest," sad, exultant, the cry for grace and for glory as old as human history, flung into the teeth of winter.

On the dais Ian Trevayne closed his eyes against the wind and the old faces around him, feeling the dislocation of being the most obviously young face among the total weight of brass around him. Had things been different he would have been just one more in a crowd. As it was, anyone could pick him out in a heartbeat, the smooth cheek and dark hair, above the rows of ribbons on his uniform. Even with antigerone treatments the other dignitaries on the platform still carried the weight of experience like a depth, just under the surface. Even though he knew better, he also knew that he projected callow youth—"an inch deep and a mile wide," his grandmother would have said. Even though people *knew* better, they still tended to react to him as if he were really that young. Something of which he would take ruthless advantage, if it ever came to it.

The piper was out high on the headland, silhouetted against the sky and sea. Invisible at this distance were the tiny cameras that broadcast the service all around the planet and recorded it for transmission through all human space . . . and Orion, as well. The Tabbies were crazy about pipes, oddly enough. He, himself, actually didn't like them (although, on principle, he'd never admitted it), but he waited for the trumpet call that would come after. "The Last Post" still raised a tear and this year he had so much more to mourn and remember, even as they geared up to fight and win this new war.

He was still wrapped in those memories, and that mourning, after the last trumpet note had dissipated into the chill air, and for a time no one saw fit to disturb him. He noticed the slow dispersal of the crowd no more than he did the chill. But finally he felt a gentle hand on his arm.

"Ian," said Miriam Ortega in the kind of voice one uses to awake a sleeping loved one.

He turned to face her. Even in her synthetically grown furs, she looked cold. *Well,* he reflected, *her body is a tad older than mine, isn't it?* He managed a smile. "Yes, I know. Time to be going. I was just thinking. . . ."

"Yes. I know. All those people who died. But they did all that could possibly be expected of them under the circumstances."

"Pity everyone in the government doesn't agree." He regretted the irritable words the instant they were out of his mouth, causing her to stiffen.

"There is a certain type of politician," she said in a tight voice, "whose stock in trade is pissing on the military people who bleed and die to enable those same political hacks to continue to avoid working for a living. And a certain type of journalist that gives them disproportionate coverage. In fact, I sometimes wonder if there's any *other* type of journalist. But nobody in the government who counts—nobody who's qualified to have an opinion—believes any of that crap."

"I know," he said, contrite. "Everyone who's read the analysis of Cyrus's report knows nothing could have been done against that kind of firepower. Especially not with stealth technology neutralized in the vicinity of this 'stealth scrambler.' And we're going to be up against those same factors in every warp-point assault in this war . . . and it's going to be a long war."

"Never a very popular thing to say," she remarked with a fleeting smile.

"Bugger popularity! It's what people need to hear, and understand. We're looking at the worst kind of war of attrition: one frontal attack after another. The only way we're going to get the Bellerophon Arm back is by building a fleet that can absorb whatever losses it takes to break through by sheer weight of numbers and material. Oh, I don't doubt that we can do it, given the combined industrial capacity of the Rim and the PSUN and the Terran Republic—and there can be no more nonsense about trying to avoid accepting their help! And these aliens have only the resources they brought with them plus those of the Bellerophon Arm. But it's going to involve the kind of casualties not even an Orion likes to think about."

"There is another type of low-grade politician," she said, all trace of levity gone, "who stays in office by telling people what they want to hear: that all problems have easy, painless solutions, and that only a meany would advocate any other kind."

"That kind of infantile self-deception can have no effect except to make a long, bloody war even longer and bloodier."

They turned together in silence and walked away, leaving the Cenotaph to its ghosts.

Mags raised her glass to the tank as the broadcast clicked off. The TRN's Veterans' Day and Independence Day weren't anywhere near the RFN's Memorial Day but the information coming back through

Arc News's embedded journalists made that ceremony imperative to watch for anyone in the forces no matter what flavor of government you saluted. It was clear to anyone with two brain cells to rub together that it was humans and allies against a new alien threat.

"Here's to them, then," Sam said further down the table. Sam Hollinger was one of Mags's friends Li Han thought was a bad influence. He was a med-tech in the Ivy Leagues Research Facilities on Sqwonk and a very attractive man. Unfortunately Mags wasn't in the mood to notice that fact, ever since she had booted George and his lover out. Her mother wasn't *always* wrong about bad friends.

She'd met George at an unpopular beach resort that she'd picked for her leave just because of its unpopularity—that meant no crowds. George had been there because of the parasailing. It had worked out between them quite well, or so she thought, aside from what she later found out was his almost pathological search for perfection (in everyone but himself) until she'd come home unexpectedly and found George and another "friend" in the shower.

She put George and Lisa firmly out of her mind and nodded to Sam. *I refuse to spoil my evening by thinking about negative people. The way things are going, no one is going to have a free evening in a long time to come. Mother would have still been on the ship, leave or no leave.*

Her exec had chased her downside to the City of Gold for a concert, held in conjunction with the Beaufort ceremonies, and Sam and his friends had invited her for a beer afterward. Phillip and Amity, the other two who'd come along after the concert, had left to claim one of the zero-grav pool tables—really a pool sphere, she thought—right after the last note of the trumpet, skipping all the closing commentary. The Slippery Men was a bar where both certain divisions of Research and the Navy drank, and the owners had wisely not followed the latest open-concept fad in design. Mags found modern design a mistake on a planet as marginal as Sqwonk. She always had the personal temperature controls cranked high in her uniform when she went out here, but constantly still felt cold.

Thankfully, the bar stuck to its roots, with tables and booths partly privacy-screened, the old shimmering fields that truly did nothing to block out sight but made everything look vaguely underwater, and wooden floors and bar. The only shiny surfaces were the taps and the antique mirror behind the bar. It was a warm place where you could sit with friends and pretend for a while that there wasn't a bloody war barreling down on them. The Beaufort broadcast had altered that atmosphere only for a time and now the somber silence had softened to the buzz of conversation again.

"So, how are things going?" Sam grinned as he jerked a thumb vaguely skyward. He wasn't truly pushing for information, since he knew that she wouldn't talk about it anyway.

They had been taking the devastators through their testing and shakedown cruise in Mothball, a system with little traffic and no habitable planets only one warp point off Snark, the sun circled by Sqwonk. It made sense to hide classified equipment in a system that had an amazing assortment of military junk stashed in it and no one would think twice about them coming or going.

"What aside from everyone working their asses off, as usual?" She didn't wait for an answer. "Nothing in particular."

"Uh-huh. And you always wear that canary-fed-cat look." He put his beer down on the table and held up both hands at her look. "No, no. Before you ask, it's not obvious. No, you inscrutable Oriental types are always impassive." He pulled at his own poker-straight black hair, grinning. "It's just me pulling your chain."

She relaxed inside, surprised to find that she'd tensed up. She'd never let anything slip about any kind of classified project. "Sam, we're just going to knock the pants off my mother in the next war games, that's all."

"Ah." He nodded, understanding dawning. Letting people figure out "secrets" on their own was a typical way of misdirecting attention. It wasn't a classified mission at all, just "war games"— which happened to be the code name for Mags's brand-new DTs; something that she obviously wasn't going to spill, even if she had anyone to pillow-talk with.

She anticipated him. "And yes, I expect it will all go by the wayside once the politicos get it together." *Because we'll be deployed.*

"There will be other war games, I'm sure." He smiled at her and she looked away from him. It would be too easy to get involved with Sam.

"And how about you?" she countered.

He waved a dismissive hand. "Same old, same old. How about we finish this drink and go cheer them on?" He tilted his head over to the games section. It was a gift of his, to always ease the pressure on her, and made it just so much easier to be around him. *Just enough interest to let me know that he's not lost interest, and putting me off what he's doing, too.* She smiled and drained her stout.

"Sounds like fun. And I'll take you on in a game of virtual archery later!"

"Loser buys a round."

As they headed over to the gaming section an irrelevant thought drifted through her mind. *Sam is one of the friends I have that Mother does like, though she pretends not to. She would never have mentioned me bringing him to the Family New Year, if she didn't.*

The new ships had performed beautifully. Slower than she'd like but the massive weight of fire-power just might be enough to stand against these aliens.

Li Han slid the old fashioned flimsy into the even more archaic envelope. *Funny how we cling to ancient rituals for these kinds of things.* The envelope went into the inside pocket of her uniform jacket. It made no sense to deliver these particular orders by courier and even though Magda was more than six decades into her life, Han still remembered the anguish she had felt when she thought she'd never have children. It made them much more precious and still inclined to such gestures.

She took the envelope out again and—she suppressed the twinge at doing something so unregulation—tucked a paper crane in with them. It wouldn't hurt. And perhaps it would help in some indefinable way.

Magda had brought the devastators home after—as Robert would have said—"testing the shit out of them" and their meeting was scheduled down on Beaufort.

She resumed tabbing up her uniform and straightened her collar, smoothed one hand over her already immaculate hair. There. Ready to face the hostile world, just as her driver commed up from the garage.

This was a meeting that would carry a mix of pride and pain, as always. For the first time since the revolution, the Fringe, the Rim, and the Core Worlds would be working in concert along with all alien allies. The actual declarations of alliance and mutual defense had been debated with record speed and the so-called MATT, or Mutual Alliance Treaty Talks, had merely been a media circus for everyone to shake hands and various upper manipulators and sign archaic flimsies on camera.

Han had been happy enough not to be in the spot light for that. Thankfully President Gibbons and President Emeritus Illyushina had taken care of the political end of things. She hadn't even had to beg off pleading business because she had actually been too busy and they knew it. At least the political arm of the TRN hadn't forgotten why the Revolution had happened in the first place. They hadn't had time to become corrupt or venal yet.

Li Han leaned back against the cushions, not out of indulgence but out of necessity. Her "car" and driver were really more like a short-hop space-to-air craft, what most people who lived on the moon used to commute to the planet, and there was always a bit of a strain for those in their second hundred when the pilot began compensating for the planetary gravity they were settling into.

She momentarily let her eyes and spirit rest on the images of the planet unfolding below, the gem tones of green and blue shot through with reds and dusty swirls of tan in the clear air between heavy cloud. That storm was a distant white sea beginning to form up slowly in the southern hemisphere, the trailing puffs of cloud scurrying to join the rest of the white herd with sun glancing off the rounded wooliness. She knew the illusion of lightness, the innocence of the upper surface, as they descended, her driver having expressed appreciation earlier that they weren't heading into that mess.

The curve of the planet was now falling away in a distance that changed as they descended into the atmosphere and her introspective mood held all the way into her daughter's offices.

She nodded at the girl—*she's sixty-four, hardly a girl*—who had the wrinkle between her eyes that she always developed when she was deeply integrated into her network, dealing with the last of the long-distance connections. Even as people figured out how to effectively shorten distances, the sheer immensity of distance between stars still slowed communications to a crawl. No one had come up with anything like the ancient stories of quantum communicators, and all of the allies were just now responding to the TRN's announcement of the production of the new DTs that Magda had been testing in Mothball.

Li Han sat down at her daughter's wave and opened her case. *If I were a betting person I would lay money on what those responses are.*

She looked up as the door opened again and blinked at the old man who entered and took a seat next to her.

Kevin Sanders had an ageless face, it seemed, but then he'd always worn his age lightly, especially since no one knew how old he really was. All anyone knew at this point was that he was over two hundred. He smiled his jaunty smile at her and gave the little wave that was somewhere between a wave of greeting and a salute. He'd retired years ago, what was he—she cut off her thought.

Of course. He saw it coming so could put himself in the place where he might do some good. As always, ahead of the curve rather than behind it as everyone military was –perforce—forced to be.

She nodded back, amiably. It was nice to know that in this war, that was shaping up to be as deadly as the Bug War, they had this man's shrewdness on their side. She ostensibly turned back to her case, her attention still on Sanders, who sat quietly, managing to give the impression of motion even as he sat absolutely still. She thought suddenly of one of her grandfather's odd sayings: "*If you stand, just stand. If you sit, just sit. Above all, don't wobble.*" His hands were the only part of him that showed his tremendous age, translucent skin over bulgy wiggles of blue veins, though they were neither liver-spotted nor tremulous.

He'd not be wearing any recording devices or wires, however much von Rathenau, the current head of the PSU's Joint Intelligence Agency, would want him to; he'd just be glad that the old master was still willing to take an active—though technically outside all of the current chains of command—role in things. Sanders wouldn't need anything of the kind.

Li Magda blinked as she disengaged from her system and nodded at the two sitting in her office. "Thank you both for coming. Claw of the Khan Jiilhaarahk'ostakjo has been delayed and will be attending, voice only, from his vehicle."

Li Han nodded and added her murmur of acknowledgement to Sanders and heard the low buzz that was the speaker from the Orion's car that signaled an open line to her. She was still very aware that most people couldn't hear that particular sound and was guiltily aware of how proud she was of her excellent hearing.

"I would like to thank the First Space Lord for arranging to come to my office, rather than having us all come up to hers." Han nodded quietly. *Very proper to acknowledge that.* "First Space Lord?" She gestured to her mother.

"Thank you." She did not get up. For such a small meeting, as important as it was, it would have seemed pompous, though she did turn slightly more toward Sanders who smiled. "I need to inform you that we have a new class of ship that we will be throwing into this war." She called up the press release and squirted it to Magda's desk so they—in the office—could see the image. "I will be forwarding all appropriate information to all allies."

"Praise to you, First Space Lord. I expect it." The voice was flattened through the translator.

"This is our devastator class. It is a ship that is more than fifty percent larger than the next smallest hull that we have, with a corresponding increase in firepower."

Kevin Sanders leaned forward, his elbows on the arms of his chair, his face intent. "It must be slower than an SMT, surely."

Han nodded, as much to her daughter as in acknowledgment of his question, and Magda took up the thread. "Yes, but it more than makes up for it. The other problem is also related to their size. They cannot traverse approximately twenty percent of warp points available." The quirk of an eyebrow was the only acknowledgement of her questions about her mother's decision. "But when it comes to hitting, whatever these babies wallop, stays down."

There was a suppressed snort from the speaker, perhaps the Orion was somewhat amused by the turn of phrase or how it was translated, but that didn't stop the question. "Is this a feasible idea? Will these *zegets* be worth building in numbers?" A rather appropriate name for the ships, Li Han thought.

"Yes." She didn't elaborate. "We have already begun an intensive construction of this new class." The silence over audio was eloquent, and Sanders didn't react at all. Li Han wondered for a moment if someone had leaked something . . . or more likely the old fox had discovered it for himself. That would account for his lack of reaction.

"Waldeck is holding Astria and we, obviously, will be deploying as fast as possible to support him and then, when we have sufficient strength, will carry the war back to Bellerophon. This is Waldeck's advice, of course, and we concur." They were all quiet for a moment thinking of what this actually meant in terms of casualties.

Oddly, it was the Orion who spoke up. "This will not be easy, but it will certainly be honorable."

"Indeed." Sanders said quietly. "'When cubs must take up their sire's claws.'" It was a quote from Khan Hiranow'zarthan, an important historical figure for the Tabbies, and they'd certainly appreciate it. The answering growl from Jiilhaarahk, the translator didn't even attempt. Li Han refrained from trading a look with her daughter, a *what-was-that-all-about* look.

"I should inform the allies," Sanders continued, "that I've been trying to analyze how the Tangri will jump, given that they like to fish in everyone else's pond. It would suit them to see us weakened by a long war. It is unlikely, in my opinion, that they will ally with these new aliens, since they by nature dislike to ally with anyone."

Li Magda chuckled. "They'd just prefer to sink their pointy little teeth into them."

"Right." He smiled at both of them. "Just to let you know that we haven't forgotten them."

Li Han allowed herself a sigh. "Our own personal thorn in our sides." She shrugged. "We'll watch out. As we always do."

"Right."

Magda spoke up. "Gentlemen—" trusting the machine to render it correctly in the Tongue of Tongues—"Sir." She nodded at Li Han. "If I could redirect you from my office to the docks I will be able to actually show you more of the new DT."

Kevin cast a glance between the two women and got smoothly to his feet. "Certainly. Jiilhaarahk, shall I meet you there?"

An untranslated growl again, then, "Yes, Sanders."

Magda nodded to him. "Mr. Sanders."

"Kevin, please."

"Certainly, Kevin. And please, call me Magda." He smiled and Han sighed inwardly at the informality. "We will be out shortly."

He didn't say anything but gave that multi-purpose wave of his and let himself out. When the door had closed behind him, and Li Han heard the carrier wave of the audio shut down, she held up her hand to forestall Magda's question.

"There is a reason we are building so many DTs, daughter." She pulled a sheaf of hard-copy out of her case and handed it to Magda. "This is something that will explain. Something the scientists are calling 'The Kasugawa Effect.' This is, of course, most secret."

Magda took it from her, but didn't take her eyes off her mother. "Of course I'll read it, but can you sum it up for me?"

"Yes. In the most simple of terms . . ." She paused a moment to collect her thought. "Two generators on two ships open a warp connection between them."

Magda stared at her, speechless for a long moment. "A *portable* warp point?"

Han nodded. "Of course the one generator has to be carried to the actual destination, but it can certainly be made to accommodate our DTs."

Magda whistled through her teeth, looking down at the copy in her hands. "Burn-*before*-reading secret then."

"I would hope my daughter would not be so foolish." Li Han pulled out the envelope that had been riding inside the uniform all afternoon. "Your orders, as well, daughter." And as Magda took them, said, "You are our task force commander to Astria." For a microsecond pride and fear together glimmered in Han's expression, the knowledge of every mother whose warrior child is entering a combat zone, before smoothing away to her usual coolness, but Li Magda was always more impulsive. She leaned forward to hug her mother, papers and all, before stepping back to snap an impressive salute.

Li Han stiffened for a second before accepting the hug and returning it and her answering salute was equally precise.

She cleared her throat but Magda interrupted her. "Come on, Ma. Let's show these guys our new toy." She swept her unburdened hand toward the door.

"Ma, indeed." But Li Han smiled slightly as she preceded her daughter out the door. *Your father would have been proud to see you now, daughter. He always was proud of you.* But she did not say it.

Li Magda paused to lock their secrets away before following. *Finally.*

CHAPTER TWELVE

In a Horse-Head's teeth

At first glance, a pre-spaceflight human would have thought he was looking at a parliament of centaurs.

But only at first glance. The Tangria race, for all its horizontal four-legged barrel and upright two-armed torso, bore only the vaguest resemblance to horses or men or any other Terran-derived life-form. The head was especially alien, with its skull-protecting bony carapace, its flat apelike nose, and the tiny eyes evolved under a type-F sun. And the short, thick body fur came in a remarkably vivid set of colors—words like "auburn" and "mahogany" and "henna" came to mind, although there were shades to which a human couldn't have put a name, almost all of them with some kind of reddish glint.

The "parliament" part came closer, for this was the hall of the *arnharanaks* or "high rulers," where the *anaks* of all the hordes met on the neutral (there was no Tangrian concept which answered to "sacred") soil of the ancestral homeworld. And since form follows function, a human would have found it appropriate-looking for such a role, and impressive in a massive, crude way, with concentric circles of raised levels accommodating the hobbyhorse-like frames that served the Tangri for chairs, from which the assembled *anaks* could look down at a circular ring.

The local notions of parliamentary procedure, however, would have been less familiar. . . .

The great chamber was designed to minimize strife. There were no weapons allowed except natural ones, and each *anak*—who knew he was the equal of every other—was isolated one from the next by decorative bars. A human would have been struck by the resemblance to ancient starting gates for horses. But the design didn't stop their version of debate.

At the moment it looked as though New Horde Daroga *anak*, Hrufely, by name, was taking the worst of the fight in the middle of the ring of places. Fyctucz, *anak* of the centuries-established Sirhogan Horde, slammed a forearm into Hrufely's face and broke out a tooth.

"Enough!" The Dominant One—the "speaker," in human terms— surged up, forelimbs braced as if he were personally prepared to make them stop, his alpha posture stopping them in their tracks. The two in the center of the ring pulled apart, both breathing hard and streaked with blood. "The winner is Fyctucz, who gains face for himself and for the Sirhogan Horde. Return to your places before calm is enforced."

Fyctucz, apparently calm again, spat to clear his mouth of pinkish foam and walked around Hrufely who stood rooted trying to catch his breath, sides heaving. They were of a height but who would have thought that a Sirhogan could stand against the beefier, heavier Daroga, even for a single breath? He shook his head and backed to his place as the servants came in to clean up. They were all youngest warriors, all without a single fight scar yet—and of course they all belonged to the Tangri race. In the center of their power, the Tangri declined to let any beasts into earshot. It was a manifestation of racial paranoia that served them well and was the frustration of those who thought to spy.

It was the refreshing finish to an afternoon of conflict resolution, using proper Horde rules rather than that endless talking and then sneaking that the beasts did. The human parliaments ran on what the Tangri considered rat's rules of order, despicable and underhanded.

"Fyctucz carries the day and we will not consider *allying* with beasts." The Dominant One's mouth worked as he spat out the ugly word *allying*. "Neither will we attack them in their war. We will study the new beasts in the field and once they and the human beasts have fought themselves to exhaustion will strike at the wounded groups." He leaned forward and showed his impressive set of pointed teeth before quoting Viztarz the Sage. "A predator who insists on preying on the healthy is a dead predator. Fellow *anaks*, do I make myself clear?"

There was a hasty wave of momentarily raised chins—exposing the throat to the alpha in submission before the *anaks* made their way out of the chamber, a jostle of dominance once they were out from under the eye of the Dominant One.

As the last of them departed, the Dominant One gave a sigh of relief he would never have permitted himself in the presence of the *arnharanaks*. He was Ultraz, *anak* of the Todenfaz, a horde of immemorial antiquity which, in partnership with the Delanden Horde, had pioneered the first ventures off the surface of this planet, more than seven hundred years ago as humans measured time. He was also getting old—too old to retain his position as *primus inter pares* much longer. He had no intention of making the common— and invariably fatal—mistake of lingering on just a little too long. But before he stepped down, he intended to see to it the *anaks* made the right decision in spite of themselves.

He heard a rustle of movement behind him, and the deep rumble of Tangrian amusement. "That was a good tactic, arranging behind the scenes for Fyctucz to take up the challenge."

"I knew he was an accomplished fighter," said Ultraz offhandedly.

"You also knew that for a Sirhogan to defeat a Daroga would impress them with its unexpectedness, and put an end to any further argument."

Ultraz did his best to conceal his gratification at having his craftiness recognized. The various hordes viewed each other in stereotypes—such as the ones that held Sirhogans to be overcivilized weaklings, and Darogas to be mighty (if not unduly bright) warriors. This wasn't the first time Ultraz had always found these stereotypes helpful in manipulating the *arnharanaks*. One just had to know how to make use of them.

The male behind him was a perfect example. Scyryx belonged to the Korvak Horde, so everyone knew he must be treacherous, underhanded, and as close to effeminate as one Tangrian could call another male of the species without provoking an instant fight to the death. So Ultraz couldn't admit publicly how closely he was allied with him, and how heavily he relied on his advice.

"I had to use whatever means I could, Scyryx," he said. "These fools had to be herded into doing the sensible thing, as usual. Left to themselves, they might even have done as those Daroga dung-brains wanted and attack the newly arrived beasts in the rear."

"There was never any real danger of that course being adopted. Everyone could see we would have had to fight our way through the force of the Rim Humans that are stranded in the Bellerophon Arm. And besides, the Darogas aren't exactly esteemed as strategists!"

Ultraz grunted in agreement. "True. But some were leaning toward the idea of an alliance of convenience with the Rim humans, as the Hurulix proposed. They always think they're so clever!" (Ultraz wasn't altogether immune to stereotypes himself.) "Couldn't they see this would involve allowing the fleets of the Rim and its allies passage through our Confederation?"

Scyryx gave another laugh-rumble. "Of course they could—and they were drooling at the thought of ambushing those fleets! But even they could guess how the humans would react to that. And they recalled that the Republic humans are among those allies." The Tangri seldom bothered to differentiate among individual members of prey species. But one human whose name they knew very well was Li Han. "Anyway, I don't think that ever really had a chance of winning acceptance either. The idea of even seeming to ally with prey—! No. It's too unnatural. The only bad idea that ever had a real chance of being adopted was the Hragha proposal of pretending to ally ourselves with these new beasts."

"Yes. Typical of the Hragha, of course. They've been stalking the Humans—especially those of the Rim and the Federation, or whatever confusing name it goes by nowadays—ever since they got their snouts bloodied about a hundred and eighty years ago. But some of the *anaks* were impressed by what we've learned about these newcomers. They don't seem to act like prey at all."

"What they *act* like doesn't matter." Ultraz made a dismissive gesture and pronounced the fundamental truism of Tangrian logic. "They aren't *us*, so therefore they're prey animals. Anyway, it was a practical impossibility. The Humans haven't been able to establish communication with them . . . and we must concede the Humans a certain talent for that sort of thing. So how could we have hoped to negotiate with them?" Ultraz gave his head a toss which actually *was* somewhat horselike—the only possible justification for "Horse Heads," the Human pejorative for the Tangri. "Anyway, it doesn't matter now. The right decision got made, and all it took was one combat. Come, let us go to Confederation Fleet Command headquarters. The *arnhahorrax* is waiting."

They departed the chamber and crossed the wide plaza under the ultramarine dusk-light of the F-class sun. In the distance, wide plains stretched away into the encroaching darkness. Those plains were typical of the homeworld, a dry planet whose landlocked seas covered less than half its surface. The lands that were not outright desert supported only the hardy but struggling vegetation known as *khunillatis*, varied by carnivorous plants like *zikkilatti* and *osamhhoru*. All the plant life, whatever its other disparities, was nutrient-poor.

And that, Ultraz reflected in a mood of introspection that was almost as rare for him as it was for a typical Tangria, had probably determined the race's history.

He had studied the humans and the other prey species that possessed some psychological process functionally equivalent to intelligence—a uniquely Tangrian attribute by definition. Most of his colleagues saw no reason to look beyond those races' military capabilities (which made them dangerous, as a stampeding herd can be dangerous) and political structures (which offered potential weaknesses to exploit). But Ultraz had delved into their histories. And in all cases, the settled agriculturalists (the *zemlixi*, he thought, with the mental sneer that was inseparable from the word) had become dominant, giving birth to the scientific and industrial revolutions, while the nomadic societies had gradually withered and died out in the face of ever-more-superior numbers and technology.

Here, though, the future had belonged to the nomads. As far as most of Ultraz's fellows were concerned, this was both result and confirmation of the race's uniqueness as the sole possessor of true sentience. Privately, Ultraz sometimes wondered. Agriculture—which, for a race of pure carnivores, could only mean growing crops to feed to meat animals—had been inherently inefficient, and had come less naturally to a race with a psychological need for space and a level of personal mobility most other tool users could achieve only with the aid of riding animals. So the *alherratogonfaloxis*, or "hordes," had imposed their pattern, and taken the traditions of raid and pillage to the stars.

Ultraz shook the musings from his mind as he and Scyryx reached the massive fortresslike building that was their destination, and passed through layers of security. They finally emerged into a large hexagonal chamber whose walls were lined with the most advanced communications and data-retrieval equipment. But the room was dominated by a circular table at its center, surrounding a holographic display of what Ultraz instantly recognized as the Bellerophon Arm and the adjacent Tangrian systems, the color-coded icons of the star systems connected by strings of light representing warp lines. Standing respectfully back from the table were staffers whose drab harnesses and certain subtle ethnic indicia evoked the thought *zemlixi,* with all the connotations of contempt it brought with it. The males who counted reclined at the table. They rose as Ultraz entered and made the submission gesture.

"Greetings, Dominant One," greeted the one who counted most of all: Heruvycx, the *arnhahorrax,* commander of the Confederation Fleet Command and thus outranking any horde's *horrax,* or war leader. He had been born into the Hragha Horde. But he was in it rather than of it, for the CFC had become a kind of superhorde for its career officers, superseding the old loyalties—to the disgust of the traditionalists. Heruvycxs' Hragha birth was ironic, for that horde's insistence on a divided command structure, instead of accepting CFC direction in its venture against the Humans, had resulted in the fiasco that had discredited those very traditionalists and enabled the great Lorvycx to realize his dream and establish a unified fleet. Nowadays, whenever a plan failed and the degrading necessity arose for explanations to the prey animals, the fleet sheltered behind the "New Hordes" that existed largely for the purpose of providing such excuses. Skeptic though he was, Ultraz had to admit that the gullibility of Human politicians was a strong argument that the species wasn't truly sentient.

"Greetings, *arnhahorrax,*" Ultraz replied as he settled onto the framework of honor that had been left vacant. Scyryx remained standing a couple of steps back from the table, even though these CFC males were far less stereotype-ridden than most. "The decision has been reached, and the advocates of the alternative plans have been humbled. We will therefore proceed along the lines previously worked out by your staff."

"Thank you, Dominant One." Heruvycx's voice held the relief common to all consummate military professionals who have to worry about the meddling of highly placed amateurs. He gestured at the holo display. "In anticipation of the decision of the *arnharanaks*, we have prepared a more detailed operational plan."

Ultraz gave a gesture of assent. The display flashed with light along the warp line that led from the Tangrian worlds to the Rim Human system of Tisiphone. (Tangrian intelligence was excellent within its rather narrow scope, and they were well aware of the names bestowed by the prey animals on their worlds.)

"This, Dominant One, is our most logical line of attack. Given the fact that the Rim Humans have doubtless rushed all the forces they have available in the Arm toward the Bellerophon system, Tisiphone should be unprotected save by its fixed defenses. Thus we could secure all the open points of the Arm. Furthermore, we may be able to make even further gains, advancing down the arm from Tisiphone."

"They would doubtless reinforce the next system—uh, Treadway—after our seizure of Tisiphone."

"To the extent they are able, Dominant One. But note that we have yet another warp connection to Treadway, through a lightly picketed starless warp nexus. Our ability to attack Treadway through two warp points would complicate their tactical problems. And in all of this, never forget our most important—and unrepeatable— advantage: the Rim Humans *won't know it's happening*, since these newly arrived prey animals have cut off the Arm from all communication with the rest of the Rim by seizing Bellerophon."

Scyryx spoke up. "Of course, if the Humans win, we could face some awkward consequences after the war."

Heruvycx brushed the point aside contemptuously. "At worst, we can always blame it on the 'New Hordes.'" A rumble of self-satisfied amusement ran around the table. Ultraz automatically joined in it, but with the mental reservation that they shouldn't rely on the Humans being the simpletons they seemed. Beasts were inherently unpredictable.

"And at best," Heruvycx went on, "by that time we would be in such a strong position in Treadway and beyond that the Humans wouldn't think it worth yet another war to get the Arm back. And, of course, if the newly arrived beasts end up retaining Bellerophon, the Humans will never know."

Ultraz considered. It seemed to hold up, even if Heruvycx sounded a little too much like a male overly inclined to see the bright side of his own theories. "Very well. So be it. But," he continued with the authority-reasserting look he had spent decades cultivating, "we will proceed cautiously. We will make no overt move until the newly arrived beasts seek to expand up the Arm from Bellerophon, drawing the undivided attention of the stranded Rim Human forces. Only then will we strike—and when we do, we will strike simultaneously at Tisiphone and the starless warp nexus that gives access to Treadway, thus laying the groundwork for our next advance. At the same time, we will inform the Rim and its allies—who will, of course, be unaware that any of this is happening—that we are declaring our neutrality in their war with the newcomers, and closing our borders to all combatants. This will preserve them in their state of ignorance. Is all of this clear?"

Heruvycx and the others made the abbreviated version of the submission gesture that indicated deference to superior wisdom.

BOOK TWO

CHAPTER THIRTEEN

No Rosetta Stones Here

Alessandro finally noticed how sick she was getting in the mornings and her changes in appetite. He stood outside and waited until she'd finished retching, handed her a glass of water before very quietly saying, "You're either pregnant, or very ill."

All Jen could do at that point was sip her water and nod. "I'm pregnant."

They were standing at the top of the stairs at this point. "How long have you known?" he asked.

"Since the invasion. I wasn't sure before then."

"What the bloody hell de ye mean, woman, not tellin' me!" His roar was enough to shake the furniture. Jennifer took her hands down from her ears where they'd muffled the noise and, despite cringing inside from the realization that the observers downstairs could probably hear every word through two floors of town house, gave back as good as she got.

"If you're going to act like a Neanderthal—which you are—no wonder I didn't tell you that we're going to be parents!" Not "I'm pregnant" as if he had nothing to do with it. Nor "You are going to be a father" as if she had nothing to do with it, but "We are now and will be parents."

He had his mouth open to go on when she said the magic word "parents" and stopped.

"Would it be easier if I were ill, the way you were worried about?" She continued. She took hold of the newel post for support—it was Damnfine wood that he'd been so proud of when they'd built the place. Her mouth was full of the sourness of bile and she just wanted to sit down.

He shook his head, wordlessly, before turning away, hands clenching and unclenching. Jennifer hoped he'd turn back, hold her, but he stood there, his broad back as unapproachable as a brick wall. *That was a low blow. Maybe I shouldn't have said that.*

It hurt that even though it was dangerous and a bad time to be pregnant he couldn't be happy with her. " 'Sandro, it wasn't just me who wanted children." Why was he blaming her? They'd agreed to try and had been hoping, before the aliens came. "I admit I didn't suggest we stop trying when the news broke, but neither did you."

He didn't turn, didn't say anything. After a long moment she turned away from him and started down the stairs. "I've said what I need to say. I'm going downstairs to have a cup of tea—the grassy stuff the medic recommended, don't worry. This nausea is lasting a bit longer than it should, but everything's okay, if you're interested. And if you have anything to say to me, I'll be in the kitchen trying to keep dry toast down."

Alessandro listened to her footsteps as she went down, unable to make himself turn around. *I should have said something. I should have done something. Now it's not just us in danger, but a child too. I'm such a hypocrite. I can do anything to fight, but present me with more to fight for and I'm suddenly frightened with the responsibility. I'd risk everything, but I still feel like I've been blindsided. I just forgot. And I've been blind. She's already showing. I just didn't see.*

He just couldn't face her. Especially not with what he'd planned. He couldn't just wait around any longer for Van Felsen's caution. He'd spoken to Wismer and Narejko and planned a raid for day after tomorrow. It was time to show the Baldies that humans weren't going to just lie down and be walked on.

I'm going to do it and I can't tell her why I'm so upset. I'll have a good excuse to be out of the house for a couple of nights. He walked out to the back balcony and went down the outside stairs. He could see Jennifer at the breakfast bar, looking into the living room and squashed a sudden impulse to go apologize. He turned and went out the back gate, determined to do what he had to, but feeling shitty. *It'll be for her and our child. I'm going to be a father. And I want it to grow up on a free world, not an occupied one.*

She heard the back gate slam, put her head down on the counter, and cried.

Ankaht was not attending the Service. In the new High City, Urkhot, the *holodah'kri* communed with Illudor and the *selnarm* flow of his and the assembled clusters would be pouring out of the new Temple, built from the specific section of ship that had been designed for it.

A human might have said that it was a spiral, somewhat like a nautilus from Old Earth, or rather more like a horn shell, since the building did rise into a cone shape. It was based on a sea creature from Old Ardu, a *Threem*. Like a *Threem* shell it was a polished creamy color that was slightly iridescent making it stand out from the reddish sandy colors of most of the rest of the city.

Ankaht was being antisocial and Thutmus had been concerned that she did not wish to participate in the Communing. She sat in a *selnarm*-isolation room in her house. Everyone had one, because no matter how much group care was essential, the individual also needed attention.

To be honest the *selnarm* flow of this whole generation disturbed her and she struggled with it in this meditation room almost daily. But the *holodah'kri's selnarm* distressed her as well. It was obvious what his opinion was.

The room mercifully stifled the wave of emotion flowing out from the Temple, the extreme ecstasy and conviction of rightness that Admiral Torhok and his *Destoshaz* so easily turned to martial action. The Circle of Sleepers was a kernel of stillness compared to that. Her problem as senior was to try and make that stillness spread. (Implacability.) This *selnarm* from the Wanderers, the Shiplings, even though they were now technically landed, reminded her of lives lived during the Great Wars period on Old Ardu. This *selnarm* sought glory and violence. It was indifferent to suffering—of any sentient creature—and it encouraged a willingness to duel and defend an honor that was as far as she was concerned as much a fiction as any cultural convention.

And Urkhot was siding with Admiral Torhok on the ruling council. The two of them had pulled all the extremists to their camp and the very few moderates on Ankaht's side were wavering. She had to prepare herself to go into Council after the Communing since that was always seen as the best time to begin any kind of meeting or negotiation. (Negative anticipation, determination.)

She laid one hand on the new statue before her, a piece that would have horrified most of the rest of her own kind. She had seen it in a park in the *griarfeksh* city and it spoke to her. (Hope for joy.) It was so smooth featured that in the abstract it could have been either *griarfeksh* or Arduan: featureless head, bipedal figure with pointed limbs, dancing, eloquent it its movement caught in time. A glossy carved rock on a pleasingly rough piece of the same material. It gave her calm in the midst of this chaos, and hope that the *griarfeksh* problem had some kind of resolution other than that of extermination.

In another *selnarm*-insulated room, the lights set comfortingly low, two heads of clusters conferred. "I'm not sure I'm going to want to present this report to the admiral (Distress, discomfort.)," Hurnefer, Senior Cluster Linguist—newly appointed out of his training as a biologist—said plaintively. "There is a regular structure to the language but it seems to violate its own rules so often that it is absolutely incomprehensible." His tentacles writhed along with his distress, coiling shut and open as he contemplated facing the admiral who was (Insisting.) increasingly intolerant of their efforts.

(Calm.) Tornat, Secondary Cluster, soothed. "He must under-stand that we can only interpret what is absolutely comprehensible. At least we are making headway with their written language."

"But that . . . even if you discount the evidence of *other languages* in the same species—possibly hundreds along with this *English* . . ." He actually paused, too agitated to continue for a moment. "Words that have identical spellings and completely different pronunciations— *tough, cough, dough, plough*—and whole families of phoneme clusters like it!" (Confusion, irritation.) "How can anything comprehensible come of such structures?"

Tornat was silent before mentally calling up his section of the report. "If one sticks to written only, and simple commands, there is less confusion; all very machinelike and only appropriate for data transmission. It is only when one delves into the masses of material they carefully preserve in their machines and in their *libraries, town halls,* and *universities*—all of which seem to translate as variations on *knowledge storage places*, mass confusion reigns."

He was flushed a dusty color. (Anger, irritation, dismay.) "A warlike Deity glorifying the hideous destruction of cities, called the 'Deity who Loves.' A word which is supposedly 'affection, attraction' but which is also given meanings of destruction, violence, jealousy, and a willingness to kill. Any emotion, or feelings of any sort, any kind of *selnarm* is either absent or totally contradictory or incomprehensible gibberish!"

Hurnefer rose and turned away, reducing pressure on his fellow linguist, who returned the favor, until the increasing spiral of *selnarm* distress dissipated. It was Hurnefer who finally turned back. "We must continue, of course. We can only report the truth and if the admiral (Unreasonable action.) blames us for these *griarfeksh*'s impenetrability then that is as it will be."

(Acceptance, resignation.) "You're correct. You may as well send it and we can go back to (Futility.) climbing the wall of language. Have you managed to collect any specimens for direct observation?"

Hurnefer flushed again. (Anger, irritation.) "A few. They appear to be older individuals out of the *knowledge storage places*. Young males and females have a universally aggressive response to attempted collection and we know already not to go near the young, even the ones apparently isolated in clusters of unwanted or neglected, as are clusters of very old." (Grieved aggression.)

"Even in the buildings where they are prolonging the agony of this life with heroic measures—utmost cruelty—I cannot comprehend what these individuals must have done to be punished in this way. . . ." He paused again, speechless. "What crimes did they do to be kept in this life, in such agony?" He closed all three eyes for a moment, shocked into complete immobility.

Tornat nodded. "They respond as though these members of society were precious as opposed to unwanted, yet if we leave them alone they ignore these individuals, save for what appears to be routine maintenance."

"Only the completely unwanted, single individuals—homeless ones, clusterless ones—are apparently acceptable for us to seize. (Condescending disgust.) Those individuals unfortunately appear to be even more damaged than other members of the group. . . . (Skin twitching visceral disgust.) They also smell bad."

(Compassion.) "We have managed to acquire two of these kinds of facilities," he continued. "But we've had to start shooting any single individuals that approach us voluntarily. They either attempt to communicate at high volume, waving various objects in one hand and a *book* in the other, or they have brought explosive material strapped to their bodies, immolated themselves, and taken the facility with them."

For a long moment the two cluster heads shared mutual confusion and discomfiture before Tornat tactfully changed the subject so they did not have to turn away to destress. "Have you lost any of your team to planetary shock?"

(Worry.) "Yes, four of my group." Hurnefer was almost a normal color at this point, tapping both claws on the table. "Filtenat had an episode right in our work. It was most distressing having to shut out his panicky *selnarm* until the mental-health officials came and isolated him." He'd screamed that it was all over him, clawing at himself, apparently trying to get the planet off his skin, but that was too distressing to convey, so it was left unsaid.

Filtenat had actually been one of the fortunate ones who could be taken back up into microgravity and a controlled environment. One of the others in Hurnefer's group had chosen to go on to the next life by trying to defy gravity off one of the taller buildings.

"And you?"

Tornat knotted his tentacles together, stilling his unnatural restlessness. (Reassurance.) "Only two. The number is dropping as people adjust to being here. It will feel like home to the next generation."

"Except for those who refuse to come down." (Concern.)

(Ripple of irony, humor.) "Then we will be two kinds of people, spacegoing and planet loving. As our lives unfold."

(Resolution.) Hurnefer tapped a control and sent a thought to the computer. It packed the report and sent it forward to the attention of the admiral's office. "Done."

"Shall we go soak ourselves in hot water before we go back to it?"

"Yes. (Anticipated relief.) We should let everyone have a short period of relaxation."

✧   ✧   ✧

"Sir," the corporal's whisper was a bare thread in his ear-mike. Alessandro was flattened under a ground vehicle, a private truck that happened to be parked on the hill above the school, giving him a perfect line of sight. He inched forward slightly to get an absolutely clear view of the perimeter the Baldies had laid around the boarding school. The truck had been parked less than an hour ago and the cooling power plant covered his own body heat in case they happened to be using bio-scanners.

The streetlights glowed yellow in the summer haze, turning the night into a smoky-looking yellowish darkness, the pavement under his chest only now beginning to give up the day's heat. Oil and dust filled his nose making him want to sneeze, and the breeze just starting up made it worse, but it would help cover their movements.

The bushes and trees rustled, the shadows shimmering on the pavement, making flickering patterns of light and dark, never the same twice. It was as good as chaff for sensors, and he was glad he wasn't defending an urban area. Almost as glad that *they* were.

He clicked his teeth together to ensure he had a good connection. "Corporal."

"We're in position and deploying the grenades."

"Good."

Wismer and Narejko had proved adept at rewiring children's toys. Each of the three of them had half a dozen remote-control vehicles of some kind, modified to carry charges, their receivers powerful enough to accept a signal from a distance vastly expanded from their original construction.

The neighborhood had been warned that something would happen. Everyone knew that the aliens had captured the school and would take the children and teachers away somewhere. Most of the houses were already vacated, though there were some people who swore they'd take their chances. For a moment 'Sandro wished he had Van Felsen's sanction on his actions so he could make them leave, but working on the sly like this . . . well, what would happen, happened.

Earlier they'd made a personal call from a mobile com to one of the teachers. It seemed that the aliens hadn't yet realized what the tiny devices were. So everyone in the school was warned and ready to act.

Alessandro sent the first of his "toys" out under the row of parked vehicles, keeping its motion random to avoid setting off detectors.

After all, they couldn't keep shooting up the neighborhood for every squirrel. His toy, his concussion grenade on treads, stopped and started, turning like a stray dog, or a near-racoon. If he hadn't had it in his sight and known what to look for he'd have lost it in the first few seconds of it trundling into the shadow under a parked vehicle. It zipped across a walkway and into the school gardens.

As the first toy cleared the bushes, he stopped it and sent in the second, third, and fourth, scattering them through the Bell lilacs. The Baldies had good sensors and caught something from one of 'Sandro's team. Five meters down the school's approach drive, the lights of one of the alien's assault vehicles snapped on, spearing into the bushes, sending harsh, eye-searing light into the trees. All around the building, other vehicles came online, turning the playing field into an alien surface, making playground equipment all but unrecognizable in the glare and stark black shadows.

"All still," 'Sandro said quietly.

"Ya." Narejko's and Wismer's answers avoided the sibilant hiss a proper "yes" would have created. Silence as they waited out the alarm. No aliens made the mistake of stepping out of their armor, but scanned the surroundings from their protection. Distantly, 'Sandro could hear one of the younger children crying inside the building, being hushed.

Some of the neighbors had helpfully left their house systems turned on, so lights and vid systems and music came on at the usual times, hopefully further confusing the aliens' scanners.

The alarm had helpfully pointed out where all the armored vehicles were and he'd carefully noted their positions. "Ten minutes," he said quietly into his throat mike. "One, take the two at the front. Two, east and north side."

"Ya. Ya."

The surreal vision of a school being advanced on by a small army of remote-control toys made Alessandro want to shake his head in disbelief, but he continued to click out directions to those cannibalized tanks and sports vehicles, each with its deadly load.

It took another handful of minutes to maneuver their mobile grenades into position. 'Sandro was sweating by the time the tone in his ear gave him a two-minute warning. The vehicle he was after was in the open, giving him no cover to get his second explosive into position. He stopped the track next to a downed teeter-totter seat but even as he did the aliens spotted it and vaporized the toy and the grenade it carried and the seesaw it was hiding behind. It began to move but 'Sandro detonated the second grenade that had just made it underneath.

The alien vehicle was engulfed in the expanding fireball and tumbled, flipped over twice before snapping off an old neo-maple, coming to rest on the shattered remains of its roof. Matching concussions on the north and east sides lit up the night, turning it into a shrieking mass of shrapnel and smoke and setting the grass and bushes on fire.

'Sandro squinted against the glare, glad of his earplugs as the massive shockwaves made the vehicle over him shudder, burned the surrounding vegetation and scorched the surfaces off the closest houses. There was a profound silence full of the ticking of overheated metal cooling, and the last pieces of debris that had been blown high into the air hitting the ground.

There were shots inside the school, where teachers turned from meek captives into killers, defending the kids, swinging improvised weapons. He didn't want to think what that took, for civilians to fight hand to hand like that. But they had assured him they would, and apparently they were. He reminded himself that the division between civilian and military was one of choice. *Lots of my buddies have this idea that the civs they came from are somehow stripped of their guts. Force a war on people and everybody becomes a grenade with the pin pulled. Just threaten their kids or their parents.*

The school itself had caught fire and Alessandro brought the last two of his remotes into play as the children, herded by the adults, began to flee the building. He could see their dark shapes against the light. As planned they began to scatter in small groups into the surrounding streets. A Baldy staggered out of the building, obviously dazed, still trying to stop them. Raising a firearm.

There's enough space. Alessandro made a snap decision and one of his remote-control air toys lost power and dropped right at the Baldy's feet. There was only a fraction of a second to respond and the alien, still stunned, perhaps by a blow on the head, didn't. The explosion was much smaller than the ones that had ripped through alien armor, but it was quite big enough to reduce the Baldy to its component parts and knock down the last group of children.

They picked themselves up and kept running, thankfully all of them, that 'Sandro could see.

"Good job, guys. Fade."

"Tomorrow."

The two corporals would work their separate ways home, blending into the crowd of people fleeing the conflagration and the expected alien retaliation, just as 'Sandro would, after dropping the remote controls in the nearest recycling bin that would flash them into their component materials.

These aliens just don't know what they're up against, he thought, satisfied. *We got the kids out, and they still don't know what hit them.* He brushed himself off after getting out from under the vehicle and walking briskly away from the commotion behind. One alley and he was shielded by another row of buildings, one more block removed from complicity.

He opened his hand, dropped his own remotes in a bin without breaking stride and kept going; the one he hadn't needed would stay behind and go off when the Baldies closed on the area. Proximity fuses were a favorite way to play merry Hell.

It was a good idea to stay on foot since the tube would be shut down by now and he'd stay on foot till he was well away, to where he'd parked a rented vehicle. The aliens would have things shut down completely for all outgoing traffic inside the next few minutes but by then he'd be safely on the way home, apparently driving *in* rather than away. Not the sort of thing he would have tried with a human opponent, but the aliens were showing a number of deficits in understanding humans and he intended to exploit every one he could. Especially now.

I have to get home and apologize to Jen. Even though he wanted to slow down, he kept up his smooth pace, one designed not to draw attention to himself.*If I don't, she'll think I'm a complete heel, not just trying to keep her safe. Not having an excuse not to be home for a couple of nights.* He felt like a complete ass, having maintained their fight to keep her from wondering what he was doing out at night without her. But it was safer that way. Even if he'd trusted her with his life, he couldn't –in good conscience—risk the baby too.

He climbed into the vehicle and got underway already planning on eating serious crow. The alien support ships zipping overhead in the same direction ignored him.

The Arduan Council chamber on Bellerophon was in silent uproar. (Fear, anger, distrust, urge to kill, shocked response.) They were mentally divided into two defensive clusters, the *selnarm* shock waves triggering and retriggering a defensive response from the *Destoshaz Anaht'doh Kainat* and *shaxzhu* both but with very different focuses.

Admiral Torhok seized control of *selnarm*, aided by Urkhot's powerful send, and formed it into (Enraged, will to destroy.). But Ankaht and Thutmus along with Treknat, Felnarmaht and Nukurhat—who was very disturbed at disagreeing with his spiritual leader—all three lesser councilors, held firm against the tide of (Rage, will to murder.) spilling from the other eight, two priests along with Urkhot and the five *Destoshaz*.

"Admiral, you do not need to destroy every one of these *griarfeksh* on the planet." Ankaht sent her strongest (Reason, calm.). "We do not know *why* they refuse to stop fighting. We do not know the *why* of ninety percent of the things they do."

"If they keep destroying our researchers then *they*, not us, will be the cause of their own destruction!" Torhok's sending was an odd sensation for Ankaht and she had to think before she recognized it. The willingness to kill blended with an eagerness that took a long moment for her to recognize it. She blinked, appalled. *Will to triumph over all opposition. Glory. Satisfaction for anticipated victory.*

She doubted that any of the other *Destoshaz* even recognized it consciously. They—*all of them,* she realized—were reacting to it on a level so deep that it almost defied description. Her own reaction was an automatic resistance to give adulation, the admiration, respect, and almost reverence that Torhok obviously was beginning to crave.

All this took only a fraction of a second for her to recognize; she blinked and cast a glance at her allies, also realizing that none of them understood what she did. They did not have the depth of *shaxzhutok* that she did and some—notably Nukurhat—were only supporting her through a vague sense of *narmata* gone awry and a stubborn refusal to assume that anything not understood was automatically monstrous.

"These fiends are not to be understood!" Urkhot thundered both verbally and in *selnarm*. (Negation, rejection.) "They should not exist! They are an insult to Illudor and our Race! Destroy them all! Cleanse the planet of their pollution, their foulness on the face of the Deity!" (Rightness, justice craved.)

Nurukhat (Resolution, determination.) said, quietly, "*Holodah'kri,*" the title for the High Priest that meant something like Born Many

Times, or Protector of the Way, "*Holodah'kri*, perhaps Illudor has brought us to these creatures for our own *holodah*?"

(Disbelief.) "You insist on questioning my judgment?" (Loathing, derision.) Under the lash of Urkhot's *selnarm* Nurukhat withdrew slightly physically, curling tentacles shut, tucking claws under, closing eyes, but refused to budge morally.

"Yes, *Holodah'kri*. I question and as my duty, continue to question. No *'kri* is above the mind of all. No one alive is infallible."

(Support.) "Indeed," Thutmus broke in. "Admiral, is the race in danger? How safe are we, really?" (Neutral inquiry.)

Illudor bless, Ankaht thought and suppressed a sudden surge of affection. That was a distraction that no one here needed. *The male is intelligent and thoughtful both. Illudor be thanked I have good taste.*

Torhok, who had merely let his *selnarm* flow as a minor support to Urkhot's emotional storm, seeming more reasonable thereby, knotted his tentacles together contentedly. "The Race is as safe as I and the other *Destoshaz* can make it, here. I feel confident that I can hold this system against anything coming. (Fierce joy, urge to fight.) These two-eyed monsters have given us an enormous amount of information to swallow in one gulp, if we can decipher it. (Indulgent humor.) And for that, I am profoundly grateful. (Irony.) I repeat, the system is thoroughly defended, and the masses of already refined materials in the vermin's shipyards have put us ahead of schedule rebuilding the defensive ships. (Chary watchfulness.) The scientists are working on what information they can glean about the use of these 'holes' in space that the *griarfeksh* use and in the future I expect we will take the fight to them." (Bloodthirstiness.)

The sense of bloody destruction from the admiral, gilded with hope, sickened Ankaht and she caught a flicker of agreement from Thutmus. (Will to destroy, six for, two undecided, five against.) The *selnarm* consensus thankfully was holding, with the two undecided, swayed by Nurukhat's unwillingness to be steered like a *Bilbuxhat* by the nose, Thutmus's neutrality and the lingering, unusual taste for blood from Torhok. It was thick in her mouth and nose, in her mind at least, and she was sure it was as mentally cloying in everyone else's, though some would more have the taste for it than she.

Ankaht's *selnarm* rose, startling a response out of the *Destoshaz 'kri* faction with its strength. She seldom "out-shouted" either admiral or *holodah'kri* but it was necessary to remind them occasionally that she had the raw power to do it if she so chose.

(Negation, rejection of blood-hunger, tranquility, patience.) Torhok looked a bit like he'd been hit between the lower eyes with a hammer. "We take no further action until we have more information. We can all feel how split we are on the subject and will maintain until something changes the balance. Give our scientists the time they need." (Fierceness.) *It will not serve to challenge the admiral directly, at this point, as much as I would dearly love to shove a claw where it would do us all the most good.* She let none of her longing for a particular kind of just violence nor her own disgust at that particular joy show, but she kept it wrapped in a core of herself to be unwrapped later.

She had not practiced *maatkah* in several years of awake time, onboard ship, but at one point, as a meditation, she had been high-ranked. It was time to begin a more active meditation, she decided. *I will need it to do what is both right and correct.* (Fierceness.)

CHAPTER FORTEEN

The Jaws That Bite

No one enjoyed duty at warp points that boasted no star. If you spent your whole watch staring at instruments, that at least was better than looking out at the dark. Humans have always peopled the dark outside the ring of light with monsters, whether that light is a campfire or a star, and the Bug War had given the unknown enormous fangs. The things out there *were* monsters and it was best to have the biggest, sharpest stick in the pile to fight them off.

When mankind found the stepping-stones from star to star, casual travelers became accustomed to the idea that there would always be a light close by to aim for, and a few light-minutes or -hours were manageable. Many who spent enough time in space, either merchant or military, tended to refer to these occasional deep-space travelers as "moths." The truth was that warp points exist in an interstellar void and physicists had yet to come up with an appropriate and generally accepted gravitational theory to explain why. BR-01 was just such a point, usually not commented on because people's thoughts blanked over it on their way through from Bellerophon to Misty much the same way that ancient travelers would close the blind on a train window and not see a whistle-stop.

The merchants who had fled the invasion had brought garbled reports of it with them, but what was clear was that they were cut off. Vice Admiral Erica Krishmahnta was bringing up every unit she had from downstream, but the RFN had never planned for this, expecting to reinforce through the warp system, and they had frighteningly few resources to hold the Arm.

One of the merchant captains, a Captain Hustapyzuk, had been pressed into service and dropped a couple of drones before she pulled back, but neither of them had managed to make warp transit with any intelligence on the invaders and Krishmahnta was doing the best with what she had.

She was well aware of her peoples' morale, and it was harder still waiting in the dark for an attack that everyone knew *had* to be coming. Even though you knew where the attack was coming from, one could never know exactly when. You could sit your watch or you could stare at the dark, knowing that there wasn't a star in light-years and the weight of the dark outside the picket ships accumulated as softly as falling snow. Drills could only keep people on the knife-edge so long before they succumbed to various ailments that the doctors and medics couldn't address with an injection, pill, or patch.

It was also a hard choice to place her flagship here at BR-01 rather than at Pegasus, for morale's sake as much as any tactical consideration.

In the privacy of her duty cabin aboard her flagship, *Gallipoli*, Erica bit her lip, a mannerism that she disliked in herself that still manifested when she was stressed. Her green eyes were worried as her light pen moved from star to star. All units that had been down the Arm had been called in and over the months what strength they had had built up slowly, but any unit that hadn't gotten here by now probably wasn't going to do them much good. The whole Arm was mostly agrarian, with specialty foods and goods, but the only heavy manufacturing capability at all was Tilghman, and that only in a very limited way. And both that worthy system's capacity and the raw materials of Odysseus were months away.

She looked at the tank showing the ships of the picket. As of 1300 today, she had twelve supermonitors when *Passhendale* and *Temuchin* showed up from Raiden. Twenty-two monitors, thirty-six SDs, and a mixed bag of CVAs and CVs all with their associated fighters.

The aliens Behemoths were far too large to ever make warp transit but the numbers of SDs they'd had was astonishing. And she had to assume that they could be modified to make warp. *No way are we going to stop them once they decide to come down the line. Not here. But if I can draw them away from Bellerophon then that will split their forces and let us counterattack from the other side. We need to spread them too thin.*

An assault was coming and every captain on every ship in the picket was aware of it. The only thing that they could do was to send recon probes through, hoping that one would give them more information. The fact that nothing came back was information of a sort but only in the negative.

She tapped the pen on her desk thoughtfully before leaning forward and keying her comm. "Liam, would you call Yoshi once he's finished his meeting with Ms. Obriko and get him to come up to see me?" It was time that she and her flag captain shook things up again; everything they could think of out of the simulators.

There had been a rumor going around that the aliens had come to BR-01 straight, and she had to show the crews how unlikely it was that the aliens could get any kind of ship through Einsteinian space to here. It was a problem even making the computers work that way. She couldn't even call up a schematic that showed BR-01 on the same image as Bellerophon; they were that far apart.

Captain Yoshi Watanabe was brilliant at setting up scenarios that illustrated what they wanted and people would, more often than not, make their own correct conclusions.

"Certainly, Admiral."

She was certain that the attack, when it came, would come through the warp point. Meanwhile, she had crews to keep on track while the knowledge of a looming attack bulked larger and larger in the darkness.

The half-dozen Arduan experimental probes, each with its individual pilots and gunners, held station in amongst the minefields surrounding the twisted places in space that the *griarfeksh* called "warp points." One needed magnification to see the minute destructive seeds scattered around the warps, tiny only in relation to the dark immensity of space that they guarded, and the warp itself showed nothing visually. The five fortresses shone *vrelish*, gleaming against the darkness; nothing like what had been there before, stately, beautiful, and deadly as they swam in the dark

The Arduans hadn't been able to use the scuttled fortifications that had been left behind, but the raw materials had been an excellent shortcut for building their own. Rather than a solid shape with missile mounts and energy emplacements, these defenses were constructed like an Arduan hand. While scanning, the long tendriled fingers waved at maximum spread. The central core contained the missile launchers while the ten projecting tentacles were packed with scanners and energy mounts. The only difference to a real hand was that normal ones only had two claws, while these had ten. Each claw end had a limited range of movement while attached, but was entirely capable of functioning independently for a short time if severed from the central command unit.

While scanning, the strands moved constantly, slowly like an anemone in shallow water, wafting back and forth, constantly changing the volume of space being scanned so the stations writhed and danced in slow motion. Whenever a hostile object was spotted the tendrils contracted, pulling in quite close but never bunched together in a closed fist; that would have ruined the effectiveness that the spread of tentacle provided in the first place.

Admiral Narrok had been present the last time the *griarfeksh* had launched a pair of machines from the other side of the warp and had been very pleased with the response. Three of the fortresses had targeted the things and the resulting explosions had made the filters in the recording devices shut down and restart. Some of the people on the planet had even reported seeing the greenish *herrm* flares in the sky, even in daylight.

The afterimages had shown the moments of destruction, silhouetting *Rin* station gratifyingly stark against the blast.

The warps in the New Ardu system were far enough out that the planets of the system were only differently colored stars, but many of the Last Generation found it comforting to know that they, and the new colonies on them, were close enough to be only hours away.

The people knew that hostile *griarfeksh* had retreated through all three of the warp points in this system and assumed that there probably more on the other side. But the idea of a warp, the idea of being able to move from star to star in less than multiple generations was stunning to the *Anaht'doh Kainat* and the number of volunteers to man the probes was enormous.

If the linguists were correct, the *griarfeksh* were scattered across a huge volume of space, tens or hundreds of planets. If Arduans could only master this technology, then Illudor's perpetual existence was assured and all limits of space were a thing of the past. The possibilities were enough to enthrall not only the theologians and strategists but everyone else as well, because the population could expand to numbers that would render the interlife less of an interminable, tedious wait. Narrok, given charge of the gathering of information about these warps, had to winnow down the volunteers to the six best for each warp—pilot and gunner for each ship— the first wave of inquiry into unknown territory.

He was also concerned as to their attitude about the nature of their missions. It was one thing to command and expect to be obeyed but the researchers were so eager to explore that he repeatedly had to rein them back, because they were so ready to fling themselves into possibly fatal situations. He was very concerned that these nonmilitary researchers would pursue their own *shotan* rather than endeavor to get back with every scrap of information that they could.

Dying would be too easy. In this case, "*Destolfi rahk montu shilkiene*"—or "Death is *not* a tiny thing!" (Emphasis.) He and his immediate cluster commanders had to keep reiterating this since the information that could be gained from a successful transit and return was of supreme importance and that living for the race was far more valuable than dying for it.

Humans would have sent unmanned probes to protect human lives, but the Arduans considered this excessive concern. If one died in pursuit of knowledge then one's *holodah* was increased, and since the landing—when the birth restrictions came off—there would be many, many more to be born anew into, so what did it matter?

The probes were actually very large armed fighters, since they could not expect anything but hostility on the other side of the warps. They were not thin, sleek, sharklike *griarfeksh* ships but more bulbous, to accommodate the energy mounts that the Arduans found so effective, but the shape of an orca is no less dangerous than that of a shark, both deadly killers when they chose to be.

The control pod where Admiral Narrok sat was at half gravity, and he leaned back comfortably, drawing his gaze away from the images of the research vessels and cast his eyes around the space with approval. He, like everyone involved, was enthralled with the possibilities and kept that at the forefront of his *selnarm* rather than his minor concerns and tensions. That was the idea for *Destoshaz*, of course, and he would never judge another on his mastery of emotional flow, least of all his colleague Admiral Lankha.

The brand new system defense ship *Neferhurukor* was actually the after third of the generation ship *Ahknemakeht* and as such was a blocky and unlovely creation, but she worked and Narrok was sure she would work well.

It appeared that the ships would have to remain in this star system but the rebuilt docks that, at a certain distance, gave New Ardu the appearance of having glittering rings, were turning out superdread-noughts in not only their tens, but as soon as it could be managed, in their hundreds. The people were at war and the number of the enemy was vast.

There was a ripple through *selnarm* as the last of the research vessels drifted into place and Admiral Narrok wordlessly sent them his approval to proceed even as he nodded at his communications tech. "Go."

"Acknowledgement from all, sir."

"Good. Now we will see if we understand this way of traveling." (Amused anticipation.) (Tension.)

"Yessir." (Willingness to fight.)

The uproar in the Council chamber on New Ardu sent if not shock waves then at least ripples through the *selnarm* of the settlers, *Destoshaz* or not, on planet or in space. The fact that the elder *shaxzhu* stood up to both the senior admiral and the *holodah'kri* was the topic of gossip and speculation even as the work of settling and rebuilding continued.

Narrok was very well aware of that and was not certain exactly how he felt on the whole subject. There was the *selnarm* of the senior admiral, for one, and his coadmiral Lankha. She was cut from the same cloth as Torhok, both of them like the many who, once presented with an enemy, considered themselves somehow like *Destoshaz* of old, the war leaders who earned their titles "Great" and "Terrible." Their *selnarm* was something unseen for more than fifteen hundred years and it was seductive, especially when there was an obvious enemy.

For himself, everything had been simple and straightforward when they were in the long deep, the quiet space between stars, and now there was confusion and destruction and just plain noise. Now everything was changed; he was inclined to wait and see rather than leap to any definitive conclusion. He was uncomfortable with simplistic responses. Across the light-hours at the other warp point, Admiral Lankha would be sending her ships through, if all coordination held true. The flow of *selnarm* from that task force was hard to pick out of the wave of feelings from the bulk of the people but the anticipation was clear.

At every warp point the first ship of the research pair made its approach and Narrok found himself holding his breath as they blinked out of existence. (Anticipation, wonder.)

Lieutenant Thomas rubbed his eyes, pinching the bridge of his nose. It was late third watch and even the most keyed-up watchers couldn't stop the dull, foggy feeling in the brain and scratchy, tired eyes. As he opened his eyes and fixed them back on the display he caught the first flicker of motion, the energetic shock wave of transit cascading into visible light from the warp point. Even as foggy as he was, his hesitation was only a moment and his finger descended on the alert pad, his voice cracking out, "Incoming! We have incoming!" even as the computers concurred and brought the ship to full alert.

People tumbled out of bunks, stuffing limbs into suddenly awkward clothing as they ran to duty stations, the quivering shock of computer launched missiles trembling even through the largest ship.

The first alien ship didn't have time to recover from transit and even as it crabbed sideways in space, missiles from *Gallipoli* and *Gallaway* both locked on. In the fraction of a second that the alien survived something got off one, perhaps two shots. Energy weapons are light-speed, faster than any missile, and a handful of mines died before the alien ship was reduced to glowing elemental remnants, sparkling as they expanded against the dark.

Lesser Cluster Captain Eraphis swallowed hard a number of times as his sight cleared, reeling from the shock that had run through him as they traversed the warp, compounded by the dying *selnarm* from the lead ship as they burst into a different space, full of dispersing wreckage and radiation. Even as he fought to settle his stomach he flung the ship—in the privacy of his own mind he'd named her

Lahatas, even though the survey ships had been deemed too expendable to name—into evasive maneuvers, her recorders faithfully, calmly, taking in the information the People needed to survive. The third ship was through now and Eraphis fought off the other ship's disorienting *selnarm* as they came through the warp. In the turbulent chaff expanding all around them he wheeled his ship in a wild, erratic, mad course, dancing with Illudor's shadow, as the human picket ships swung their clubs at the gnat buzzing around them.

The third ship tucked in below him until its pilot recovered, before it peeled off in as wild a course as he. It darted in a widely divergent course, as planned, and they were aware of the excitement, tension, and fear from their fellows, but couldn't let it influence them. In a small part of Eraphis's mind, he could only faintly wonder that he and his gunner, Sehtsurankh, were still alive. What kept them alive was his piloting. He couldn't afford a millisecond's distraction. Seht blew them a path as they corkscrewed crazily around the mines and floating debris.

Missiles locked on them, and as Eraphis forced them to lose lock he could hear and feel Seht cursing as his course flung them against their harnesses and gel cushioning. "Hold on, my friend. We may even make it back." The two of them had been getting into trouble together even in their nursing cluster and though neither of them were *shaxzhu* and could confirm it, were convinced that they'd known each other in many lives before. "Shut up and fly," was Sehtsurankh's grunted reply in the ear-speaker, the flow of his *selnarm* undisturbed, even as his body tried to brace itself.

They had to stay in this new space a certain amount of time before trying to make it back. Had the timer been damaged? What if —

A clicking in Eraphis's ear hole–speaker let him know that it was time to run—if he could. It was now his duty to get them home safe. "Do you know that you hum if we are in deep shit?" Seht grumbled. They'd never been in true combat before, so he hadn't known. Eraphis grinned to himself.

Thank Iludor these tiny ships had the drive that let them start and stop on half a heartbeat. The whole ship jolted sideways and "rang" somehow. He couldn't see what caused it. It couldn't have been a hit or he'd be on to his next life. Damage indicators flared into vision on his board. His tentacles locked tight around the control sticks, bracing himself against his gel he wrenched them around and hurtled through the shrieking remnants of the last ship that had just been vaporized, clenched his grinders against the emotional surge of the two deaths, riding the shock wave these ships were supposed to be immune to, before hauling what felt like the whole ship up through the mess and down, back into the warp point.

Admiral Torhok clenched his tentacles into fisted knots on his knees and closed his eyes to cut off his (Rage.) uncharacteristically mobile for a *Destoshaz*. *I could take them. I could take every* griarfeksh *on its own ground and make Illudor safe. I could make my name, my holodah, and these chattering* flixits *want me to stay* here *as opposed to leading this fight!* He forced himself still and blinked slowly, refusing to look at the eldest speaker. (Consensus 18, Dissent 1.) He turned sideways in his seat to regard the new piece of artwork to the left. A rough granite lump the size of his torso, with random planes of various textures polished into its surface standing on a *vrel*-colored glass plinth. He surged to his feet and heard old Tefnut-ta-sheri startle back at his abrupt movement.

There was a polite rustle all down the curved table as the others in the Council also chose to appreciate an artwork. It was Illudor's blessing that they again had a whole planet's worth of space to spread out in. Torhok ran his hands up into the slots in the stone, appreciating the subtle texture under his tentacles. The *selnarm* roil in the room calmed.

When he turned back toward the low table he refused to look at *Shaxzhu* Ankaht. It would only enrage him and make his argument less effective; any rage made him less effective.

Even though Ankaht hadn't said much, he knew she had to be behind it. She'd been blocking him at every turn, from the moment they'd known of the aliens. He turned his gaze to the *holodah'kri* who was still apparently contemplating a feathered tapestry though everyone knew his attention was focused on the room behind him. The man was becoming a liability instead of an ally, since you couldn't count on him to back you to do the sensible thing. Torhok shrugged mentally. If it had to do with the preservation of his thislife, an odd perversion to be sure, the priest would always take that course. (Consensus.)

"I'll bow to the consensus, of course. (Dutiful agreement.) I am sure the honorable admirals will bring about the victories we need." *My admirals will have to be my* holodah-ra-nekt—his honor carriers.

"And all glory will accrue to your name as senior commander," Ankaht said quietly. (Compassionate understanding.) She couldn't understand his need for conquest and victory, but she could honor it.

Torhok was rigid with anger and disgust but put it aside with (Water Flowing Down the Mountain) a mental discipline he was resorting to more and more in her presence. *How dare she sympathize!* She was arguing more for *griarfeksh* and less for the People as he saw it and anything that endangered the People disgusted him. The solution was to fight and to win over these aliens.

"I bow to the elder speaker's word." (Irony. Anger.) The fine edge on his *selnarm* making it clear that it was the last thing he wished to do. "I am needed here in this star system." He acknowledged their demand and left the council chamber more abruptly than was politic. They held him here, at New Ardu, but they couldn't make him like it, these cluster-nursing builders and suppliers, rather than doing what he found he did best—fighting. Narrok and Lankha would need all the help he could give them now that he wouldn't be leading either assault. It changed all his plans and everyone would have to scramble to adjust.

Now that the People *knew* they could use these warps it made him feel enclosed in a way that he had never noticed before. *We have a way to travel from star to star and the closed-clamshell minds back there want to keep me confined to merely one? They talk of battle, of defense of the race as "rash," "over-ambitious," and even "vain." Illudor's claws and tentacles, if the* shaxzhu *have their way the Race will become dull, defenseless herbivores that the next predator along will finish off—and then Illudor dies. Do they* want *the universe to vanish in a popped bubble of ennui?*

Lankha would take the warp their young pilot had returned from. All the others hadn't come back, but that actually had been expected. The second wave of research ships had been ready if the first wave had brought no information back at all.

If Eraphis hadn't made it back they wouldn't have known that it wasn't the act of transferring through the warp that had killed them in the first place. They couldn't assume that it would all just function as predicted and that the *griarfeksh* had immolated them. But one ship had made it back and even if the two aboard were more than tired of being examined for possible ill effects and questioned about the experience, they were still gamely answering researchers questions.

Narrok would take the other. The mild rivalry that Lankha maintained—though he knew that Narrok saw such games as just that, games—would give them both incentive to take the war to the *griarfeksh*. If they held one or two star systems or more then the actual physical distance provided stronger walls than mere ships.

He stormed into his ground-side office, his *selnarm* rage boiling before him, sending lesser support staff scattering long before he actually appeared. This nonsense was at least picking out his more timid staff. The ones who did all their work and more—with clear consciences—stayed serene, confident that they were not the focus of disgusted anger.

"Call Narrok and Lankha, conference communication in a hand of minutes." (Endurance.)

"Yes, Sir! (Obedience. Awe.)

CHAPTER FIFTEEN

The Claws That Catch . . .

When the alien attack came the defenders weren't quite as worn from waiting as they had been previously. As shocking as it had been the probe ships had given them actual targets and had ended the waiting. Only one ship had escaped back through the warp point, but that was all it took. Then the waiting started again. Now that they had their information, how long would it take for them to follow up?

Lieutenant Thompson was on duty again, this time in the middle of the shipboard day, supposedly much more alert than in the dead hours of the night, and the computer still beat him to the alarm, this time.

Krishmahnta was long past the "drop everything—literally—and run" mentality of her days as an ensign. It never did anyone any good for officers to arrive on deck disheveled, panting, looking as though they'd just fought off an Orion *zeget* or an Earth tiger to get their uniform back, wresting it out of needle-fanged jaws. She'd had one captain who did just that, almost every time, and while he was a good officer she'd certainly learned that it always played merry Hell with morale. It still took her under a minute to take her place on *Gallipoli*'s command deck.

"Admiral, they're coming through in force!" The one thing she didn't do was sit down. She was so keyed up that she stood rather than sitting in her command chair, but she didn't pace, clasping her hands behind her back, taking in the glittering tank with blip after ominous blip emerging red from the warp point. They began blinking as the mines engaged, and began to vanish, but slowly the inexorable pressure of ship after ship began forcing the defenders back. The space around the BR-01 warp point was a hellish expanding bubble of wreckage and radiation. The tank in the command center of the *Gallipoli* was having a hard time compensating for the background glow and still give enough contrast to let Krishmahnta and her staff discern what was happening. It hiccupped and suddenly the display came clear.

It was an ugly, brute-force assault, with the aliens showing themselves utterly willing to spend their ships and themselves in a way that chilled everyone watching, raising the specter of the monster under the bed, the monster in the dark. There were not enough mines and when the last had taken an SD with it, the alien assault force began to expand faster. The defenders had already been pushed back a full dozen light-seconds.

"Commander Williams' com-net has gone down, Admiral."

Damn. Damn. Damn. She didn't let that get off her tongue. Without the net to coordinate ship movement more of her people were going to get killed. "All units pull back. Retreat to point Alpha."

The fighters from *Celmithyr'theaarenouw* were the last to break off, even accounting for the lag—like all Tabby fighter jocks they always rode the edge—and before their final attack group peeled away they managed to take another alien SD out, but the explosion wiped out most of the group as they fled the expanding blast. Krishmahnta had held *Celmithyr'theaarnouw* out as far as possible and she had orders to retreat through the warp point once she had all her fighters back, at least all those who made it back. But it had been hard enough to get the Tabby captain to hold back so far.

The older carrier had been halfway through her refitting and had been withdrawn to join up with her forces with human engineers still working as they withdrew. She was just as glad that Kiiraathra'ostakjo was used to working closely with humans, especially out here. It was sheer fluke that she had *two* Orion CVs, counting the damaged one that had brought them the images of the first battle, to try and retake Bellerophon.

Most people believed that the fighter was little more than a distraction against the heavy metal of the ships of the line, but the fighter primary beam still made them formidable, especially in numbers against an alien foe who'd never had to deal with such tiny, agile foes. It was somewhat like a knight in full armor being swarmed by wasps; one or two would annoy, dozens or hundreds would kill. Erica could almost imagine the Orion howls of victory, even though none of that would be transmitted.

Erica sat down as she watched the tight group of Commander Williams' command drift apart, captains attempting to maintain the cluster that made both their offensive and defensive fire so deadly; trying and failing.

Against all his instincts Least Claw Kiiraathra'ostakjo pulled the *Celmithyr'theaarnouw* back as ordered, restraining the thunderous rumble in his chest as Orion and human engineers struggled to find the glitch that had caused the failure of the com-net all down the line. The acrid stench of burnt insulation in the air made everyone's fangs visible as their noses wrinkled, but they ignored all of that, even as they ignored the technicians frantically pulling panels, struggling to keep the carrier's missile fire as coordinated as possible with the rest of the group. "Least Claw! We have it! We have it! Com coming back up. Commander Williams, Sir!"

"Good. Kiiraathra'ostakjo here."

The translation was broken but clear. "Regrouping as ordered, Good work, Claw. We've lost *Arbalest*. *Longbow*'s closing to cover your flank."

"Acknowledged." Kiiraathra'ostakjo watched his plot as the alien ships continued to warp in, in a never-ending stream. The odor in the air had nothing to do with how much fang he showed.

The aliens were still bringing up units. *Dammit,* Krishmahnta thought. *Where are they coming from? How could they have built so fast?* Superdreadnought after superdreadnought came through so close that several annihilated each other; yet they were still coming through the carpet of missiles she'd laid down when the alarm blared. Tension in the picket had ratcheted up once the probe ships had zipped through the warp. They knew they hadn't destroyed all of them and she and her staff had planned their best with what they had.

The aliens were treating SDs like fighters that could make warp and the human defenders were starting to feel like people trying to plug a hole in a dyke with their palms, against the weight of the sea.

When it hit the fan and the first alien ships came through, she'd wished to be at Pegasus rather than downstream of Misty. But she could hardly go back four star systems and around another four just to make herself feel better. It didn't matter.

She'd had to assume that the aliens were now using the warp points and would be attacking through both of them and she could only hope that Vice Admiral Yoshikuni was doing better over at Pegasus. On some level every human was somehow reassured now that they were fighting a war whose shape they understood, even if it raised all the horrors of Bugs anew from everyone's nightmares.

She bit her lip, but pulled her mouth straight, refusing to be distracted by her own concerns and concentrated on the mess that was the battle. The faint, almost subliminal twitch told her gut that her ship had fired again.

"They're still coming." The channel broke up in an aural shower of static before coming back, the voice as flat as suppressed panic could make it. "They don't give a damn, sir." Even over the light-minutes the officers on the *Gallipoli* could see it. The alien SDs were coming through with the same disregard for their own safety as they had before. The red enemy icons continued coming through, an expanding bubble as they forced a space around the warp point.

Given enough weight of ships and willingness to throw them through a warp point, a toehold could be forced. You couldn't put mines right *on* the warp point—they'd only be torn apart by the stresses and you had to back off to a certain extent. That was what had allowed the small ships to get in and out again to give the aliens their information.

"Admiral—" The *Norfolk*'s icon was beginning to flash yellow.

"—I see it, Mr. Aetlan, thank you." She leaned forward unconsciously, as if she could pull the ship in trouble out with her will alone, but as she opened her mouth the Omega code flashed. She heard a muffled sound from the exec that could have been a curse.

If the aliens were following true to form they would not pick up life-pods or try to save those aboard a disabled ship. "All command groups. Fall back. Fall back. Pick up as possible. Repeat, as possible." In the holo tank the green dots of the defenders began breaking free of the ugly swath of red in the center, falling back in their command groups. There were so few of them compared to that red tide.

They had planned for this, trained to make their withdrawal as costly as possible for the aliens. She thought of Misty, and hoped like hell that they could stem this tide, this god awful, relentless flow of alien ships. She turned to the image of the hideous flood still coming through the warp point. Ship after ship after ship. *Dammit. Dammit. Thank the gods that they don't seem to have anything like the Desai Drive. In a straight run for the warp point, they can't hope to catch us.*

(Self-satisfaction.) Torhok looked along the Council table, sending the cascade of his elation out freely. His supporters, at his end of the table, picked it up and amplified it without needing to know the contents of the reports resting under his right hand, bracketed by his claws.

It was all but impossible for one of the People to completely hide what he or she felt, but Senior Speaker Ankaht nearly managed. It was one of the things that irritated him. *Well, we will just see her react once I let her and the rest of the rock-bound idiots know.*

"Admiral," she said quietly. "I understand you have your reports for us?" (Polite inquiry. Tiredness.)

"Indeed, Elder." He fanned out the information wafers with his hand and handed them to the *holodah'kri* for him to take his and pass them down the table. People inserted them in the readers and the central display showed a diagram that the People had never seen before, a tree with miniature images of stars at each junction. "For everyone's perusal." He paused and uncharacteristically showed his grinders in a physical display that gave his *selnarm* far more force. "Admiral Narrok has seized another star system with more warp points leading on, though he is being blocked by the *griarfeksh* at one of them, others have been explored. The People now have access to six more stars." (Intense satisfaction.)

"Admiral Lankha on the other hand has seized and is holding seven star systems against very heavy resistance and hers is the *holodah.*" (Personal regret.) Councilor Amunhershepeshef tapped one claw gently on the table to call attention to himself. (Concern.)

"Admiral Lankha has also lost a great many trained souls to the Race."

Torhok restrained himself with effort. Obviously *she* had been working on undermining his efforts for the People. It didn't matter. Most of the Council believed in the *Destoshaz* way. *We are now truly Star Wanderers, and Illudor's Glory will be our* sokhata.

"I am, of course, pleased with my admirals." Torhok said quietly. "But I find that Lankha has more—shall I say—momentum. (Admiration.) Narrok is more cautious." (Mild distain.)

Amunhershepeshef merely repeated his mild claw-tap. "Yes. Yes. (Approval.) But we are not yet able to spread ourselves so thin, so fast. I repeat, 'trained souls.' It takes time to train someone, even in the *Destoshaz*." (Approval 5, Distain 10, Uncertainty 4.) Ankaht also tapped gently to call attention to herself. "Your reports, Admiral, also mention that there are few planets habitable to us, or with abundance of refined materials. We know we can build fast, but can we build fast enough?" (Mild inquiry.)

"Yes, Senior, we can. There are many who are working in orbit— also solving some of the problems you are having on the planet. There are numbers of people clamoring to get back into space." (Derision.)

"Have you been down to the planet surface, yet, Admiral?" She was still as the statue she sat next to, nothing in body or *selnarm* to give offense.

"No, Senior. I have not time for pleasure jaunts." (Suppressed anger.)

She looked away politely. "Of course, Admiral." (—.)

Torhok and other councilors registered confusion, but let her blankness pass uncommented on.

It was a G-type star that humans called Raiden and the habitable planet—Polixenes—was very dry, showing a tan and blue eye against the dark. The terminus on the planet's face showed habitation more, as a jeweler's display case of lights on black velvet followed it around the world.

No one in the vice admiral's briefing room was looking at the display screen on the wall that matched the planetary image. They were focused on the hologram over the briefing table that flickered into a the familiar shape of the warp tree. Everything "upstream" from Raiden to Bellerophon and from Andromeda to Bellerophon was an angry shade of enemy red.

The briefing room aboard the *Gallipoli* was silent, their faces still, as Captain Watanabe Yoshi drew a breath to continue. "We only have seven supermonitors left in fighting shape and we're hoping that we can get repairs on *Temuchin* done before the next week, if we have that long."

"So what you're telling us is that we've lost twenty-two percent of our forces," Krishmahnta said quietly.

"Yessir." Watanabe sat down as she turned to Kiiraathra'ostakjo's image to her left.

As she turned he spoke, the hissing rumble of Orion translated in the transmission. "Vice Admiral, the fighters Zteeffwiit'gahrnak and I have taken on, when *Norfolk* and *Anne's Revenge* were destroyed have settled in well enough. Fighter pilots seem to be alike across species." The black humor still managed to come through the machine.

"In other words," she continued, "they're all crazy—no offense to your race, Least Claw—"

"None taken." He nodded, smoothing one side of his whiskers.

"I'm glad to hear that they're integrating well enough." They didn't have enough CVs to have human- and Tabby-only ships any longer. In the slow, prying, one-finger-at-a-time battles for each star system, if a fighter's carrier was destroyed, *any* fighter berth space was welcome. One couldn't afford to be too fussy, even if cross-species lighting gave you a headache, the temperatures were all wrong, and the food didn't have the right trace elements. It was better than trying to breathe vacuum or get left behind because the aliens wouldn't pick you up. Though it wasn't the first time multiple species had been forced to share ships. This, too aroused nightmarish echoes from the Bug War.

"Commander Mackintosh, your analysis on our current situation?" She leaned forward and sipped at her coffee cup, realizing even as she lifted it, that it was already down to the dregs, set it down with a click.

Samantha Mackintosh was silent for a moment, but then she seldom spoke up quickly—except in emergencies of course. "Not good, Admiral. We simply don't have enough firepower to defend the Arm. We're already spread thin as a meniscus and Admiral Yoshikuni is holding Andromeda by the skin of her teeth."

"Anyone want to comment on that?" Erica looked around the table and met their bleak looks and grimaces as they shook their heads slightly. It was all on her plate. Well.

She'd already thought about it and hoped that someone would give her the extra piece of information that would let her pull a rabbit out of the hat . . . though she couldn't imagine why she would want a rabbit in a hat to begin with.

"Ladies and gentlemen, we do have a problem and at this point only one solution I can see." She leaned forward and put her hands flat on the table. "We have to pull back and set our backs to a wall of some kind. If we fight each system back along the warp line we'll lose them and lose our people to no effect." The image of the warp tree glowed in front of her face glittering like an absurd firework. It was haunting her dreams.

"I would prefer to hold the Bellerophon–Hotspur line." She traced it up, her index finger glowing briefly as she drew it through each star image, skipping up the line—Andromeda, Charlotte, Demeter, Hera, Athena, on up to Hotspur.

"We couldn't hold anything south of Treadway," Commander Mackintosh said quietly. "We could be outflanked through Mangus–Zhi." She indicated with her pen.

Krishmahnta nodded back at her. "Yes, thank you, Sam. We have only a bad choice her, people. We're going to hold the westernmost arm if we can. We'll be falling back—for once, not under direct fire—to Suwa. I will be sending orders for Yoshikuni's task force to withdraw to Charlotte and hold there, to forestall a flank from BR-01 through Polo. If they cannot hold there she is to retreat further to Beaumont, where we will be guarding their backs."

She paused to let them take in what she was proposing, feeling the sourness in her gut. She'd be commanding Miharu to leave the population of Cetus, the habitable planet at Andromeda, to the invaders, as well as the two hundred million people here in Raiden System.

"We'd be abandoning three hundred million people." That was Lieutenant Wells, one of Samantha's aides. He'd gone white.

Krishmahnta nodded at him slowly. "In effect. But we cannot defend them. It would be suicide and that is not our duty." She took a deep breath. "We are going to regroup. We have to get over heavy space, people, consolidate our position and defend what we can.

Single warp point access is what we can defend given the weight of metal the aliens have so far shown us they have."

All around the table people looked sick but were nodding as they took in the possibilities and Commander La Mar had shredded most of the flimsy pad absently between his fingers.

"Samantha." The analyst looked up from the tabletop. "You and your staff are going to be the busiest people onboard. Because I need the largest evacuation plan ever attempted."

Mackintosh brightened and looked daunted, both at once, and Lieutenant Wells had positively blanched, if he could go any paler. "All those merchants that came from Bellerophon is where I'll start, then," she said. "All that haven't tucked themselves into mouse holes, or just run down the lines."

"Ms. Dafey. I want you to start finding, and moving every kind of industry we have. I'm aware that the bulk of this arm is agrarian, but someone has to build and repair the heavy machinery. I want it all moved down to Tilghman. If the relief force hasn't arrived yet, it will be months before it does."

If the silence had been profound before, it was deadly now. Kiiraathra'ostakjo's booming growl startled everyone. "This is stuff for the so-called 'long haul,' Ahhdmiraaaal."

She turned slightly toward him. "Yes, Least Claw." A slight feedback trick had her words, translated, echoing back through the link. "We are cut off and we will hold this space." The sound from every throat around the table in response to her declaration was atavistic; not a cornered sound but one ready to carry the fight to the enemy. A sound that the Orions could appreciate. They had been beaten back and had lost friends and lovers while being forced to retreat. That had to stop.

Erica symbolically drew a finger across the table in front of her, for all the world like she was drawing a line in sand. "This far. No further."

CHAPTER SIXTEEN

As Useful as Tits on a Bull

The observation hall was in orbit, twenty thousand kilometers from Novaya Rodina, giving a wonderful view of the planet below. A white and turquoise marble shining against the black, surrounded by a glittering cloud as ships and satellites moved in and out of its shadow. The hall itself gave the impression of a flattened sphere with an observation band from floor to ceiling all the way around. It wasn't any kind of window but rather a holo screen that gave the illusion of an immense wall of glass.

The shipyards were much closer than the planet but not visible behind the opaque screens around the back three-quarters of the room. The swivel chairs were empty, tilted to the right or left, bereft of human direction, except for one where Li Han sat quietly in her dress uniform, with all the braid and medals, so the delegation from the PSUN would understand which of her roles was more important as far as she was concerned, soldier or diplomat. Her heels were together, one hand loose in her lap while the other rested on the table to her right. Though she faced the magnificent view, her eyes were closed and her breathing slow and measured as she waited in a light Zen state. Magda Windrider set a bone-china mug next to her hand on the table and a hint of steam pooled just above it before drifting lazily upward in the lighter gravity of the hall.

"You have about ten minutes before the delegation shows up," Magda said as she sat down comfortably next to her. Another, deeper breath brought her eyes open, full of calm as she looked out over what would be their opening display. She picked up the cup and nodded her thanks. "And you are planning something," Windrider said.

"Would I do such a thing?" Li Han said blandly and was answered with a snort.

"In a heartbeat."

The door chimed and slid open to reveal a tall, elegant woman whose face was a blend of Northern European and Indian from Old Terra, a pale Brahmin's face. Some would have called it severe and harsh, but it was the kind of face on which age rested well and transformed mere severity into an immense dignity. Her dark hair was threaded through with gray and fell in smooth wings from a center part.

Admiral Sonja Desai, TFN/PSUN, retired, smiled briefly, and nodded at the seated women. "Hello, Ms. Windrider, First Space Lord."

Li Han rose to face Desai, her mind flickering back to a much younger image of this woman on a ship screen, her vac suit spattered with blood. For a moment it was as though eighty years had vanished.

"I've enjoyed our letters, Admiral," she said quietly. In the peace that they had initiated at Zapata, they had been able to correspond over the years. Each would have been surprised that what they thought of each other was so similar, if someone had mentioned it: *Impressive woman. Stubborn, too.*

"Sonja, please. We've gotten to know each other well enough, don't you think?"

For a moment, Li hesitated as though wondering if it would be quite proper to be so informal. Windrider could almost see the mental shrug as she conceded that it would be. "Sonja, please call me Han."

"I thought I'd come a bit early and have a chat before the rest of the mob shows up," Dr. Desai continued. Li shook her hand and they all sat down again.

"Mob?" Windrider asked. "Do you feel as though younger people sometimes have more energy than is easy to bear? I know I do and then get concerned that I'm acting the old biddy."

Desai smiled slightly. "I do find that most younger people have far too much energy for inconsequential things. They 'vibrate' even when they sit still." The staff began filtering in carrying briefcases, setting out water, and clattering around the coffee station with what seemed to be a lot more noise than necessary, breaking up the natural hush of the hall. The three women exchanged looks at this unintentional proof of her statement.

"Ah," Magda said. "Yes. It's been nice to meet you in person, Dr. Desai."

"You're welcome. I've quite enjoyed the whole experience, myself, even though Daniel would prefer to keep everything as formal as possible. Since it will annoy him, please call me Sonja."

"Then you'll have to be familiar and call me Magda."

"Of course." Desai leaned back slightly and smiled. "Well, I hope that your asking to have me along with this delegation hasn't disarranged anything for either of you. I'm curious as to why you requested me particularly." She regarded Li Han with a look of pleasant inquiry on her face, but a hint of command steel in her voice. "I am hardly indispensable in this delegation. I've been letting the younger ones do all the tours. I'm a theorist, not a technician."

Li was impervious to the voice. "I have my reasons, Sonja. But I do promise you'll find out today, on that you have my word."

"I will be very content with that—as before. A few more minutes won't make me explode." She looked around at her staff and that of the rest of delegation's support. "The rest of the youngsters—" She waved her hand to encompass anyone under a hundred. "—are inclined to look sideways at me, thinking I'm going to start spouting physics like some theoretical oracle."

The three women were very aware of the reactions of the so-called youngsters, even the fancy executive secretaries who supposedly thought themselves above things like hero worship. Even now as Li Han's staff finished prepping the room and the support staff for the delegation started arriving, there were furtive and speculative glances at them.

Li laughed and shook her head. "No, but your lofty status holding down a physics chair does make some people light-headed."

Windrider threw up her hands. "A physics chair she says; the Einstein Chair at the University of Athena no less. The woman even has to downplay her peers' accomplishments as well as her own." Li loftily ignored this aside, as hard as that was for someone as short as she was, and rose again as the rest of the PSUN delegation, headed up by Daniel Bortollotti entered.

He came up to shake all their hands as his delegates got themselves sorted out. "First Space Lord Li, Director Windrider. Dr. Desai, you're here early." His tailor was good, but no tailor in the galaxy could ever make him look tidy. He looked as though his suit should have a pocket protector in it rather than a decorative pocket square. Everything about him was just slightly rumpled and askew.

One corner of Desai's mouth twitched narrow lips into something like a half smile. "Daniel, you know that I am a law unto myself." She nodded at Li Han's china cup being whisked away. "And surely you don't read anything into having a cup of tea with friends."

His look was ironic for he saw deep meanings in everything, trying to be the politician he thought he should be instead of an engineer with grafted-on people skills. Of course he was young to be heading up the technical delegation—only fifty-eight. "Ladies." He nodded and offered his arm to Dr. Desai. "Don't let us hold up your presentation, First Space Lord, Director." Sonja tapped his arm lightly but didn't take it.

"I'm not so decrepit that I need support, Mr. Bortollotti." He colored but changed his gesture to a sweeping one, letting her proceed. As they settled into their chairs, Li turned and brought up the holographic screen for her notes, not saying what they were thinking. *Who does he think he's politicking, here?* Windrider took her seat and leaned back. She knew that Li Han was up to something but hadn't confided in her. But she knew her friend well enough to enjoy whatever was coming down.

"Ladies and gentlemen," the First Space Lord said quietly and waited the half beat until everyone settled. "We've introduced you to our new ship type, the devastator." At the touch of her finger the last of the opaque screening faded and revealed *Taconic*, all two million tonnes of her. She'd been brought up to close magnification, so it looked as though she were in orbit right outside the hall. Sparkling beyond her were visible a hundred miniatures of her, toys that shone silver against the dark velvet of space. Everyone turned toward the ship, almost unconsciously drawn to her graceful lines.

With no perspective to give an indication of her size she was light and elegant, giving the impression of splendid motion, even at rest. "You've seen the specs, you've watched her performance, now I understand that you have some reservations, especially about how many of these ships we are intending to build."

Dr. Emil Roberts, an R&D engineer from Galloway, was the first to speak up. He stood. "First Space Lord Li, Director Windrider, you have an enormously powerful ship here." He paused to let his eye linger on that beautiful piece of engineering, before coming to his first concern. "She's so big that she cannot maneuver very quickly."

"Like trying to park a swimming pool," someone muttered. Dr. Roberts shot a quelling look at the miscreant before accepting the description.

"Let us just say, slow to turn. But I find it astonishing that you would commit this amount of effort to a ship that has so little use in the normal warp network."

One of his staff chimed in with "It could be that twenty percent of all warp points couldn't allow passage to this vessel."

"Ah," one of the others commented—Nora Ishisu, that was her name—in weapons design. "But how big a punch she can throw."

"But if you can't get the punch to where you need it, or someone gets into your blind spot it isn't worth spit—"

Bortollotti cut them off. "I'm sure you all would love to continue arguing the pros and cons of this ship's size, but I would like to ask the First Space Lord why the Republic intends to build so many of this class? Given the drawbacks?"

Over the decades Li Han had finally made her most inscrutable face, the china doll, the mask she'd wanted it to be. To everyone but her close friends, though. Windrider raised her chin as if to get a better view. *Here it comes. She's got too much of an air of canary-fed cat about her.*

Li Han tilted her head to one side and smiled. "I'm glad that your coterie does not include Orions or Ophiuchi, or I'd be hearing variations on 'How many fighters would that hull hold?'" She got the laugh she wanted and before it died down turned to Desai.

"In answer to your question . . . if I could ask Dr. Desai to brief the staff by explaining the Kasugawa Effect?"

Sonja sat silent, completely stunned by the request. *How in hell did their ONI find out about it?* The others around the room gazed at her expectantly, or curiously since no one in this room but her had known about it. At least that was what she'd thought a half second ago. A rather large mistake. "Ah." She closed her lips, opened them again. "Well. I wouldn't want to get too technical—" She looked over at Li Han, sitting, watching. *I could smack you silly for springing this on me, woman!* "It's . . ." She threw up her hands. *If I were old and decrepit enough to even consider a cane, I'd hit you with it.*

"Dr. Desai, perhaps I can help you," Li Han said. "Since I don't have the technical expertise, I should be able to put it in layman's terms." She had her chair tipped back with her fingers laced together over her middle. Desai just looked at her, still gathering her thoughts. Everyone's eyes were on the two of them, aware that something momentous was happening but not sure exactly what. Sonja Desai's lips thinned, as Li Han went on.

"The Kasugawa generator is an offshoot technology of the Desai Prime, actually, which is one reason I specifically asked her to be here." Sonja's eye narrowed as she listened. "It creates a massive gravitational disturbance in the space-time continuum . . . in effect a very short-lived black hole. One of my analysts has a sense of humor and tells me that if one could find an enemy stupid enough to come close to the generator it would make a dandy weapon, but since gravity is inversely proportional to the square of the distance, I don't think we're going to try anything that suicidal." She startled a laugh out of the engineers and even Sonja smiled. "That's as technical as I care to get at the moment, but one real effect as I understand it, is to 'dredge' existing warp points and make them large enough for our new 'baby' out there."

Another long moment of silence before a confusion of babble broke out. "—unprecedented—" "—but the power consumpt—" "—ink of the poten—"

Li Han let it go on for a moment before she placed one finger precisely on the attention button on the arm of her chair and held it there. The insistent peal finally silenced them all. "And," she continued, "if one pairs two generators, a warp line is created between them."

Bortollotti quietly signed himself. "Santa Maria," he said quietly. "Dios."

Li Han nodded. "Of course it means that one has to actually, physically get a Kasugawa generator on either end of where one wants a warp line, but I think we can live with that," she said.

Desai sat rigid, heels together, hands clamped in her lap, her entire body snapped shut as Li Han finished. "There are other effects, I'm sure, but that is the layman's gist of it." She made a small "over to you" gesture to Desai who was still glaring at her.

"Sonja," Li said gently, a faint twinkle in her eyes. "You remember the last time you and I creatively interpreted our orders." There was an almost subliminal sigh in the room as people remembered. Eighty years ago, at the Battle of Zapata, these two women had changed history.

Sonja Desai, the highest ranking unwounded commander of the Terran Federation and Li Han of the Terran Republic, had been locked in a bloody, Pyrrhic battle. Li on one side had just lost her third flagship and her friend Admiral Tsing Chang, while on the other Sonja Desai had just whipped a piece of cable around Joaquin Sandoval's severed leg, to save his life.

Desai had signaled Li to parley and in the furious, bloody, ruinous, godawful mess they had made the first moves to peace.

I had Ian Trevayne, dead or dying in sickbay. The only person who'd ever managed to defeat and capture Li, Desai thought, remembering. She hadn't been able to make herself contact the resurrected Ian even though he'd contacted her. He'd meant so much to her that she didn't think she could bear dealing with being the "old lady."

In that war we couldn't win. Nobody could, she thought. And now they were doing it again, only this time they were on the same side. *I don't even want to think of how she reacted when the man who handed her her worst humiliation came back from the dead.*

Desai maintained her silence a moment longer before she relaxed and shook her head, not in denial but with ironic respect. "I suppose I should know by now that secrets aren't." She took a deep breath. "Yes, Han, you are essentially correct. We will be able to move that enormous ship through any warp point we need to." She actually smiled at Li then. "That's why you're building so many."

Li was upright now and nodded at her old enemy and friend. "We're going to need every one. But now we'll have them."

CHAPTER SEVENTEEN

"My God, there are more of them!"

The Zarzuela System had an unusual amount of cometary material in its Oort cloud and Thirty-Fifth Great Claw Howaarmaiis'jothar'kriana loved having his drills out there, especially now that there were new aliens attacking the Rim Federation. He was young for his rank, with two honor names to live up to, and while he was levelheaded for his species—he wouldn't have gotten so far if he were not—he prowled his dreams hunting honor. He told himself it was good that this minor arm of the Pan-Sentient Union was alerted to the possibility of another alien incursion, but some part of him yearned for a fight. Zarzuela was on the list, but the system was only on a low amber alert.

"A minor target," Howaarmaiis growled to himself, his thick cream-colored pelt faintly marked with slightly darker cream and gray spots, like the cloudy coat of a snow leopard. He stroked his impressive mustaches. "And I'm supposed to be glad that a handful of other stars are more likely to be attacked."

He leaned forward flexing his claws as he watched Commander Simmons's red squadron in the holo tank. If Least Claw Thraaiewlahk'gahrnak didn't watch his tail he was going to stalk straight into Simmons' reverse ambush. The command view gave him the overview of the scenario unfolding—Thraaiewlahk had taken the part of an enemy, a straightforward smash and grab, with the human scanning to find the potential ambushers.

The least claw had sprung the trap neatly, but Simmons had seen it coming and his ships leapt to full speed an instant before Thraaiewlahk fired, fleeing, some scattering to draw fire, some bunching to support each other. The dust and space junk was thick in the exercise area and Simmons was taking full advantage of that.

Thraaiewlahk had lost track of Red Squadron when pursuing Simmons into the heavy dust and Howaarmaiis could see that Blue and Green Squadrons were laying down a confusing, shuffling pattern to hide that fact. Actually, it looked like Simmons's fighters were not only mimicking inert rocks; one or two gave off signals imitating the random tumble of icy planetoids. *If this works, I will certainly ask which genius came up with this idea so fast. Typical human sneakiness, but ambush and pounce are now seen as part of a warrior's way.*

Simmons was ruthlessly taking advantage of the least claw's tendency to see only what he thought could be there, and the human's strategy profited from the amount of debris in the drill area. *One minute twenty-two seconds and Commander Simmons will... what was the human expression? Ah, yes, clean his clock. The least claw will certainly snarl at me later.* Howaarmaiis bared his teeth. It wasn't easy keeping the coordinated defenses working smoothly and it was time for Thraaiewlahk to bow to the claw again. Simmons was the being to do it, too.

Thraaiewlahk's squadrons, Gold, White, and Brown, swept straight up Simmons's wake, not even peeling off flankers, believing that he needn't. Thirty seconds before he'd be the one englobed. Twenty seconds. There.

Red Squadron announced its presence with a salvo that ripped up Thraaiewlahk's fighters from behind as Blue and Green swept up and back into the teeth of their pursuers. Fifteen seconds later 82 percent of Thraaiewlhk's group were "killed," the howls from the fighter jocks—of victory or frustration—were similar whether they were human or Orion. White Squadron did manage to take 20 percent of Simmons's with them, which was to their honor.

He tapped one claw on the screen and twitched an ear at the slightly annoying click the translator had developed as it kicked in and hoped the engineers would see to it soon. "Debriefing in one hour, here on the *Heavyside,* my claws. Flag, out."

"Acknowledged. Yes, Great Claw." Even the flattening effect of translation couldn't disguise the satisfaction in Simmons's voice and the swallowed snarl from Thraaiewlahk.

The briefing room aboard the supermonitor *Heavyside Layer,* a carrier/main combatant, was the compromise the Orion engineers had come up with, too bright and harsh for one species, somewhat dim and fuzzy for the other. The whole ship was an experiment in many ways, with accommodations for both races, and so far it had worked well enough, with translator networks seeded through the wall coatings and woven into clothing, so everything worked as though the two races actually had a common language. And as for the brightness an ancient form of amber-colored eye protection had become the norm for humans; some wag had dredged up an ancient name for them—"aviator shades."

"Great Claw," Commander Simmons spoke up almost the moment Howaarmaiis entered the room. Unfortunately to Orion eyes, his hair was thin and beard almost nonexistent, his narrow face tight with a concern that was surprising. Howaarrmaiis would have thought he read human faces a bit better than that.

"Yes, Commander Simmons." He settled down into his chair. "Something's wrong?" He wondered if Thraaiewlahk had taken his failure harder than he should have and his ears began to flatten, even though the least claw looked confused.

"Nothing to do with the exercise, Great Claw."

"Go on."

Simmons tapped a finger on the table to bring up a small file, grainy, heavily filtered, obviously downloaded from the small sensory suite onboard a fighter. "Mai Shi Hui was one of my ambush and while she was powered down, her passive sensors picked this up. She didn't just put it down to a glitch and reported it. We got a similar reading . . ." He called up another image, even fuzzier. "This was from Shu Han's red box and even though no one else recorded it, it's not a glitch."

The images glittering above the table were mere pinpoints of light magnified. Commander Simmons looked grim. "I believe—and the computer concurs—that those match the parameters for alien drive flares." Through the rising growl from Thraaiewlahk he concluded. "The computer analysis estimates—if these are the same aliens holding Bellerophon—that we have about eighty days before they get here."

The command pod in the generation ship *Ptahtoranknefer,* Second Diaspora, was dead quiet in the wake of Senior Admiral Amunsit's order, the officers taking on ritual immobility so as not to draw attention. "Illudor's Claws and Tentacles!" (Rage.) "Do I need to repeat every order I give? Do not, and I repeat, do not unfreeze the Sleepers!" (Disgust tempered with determination.)

She tucked herself back into her command niche and glowered at the image of the unfortunate senior physician, down in the ship's revivication space. "Rest assured, senior physician, I am not in need of the attentions of a *narmata* healer. In my opinion, this discovery of creatures mimicking intelligence is a matter for *Destoshaz* not *shaxzhu*. In this emergency situation I must retain control to bring about safety for the Race. I will bring the honored Sleepers back to a peaceful colony world." (Willingness to fight.) The end of that sentence—"or not at all"—she left unsaid. The Sleepers represented a world that no longer existed except as part of an expanding star, and as such just kept getting in the way of people who actually knew what they were doing.

"Understood, Senior Admiral." The senior physician was very precise in his response, recognizing that anything less would trigger a challenge to *maatkah* duel. "Revivification, out."

Amunsit gazed around at her officer who still had not moved. "The *holodah'kri* and his can worry about what this all means in the greater scheme of things. Our jobs are to ensure the continuation of the race and we *must* act as though none of the other Fleets survived." She laced her tentacles together, obviously reducing threat, even though she had no intention of engaging in challenge of any kind. (Willingness to duel.) She didn't need to add overt physical gestures to make her point. "Pass my orders along, Uatchet." (Impatience.)

Her second snapped out of his stiff posture. "Yes, Senior Admiral. Comm, pass the word to the rest of the Fleet. Senior Admiral's orders under the present state of emergency. Do not revive the Sleepers."

❖   ❖   ❖

The noise in the fighter pilots' ready room was astonishing. Even with sound-dampening baffles, scarred up by countless attempts at surreptitious graffiti by pilots even in the short time since *Heavyside* had been commissioned, Simmons wished for a moment he could flatten his ears. Over the past few weeks people had been working under need-to-know. But everyone who had two brain cells to rub together figured that things were going to go about as badly as at Bellerophon, and morale was a wild mix of "wanting to go out and shoot things" and numbness. Both of which brought out the worst in fighter jocks, both human and Orion.

"Listen up, people!" His voice snapped out and brought the room to attention that was at least quiet. He looked over the mix, not caring any longer whether the pupils that looked back at him were human round or Orion slitted, in a naked or furred face. They were his people and he hated to lose even one. Other officers would be doing this same briefing, he knew, dealing with the jocks with less spit and polish because they just wouldn't buy that kind of bullshit.

The task force that Great Claw Howaarmaiis—and his brain kept wanting to translate the Orion name into "Howard"—had scraped together from every system who could reach the Zarzuela Arm in time, waited for the aliens to close. With the original picket they now had two dozen supermonitors and forty-two superdreadnoughts, ten assault carriers, fifteen fleet carriers along with eight archaic monitors and sixty-one battlecruisers.

"This is the word from on high. Apparently the reinforcements that were sent to Dogpatch, Pogo, and Amadeus are just too far away to reach us in time. What we had, we have, amen."

"All hail the analysts." That mutter was from Naguya, a jock whose attitude had gotten him busted more times than he cared to recall. It was not meant to be heard, so Simmons ignored it.

"This alien fleet has twenty Behemoths rather than the twenty-six they had at Bellerophon, but they're bigger. They are also moving faster. Which is why I'm here wagging my jaw at you sixty days after we first spotted them rather than the eighty we initially estimated. You fighters aren't going to be let out of your cages until the aliens release their parasites—"

"That's because we're vermicides, Commander."

"—because," he continued resolutely, "we all know you can do the impossible but would like you not to try."

"It would just take us too frikkin' long." There was a low buzz of derision and a bilabial fricative.

"Stuff a sock in it, Naguya," Simmons said, not looking up from his briefing notes.

"Sir, yessir."

"Commander, have we gotten any responses back from our hails?"

"Negative, Guitano." She was a squirrelly little woman from Brazilica in the Parone System, very quiet for a jock. "We've been trying to get a response almost from the beginning."

"Damn, and I was hoping we'd all have a beer together."

"Not a chance." Simmons looked around at them all, flight suits and helmets perfect, with attitudes that any psych would insist needed adjustment, showing their evolutionary roots. Humans deriding what they were about to fight, hurling verbal sticks and rocks like a troupe of baboons. Orions growling an almost steady tigerish rumble and it wasn't a purr. "Get ready for things to get hot."

"Behemoth steaks coming up, Commander." That was Jiilhaarahk'edohan showing all his fangs.

"Just bring the heavy fighters back, okay? Maintenance gets shirty if you scratch the paint."

The laughter was a relief and brought on a barrage of obscene suggestions as to what Maintenance could do.

Curled into her command niche Amunsit waved one of her claws at the screen as the Fleet neared the system. "There, Uatchet! Look at that. They're preparing to attack us! See this? That's an attack formation or I'm a flixit dropping." (Disgust.) She was as angry as if she'd already been attacked.

"Sir." Uatchet kept his *selnarm* very subdued. Many thought it was because the senior admiral was so volatile.

"The researchers say there are two planets that could be livable, or made livable in this system. Two! And these . . . these babbling vermin are swarming on both of them! Illudor bless, what was He thinking?" (Nausea. Outrage.)

"Sir. Perhaps these creatures truly are intelligent? It looks to me like a defensive formation. Perhaps their incessant signaling has been an attempt to—" (Reason. Calm.)

She was staring at him as if he'd gone crazy. "Stop right there, Fleet Second. (Determination.) You are starting to sound like one of the needlessly cautious, terrified *shaxzhu*. Should I put you into freeze with them and promote Binthanath?" (Defensive anger.)

"No, Sir. I was pointing out an option." (Logic.) She stared at him a moment longer before dropping it. She turned back to the screen and the cluster of threats to the Race on it.

"Battle stations. We will win this system."

"Sir!"

Howaarmaiis turned his command chair toward the comm. "Any response, Yiraanthu'astahal?" He asked quietly, watching the screen with its interlocking snowflake pattern of enemy ships. Not only was it a crystal pattern but a hollow crystal, with the smallest oncoming ships around the edges. It was an unorthodox formation but certainly allowed the Behemoths, which could not turn, maximum flank support.

Someone had thought this out a long time ago for these ships, moving at such a fraction of light speed, would either have had to start in that formation or taken years to move into position.

These ships were different from the ones at Bellerophon. Rather than cylindrical, they had a pinched waist about two-thirds of the way down their length, but they were similar enough from the images he'd studied. They were the same aliens.

Commander Simmons was onboard the *Spyridon* coordinating battlecruisers and fighter squadrons, while his Orion counterpart on the SMT *Lareina* took the left/above flank. *Between us,* Howaarmiis thought, *we'll savage them.*

"No, Sir."

"Fire on my signal."

"Aye, Sir."

"Aliens launching SDs! Multiple launches!" Lieutenant Stills, tense over his sensor boards, sang out.

"Fire missiles!" Howaarmiis snapped. "Simmons!"

"Aye, sir, launching!"

The only thing he could do was to use his waves of fighters against the alien parasite ships while his heavies targeted the Behemoths before they could launch more. His HBMs roared out, targeting the obvious drive ends on the generation ships, the heaviest missiles he could throw, even if they had no sprint mode.

"Hits! Sir, multiple hits!" The screen sparkled for a moment as it recorded the multiple hits but it was like smacking boulders with a sledgehammer. He had to keep pounding them and as the aliens fired back the damage codes for his ships began pouring in.

The damage reports were pouring in. Amunsit looked at her second in command. (Bitter satisfaction.) She opened her mouth to speak, just as the screens blanked, completely overloaded, the shockwave from the explosion of *Amunsehkanhk* and *Ma'atptah* enough to even rock the vast bulk of the flagship. The *selnarm* shock was more devastating, but they were *Destoshaz* and fought through it. The sudden death of almost a million civilians was enough to slow everyone but also ignited a rage that hadn't been felt in hundreds of years. Latent, quiescent, and without the mitigation of *shaxzhu* and their memories, the group rage locked them into a fighting unit that included every *Destoshaz*. Showing more physical emotion that any Arduan had for centuries, they recklessly flung themselves on their enemies. (Blinding rage. Survive, survive, survive. Consensus.)

Howaarmaiis ignored the Omega codes lined up like grinning fangs along the edge of his screen. The acrid stench of burnt insulation in his nose was a vileness the scrubbers couldn't quite clear well enough for the Orion sense of smell. His lips pulled back in a soundless snarl.

He couldn't hold. He'd lost 20 percent of his force already and the aliens had lost—another polarizing glare from the screen—they'd lost three of the big ships and half a hundred parasites.

"All ships, all ships," he snarled into the channel. "Pull back to missile range. I repeat. Pull back. Fire plan Alpha, or I will bite your heads off!" The monitors *John Ericsson* and *Bruno Togliatti* were going in like fighters, raking two Behemoths with capital beams— "*Zeerloweer dirguasha!*" The obscenity ripping out of his mouth as they both vanished in a blinding boil of light and two more Omega codes flashed onto his screen. "Withdraw." The word bitter in his mouth as he spoke it. "Withdraw. All ships, withdraw."

Even though he hadn't liked it—despised it, even—he'd planned for a route of retreat. He was leaving two planets, even sparsely settled, it was still close to three quarters of a million beings in the hands of the enemy. His claws dug into the arms of the command chair as his battered, bleeding force limped away from the equally savaged Behemoths.

"Withdraw through to Santa Evita." Even the most stalwart warrior had learned the human idea of *theernowlus*: *Live to fight another day.*

CHAPTER EIGHTEEN

"She's come back to haunt me."

The day was blustery enough to raise whitecaps on the ocean out beyond the Alph estuary, but Waterside was shielded from the wind, and the wan light of Zephrain A was reasonably warm. At any rate, Ian Trevayne hardly noticed the weather as he sat sprawled in one of the wrought-iron chairs on his terrace, eyes closed, absorbing sunlight and Scotch.

"You look exhausted," commented Miriam Ortega from the other chair. "Don't burn yourself out with overwork."

"Thank you, Mother," Trevayne sighed without opening his eyes.

Miriam gave an unseen smile. The jape held a larger grain of truth than its speaker knew.

It had taken time, but Trevayne had come to an emotional acceptance of what his forebrain had told him from the first about their relationship. The woman in her thirties he had known was dead. They could no longer be lovers. But there could be no escaping—even if they had wanted to escape—the knowledge that they *had* been lovers. Their love would always be there, imperishable and incorruptible, but now it was of a different quality. And she herself had been startled by the realization that it held, on her side, an undeniable element of *motherliness*. But why, she had asked herself, should it be so startling? After all, he was younger—both biologically and in terms of total conscious life experience—than either of her sons.

Motherly, hell! she thought. *It ought to be* grand*motherly.* But then her eyes rested on the reclining body, a younger version of the one she had known so well. *All right, maybe not grandmotherly. That's a little much. In fact, maybe not even entirely.... Oh, stop that, you dirty-minded old biddy!*

She took a sip of her own Scotch. "You know, you got me hooked on this stuff. I used to be considered a cheap date in my youth. But for the last eighty years I've had to pay through the nose for the genuine article, imported all the way from some island on Old Terra."

"And quite rightly, too!" Trevayne opened his eyes, sat up, and took a patriotic pull on his drink.

"I should have billed the trust, all those years," she said accusingly.

"Then I would never have been able to afford this place," Trevayne retorted.

They grinned at each other. She had had the advantage of years in which to prepare herself for the situation into which he had been abruptly thrust. But they'd both had some adjustments to make. Now they had, in their own ways, both come to terms with the realities of their relationship. The earlier perplexities were gone, leaving a deep and uncomplicated comfort in each other's company.

"At any rate," Trevayne continued, "you've had your revenge with the 'refresher courses' I'm having to undergo. You're bloody right about me being exhausted!"

"I know there's a lot to cover."

"And not enough time to cover it in. I'm being hurried through all the technology that's new to me without being given a chance to assimilate the theory underlying it."

"But you're at least getting a grasp of the capabilities, aren't you?"

"Oh, yes. I know what things will do, even if I don't always understand how they do it. And I suppose that's all I really need to know. I'm not expected to be a technician. The applications—the tactical possibilities—are going to be my business. And I've begun to have a few ideas...." Trevayne's eyes lost their focus as his mind started to slip into a realm of vast spaces and vaster energies, of whirling abstractions representing gigatons of metal and thousands of lives, knitted together into coherency by threads of technical parameters.

"Well, that's good," said Miriam, hastily hauling him back. "Because things are happening. In fact, that's what I'm here to tell you about. The Terran Republic Navy task force for the counteroffensive is en route now. And it's going to pay a call here at Zephrain in two weeks." She paused and watched Trevayne's expression. It was as ambivalent as she had expected. Ever since the failure of Cyrus Waldeck's attempt on Bellerophon, he had been insistent that the Republic's aid must be accepted unreservedly. And yet . . .

"Well," he finally said, a little too briskly, "this should be quite an occasion. The first major reinforcement from the reb— from the TRN."

"And its first-ever *peaceful* appearance in this system," she added for him with a smile. "All you remember are the not-so-peaceful ones."

"Yes. And unlike everyone else in the Rim Federation, I remember them as recent events." Trevayne fell into a silence that Miriam hesitated to break. His eyes held a brooding expression that was incongruous on such a youthful face.

You became a legend by smashing those two invasions, Ian, she thought. *And the first one included a certain Lieutenant Commander Colin Trevayne, who had joined the Fringe rebellion. The son who alone remained of a family that had otherwise been vaporized when the rebels nuked the civilian housing at Jamieson Archipelago on Galloway's World.*

And you knew his ship was there, among those whose obliteration you were orchestrating.

"Anyway, Ian," she said at last, "you're right about it being a major occasion. There's going to be a big-deal reception for the senior TRN officers at Government House."

"Which I will of course be expected to attend," he said quietly.

"Of course," she echoed, just as quietly.

Only a brief silence passed before he tossed off the last of his Scotch and smiled at her. "Well, I've been wanting to talk to someone about this new 'devastator' of theirs."

At six supermonitors, eleven superdreadnoughts, three assault carriers, eighteen battlecruisers, and assorted lesser ships, the TRN contingent was a little on the light side to be called a task force. "Task group" was a title it might have worn more comfortably. But there was general agreement that no useful public-relations purpose would be served by minimizing the Terran Republic's contribution to the Rim's war effort.

The newcomers slid peacefully into the system their grandparents had tried and failed to fight their way into, and took up orbit around Xanadu. A major ceremony of greeting in space had been rejected in favor of moving such displays to the surface, where all the amity would be on full display for the populace. So the TRN brass were transported down to Prescott . . . in RFN shuttles.

Since becoming the seat of government for an interstellar nation (however stubbornly the Rim Federation resisted calling itself that) rather than for a single system, Government House had necessarily undergone expansions and renovations. Most notably, a reception room and dining hall now extended back into what had been formal gardens. Here the Rim's new allies would be wined and dined.

Trevayne arrived as late as possible, or perhaps just a tad later than that. The reception room was already crowded with formally dressed VIPs and suffused with a low hum of conversation. It was as impressive as he had been led to believe: an enormous square chamber with a predominantly gold color scheme enhanced by the melting light of great chandeliers. The walls were lined with furniture of antique elegance, alternating with marble-topped side tables. A wide, shallow flight of steps descended to the equally vast dining hall, through whose thirty-foot windows the remains of the formal gardens could be glimpsed in the twilight.

But what caught Trevayne's attention was the flag of the Terran Republic, draped on a wall in honor of the guests. It was something he'd never thought to see on Xanadu.

Ah, well. Times change, he philosophized. He studied the ebon banner with its gold starburst, and the bloodred creature—a manifest zoological impossibility—that coiled around the star. Trevayne had always wondered about that last.

"There you are!" Miriam Ortega emerged from the throng. "Come on over here. I want you to meet the Republic commander. And she's eager to meet you!" Was he imagining things, Trevayne wondered, or was there a twinkle of mischief in her eyes?

He allowed himself to be led across the floor, pausing repeatedly to acknowledge greetings and to snag a glass of champagne from a waiter. Ahead was a cluster of TRN full dress uniforms—a rather elegant confection of deep-blue and white, edged with gold, in a traditional military style. A figure emerged from the group.

Trevayne's lower jaw didn't quite hit the golden-brown–carpeted marble floor.

Good God! he thought, amid his roaring mental chaos. *She's come back to haunt me!*

But no, of course it wasn't Li Han. Li Han must be in her 120s and a fleet admiral. This woman with rear admiral's insignia appeared no older than Trevayne himself did—not that that necessarily meant anything in this day of antigerone treatments. And she was taller than Li Han. (Actually, almost everybody was taller than Li Han.) And her features held a hint of the aquiline look traditionally associated with Japanese noble families, while Li Han's were uncompromisingly Chinese.

For all that, the resemblance was eerie. Perhaps, he thought, it was the eyes. As a rule, eyes described as "black" are actually dark brown. But Li Han's were literally black. And so were the eyes that now met his with frank curiosity. They were exactly like the eyes he had once stared into in a comm screen, hoping that their owner would give him an excuse to kill her.

"Admiral Trevayne," he heard Miriam Ortega say, "allow me to present Rear Admiral Li Magda of the Terran Republic Navy." Her voice was formal, but there was no longer any doubt about the nature of that twinkle.

She'll pay, Trevayne thought darkly. He inhaled his champagne and glanced around rather desperately for a waiter. Seeing none, he extended his hand. "Li Magda?" he managed, with a stress on the surname.

"Yes, Admiral," she said, taking his hand. "But my friends call me Mags—though not in my mother's hearing!"

Any illusions based on physical resemblance shattered as though they had been dropped on the floor. Trevayne's imagination failed at the thought of Li Han saying something like that. But ... "Your mother?" he queried.

"Yes." She nodded. "My mother is First Space Lord Li Han. And may I say, Admiral, that I've heard a lot about you all my life."

"I can just imagine," said Miriam Ortega sweetly. "Actually, Admiral Li, I once met your mother."

Li Magda showed her surprise. "When was that, Madame Chief Justice?" She had, Trevayne decided, been very well briefed.

"'Miriam,' please. It was after the Second Battle of Zephrain."

"Yes," Trevayne piped up. "Your mother was here on Xanadu at the time, as . . ." He trailed to an embarrassed halt.

"As your prisoner," Li Magda finished for him helpfully.

"I was laboring under the title 'Provisional Grand Councilor for Internal Security of the Rim Systems,'" Miriam explained, rescuing Trevayne. "I was touring the POW camp, and I interviewed her in her capacity as senior prisoner. She seemed to appreciate my interest in conditions there. We got along very well, I thought, although she was extremely—" Miriam sought for the right word. "—earnest."

"That's the general consensus," Li Magda acknowledged sadly. "Mother can never understand why nobody thinks she has a sense of humor. *She* thinks she's a stitch."

Trevayne wisely refrained from remarking on the commonness of this delusion.

"I think she was also a little embarrassed," Miriam continued. "She correctly inferred from my surname that I was the daughter of Admiral Sergei Ortega, who had died in First Zephrain."

"Oh." Li Magda was silent a moment. "I suppose a lot of people had deaths to get over in those days. My generation will never really know what it was like. But now . . . well, just the fact that I'm here, in this system—"

"Yes," Miriam agreed. "We've very grateful to have you here now."

"Especially," Trevayne interjected, "in light of this new ship class the Republic has developed."

"The devastator, you mean. There aren't any in my task force, as you know; we wanted to get reinforcements here without further delay. But later elements will undoubtedly include them, as they're well into mass production now. I had some input in the design stage."

"*Did* you?" Trevayne perked up.

Miriam sighed. "I can see you two want to talk shop. And you know, Ian, how hopelessly unmilitary I am. So I'll just go and touch base with a few more people." As she vanished into the crowd, Li Magda's TRN subordinates took the hint and drifted away, still staring at Trevayne with fascination. The two of them were left to themselves in the center of the golden room.

Li Magda spoke first—but not of the devastator. "You know, Admiral Trevayne, I knew intellectually about the . . . circumstances of your revival. So I knew, or should have known, what to expect. But I still can't get used to your being so young, in a physical sense."

"Not an uncommon problem," he replied drily, thinking of some of the high-ranking Rim officers who now found themselves junior to him. "I must say that you also seem quite young for your rank, and considering your mother's age. . . . Ah, that didn't come out very well, did it? Please excuse me. I'm not always this socially inept. Blame it on the fact that I *wasn't* prepared in advance to meet you."

"Point taken." She laughed. "And it's quite all right. As a matter of fact, I'm sixty-four Standard years old. But I've had access to the full antigerone regimen from an early age, and I'm one of those who take to it very well. Physiologically, I'm only about twenty."

"As am I," Trevayne nodded. "I can understand why my current appearance must be difficult for you to reconcile with all those stories you said you've heard. It's not how one usually visualizes a monster."

"Oh, that's not really how people in the Republic remember you." She paused to frame her thoughts. "I think they regard you as a figure along the lines of Irwin Rommel or Robert E. Lee: a brave, honorable, and, yes, frighteningly capable soldier for the wrong side."

A perceptible moment passed before Trevayne could respond—and not just because it had been a long time since he'd spoken to anyone besides Genji Yoshinaka with any knowledge of Old Terra's history. "Actually, I like to think of myself as having been on the *right* side."

"Again, point taken," she said ruefully.

"But I must say I find this viewpoint refreshing. The attitude of people in the Rim can be somewhat . . . well . . ." He wondered how to describe near-adulation.

"I think I understand what you're trying to say. And yes, I can definitely understand how it might be that way." She blinked, and abruptly changed the subject. "Anyway, you expressed an interest in the devastator. I don't know how much you already know about it."

"Only the basic statistics. Two million tonnes displacement, and still as fast as a supermonitor—or, I should probably say, no slower than one. I understand, though, that it's even less maneuverable."

"True. But still, with two-thirds again the hull capacity... well, let's put it this way. It represents as great an increase in fighting power over the supermonitor as the supermonitor did over the monitor when you introduced it."

"Well, it will be the last quantum leap of that sort. You've run up against an absolute limit: the largest hull that can transit a warp point. It's rather like the United States Navy in the early twentieth century; they couldn't build a battleship too big to squeeze through the Panama Canal." He watched her eyes for the blank look he usually saw when he said something like this. He didn't see it now. But there was something else—a closed look, as though she was withholding something. He was about to probe deeper, but dinner was announced.

He was seated across the table from her, a few seats down, and they were able to exchange no more than occasional bits of conversation. They were both natural centers of attention—Trevayne as he always was, and Li Magda as the living embodiment of the new alliance. So each of them was the focus of a sycophantic cluster of personages too exalted to be brushed off. At least Trevayne wasn't called on to make a speech; the politicians were only too willing to perform that function.

Finally, dinner ended and everyone filed out through the reception room. Trevayne looked around for Li Magda, and found her beside the Terran Republic flag.

"I imagine it must seem strange to see *that* here," she said.

"I can't deny it, Admiral Li. By the way, perhaps you could answer a question about this flag that's always puzzled me."

"I may be able to. After all, my maternal grandfather was largely responsible for designing it."

"Really?" This woman was, Trevayne reflected, full of surprises.

"Yes. Li Kai-lun was head of the Hangchow delegation to the constitutional convention of the Fringe provisional government, which became the Terran Republic. He chaired the committee that designed a new flag. But what's your question?"

"Well ..." Trevayne pointed at the creature that sinuously encircled the starburst. "What *is* that?"

"Oh, that's a doomwhale."

"A ... doomwhale?" Trevayne echoed faintly, recalling the ferocious thirty-foot-long snakelike denizen of Beaufort's oceans, whose pharmaceutical byproducts had brought wealth—and conflict with the Corporate Worlds—to that harsh Fringe planet.

"Yes. The whole flag, except for the starburst, is patterned on the Beaufort planetary flag, since that was where the Fringe Revolution started."

Trevayne spoke in the painstaking way of someone who feels sure he must be missing something. "Uh, but Admiral Li . . . doomwhales *don't have wings.*"

"The Beauforters pointed that out to my grandfather at the time," she said, deadpan. "He explained that—oh, how did he put it?—the wings 'indicate the sweep and power of our new star nation.'"

"Hmm . . ." Trevayne sounded dubious.

"The Beauforters eventually came around. Of course, they and everyone else wondered why the Hangchow delegates smiled so much afterwards." Seeing that Trevayne was also wondering, she explained carefully. "If you put wings on a doomwhale, it bears a certain purely coincidental resemblance to a—"

"A *dragon!*" Trevayne guffawed, startling those nearby.

"A li ying *lung,* as my grandfather would have said," she corrected primly.

"Well, Admiral Li," said Trevayne when he'd gotten his breath back, "you've given me yet another reason for never underestimating your family!"

"I do wish you'd call me 'Mags,' Admiral Trevayne."

"If you don't mind, I think 'Magda' is as far as I'm comfortable with going just yet. I hope you'll be comfortable calling me 'Ian.'"

"All right . . . Ian," she said as though trying it on. A slightly unsteady laugh escaped her. "And you thought seeing this flag here was a strange feeling!" Then she was gone, to rejoin her officers. Trevayne watched her go. At the door, she turned and gave him a smile over her shoulder and then was gone.

After a moment, he became aware of someone beside him. "So," Miriam Ortega asked innocently, "how did it go?"

"Well . . . she compared me to Irwin Rommel and Robert E. Lee."

"Oh?" Miriam raised one eyebrow into an arc of polite inquiry. "Relative of hers?"

It is a terrible thing to see a grown man cry.

CHAPTER NINETEEN

"Will you walk into my parlor?"

"Michael 2, give me a nudge on that lateral thruster," Captain Paulo Velasquez said quietly, splitting his attention between his partner and the rest of his crew. The thrust moved the armor up against the bulk of the fort with a soundless stateliness until the targeting dot lined up perfectly in his sight. Since he wasn't standing on the hull of Fort Los Dios, he wouldn't have felt the shock wave when the two pieces lined up.

He'd been a yard dog at Bellerophon and never expected to be doing major repairs and refurbishments in deep space. He reached out one hand and the titanic waldo slaved to it, mimicked his motion. His powered work suit was a very large suit or a very small ship, called an "arc-angel" for some reason. His waldo closed on the armor of the fortress and steadied it in place.

"Roger, Michael 2 copies."

It was very strange to be working outside the safety of dock webbing, where anything dropped would be safely caught before it could head out on a trajectory all its own. Out here around the warp point it would eventually to fall into it, whether it was a tool or a person. He kept his mind on the job at hand rather than think about it. He also had to make sure his crews didn't think about it either.

He tabbed through the four main channels, hearing the soothing buzz of construction chatter, even while he applied the Rosy to the armor in front of him. He'd taken an interest in ancient forming techniques once and was still fascinated by the archaic art of welding, but it had nothing to do with modern techniques.

"Rafe 16, get your ass out of the way."

"Roger that. Up yours, Raphael 8."

That kind of sound was typical. It sounded like everyone, working tired, working frantically to put Admiral Krishmahnta's plans in motion, had adjusted well to working out here. There. That was done.

Time to get the crews in, let the flyboys play with their new kludged-up remote-control toys. "Gabriel, Michael, Raphael, Uriel. On the mark. Finish up and get inside, gentlemen." It was a monstrous mess, but it would work.

"Copy. Uriel all present, coming in."

"Gabriel, copy."

"Raphael, copy."

Against the velvet darkness the fort's armor was the only reflective surface under the work lights, the clusters of lights that twinkled starlike were his people moving inside to the relative safety of the ships they'd been assigned to. In the flight from Bellerophon the work shuttles, designed to hold racks of arc-angels, had fit neatly into the capitol ships' pinnace slots and they'd managed to get the work crews out before the aliens moved in.

He caught the double click from Abijit, rounding up Section Michael's lambs. "Good work, people. Let's not keep our ride waiting."

The duty cabin had the slightly tense, stale air of a room too often occupied by nervous, sweating humans. Krishmahnta had the lights lowered, rubbing tired eyes. She put down her cup in the clutter on her desk with a slight mental apology to her aide who would have to clean up, and turned to the captain of the *Gallipoli*.

Yoshi Watanabe looked just as tired as she felt, his lips pursed thoughtfully as he paged through the images they'd cobbled together. Flicker. Flicker. Flicker. He paged through the whole thing before stopping page one.

"We've based all this strategy on this assumption, Erica. I'm nervous about that." She leaned forward and indicated the recording of alien forces coming through the warp point, and tapped to bring up the battle report from Vice Admiral Miharu Yoshikuni at Andromeda.

"Run comparative," she said quietly, and the machine obligingly ran the tank images from both the assault through BR-01 and Pegasus. As the two battles silently ran through their courses she let the images speak for themselves but turned to him once they stopped again. "You and I spotted it together. Each of the two alien commanders have a distinctly different style. The one is far more profligate with its people and equipment than the other. You see Commander Yoshikuni is facing the more dangerous opponent because it is more careful of its resources." She absolutely refused to refer to the alien commanders as either he or she. "At the risk of assigning anthropomorphic tendencies to aliens, I think we can sucker the one we are facing."

"And with this plan, fewer of our people get killed doing it." His smile was sharp edged. "I see it. I was trying to be devil's advocate for you."

The attention chime sounded before the admiral's aide, Liam, spoke. "Admiral, Captain Watanabe, the work crews are reporting in."

"Thank you, Liam. Aren't you a bit over your watch?" Even over the voice channel she could hear the young man blush when he responded.

"Just going off, sir. Kausalya is coming on." Erica smiled. Liam Howitt was very inclined to overdo to see that she was looked after.

"Thank you, Liam."

"Sir."

She turned back to Yoshi. "And that gives us the first part of our trap." She spread her hand through the display and made a fist. "I'm willing to accept the loss of responsiveness to save our people."

The warp forts at Jason-Castor had now all been linked into the datanets of *Gallipoli, Passhendale,* and *Temuchin* and were entirely unmanned. They had also been loaded with the largest damned antimatter warheads that anyone had ever devised.

"And if this commander is still the one that doesn't mind interpenetration losses we should be able to keep them bottled up on the warp point."

"That's the idea. Then there's your brainchild." With a snap she wiped away the tank images before calling up Spiderweb, and Yoshi's cutting smile took on a molecular edge.

"If it works," he said. Spiderweb was within fifteen degrees of the ecliptic as though it was a warp point or some other important area in space. Which it wasn't. But the aliens couldn't know that. "Once they deal with the warp point, I'm betting that the alien commander is as much of a glory hound as it seems to be and will follow us here."

"Howling for blood, of course."

"It'll get plenty of that."

When the alien assault on Charlotte came, Vice Admiral Yoshikuni was almost prepared for it. The alarm sounded as she put her fork down. "Here we go," she said to the rest of the table who were getting up with her.

"Aye, Sir."

When she sat down in her command chair two minutes later, clipping her helmet into its brackets, the main tank already showed a split image. Both Andromeda and Demeter warp points were breached. That meant both Commanders Way Lem and Armand Dupres-Pacey had their hands full. "All right, Armand, Way. You've got them bottled up so far. Let's keep them that way."

"Yes, Commander."

With the drone from the vice admiral, Yoshikuni had an idea what tactics she'd face, and sat with a face of iron as the red icons gradually swelled out from the warp points until, despite the defenders, broke open like boils bursting. She ignored the flashing codes signifying damage and refused to see the Omega codes in amongst them.

"Commander! Some of those ships have the Desai drive!"

"How many? Numbers?" She leaned forward, fingers tapping against the arm of the command chair. Her face was calm but she could feel and smell her own nervous sweat wafting up the neck of her suit as her body fought the scrubbers built into the smart fabric.

"Only four, five now, Sir . . . Numbers are going up. It looks like eleven, Sir. Positive identification on eleven alien ships."

"Target them." She could see that Lem was going to have the worst of the mess on his hands. The aliens had sent the bulk of their faster ships through Polo and Demeter.

It was only the unified actions of the defenders that made the defense possible, with ships coordinating their fire and their actions. They stood off as best they could and smothered the aliens with missile fire, but they didn't have infinite ammunition. *Kirin*, Commander Lem's ship, vanished in an expanding bubble of energy. Omega code for everyone aboard. More ships dying. More people dying trying to hold against two fronts. Vice Admiral Yoshikuni drew a deep breath and spoke over the command channel.

"All ships fall back to Beaumont."

"Acknowledge, Admiral."

It was always a bitter thing to be forced to retreat but she had to back off again, for now. Her task force was a shambles and she hoped that Vice Admiral Krishmahnta had a better reception for these bastards.

Her wounded ships staggered away from the oncoming enemy, able to outrun all but a handful and those ships did not pursue.

Vice Admiral Krishmahnta was on deck when it came. The alien transits were simultaneous and the alien commander lost half a dozen ships interpenetrating the space where they emerged. The rest advanced into a hail of missiles from the forts. She smiled as the savage firefight erupted into space, light and radiation sheeting out in waves as the alien SDs pounded at the forts. She hadn't lost anyone yet, not one.

"Captain Watanabe, have you ever heard of a Marshal Zhukov?"

He turned and looked at her, wondering why she'd bring this up, now. "No, Commander."

"Ah. Well, there is something about this alien commander that reminded me. He had a 'thing' about how many losses were acceptable. But then he had enormous amounts of cannon fodder available." She shook her head. "Not important."

"Fort Zulu's just gone off-line, sir. It's dropped out of the net." Almost the moment the words were out of the comm officer's mouth the fort in question visibly moved in space from the impact of alien missiles. It was even visible in the tank and, for a moment, withstood the pounding before it vanished in a Hell-bubble of light.

On the *Montuhoteph*, Admiral Lankha's *selnarm* was enough to catch up every one of her command crew in a harmony full of emotional halftones, shrilling wild through everyone in the ship and beyond, an emotional wave roaring through and submerging anything else. (Glorious victory.) (Defensive rage.) (Love of battle.) The deaths were felt, but absorbed into the defensive rage. Everyone could see on the screen that the defending forts were firing more raggedly, somewhat less tightly coordinated than any they'd faced before. The *Montuhoteph* had come through on the second wave and Lankha felt she rode her ship as it shuddered, shaking off a near miss.

"Sir, they are holding our ships at the warp point."

The admiral dismissed the report, curling into a gleeful knot in her command niche. "Not for long. We're driving them ahead of us and they're tired. It's not as though they are truly thinking creatures. (Righteous fanaticism.) Bring up the reserve."

"This time I want you to bring every ship you have," Krishmahnta said softly to the red codes glowing so malevolently in the heart of the tank. She'd only lost hundreds of her people, not thousands, and she was almost ready to close the jaws of the trap. It wouldn't matter so much if equipment were destroyed, once Samantha Mackintosh got *some* industrial capacity running at Tilghman.

It was hard to wait and watch the aliens hammer at the unmanned forts, waiting for them to bring up more of what ships they had. They had to be running out of people, out of ships, out of will to continue. They couldn't have had more than thirty million on those Behemoths to begin with. How could they just fling their own into the furnace like this?

"Admiral." At that scale, the tank couldn't show individual ship icons and the center of the area was a solid core of red. The tank blinked and adjusted its internal contrast to bring the ships clear again. The actinic light from the tank glanced off Captain Watanabe's face giving him a surreal look. "I believe that could be the best we'll get."

Krishmahnta nodded. "Tell the last of the hotshots to break off, Yoshi. I don't want them to get their tails in the vice when we snap it shut. No use saving all those lives and having the idi—ah, eager... pilots waste it."

That startled a smile out of him as he passed the word and the SMTs controlling the forts and providing bait moved back smartly.

The anticipation was thick, even though no one smiled openly. They had all bled at these aliens' hands and it was time for getting some of their own back. Erica flipped the cover off a small button on the arm of her chair, put her finger on it and pushed down, gently.

Since they were almost five light-minutes from the warp point they waited, watching the SMTs continue their flight toward them. Time for the signal to travel in space. Time for the image to return. In human perception on the battlefield, a long, long time to gaze into the past.

The forts had been loaded with enormous antimatter warheads and the computers onboard had no quibbles about self-destruction. When the code came, every single fort surrounding the warp point and the alien invaders vanished in an explosion big enough to rival the destruction of a pinhole drive; a twisting glare that sent a pulse into the warp point itself. Radiation sheeted through space and time and dozens of the alien ships didn't merely explode, they *sublimated,* translating from matter straight to energy.

Those further out from point zero reeled in space, crippled, hulls damaged or outright holed from the force of debris driven at almost light speed. Then came those "dead in the water" with their drive busses melted, leaving them unable to maneuver.

A spontaneous cheer started up from the ensigns on the command deck of the *Gallipoli.* They hesitated and realized a ferocious "Yes!" still hissed around the deck from the admiral who watched the Omega icons wash over the enemy icons in the tank, fist clenched on the arm of her chair, eyes alight.

The *Montuhoteph*'s gravity compensators hiccupped, flipped off before coming back at three-quarters their former strength sending everything that hadn't been secured raining down onto the decks.

Admiral Lankha clutched the edges of her command niche, her claws dug into the edges, holding her in place, staring at the screen as damage and injury reports began pouring in. (Pain. Minor injuries. Deaths. Humiliation.) Her command. Her beautiful command, that would overwhelm the *griarfeksh* with numbers, was decimated. She blinked her eyes closed for a second, reaching to seize the confusion of *selnarm*. (Reassurance. Calm. Will to fight. Rage. Humiliation.) It served to stabilize the embarrassment and disorder in her ship, spreading out to the others that had escaped that hellish trap.

"Admiral Lankha," her surviving third officer, Teti, spoke up, already showed a bruise rising dark against the pale gold on the side of his head. Medics had just bagged Uatchet where he'd been flung when the gravity had fluxed. "We're down to 50 percent strength." (Numb.)

"Illudor's claws and tentacles." (Humiliation.) All three of her eyes locked on the cluster of *griarfeksh* ships, running, still running. "We will repay this *at'holodahk*! They will regret trying to shame the people. Get us underway, Teti. Lesser claws, new orders. Pull into wedge wall. We go in pursuit. Many heroes will be reborn this day."

"And now we find out if we've pissed them off enough," Yoshi said, watching the alien ships sort themselves out. Krishmahnta laughed, shortly.

"Oh, I think so." She turned in her chair slightly. "Now comes your half of this little charade, Paulo. Are you ready to throw rocks?"

Captain Velasquez nodded from where he was sitting, at a board so hastily put together the joke was no one was to breathe on it. "Spiderweb's ready, Admiral."

"Good. Now drop our speed a bit, Yoshi. We want to present a suitably crippled duck profile."

"Acknowledged." He looked over at her. "A crippled duck?"

"Earth waterfowl."

"One crippled duck coming up, just fast enough to not let them catch us."

Ahead of them in space, ranged around a mythical warp point was a minefield seeded with missiles and the nasty surprise Velasquez had modified from the asteroid minefields.

The ecliptic of any star is often full of small space junk at fairly regular intervals, small nickel/iron dirtballs ranging from a cubic meter or so up to planetoids. Mining was about getting the raw ore to the refining ships as cheaply as possible and small reactionless motors designed to move these small chunks of rock around were cheap and had been regularly used since the Bug War. Set the refining ship in the right orbit, send out the robotic motors programmed to latch onto the asteroids and bring them back.

Velasquez had thrown his idea out, not thinking it could be used at all against modern warships, but the admiral had seized on it. The motors were all out there, with all their governors removed. Each one locked in place, cuddled up to an inert partner, no piece bigger than a hundred tons or so.

They had pursued and closed with the *griarfeksh*. Admiral Lankha could almost taste the victory she would snatch out of the shameful defeat they had handed her. She leaned forward as if she could somehow urge her ships along with the motion, an odd enough action that she could feel the nervousness swelling in her junior officers.

"We have them. (Confidence.) We are both converging on that warp point where they are running." (Revenge.) She let the *selnarm* flow as she spoke to whip up their *matsokah*. "We will crush—"

"Admiral! *Hapshet* is reporting—is gone, Sir!" (Shock.)

"Mines! Ware, mines!" (Fear. Fear.)

All around point sources sprang to life and her ships found the minefield the hard way, as first *Hapshet*, then *Anknefhotep*, *Pertetis*, and *Nunefankh* found mines.

"Incoming! Missiles at zero one, zero three, zero five . . . all around, sir!" (Concentration.)

And that was when Paulo Velasquez triggered his mining tools. The rocks, without shielding, cheap and plentiful, with the crudest of guidance, leapt from motionless to five hundred meters per second.

The iron in the asteroids melted almost instantly, from compression alone, and the shooting-star trails of ionized particles drew together, clearly visible, a silvery network whose endpoints all converged inside alien ships.

At that speed, at that distance, no countermissile defense was possible if one could even lock onto something as crude as a rock. Arduan ships blew up at the center of each of the spiderwebs of glowing iron. In the first thirty seconds three quarters of the remaining ships where scrap, or fast expanding radiation including *Montuhoteph*.

The last remnants of the force Admiral Lankha had led into Raiden tottered out of the second ambush and retreated. Of the ships that attempted transit back through the warp, under Junior

Commander Osirii, only one in three made it, for the point itself was disturbed.

CHAPTER TWENTY

"They have the Desai drive."

The main briefing room of RFNS *Zephrain*—more like an auditorium, really, on this flagship-configured supermonitor—was full, because this time Cyrus Waldeck wanted to have all of Second Fleet's flag officers down to task-group level, and their chiefs of staff and ops officers, present in the flesh. Flesh and fur, actually, for the PSUN contingent had grown with the steady arrival of heavier units here in Astria until it was a full-blown task force, and Least Fang Zhaairnow'ailaaioun and several other members of his species were on hand. Waldeck had double-dosed on allergy pills, set the air filters on maximum, and hoped for the best.

And at any rate, he thought, his eyes straying to an all-human cluster of deep-blue uniforms among the black-and-silver of the Rim and the Pan-Sentient Union, *I'm not sure it's the Orions I'm most allergic to.*

He chided himself for the thought. More of the Terran Republic's heavy units had also had time to lumber into Astria by now, and Li Magda, rear admiral though she was, commanded a genuine task force—officially, Task Force 23. Those heavy units didn't include any of the new devastators; those monsters required a *long* time to build, and afterward would take a while getting anywhere thanks to the tortuous warp-line routes they had to take, avoiding warp points that could not accommodate their mountainous bulk. Still, it was a formidable TRN task force indeed—nineteen supermonitors, thirty superdreadnoughts, nine assault carriers, and forty-two battlecruisers—and Waldeck knew he ought to be glad to have it. And he *was* glad to have it. Only . . .

That *only*, as he was well aware, worked both ways.

Waldeck didn't delude himself that he was the most sensitive of men. But even he had been able to perceive the stiffening in Li Magda at the mention of his surname when they'd met. It could hardly have been otherwise. In the drama of the Republic's birth—at least as understood by its own citizens—the Waldeck dynasty of Corporate World plutocrats were cast as villains of the deepest dye. Hector Waldeck, chief delegate from Christophon to the old Terran Federation's Legislative Assembly, had been up to his choleric jowls in the maneuverings that had led to the assassination of Fiona MacTaggart of Beaufort, igniting the rebellion. Afterward, another relative—as little as he liked to admit any relationship to that unutterable jackass Admiral Jason Waldeck—had occupied Novaya Rodina and proceeded with a series of executions whose clumsy pompous brutality had seemed to confirm the worst the Fringe Worlds thought of the Federation and the Corporate Worlds that dominated it. The rebels, Waldeck had often thought sourly, might at least have been grateful to him for providing them with a matchless *cause célèbre*—and for losing his task force to them intact. He had, if nothing else, been consistent in his stupidity.

As for Cyrus Waldeck, he had looked at Li Magda and seen not just an admiral of the Terran Republic—he still had to suppress his gag reflex at that name—but the daughter of the woman who had been instrumental in the rebellion's success at several crucial points, culminating in the climactic carnage of Zapata where she had fought Ian Trevayne himself to a standstill. That bloodbath had left the Federation without the will to continue the struggle.

Yes, he thought, *there's a lot of history to be overcome here.*

But it must *be overcome. And as commanding officer here—a Waldeck commanding a Li—mine is the primary responsibility for overcoming it.*

He stepped to the podium in front of the wide viewscreen and cleared his throat, hoping his need to do so wasn't a harbinger of an allergy attack. "Ladies and gentlemen," he began without preamble, "most if not all of you are already aware that our recon drones have been probing Bellerophon for some time. Many of you are not aware"—*except through Rumor Central*, he mentally qualified—"of just how that is possible. I will ask Commander Koleszar to explain briefly."

The ops officer stood up and took the podium. "In essence, we were able to devise a temporary way around the aliens' stealth scrambler. It is, in the simplest terms, a modification of the stealth field which 'bends' the scrambler's effect around the outside of it, just as it normally does various other wavelengths—most famously, that of visible light. I call this solution 'temporary' because there is no room for doubt that aliens will become aware of what we're up to and adjust their scrambler."

"But won't we be able to switch our frequencies in response?" someone asked.

"Certainly. And they'll do the same thing again, and so on. It's an old story in the history of electronic countermeasures and counter-countermeasures. But for the moment, they evidently haven't caught on. So we're not going in blind—no, worse than blind: relying on false assumptions—like we did last time. We believe we have a fairly complete picture of their close-in warp-point defenses. Of course, we don't know everything we'd like to know." Koleszar paused as though hesitant to bring something up. "For example, our drones have yet to observe one of their system-defense ships underway, and we therefore have no performance figures for them."

An uneasy muttering suffused the room.

"We all know the basic facts about them by now," the ops officer resumed, deciding that the subject had better be faced forthrightly. He activated the viewscreen to show a digitally enhanced but still blurry image of a blocky, unlovely conic section against a starry black-velvet backdrop, with nothing to give a sense of its size. "On the basis of their shape, we believe the aliens have broken down some of their smaller generation ships—quite possibly they had a modular design philosophy built into them for this very purpose—into hulls of roughly a billion tonnes." He didn't add, five hundred times the tonnage of a supermonitor. His listeners could figure that out for themselves. "Of course," he hurried on, accentuating the positive, "these are basically transports, not purpose-built warships, so their actual fighting power must not be nearly proportional to their size, in our terms. Furthermore, we believe that, like the original ships from which they were cut down, they use reaction drives."

"How sure are you of that?" demanded Vice Admiral Alistair McFarland, RFN. A scion of a political family of Aotearoa, he commanded Task Force 21, the segment of Second Fleet which contained the Rim's own contingents—twenty-three supermonitors, twenty demothballed monitors, forty-four superdreadnoughts, fifteen assault carriers, eight fleet carriers, and sixty-three battlecruisers.

"As sure as we can be without actual confirmation, Admiral. As I mentioned, our probes haven't observed them underway. But it's a reasonable inference from their sheer size. And we feel their immobility is strong negative evidence."

"That means that they will not have 'blind zones,'" Zhaairnow rumbled. He commanded Task Force 22, the PSUN elements. Like all PSUN forces, it was heavily fighter-oriented—sixteen supermonitors (mostly of the carrier/main combatant variety), thirty-seven super-dreadnoughts, twenty assault carriers, thirteen fleet carriers, and fifty-six battlecruisers. As always he was thinking first and foremost of his beloved fighters, whose tactics had always aimed at getting into the area astern of a ship under reactionless drive, where spatial distortions prevented it from targeting its weapons.

"Admitted, Least Fang. But by the same token, they will on our standards be effectively immobile—little better than orbital weapon platforms. There's no escaping the fact that we'll have to take some extremely heavy missile fire from them in the early stages. But after we're past them, they'll be left behind." Privately, it bothered Koleszar a little. Why had the aliens—they *had* to come up with a better name for them than that!—even bothered to break up generation ships into things that could do little more than what the generation ships themselves could: sit back and launch immense salvos of long-range missiles? To be sure, the system-defense ships must be somewhat more maneuverable than the generation ships, even the smaller ones. But on the standards of reactionless drives—especially those in use today—the difference was scarcely noticeable.

"At any rate," he resumed, changing the subject, "we have their positions plotted out, and also the minefields and weapon buoys covering the warp point. We have also confirmed the aliens' possession of strikefighters." That didn't cause a stir. They had been fairly certain of it already. And nobody saw fit to remark on how many fighter launch bays one of those system-defense ships could accommodate. "We have also established the location of the aliens' main asteroidal shipyards. The last was particularly easy for the drones, due to neutrino emissions—and it forms the basis for our strategy."

"Thank you, Commander," said Cyrus Waldeck. "And now I will ask the chief of staff to outline that strategy."

Captain Julia Monetti stepped to the podium and, to the general relief, turned off the image of the system-defense ship. Replacing it on the viewscreen was something they all knew by heart: the Bellerophon System.

A two-dimensional display was quite sufficient for a planetary system, since warp points (for reasons as obscure as everything else about them) always occurred more or less in the same ecliptic plane that held the planetary orbits. The sun of Bellerophon showed as a golden dot at the center of the screen. The orientation was an arbitrary one, with the purple circle marking the warp point through which they must enter from Astria directly below the sun—at "six o'clock" on the clockface that humans always mentally superimposed on such displays—a little less than halfway to the screen's lower edge. Three other purple circles occupied positions at three o'clock, ten o'clock, and eleven o'clock, at various distances from the primary. Planetary orbits showed as blue concentric circles around the sun. One of these, representing the system's mineral-rich asteroid belt, was dashed; it circled the sun out beyond their warp point, at an average orbital radius of twenty-two light-minutes. Two light-minutes in from that—but still four light-minutes outside the Astria warp point—was yet another concentric circle, this one in brown. It was a relatively new addition to displays like this, for it represented the Desai Limit, within which the Desai Drive would not function.

"In light of the recon drone data," Monetti began, "we believe we have a realistic chance to break into the system. In particular, our detailed knowledge of the minefields and buoys will enable us to employ our new AMBAMMs to good effect." There was a general sound of agreement. The improved AMBAMMs, better shielded and built on larger hulls, had been arriving for some time in wholesale lots, for Waldeck had refused to even consider another offensive until he had accumulated enough of them for a truly lavish preliminary bombardment. "Once we've won free of the warp point, we can make use of our greatest technological advantage: the Desai Drive."

"But," someone protested, "our warp point of emergence is within the local sun's Desai Limit. And the planet of Bellerophon is even more so, at only seven light-minutes from the sun."

"The planet is not our primary objective." Monetti touched the podium's control pad, and a flashing light appeared along the broken circle of the asteroid belt, and about four o'clock. "This is the location of the enemy's primary shipyard—or, to be precise, it will be its location at the time for which our attack is scheduled. We are going to destroy it.

"The details are in the data chips you have all received. We are going to put together a special fast strike force built around Task Group 21.4." Behind McFarland, Rear Admiral Aline M'puta sat up straighter. She commanded eight of the RFN's assault carriers, escorted by thirteen battlecruisers and an array of the heavy and light cruisers that weren't even counted in a tally of capital ships in this day and age. "It will be reinforced by PSUN elements from Task Force 22, selected by Fang Zhaairnow, to include only carriers and escorting cruisers. As must be obvious from this force composition, speed is of the essence. This is to be a raiding force. After the heavier but less mobile elements have secured the warp point, Admiral M'puta's force will proceed outward from the primary until it is outside the Desai Limit. It will then proceed on Desai Drive to the shipyards—which are also outside the Desai Limit—and destroy them, thereby crippling the enemy's capacity to repair damages and make up losses. It will subsequently exit the Bellerophon System— unless the situation has developed in such a way as to indicate that we can establish a permanent beachhead in the system. Flexibility must be our watchword."

M'puta spoke up thoughtfully. Like all carrier admirals, she was an ex–fighter jock. Unlike most of that breed, she was not notorious for hair-raising cockiness—which was precisely why Waldeck had picked her for this mission. "We will, of course, not have the advantage of Desai Drive in the last stages of our return to the Astria warp point. And the enemy will know that's where we'll be headed."

"True, Admiral. It may prove impracticable for you to fall back to Astria. But we have an alternative plan for that eventuality." Monetti manipulated the controls again, and the purple circle on the three o'clock bearing flashed on and off for attention. "The warp point leading to Pegasus is outside the Desai Limit—twenty-four light-minutes from the primary, to be exact—and is just outside the region of the asteroid belt where you will already be. If you find that the enemy has interdicted your return to the Astria warp point, you will proceed there on Desai Drive and transit to Pegasus."

"And once there . . .?" queried M'puta in a steady voice.

"You will do as seems indicated in light of the situation you find in the Arm out beyond Bellerophon—of which, obviously, we have no knowledge. Your objective will be to reinforce the Rim units still holding out there." If any, Monetti did not add. "You will also be able to provide them with the doubtless welcome news that they are not forgotten."

Cyrus Waldeck watched M'puta's dark face closely for her reaction to orders that normally would have taken the form of a call for volunteers. He saw nothing but her trademark equanimity. He didn't even need to look at Zhaairnow. The Orion would, as a matter of course, try to appoint himself to lead the Task Force 22 elements that would take part in M'puta's razzia across the Bellerophon System and into the unknown, even though it would mean putting himself under the tactical command of a rear admiral. Equally as a matter of course, Waldeck would refuse his request; his duties lay here with Second Fleet. But after getting over his sulks, Zhaairnow would pick another of the Orion PSUN officers for the assignment, which resonated so well with the honor code of the *Zheeerlikou'valkhannaiee*. (Waldeck was far from being the first human to give thanks that the Khanate's homeworld lay in the constellation of Orion as viewed from Old Terra, providing a humanly manageable name for the race.)

Actually, Waldeck had planned it this way from the first. The legendary skill of the Orions at the fighter operations they loved could only increase the mission's chances of success. And if—as Waldeck privately considered very probable—the raiders had to flee to Pegasus, there was something to be said for having an Orion PSUN element among them. The populations of the Bellerophon Arm needed to know how many nations and races were struggling to break through to their rescue.

Of course, adding a Terran Republic Navy contingent to the raiders would have further emphasized that last point. But Waldeck hadn't done so. He could justify that decision: the TRN's strong suit was battle-line tactics utilizing their "generalist" supermonitors, not fighter operations. But he knew that wasn't the real reason.

In some fortunate cases, living outrageously far beyond the Biblical threescore-and-ten courtesy of antigerone treatments had the effect of intensifying the individual's redeeming features. Cyrus Waldeck's redeeming feature had always been ruthless honesty about himself to himself. And he was not about to start indulging in self-deception now. He acknowledged his very mixed feelings about Terran Republic units in Second Fleet. And having them commanded by the daughter of Li Han didn't help in the least. He could recognize the feeling for what it was, and do his best to combat it. But he couldn't deny it.

And, he reminded himself, he at least wasn't sending Li Magda's supermonitors through the warp point first, which would have placed them in maximum peril. They were to follow in subsequent waves, where their mixed armament would make them well able to deal with whatever tactical situation had developed in Bellerophon space by then.

"Thank you, Captain." He stepped to the podium as Julia Monetti relinquished it. "Please review your data chips and submit any questions or comments to Captain Monetti so they can go on the agenda for the final meeting. It is essential that we adhere to the schedule, as it is predicated on the orbital position of the asteroid shipyards relative to the system's warp points. Are there any questions before we adjourn?"

There were none. Everyone wanted time for study first. Waldeck watched Li Magda closely. She had no comment to make. But she looked very thoughtful.

The torrents of improved AMBAMMs that opened the Third Battle of Bellerophon were without precedent, and they were directed in accordance with accurate probe data. The dense minefields and serried ranks of weapon buoys largely vanished, as though burned away by successive waves of cleansing flame. Interspersed with the AMBAMMs were accurately targeted SBMHAWKs in such numbers that they were able to send a perceptible shake through the monstrous bulk of an SDS.

Only then did the first crewed starships begin to transit into the spaces so recently wracked by inconceivable energies. Waldeck's tactics were different this time. The initial assault waves were a combination of expendable monitors and a mix of supermonitor types, including a generous allotment of the PSUN carrier/main combatant classes. It was still too risky to commit the relatively fragile purpose-built carriers. But at long last the Orion fighter pilots got the action they craved, as clouds of fighters swarmed forth from the SDSes, each of which carried four hundred or more of them, piloted—not though the allies knew it—by beings who saw death as a temporary inconvenience.

But the pilots of the Rim and the PSU were flying the new space superiority fighters, capable of engaging their oncoming opponents at long range with fighter-launched AFHAWKs supplemented by salvos of capital AFHAWKs from the supermonitors. Those enemy fighters that got through were taken at close range with sleets of hypervelocity powered flechettes. Blood-chilling Orion howls of triumph began to echo over the comm channels.

But the defending capital ships—including new heavy superdreadnoughts, halfway between an ordinary superdreadnought and a monitor in size—began to close in and coordinate their fire with the staggering missile salvos from the system defense ships. The region around the warp point became a holocaust of dying ships.

But even in the midst of this saturnalia of destruction, the automated sensors of Second Fleet's ships continued, with a single-mindedness impossible to their organic masters, to observe. And courier drones continued to flow back through the warp point with the data Cyrus Waldeck's intelligence analysts needed.

As the initial shock of the attack wore off and the enigmatic aliens began to rally in response throughout the reaches of the system, those courier drones brought two pieces of bad news.

(At last.) The fight that Torhok craved came to him. The initial assault out of Astria seethed out of the screen at him like a boil bursting, carrying the shattered pieces of the warp defenders with it. He turned to his comm officer and said quietly. "Call in system-defense ships and all support." He knotted his tentacles together and watched the alien ships come. (Anticipation.)

"Iakkut."

"Yes, Sir." His second uncoiled from his niche slightly, acknowledging with *selnarm* and voice but not letting his attention stray too far from his boards.

"I think these creatures are about to get a surprise."

(Anticipation. Will to fight. Bloodlust.)

✧   ✧   ✧

Cyrus Waldeck surprised himself with the steadiness of his voice. "So they have the Desai Drive?"

"I'm sure they themselves don't call it that—" began Commander Lester Jardine, the intelligence officer. Nathan Koleszar gave him a silencing glare. Jardine was an expert within his specialty, but devoid of common sense in social interactions. Koleszar recalled the word *nerd* from the historical fiction of which he was fond.

"Yes, Sir," Koleszar took up the report. "There's no doubt of it, now that they've begun to summon reinforcements from elsewhere in the system—including the Pegasus warp point." He indicated the readouts that showed the velocity at which those reinforcements were streaking inward. "Of course," he ventured, hoping he wasn't sounding too much like Jardine, "this will leave the Pegasus warp point largely undefended, increasing its practicality as an alternative means of egress for Admiral M'puta's raiding force."

"Yes," said Waldeck, more to himself than to the ops officer. "Save for the fact that Admiral M'puta's raid is now out of the question. The assumption on which it was based turns out to be false "

Koleszar swallowed hard. "Yes, Sir. Uh . . . Admiral, there's more."

"More?"

"Their system-defense ships have started to move. And from the nature of their motion, it is clear that another of our assumptions must be abandoned. Those ships aren't using photon drives, Admiral."

"You mean—?"

"Yes, Sir. Their maximum velocity is only a little over half that of a supermonitor . . . but they went to it instantaneously. The enemy has managed to build reactionless drives into those monstrosities. Judging from the data we've gotten so far, they're even more cumbersome than they are slow. Turning must be a major project for them."

Waldeck had stopped listening. He blinked away his shock and spoke with his old crispness, verging on harshness. "Commander, abort all further warp transits. All elements now in Bellerophon space are to withdraw to Astria as soon as they can recover all their currently deployed fighters. And tell Admiral M'puta to stand down." His tone softened just a little. "Her day will come. But I'm not going to commit relatively light units like hers to a combat environment that's deadly even for supermonitors."

"Yes, Sir. Ah . . . Admiral, most of the surviving units of the initial assault waves have sustained heavy damage."

"Well, the most recent arrivals will have to cover their withdrawal. Who would that be?"

"Admiral Li, Sir, with the first few heavy TRN battlegroups."

"I see," said Waldeck after a pause so brief that some would have missed it altogether. "Well, she'll have to do it with those battlegroups. Prepare the courier drones at once. Tell Admiral Li she's in charge of extricating us from Bellerophon."

Eraphis's beloved little research fighter had been upgraded with heavier armerments since he and Sehtsursankh had made it back through the warp with the data and he'd actually resented being left with the SDS'es in the reserve.

(Glee.) Was his response when the commandship's call came. With the new engines in the fighters and heavies it would be possible to still get into the fight, even from so far away.

He locked his eyes on the screen in front of him, as he sent the ship hurtling toward the fight. *Oh, you are a sweet little thing to fly.*

"You're humming again," Seht grumbled as they closed on the *griarfeksh* fighters withdrawing to their carriers.

"I'm not," he snaped back absently, fists tightening on his control. The image on his screen whirled to the left, real-time, as he sank into the gel. That sucked. It didn't give him enough to brace against. The alien fighter dodged in front of him, dancing like a kreevix fly over a hazy stream. He felt it when Seht launched missiles. (Wild exhilaration.)

"You are *ranarmata*, you idiot," Seht said. (Affection.)

"Am not." But there were no more enemy fighters to engage. (Disappointment.)

Fighter action had almost entirely petered out. The defending system defense ships had shot their bolt in that respect, and Second Fleet's retreating units had recovered their fighter groups for good, unable to afford the time for any further launches to cover their backs as they limped back to the warp point and the safety of Astria at a rate limited to the speed of their slowest units . . . some of them very slow indeed, with the damage they had taken to their drives. And Li Magda was resolved to leave no ship behind.

Now that resolve was about to be put to the test, as she watched the holographic display tank on TRNS Implacable's flag bridge and saw the line of scarlet enemy icons moving in on a course intended to intercept the retreating cripples.

At least the system defense ships couldn't hope to catch up, although they could and did continue to pour in seemingly inexhaustible missile fire from long range. But those approaching icons were the enemy's new intermediate ships, as fast as superdreadnoughts but approaching monitor size. Individually, they were no match for supermonitors like the Impregnable-class ships Li Magda commanded. But the numbers she saw in the tank more than compensated for that, and they came under the missile umbrella from the system defense ships that saturated the supermonitors' point defense and battered their shields and armor.

"Commander de Chaleins," she told her chief of staff, "order all ships to concentrate their missile fire on these incoming SDHs. And while they're doing it, we will change course, thusly." She pointed a wandlike device, and the string of green light in the holo tank that represented her battle line's course curved sharply inward toward the warp point.

De Chaleins stared. He was a hereditary aristocrat from Lancelot, and had a sternly suppressed tendency toward rashness. But this startled even him. "Admiral, this brings us in toward the warp point much sooner, reducing our margin for covering the retreating ships."

"Do it anyway, Commander." She relented enough to explain. "I want them to think we are predominantly missile-armed ships, trying to keep the range open as long as possible. They, of course, will be eager to close the range. When they come into energy-weapon range, we will engage them with everything except our energy torpedoes, until I give the word."

Understanding dawned in de Chaleins's eyes. "Yes, Sir!"

Li Magda dismissed him from her mind and stared at the tank. It would be risky. If she failed, those fresh SDHs would be in among the battered, exhausted ships she had been ordered to protect. But if it worked, it would enable her to spring a technological surprise on the enemy in a particularly nasty way.

The *Impregnable* class was the newest of the Terran Republic's "generalist" supermonitors. It had been fitted with heavy batteries of the new energy torpedoes in place of many of the older designs' beam weapons and some of their missile launchers, for it partook of some of the characteristics of both.

Essentially, the energy torpedo wrapped plasma, at near-fusion temperatures, in an envelope of force and sent it out as an unguided ballistic projectile at near light speed. Its maximum range was actually a little longer than that of a standard missile, although its chances of actually hitting anything moving at space-combat speeds was very problematical at that range. And it could, with difficulty, be interdicted by antimissile defenses—but only if it were fired from more than about nine light-seconds, giving those defenses time for a targeting solution against something crowding the heels of light. Within that range, it was unstoppable. And it had one other interesting capability. . . .

"Commander de Chaleins," Li Magda called out over the increasing drumroll of noise as the missile bombardment intensified, "an addendum to that last order. When I give the order to open fire with energy torpedoes, they will be launched at their maximum rate of fire."

"Aye aye, Sir," the chief of staff acknowledged after a brief pause. Li Magda heard the pause—and understood it. She knew the possible consequences of spitting out energy torpedoes at twice their normal rate.

"I know, Commander," she said. "But we can't worry about burning out our capacitors now. This engagement is going to be over in a very short time, one way or another. So send the order."

"Aye aye, Sir."

Li Magda continued to watch the curving strings of green and red icons converge. She also listened to more and more damage reports from her ships as they replied as best they could to the missile salvos that battered them. The aliens must be wondering why that reply was so weak, coming from ships whose behavior suggested that missiles were their primary armament.

Then the converging icons slid together into beam-weapon range. The shuddering of *Implacable*'s hull, and the stream of damage reports, both intensified as the alien SDHs brought their energy weapons into play—mostly force beams, as expected. And now they must be certain they were dealing with specialized missile ships, given the light reply from the limited force-beam batteries of the

Implacables. Space-twisting energies gouged at Li Magda's ships and sought to gut them.

Just a little longer, she thought as the din rose to crescendo.

RFNS *Indomitable* reeled, sending the damage control parties sprawling as they worked amid the smoke to contain the results of the last missile salvo. Captain Fergus Thorsen was thrown against the restraints of his crash couch. He was from Beaufort, and had the kind of build that high-gravity world had bequeathed to its children. But even his consciousness wavered. He might have passed out altogether but for the hideous din of twisting, tearing metal as the force beams went to work on a ship no longer protected by force shields.

As the inertial compensators reasserted themselves and the deck steadied, his executive officer staggered up to face him. Commander Rafael Gravina's right arm hung bloody and limp, and his face was ashen. But his eyes held a wild light.

"Captain," he shouted above the noise, "the weapons station reports that we'll soon lose the ability to target the energy torpedoes. We've got to use them while we still can!"

"That's a negative, XO," Thorsen yelled back. "We're under strict orders to employ them only on command."

"Captain, they're all we've got left! We can't just let this ship be torn apart when we still have something to return fire with!" The light in Gravina's eyes blazed up into something Thorsen had never expected to see there. "Captain, I must insist that—"

Ever since the boarding actions of the Theban War had caught the Terran Federation Navy unprepared, laser sidearms had been a standard item of space-combat attire. Now Thorsen's hand went to butt of his. "Commander, that will do! We will obey our orders and withhold energy torpedo fire. Is that understood?"

Their eyes locked, and Thorsen thought he saw the mutiny begin to die in Gravina's.

But then the ravening force beams found the bridge, and it didn't matter anymore.

"Code Omega from *Indomitable*, Admiral," De Chaleins shouted to make himself heard.

"Just a little longer," Li Magda called back, walling off her mind against the thought of a supermonitor's death. Instead, she thought of the damaged ships of the earlier PSUN and RFN waves that were beginning to commence warp transit back to Astria. And she watched the crawling multicolored icons in the tank.

"Admiral—!"

"Almost." She felt a strange psychic proximity to the aliens as they drew closer and closer. *What kind of beings lurk inside those ships?* "Are all units locked on?"

"Yes, Admiral."

"Good." As Li Magda watched, those red "hostile" icons passed an invisible line. "Then they may commence firing with energy torpedoes . . . *now!*"

Most energy weapons are invisible in the vacuum of space. But the packets of star-hot plasma that now shot out from the Terran Republic's supermonitors were blinding. And at their speed they looked more like beams of dazzling light—beams of a peculiarly stroboscopic sort, as new torpedoes were punched out at a rate that could not be maintained for long.

Even if the Arduans had known with what they were dealing, they could not have intercepted those immaterial wads of death in the nine seconds or less they took to flash across the intervening space. And when they struck—as they generally did, at these ranges—they struck with the destructive force of a capital missile antimatter warhead.

Shields went down, armor buckled and vaporized, and SDHs exploded outward in series of secondary explosions, fissuring and splitting apart in eruptions of hellfire. Even the ongoing missile storm from the now-distant system defense ships abated as though in shock at what they were witnessing.

"They're pulling away, Admiral!" exclaimed de Chaleins. "They're breaking off the engagement."

"I see they are," said Li Magda in a voice that sounded as drained as she felt. She had read the reports describing these aliens' seeming indifference to death. But evidently they couldn't be indifferent to losses.

"Get us turned around, Commander," she ordered, straightening up. *Plenty of time for exhaustion later.* "We'll transit after the last of the damaged ships."

✧　　✧　　✧

Cyrus Waldeck watched grimly as the last of the PSUN and RFN units limped through the warp point, followed by the TRN ships that had enabled them to do so.

He steeled himself against disappointment. Once again, the objective had proven unattainable; but once again they had gleaned invaluable information about the enigmatic enemy. And, while it was difficult to be precise about the losses suffered by an enemy who was left holding the field, all indications were that this time they had given at least as good as they'd gotten.

"The last ship is transiting, Sir," Nathan Koleszar reported. "It's *Implacable*, with Admiral Li."

"Ah. Yes. Please establish a comm link with *Implacable*. I wish to speak to Admiral Li personally."

Admiral Li. He distinctly remembered that he had been of two minds about having someone with that name in Second Fleet. But he was finding it harder and harder to recall how that had felt.

CHAPTER TWENTY-ONE

Art Is Either Plagiarism or Revolution

Ankaht opened the window and leaned out, trying to let the wind and soft rain blow some of the mental stench off. It soothed her, but did little to ease her spirit and it was getting her office wet. She shut it and want back to her cushion and her desk, not bothering to wipe the droplets off her skin.

It wasn't truly raining that hard and she tried to tell herself it was all right, she'd get used to the subtle wrongness of this planet. She appreciated it, truly, but it wasn't and would never feel just like home to her. She'd have to wait till the next life when she could be born into a space, a place, which was home. She didn't want to be back in that box of a ship either. It was a feeling that had no help. It was what it was. The rain outside her window grew heavier, blowing away from her down the street, at least washing the dust off the plants that were the wrong shade of *herrm*.

The episodes of mental trouble in the city clusters had leveled off and people were starting to adjust to the vagaries of weather and the immutability of planetary gravity, but the attacks on the People hadn't stopped despite the attempts the Council made to discourage them. She was truly starting to think that if you killed these creatures the survivors fought harder as though death were somehow terrifying. *I will have to think on that some other time.*She squeezed her eyes shut hard and massaged the sides of her head, trying to stop the ache behind her top eye. (Depression.)

Even though these aliens—she refused, even in her mind, to call them *griarfeksh*—were *selnarm* mute she was convinced they were truly intelligent and worthy of communication. If only Torhok and Urkhot and their cronies weren't so strong on the Council there was a chance a more moderate view could be achieved. (Exhaustion of spirit.)

Without peace with these things there would never be a safe place for Illudor's people and that fear was exactly the emotion that would fuel the brutal drain on the People. (Resolve.) She pushed herself up from the cushion, determined to break out of this mood. A walk would do her good; let her skin be soothed by the warm rain.

This cluster had been cleared for Arduan use weeks ago so she was safe enough during the day and she walked out past the buildings most of the People had commandeered. The buildings here were open, empty, and the rain fell on her and the pavement under her feet. She paused under a cluster of trees planted in pots that actually had a pleasing contrast of texture, and in the midst stood a construct for which she could see no reason. It was an alloy-of-white-metal representation of a grazing creature of this planet poised on the edge of a pool that bubbled out of a pebbled depression in the walkway. Ankaht stood regarding it, wondering just what such a thing would represent to an alien.

In a wandering line more creatures were depicted and, curious, she followed the path so marked out. A small hunter crouched on a boulder. A water creature emerging out of the stone. The path of creatures led to a large typically ugly alien building, all straight lines and vile angles. The door opened itself for her.

She almost didn't enter because behind the door was one of the foulest tapestries she'd ever seen. *Vrel* woven through red. *Herrm* and *crivan* overlaid on orange. She shut her eyes and pressed on.

The hall beyond that excrescence was actually pleasing. The ceiling vaulted up in smooth curves and suspended in pools of light were the crazed color blotches of madness. On display. *Why?* Did they find this disharmony, this *ranarmata*, soothing?

She was stopped by a locked case showing a single black-and-white depiction of a human hand drawing itself. *I did not believe I would find* sulhaji, *here. I shotan that.*

The three-dimensional depictions were more often better, but even they weren't always well colored. This was not helping either her eyes or her head but her stubborn curiosity kept her from just leaving. *I found* sulhaji *once. Perhaps there is more here. And if these creatures have any kind of* shotan, *then it can be argued that they are not just pests on our new planet.*

She turned another corner and was rewarded with a lovely little room with a series of small grav plate–suspended fountains, each apparently representing a season on planet, day and night and in a number of weathers and it was a very clever trick that made it look like each fed into the next perpetually. Why was this here in amongst all the ugliness? Sulhaji *again.*

There was a faint disturbance, as if someone were distantly shouting, something like a faint whiff of a sweetness, a sense of *selnarm* from someone asleep or unconscious. She followed the sensations and though they got no stronger, she found herself in a hall with three sculptures along its length. The first was a column of blue-black and as she stepped up to it, she realized the *shotan* of it. Night. Mystery. Danger. Holding on.

The second looked the same except for a sliver of red/orange/ *crivan*/white. Dawn. Hope. Relief.

The third smooth column was solidly *crivan*/white. Day. Reality. Safety. And a faint suggestion of Dullness.

She had no idea how she knew what they meant. It wasn't *selnarm*. She turned and looked down the hall she'd just walked and the alcoves and rooms and knew what it was. Simply put. A gallery. Unemotional creatures did no art. Here was her proof that the aliens were not dispassionate machines, oblivious vermin. This was not just opinion, or theory that could be argued away as Ardupomorphic or her wishful thinking, was it? She had found enough *sulhaji* in amongst the *ranarmata* to make an excellent case.

There were other works like the three that had spoken to her and on some level she could feel them, sense them to varying degrees but came back to the original three again. There were alien artists who could speak, however crudely. They saw true. And one of them had made something that gave her hope. True comprehensibility might be attained. She took a recording of the identifier code she found with Night, Dawn and Day. Jennifer Pietchkov.

✦   ✦   ✦

The Council chamber lighting was subdued, but not so much as the emotion around the table. Torhok restrained his impatience as the *narmata* refused to settle. Urkhot, the rest of his staff, and many junior *'kri,* were off to the star they were calling Asth after the continent on Old Ardu, where Narrok consolidated his forces. That significantly cut down on the number of councilors he could rely on not to be swayed by the innate wrongheadedness of the Sleepers and *her.* The *shaxzhu* were honored for all the wrong reasons. They held these ideas that were going to get people killed, they obstructed the clear path to *Destoshaz holodah.*

And Narrok. He was so cautious. Why had *he* not been the one killed? *Lankha and I understood one another,* he thought. The *narmata* of the forces that had lurched out of the warp point, some of them air-bleeding wrecks that it was easier to scrap than rebuild, had been shaken. The *Destoshaz* under Lankha had never questioned her *sulhaji.* Or his.

Now that portion of his forces questioned all of it. Could unthinking creatures so outguess the admiral? How had they known to set up traps like that?

He shook off the questions they had put to him and that he had not yet answered. There was a reason for it, just not the patently false idea that the aliens could actually feel, or understand. This did not make them incapable of being either malicious or dangerous.

Ankaht sat, arms folded, eyes almost closed, the image of a *'kri* in meditation. He tried to discern her *selnarm* state, but failed. She was keeping everything down to a minimum. He didn't trust it.

"Councilors," Torhok said. "I propose First Claw Appep be promoted to admiral and sent to rebuild our forces in the *Fetket* system. (Problem solved.) To replace Admiral Lankha." (Mild regret.)

(Consensus.) *Well that was easy, but I didn't expect anyone to question my* Destoshaz *judgment.* (Satisfaction. Preparation.) "That concludes my contribution for now." (Tension. Anticipation.)

"I have a proposal to make." (Determination.) Ankaht spoke up from her end of the table, a claw clicking slowly on the table.

(Interest 12, Dismissal 3, Indifference 5.)

"Recently evidence has come to light that some aliens may have a rudimentary ability to communicate something faintly like *selnarm.*" (Excitement. Anticipation.)

(Interest 16, Dismissal 3, Indifference 1.)

Not this nonsense again. Torhok felt like he'd already killed this problem a dozen times and each time it was reborn immediately. There was no rest period, no waiting time. Ankaht brought it back to him each time and he was trying to curb his dislike but it kept sliding over toward hatred and it was more and more difficult to mitigate when in her presence and in the presence of others. She was disaster incarnate. *But she brought this up again because so many of the right-thinking councilors are away.* He unobtrusively rasped his grinders together. It was terrible. He was developing more and more physical expressions as he closed off his connection to *selnarm*.

"Elder," he said mildly, succeeding in mastering himself. (Interest.) "This is fascinating news. Does it look as though we may be able to actually get through to these creatures?" (Polite inquiry.) *I am thinking of naming the next few griarfeksh after you and ripping their throats out.* He didn't move, sitting and waiting, his hands still on the table, but startled himself with the virulence of his inner thought. *This is, perhaps, too extreme. I can't let her upset me this way.*

"I found that the aliens have displays of art." She waved a hand around the chamber to indicate and encompass the display pieces that served them all when discussion became too *ranarmata.*

Hachette sent (Negation.) before he began speaking. "I've seen their 'art.' It is as incomprehensible as the rest of their works. Ugly, discordant daubings." (Disagreement.)

(Confusion 4, Open to thought 15, Rejection 1.)

"But the point is that they produce it at all. Machines have no need for art. Animals do not create art." She actually leaned forward a fraction, she was so intent on her argument. "I propose we assemble a number of the creatures' artists and attempt to communicate with them." (Surety.)

There are too many here who are interested. With Admiral Lankha's death and our defeat, I just do not have the weight of hand to bury this idea again. But the wise warrior uses everything.

"I must concur with the Elder." Torhok said. (Support.) "The People bleed when we cannot achieve even basic understanding because the aliens' maddening behavior."

(—.) His abrupt support of an idea he'd fought and despised for so long, was so stunning that the *selnarm* almost stilled in the room. "I believe that the elder is the very Arduan to head this project, personally. Her other duties have been ably and capably dealt with and can be safely given to a junior for the short time I'm sure it will take for her to find our talking aliens." (Support. Wry humor.) "In fact I am certain that this act of *sokhata* on the part of the eldest will lead to the highest *matsokah.*" *I'll get her shuffled off to one side, tangled in her impossible task, and pried off the back of my neck, finally.* With that thought, he could let his real *selnarm* flow. (Intent to aid. Satisfaction.)

"I'm willing to oversee this, of course," Ankaht said carefully. (Startlement.) "I admit I didn't think to look for your support, Senior Admiral." (?)

"All it takes is *sulhaji*, the true seeing. That is our *narmata.*" (Concern.)

(Consideration 19, Uncertainty 1.)

Torhok looked over at Mahes, councilor for Civanrock. "Did you think, my friend, that our elder speaker isn't capable of this *matsoka*?" (Belief.) *I will see that she doesn't bother us again.*

Mahes was one of the strongest supporter that Torhok had here. And he was obviously too surprised to fall in line immediately. (Embarrassment.) "Of course not, Admiral. I was merely uncertain. I am no longer." He turned to Ankaht.

"I think that you and the senior admiral are right, Elder. You have my agreement."

(Consensus.)

"I will send you the *Destoshaz* to assist your staff in rounding up these so called 'artists' of yours, Elder," Torhok said. (Amiable.) *If I send some of the younger claws who are nervous of griarfeksh, I'm sure I can help start her project on the best possible course.* He smothered the gloating he felt when he imagined the *ranarmata* she would have if she had to restrain a hundred of these wild things. (Minor satisfaction.)

She stood. "Then since I have a new project to begin, and have consensus, I ask leave of the Council to begin." (Anticipation.)

"Of course, Elder." Torhok took it on himself to answer where Mahes would have. It sent a message of course, that he was letting no military setback diminish him. (Will to direct.) "Councilors, I should also inform you of new deployments I have in mind for Asth. Narrok will need a considerable force to pursue his style of assault and I propose there is a way to give it to him." (Intensity.) He heard the click as the door closed behind Ankaht as he began outlining his plans for the systems Narrok held. *Let her have her impossible project. She will be thoroughly closed out of the decision-making from now on.*

Jennifer leaned her head into one hand, tapping her stylus against the table as she listened to Lewis's vile "please wait" music. Click. "I'm back, Ms. Pietchkov—"

"Hey!" She had to interrupt him. "Since when was I Ms. Pietchkov to you? I just need access to Crossingford Gallery for a few hours. The pieces of mine that they have aren't too big for my truck to handle and Alessandro will help me get them. . ."

"Jennifer. I'm trying. No one is allowed into an area the aliens have claimed, period, even if they've stopped just shooting people. I for one am not going to test the canned warnings they have broadcasting. Jesus, I don't want to get you killed. It's not like they're burning or bombing anything in the cleared zone. Your artwork is probably safe enough in the gallery. Please don't ask me to try to get in there."

Jen sniffed, vainly trying to clear her sinuses. No one had warned her she'd have postnasal drip as a symptom of pregnancy. She was tired and could see it in her picture inset into the call screen. And she looked puffy again. "At least not until the end of next week. Thanks, Lewis."

"Sure, Jennifer."

She shut down the connection and eased back in her chair. Her kitchen table was covered in the stuff of business and a couple of empty cups, a half-eaten piece of pie. At least her ravenous appetite had eased up a bit. *Thirty-seven weeks. All I have to do is deal with another three-seven. Mom always said that pregnancy was two months too long.* The baby readjusted himself inside, running a heel or an elbow along the inside of her uterus, making her aware of how thin her skin and flesh really was at this point. "I'm a skin envelope, huh, baby." She was talking to the belly again. "Boy, will I be glad when it's just me in here again." More oil on the belly tonight.

Sunlight slanted through the sliding door at the back of the house and she could just see Alessandro outside, messing with his newest hobby. How and why he'd gotten into building remote-control vehicles, she just couldn't understand, even though he had no formal "work" he hadn't had time for hobbies for a long while. That's why they'd given up the historical re-creation.

But he had to do something. His company had just shut down and laid everyone off after the aliens came. There was just no point in trying to get out to the mothballed and hidden extraction facilities. No human traffic was allowed off-planet. The strange thing was that as long as the aircraft was on the ground the Baldies didn't trash it, but if it fired up its engines—zzzhpt—gone.

She felt tears welling up in her eyes as she watched him. They'd never gotten over that first argument, that first time he'd gone so distant and cold and it hurt. Jesu, it hurt. He was still there and sometimes at first, she'd thought they'd get over it. Even now she caught flashes of the old 'Sandro, when he rubbed her back for her, or made something to eat that she could actually stomach. Then he'd go icy again and storm out without saying anything and when he got back, at whatever time, he'd sleep in the guest room.

The entertainment unit in the living room turned itself on and brought up her favorite classical music program, Ijaba Danladi's *Phoenix Sonata* soothing her with its peaceful opening.

Jennifer laced her fingers together around her belly, feeling her baby bump. *I'm so weepy lately. I just lose it. Whether it's 'Sandro, or a stupid media presentation.* She tried to smile, even though she was still crying. Her dad would have said she didn't know her butt from breakfast. She didn't have any way of sending a message, so her parents didn't even know they were about to become grandparents. They had to be worried sick, but there was absolutely nothing she could do about it. No way to send mail to sunny Palma Brava, where they'd bought their retirement home.

"Illudor's claws, this list sucks," Enforcement Officer Shesmetet grumbled, waving the list reader under her partner's nose. (Frustration. Fear of *them*.)

"Yes." Tatenen pushed it back with one hand, driving with the other. "You would have to make things more difficult. You shoot one and the rest go nuts. Do you want to get this detachment killed? It would inconvenience more than just us. Don't kill any more of them. That's the orders." (Indifferent irritation.)

"But this list of identifiers. Half of them aren't here. Escher. Michelangelo. Kresaarkal-jahr'tergit. How can these be identifiers?"

"Illsblood! How should I know? Check the monitor, make sure those things aren't waking up." (Nervousness.)

Shesmetet turned toward the images she was getting from the back of their containment vehicle. "You think I'm not keeping an eye on the creepy little things?" (Anger.)

"Not so little, and I know you don't like lookin' at them." (Annoyance.)

She pulled back on her *selnarm*, refusing to give him her emotion, but continued checking the condition of the *griarfeksh* in the back. "Temperature and air circulation good. Still alive. Still unconscious."

"Good." (Petty annoyance.)

As the heavy rumble of alien trucks made itself apparent on the street, Jennifer was just stepping off the bottom stair. She paused, looking out the front window, seeing the Baldy vehicle stop in the street—a gold-skin and a dark-skin were getting out of it, while a third sat shotgun up on top. She'd never seen any of them close up since the invasion, only on vid, and it was amazing how much was lost on screen. To her they looked somehow more vital, more real somehow, yet at the same time more expressionless all at the same time.

"What's going on?" Alessandro asked, coming across the living room. Jennifer, from her position, still on the last step, put her hand on his shoulder.

"I don't know."

The two Baldies walked up the street so they couldn't see them from the window any longer.

"I hope to hell they go away." 'Sandro's voice was strained and he'd broken out in a sweat for some reason. Jennifer put her arm around his neck and he pulled her a bit closer but not enough to unbalance her; that was when the front gate squeaked and a second later, someone tried the door.

"Shit! I forgot to lock it!" Jennifer's other hand was over her mouth as the two Baldies walked in. She could feel 'Sandro tighten up rock hard as he stood still, as though confronted by a rabid dog.

"## ### ### ##### of Jennifer Pietchkov ### ###," The gold one said. The small dark one was looking at its hand screen, one hand on its sidearm.

"What?" He looked startled before shaking his head. "No," Alessandro said through clenched teeth. "No! There is no Jennifer Pietchkov, here!"

"### Come with ## Jennifer Pietchkov," Gold said. Dark unclipped the holster and was pulling out the weapon, when Jennifer stepped down in front of 'Sandro and spoke clearly.

"I'm Jennifer Pietchkov."

"Dammit, Jen!" Alessandro shouted and the two Baldies stepped back.

"I'm not letting them shoot you, love. That's what they do if you buck them, right?" She walked forward one step and then another when Gold reached out a hand toward her. It wrapped its tentacles around her wrist and she noted absently that it was like being touched by a warm, dry, extremely flexible leather belt. The claws lay neatly in callused slots when the hand closed, she noted. *I'm so frightened, I couldn't spit. I don't know what to feel.*

Behind her she could hear an anguished sound and half-turned as 'Sandro lunged to snatch her away from them. Dark couldn't pull the weapon out, they were standing too close, but Gold brought its other arm around, hand fisted around a metal tool.

It cracked into 'Sandro's forearm where he'd grabbed at Jennifer's, slid forward to punch into his belly, and snapped up into the middle of his face with a sound like a hammer hitting a thumb. 'Sandro, stepping back, hand up to block, his weight coming full on Jennifer's arm for only a second, crumpled to the ground streaming blood from nose and forehead.

Jennifer drew breath to scream when Dark brought up a canister and sprayed it in her face. Gold caught her as she collapsed, carried her out the door, and loaded her into the back of their vehicle.

Phoenix came to its thundering conclusion as the truck drove away, sending a plume of dust drifting in the door they'd left open, the fine yellow grains floating on the fresh blood on the floor.

Across the road the curtains twitched as a neighbor backed away from the window.

Her head felt as thick as two short planks and hurt like someone was hammering on them. Jennifer realized she was lying in such a way that her arm had fallen asleep and while her mouth was open, her eyes were closed.

The baby! was her first thought and her eyes snapped open, hands cradling her belly. The baby moved inside, kicking, reassuring her even as she sat up, looking around for 'Sandro. *'Sandro? They...*

they'd hit him. She could remember the beginning of the fight. The alien had moved fast. Either they'd taken 'Sandro too, or they'd left him and the team in the basement would have made sure he was okay after the aliens had left. She scrubbed her hands across her face. It had to be either of those two outcomes. Both of which left him alive. It just had to be.

There was no one else in the room. Two closed doors. No window. It looked as though someone with absolutely no color taste had tried to furnish a small bedroom. The bedspread under her was a bilious orange and she closed her eyes against the red pattern on the cushions, suddenly unsure whether her nausea was because of whatever drug they'd knocked her out with or the sickening toile.

There was a small drafting table and chair with a professional-quality lamp bolted to it. No window. She was fixating on that. A pitcher of water on the bedside shelf with a wineglass next to it. She picked it up and sniffed and tasted. It seemed to be water.

They've already drugged me once. If they wanted to poison me it probably wouldn't be like this. She drank straight out of the jug, suddenly realizing her thirst, her initial restraint thrown away with the first taste of cool water. The baby jumped. *If they've hurt my baby with whatever dumb, alien thing they're doing, I'll kill them with my bare hands. If they've killed—* She stopped, unable to complete the thought, still too dehydrated to cry easily. She set her teeth and put the jug down at the same time.

If they've killed Alessandro—once this baby is born— She couldn't even think of that. *One thing at a time. This baby has to be safely born, first.*

However dry she still felt, she needed to empty her bladder. *Quit jumping on mama's internal organs, junior.* That was when she felt the tears well up, as she tested both doors, one locked, the other opened on a bathroom, to her great relief.

As she washed her hands and face after relieving herself, she scanned the shelf over the tiny vanity. Some alien had apparently swept off several shelves in a drugstore. Shampoo, contraceptives, a can of cheese spread, party body-mod make-up. Bathroom tissue, toothpaste, eight toothbrushes. No hairbrush or comb. Hair-restorers, menstrual pads and sponges, a handful of random greeting cards and magazines. Jennifer dried her face. Thankfully there were towels, and facecloths. She stood, leaning her forehead against the wall, looking down at a box of Band-Aids, a bottle of children's cough syrup and a rubber doggie chew toy, and felt the weird urge to giggle. *Take us to your mall,* she thought, and started to cry. She scrubbed the tears away more roughly than she had to. *Stop that. Think logically. Why did they take me? I don't know. Where am I? Also an I-don't-know. But they've gone to some trouble to try and make me comfortable . . . with an ineptitude that says something about their experience dealing with us. Or anybody else?*

When the outer door opened, she froze for a second and turned as a female Baldy came in and stood in the center of the bedroom, looking through the door at her. She was one of the short, dark variant, wearing a robe that looked vaguely linenlike, but Jennifer, for all her eye, couldn't name the color exactly. Very unlike the limb-covering uniforms everyone had seen until now. There was gold in it, and green, and an odd violet.

Jennifer realized she was focusing on the clothing rather than look the alien in the eyes, those three eyes. She raised hers. The Baldy stared at her, impassive, unmoving as they seemed to do, the machine-in-idle-mode quality less pronounced somehow. The tentacles on the hands twitched finally and it went over to the chair at the desk and sat down, knotting the hands together in the lap.

It's acting like it's in the room with a potentially vicious dog, Jennifer thought angrily. *And it is what set this all up. If 'Sandro's hurt, I'll show her just how vicious I can be.* She set one hand against her belly and slowly came into the bedroom, easing sideways along the wall, as far from the Baldy as she could get, before sitting down on the end of the bed. It just watched her with that peculiar intensity.

Jennifer's scalp and neck tightened up and started itching; she shook her head and stared at her visitor. "Who are you and what do you want from me?" She shook her head again and ran her hands through her hair. "Where is 'Sandro? Is he all right?"

She knew that the Baldy couldn't understand the questions but had to ask. Then she shrugged and fell silent.

The Baldy finally said "### you ### ### ##### Jennifer Peitchkov?" The translator tried but that was all that came through. The dark skin of her arms and face flushed darker for a moment, then paled to almost a latte coffee color. It happened a moment after she spoke and didn't seem to be associated with the words.

"Yes. I am Jennifer Peitchkov." Jen tapped herself as she said it. The Baldies didn't seem to notice, or pick up on body motion, but it never hurt to try again. As long as they weren't shooting you out of hand. She tapped again. "Jennifer."

The Baldy sat, color shifting on her skin almost in waves, as still and foreign as a statue. Jennifer suddenly felt hot and that scalp itch was back. She scratched her head again and wished for a window. She got up and retreated to the bathroom, uncomfortable being still. She didn't even care that the Baldy actually twitched when she moved.

Jen ran more water over her wrists and drank some. She didn't want to go back into that room but there was nowhere else to go. She returned and sat down, staring at the Baldy with all the anger and discomfort she felt.

The alien hadn't moved other than the once. Now one hand unknotted itself from the ball of clenched tentacles on her lap and rose, almost uncomfortably, to tap herself on the chest, an awkward motion mimicking Jen's. "Ankaht," she said. "## #### ## talk."

Well for goodness sake, it's about time, Jen thought. *Someone at least has some sense. The only way I'm going to get out of here and get back to Alessandro, is to talk. Maybe we can even put a stop to the fighting, in the long run.* She pointed, since the Baldy seemed to be trying to understand gestures. *Hopefully this will get through the machine.* "Ankaht. Hello. You're right. Talk."

CHAPTER TWENTY-TWO

"Welcome to Zephrain, Admiral Li."

As her interorbital shuttle nosed its way into the hanger bay of the main space station of Xanadu Skywatch, Li Han examined her feelings with clinical detachment and realized, to her intense annoyance, that she had butterflies in her stomach.

Absurd! She made adjustments to the gold-edged deep-blue-and-white dress uniform she was wearing for this occasion in preference to the more usual civvies of her First Space Lord persona—and then became even more annoyed as she became aware she was doing it. *Self-consciousness too? Really, Han! You're acting about a tenth of your age.*

She had thought she was doing well on emergence from the warp point into the light of this sun that held so many bitter memories for her. The choice of Zephrain to host the first meeting of all the allied fleet commanders in chief had been a political one. The Rim Federation, after all, was the first star nation to be attacked by this new enemy-without-a-name. But she knew there was more to it than that. There was also the near-mythic status of the man who was about to welcome her to this system, where he had once held her captive.

She dismissed the thought defiantly. At least the Terran Republic's politicians had insisted on a compromise. The Rim Federation's capital system would host the conference, but it would actually take place aboard the TRN flagship. Han's lips formed a grim smile. TRNS *Taconic* had doubtless already caused eyebrows to raise and jaws to drop as she had eased into orbit around Xanadu. And she hadn't even shown them the inside yet. She was looking forward to that.

But first, of course, formality demanded that she first pay a call on her host. She anticipated a certain sense of unreality.

The shuttle came to rest and the hatch wheezed open. Li Han stood up, motioned to her entourage to wait, and stepped out onto the ramp all alone.

At once the cavernous hangar bay's sound system broke into the Terran Republic's anthem—a nice courtesy, she had to admit—and an honor guard of RFN Marines clicked to attention. The last time she had seen those forest-green tunics and black trousers, they had clothed her jailers. But she had no eyes for them. Her attention was riveted on the figure who stepped forward from a multispecies group at the foot of the ramp—a tall figure in the black-and-silver of the old Terran Federation Navy, but with the Rim shoulder flash. She descended the ramp to face him.

She had prepared herself for the fact that he would look no older than his early twenties. Reconciling that with his fleet admiral's insignia wasn't as hard for her as it would have been for someone from the centuries before antigerone treatments had blurred traditional notions of how authority figures were supposed to look. But it *was* hard to reconcile with her memories of a man who'd been older than her and looked it.

She wondered how he was coping with her pure white hair and general sixtyish appearance—and with the fact that now she too was a fleet admiral. But legally he had more seniority, even though she had more life experience, to the tune of what were traditionally called generations. And she was, of course, coming aboard *his* space station. So she saluted him with scrupulous correctness.

He returned her salute. "Welcome to Zephrain, Admiral Li." Yes, it was the same voice, even though formed by a physiologically younger throat. And his features were recognizable, though unlined. The absence of a beard and the presence of thick hair (*He must have loved that part,* she thought tartly) took some getting used to. But yes, it was he, beyond any possibility of doubt.

For an instant, they stood armored in formality.

Well, she decided, *someone has to make the first move. And I'm the older and—I like to think—wiser.*

"I imagine, Admiral Trevayne, you never expected to say those precise words."

"Actually," he said with the dryness she remembered, "I've had some practice. You're the *second* Admiral Li we've welcomed to the Rim Federation. And since Third Bellerophon, we've been very glad to have the first one."

"Thank you, Admiral," she replied, determined to keep up the badinage. "I hope I don't turn out to be a disappointment by comparison with my daughter."

"I hardly think so. I'm only glad our warp point was able to accommodate your ship."

She smiled in spite of herself. "Yes, that would have been awkward, wouldn't it? But we naturally took it into account. And I'm looking forward to receiving you and the other allied commanders aboard *Taconic.*"

"Not as much as I'm looking forward to touring the prototype devastator," he said with an unaffected eagerness that seemed more in keeping with his apparent age than his actual one, however defined. "But first, let me introduce you to my colleagues."

First Fang of the Khan Thraaiewlahk'gahrnak was currently Sky Marshal by virtue of a tradition that alternated human and Orion officers in the post of the PSUN's military commander in chief. His whiskers were luxuriant, his coppery pelt beginning to show the silver that betokened age in a race for which no equivalent of the antigerone regimen had ever been discovered. Li Han made a point of being especially courteous in exchanging salutes with him, and took care to demonstrate her understanding of the Tongue of Tongues. The Terran Federation's proposed amalgamation with the Khanate had been the proximate cause of the Fringe Revolution, and the people of the Terran Republic still had a reputation—which Han knew to be false, albeit understandable—for anti-Orion bigotry. But the old Tabby lost no time in relieving her of any anxiety she might have felt.

"Ahhdmiraaaal Liii, I am honored to meet the First Fang of your nation—and even more honored to meet the mother of your daughter.

Least Fang Zhaairnow'ailaaioun has related the tale of how she made possible the escape of many of the *Zheeerlikou'valkhannaiee*, at great risk to herself, while taking a heavy toll of the *chofaki*. Our claws are hers," he concluded formally.

"I am honored, First Fang, as I am sure she would be." Li Han meant it. She didn't claim to be an expert on the Orions, of whom there were none in the Republic, but she knew what that last expression of honor debt meant. If Mags ever needed anyone killed, she had only to ask.

Thraaiewlahk introduced her to his staffers. They included both of the PSU's principal races, and one Gorm, Tolkaru, known as "Task Force Leader" among a race that had no structured system of military ranks. The gray, thick-hided centauroid was standing at his race's equivalent of "attention," on the lowest pair of limbs alone, which brought his eerily humanlike face to a height of three meters. But Li Han controlled her annoyance at having to look even further up than usual. The race's status inside-but-not-of the Khanate had always puzzled humans, and its relationship to the PSU was almost as ambivalent as the Rim Federation's. There was no ambivalence about the respect in which the massive heavy-planet dwellers were held as fighters, however.

"Fleet Admiral Zhwaaraa of the Ophiuchi Association Defense Command," Trevayne concluded the introductions. Li Han recalled that Terra's long-standing allies the Ophiuchi had adopted the human naval rank structure. She also recalled that they had broken out of the warp cul-de-sac that had long confined them, by unintended courtesy of a race called the Sedua who had been ill-advised enough to attack them through a closed warp point. So their traditional minor-power status was now rapidly becoming a thing of the past. And they had always been handy in a fight, for the simple reason that they were the best fighter pilots in the known galaxy, not excepting the Orions. Descendants of avians, they had evolved into tool users at the cost of the ability to fly—but *not* at the cost of the innate sense of relative motion in three dimensions that was their heritage. Once again, Li Han had to strain her neck to look up into Zhwaaraa's beaked and crested countenance, for his feathered, hollow-boned body, somewhat similar to that of an emaciated humanoid, lifted it two and a half meters.

Li Han introduced her own staffers. "In addition," she concluded, "I asked Dr. Kasugawa to accompany me. He agreed, even though

Dr. Desai could ill afford to spare him. You'll be meeting him aboard *Taconic*."

"Ah, yes." Trevayne nodded. "I'm definitely looking forward to making *his* acquaintance, in light of what we've all heard. Ah ... I gather Dr. Desai herself has not accompanied you."

"No," Li Han said carefully. "Strictly speaking, she is *Admiral* Desai now. She is back on the active list, and is working with the PSU's Bureau of Ships. The press of her affairs made it impossible for her to come."

"Too bad. I'd looked forward to seeing her. She used to be my chief of staff, you know."

"Yes, I know," said Li Han, who also had a very good idea of the real reason for Desai's absence—although, she reflected, Trevayne's impossible physical youth might, paradoxically, have made it easier. "And now, let me invite everyone aboard *Taconic*. We are rather proud of her, you know."

The allied brass were still looking somewhat dazed from their tour of *Taconic* when they took their seats (or whatever; Li Han mentally congratulated herself for remembering to lay in some of the saddlelike couches the Gorm used for chairs) in the conference room.

Some of them looked a bit puzzled as they took their places on the crescent-shaped terraces that overlooked the vast holo tank in which floated an immaterial warp-line chart of the Bellerophon Arm and a great deal else besides. Why, they wondered, was a three-dimensional display needed?

Li Han took her place at a table facing the guests from across the tank. Dr. Kasugawa shared the table with her. He was, she could tell, even more of a focus of interest than the holo tank, for by now all of these people had heard of his and Sonja Desai's work.

"Admiral Trevayne," she began formally, "as most senior officer present, and as military commander in chief of the Rim Federation, the first victim of these beings' aggression, I will ask you to open these proceedings by summarizing the situation with respect to the Bellerophon Arm."

"Thank you, Admiral Li." Trevayne stepped around the holo tank to take her place at the table, moving with a jauntiness appropriate to his apparent youth. But when he spoke, any illusion of callowness vanished. "Not to put too fine a point on it, the 'situation' is bloody awful. You've all been provided with the statistical summary of Admiral Waldeck's latest attempt to break into the Bellerophon System. I and my staff have analyzed it, and have concluded that no blame can be attached to him or anyone else for its failure. I have so informed the cabinet of the Rim Federation. I believe the same can be said for the more recent attempt to counterattack the incursion into the Pan-Sentient Union." A growl of gloomy agreement came from Thraaiewlahk's direction. "In both cases, we inflicted heavy losses on the enemy, partly due to our neutralization of the 'stealth scrambler.' We are, of course, routing reinforcements to Second Fleet in the Astria system, and can continue to build up our force there practically ad infinitum. But while we're doing so, the enemy is breaking up more of his smaller generation ships into system defense ships."

There was a heavy silence. *Taconic* had, in an odd way, brought home to these people the system defense ships' almost inconceivable size. Touring the devastator, they hadn't been able to forget that an SDS was *three hundred times* its tonnage. Trevayne let them think about it a moment before continuing inexorably.

"All the quibbling in the galaxy about the relative inefficiency of the SDS's design can't alter the firepower advantage it gives them. And while its lack of speed and maneuverability would put it at a disadvantage in a war of movement, we have to break away from the warp point before it can *become* a war of movement. That's what Admiral Waldeck tried to do. And we know what came of it."

"Yes," Thraaiewlahk acknowledged. "Their fighters are no match for our space superiority fighters at anything like even odds—that much was demonstrated. But we all know the difficulty of launching fighters in sufficient numbers while a warp-point assault is still in progress. That is even more true with these monster ships. They can smother the transiting ships with missile fire from long range like the *chofaki* they are." He barely troubled to keep the contempt out of his voice. *Chofaki*—delicately translated into Standard English as "dirt eaters"—meant beings too inherently honorless to be amenable to the warrior code of *theernowlus*. "And because our ships must be able to make warp transits, there is no escaping their crippling disadvantage in size—even with this awesome ship of yours, Ahhdmiraaaal Liii. No," the old Orion continued, drawing himself up and visibly mustering the moral courage to face up to an intolerable truth. "I see no way to carry out a warp-point assault without incurring totally unacceptable casualties."

There was dead silence. Everyone knew what it had cost Thraaiewlahk to say that. When an Orion called casualties "unacceptable," he was taken seriously.

After a moment, Li Han spoke with the diffidence she had never managed to entirely lose, even though she knew not everyone found it either convincing or endearing. "Admiral Trevayne ... First Fang ... Admiral Zhwaaraa ... I gather we are agreed that we find ourselves at an impasse." No one broke the gloom to contradict her. She stood up. "The Terran Republic—with the help of the Pan-Sentient Union—is prepared to propose a way to break that impasse."

She could tell she had their undivided attention.

"You have the floor, Admiral Li," said Trevayne.

She stepped around the table and pointed a remote at the warp-line display in the tank. An icon in the Bellerophon Arm began to flash on and off for attention. It was a backwater: a cul-de-sac system with only one warp point, at the end of a "spur" connected to the main arm through a starless warp nexus.

"The Borden System," said Li Han. "A red dwarf star with no habitable planets." Leaving her audience to wonder why she had even mentioned such a worthless bit of cosmic detritus, she walked around the perimeter of the tank to an area where the spreading warp network extended into the Terran Republic. She pointed her remote again, and another icon began to blink. "ZQ-147," she stated. "A starless warp nexus."

The general puzzlement deepened, as the two icons flickered across the tank from each other.

Li Han permitted herself a smile which, in anyone else, would have been called mischievous. "Our programmers are very proud of themselves for this," she murmured, and pointed the remote again. . . .

Chaos!

There was a collective hubbub as everyone rose to their feet to stare down into the tank, where the string-lights of warp lines had vanished and the icons of star systems—far fewer icons, it seemed— were scrambled into a pattern with no resemblance to the former one, with the colors of the various star nations all intermingled.

The only apparent connection between the new display and the former one was the two blinking icons. But now they were side by side, practically touching.

"What you are seeing," Li Han explained, "is something no one except astronomers has given any thought to for centuries: the *real* arrangement of the stars in three-dimensional space—the space of Newton and Einstein. Only a fraction of those from the warp line display show at all, for the simple reason that most of them lie outside the volume of space this display includes—*far* outside it in many cases. But the important fact is this: the Borden system and the ZQ-147 warp nexus lie only 2.21 light-years apart in real space." (She used the traditional measure of interstellar distances, based on the year of Old Terra.)

"Ssso we sssee," said Zhwaaraa in the silibant tones his race gave to Standard English. "But the relevanccce . . .?"

Li had restored the warp-line display, to the general relief. "We propose an expedition from ZQ-147 to Borden . . . an expedition across normal space."

"Across *normal space?*" someone blurted. A low hubbub arose at such an unheard-of idea.

"Precisely. The purpose will be to transport a Kasugawa generator." The confused buzz halted abruptly. "You are all aware by now of the work Doctors Kasugawa and Desai have been doing. You know that paired and aligned Kasugawa generators, activated simultaneously, can in effect punch a hole in the continuum"—Dr. Kasugawa winced as though in severe intestinal pain—"and forge a new warp line between them. We meant to take advantage of this. Once the generator is in place in the Borden System, we will use it to open a direct warp link—the first *artificial* warp link in history— between that system and ZQ-147, where the second generator of the pair will be located." She pointed the remote again, but this time it was like a sword thrust. A very long string-light appeared, stretching more than halfway across the tank from one flashing icon to the other. "I will then undertake to lead a fleet of devastators through this warp link into the Bellerophon Arm. As I'm sure you all agree after your tour of this ship, the devastators are far more formidable than anything the enemy has except the system defense ships—and those are confined to the Bellerophon System by their sheer size, which makes warp transit out of the question for them. We will retake all of the Arm except Bellerophon itself, into which the enemy will be sealed. They will, of course, continue to strengthen the defenses of Bellerophon, but they will have only the finite resources of that system to do it with. And those defenses will have to be split between two or more warp points rather than concentrated on one. We will finally be able to fight our way into Bellerophon and liberate it, which of course is our primary objective."

The basso profundissimo of the Gorm's otherwise astonishingly good Standard English broke the silence. "I can see certain problems with this," said Tolkaru, even as he rapidly manipulated the minicomputer strapped to one of his massive primary arms. "First of all, the route from Borden to the main Bellerophon Arm leads through the starless warp nexus BR-06 to the Mercury binary system. And that warp connection is impassable even to a supermonitor, much less to a devastator."

"Evidently, Task Force Leader, you have not been exhaustively briefed on the capabilities of the Kasugawa generator. It can be used to increase the capacity of existing warp points—'dredge' them, as Dr. Desai put it, using a term derived from Old Terra's wet-navy history—to up to twice that needed to accommodate a devastator. Our fleet will carry additional generators for this purpose."

"All very well," hissed Zhwaaraa. "But the fact remainsss that the Desai Drive's top ssspeed is only one half that of light."

"Precisely," said Thraaiewlahk with the nod he had picked up over many years of association with humans. "So the crossing you propose would take four point four two Standard years. Of course, the crews would enjoy some relativistic time-dilation advantage—"

"To be exact, First Fang, the voyage from ZQ-147 to Borden would take three point eight five subjective years at the zero point five c possible to the Desai Drive." Li Han raised a hand. "Before anyone draws any conclusions from that, I would ask that Dr. Kasugawa be heard, for I have asked him and Dr. Desai to turn their attention to the problems inherent in my proposal."

There was no objection, and the elderly scientist stood slowly up. "Elderly" was a word that came naturally to people, even though he was well under a century. He had come to antigerone treatments fairly late, and had the look that humans still tended to associate with mature wisdom.

"First Space Lord Li already knows what I am about to tell you, as a result of the PSU's new policy of information sharing with the

Terran Republic. But I must ask you to regard it as sensitive beyond even the overall classification of this meeting.

"Briefly, and in nontechnical language, Dr. Desai and I believe it will be possible to achieve very significant improvements in performance over the Desai Drive. We have dubbed this new application the 'Desai Prime' drive. It is an 'all-or-nothing' drive which can only operate at its top speed, attained instantaneously, of approximately zero point eight five c." Kasugawa waited for the gasps to die down before continuing in somber tones. "There are drawbacks. The most obvious is that the drive has no tactical applications, as it is moving at maximum velocity or not at all. More seriously, this velocity is at the very limit of radiation and particle shielding's ability to protect a crew. Nevertheless, if the drive proves to be practical—"

"If?'" someone queried.

"—as Dr. Desai has every confidence that it will, the duration of the expedition Admiral Li proposes will be reduced to two point six Standard years from the standpoint of an outside observer, or only one point three seven standard year as experienced by the crew."

"Thank you, Dr. Kasugawa,' said Li Han, perhaps a little too hastily. "I should point out," she continued, addressing the audience, "that the transit time, while admittedly very long compared to the interstellar travel times to which we have been accustomed for centuries, is in a sense no disadvantage at all. It will take very nearly that long to complete the construction of the devastators we have earmarked for the offensive anyway."

Tolkaru was not to be sidetracked. "Let us discuss the crew of this expedition," he rumbled in the inexorable Gormish way. "One assumes that they will be volunteers—"

"Naturally," Li Han interjected.

"—and that they will be provided with the best shielding and armor modern science can provide. Nevertheless, on the optimistic assumption that they survive the voyage, we must consider what will happen when they arrive. What if the Kasugawa generator fails to work? They would be stranded, would they not?"

"That is correct, Task Force Leader," Li Han replied unflinchingly.

Thraaiewlahk spoke up . . . and in tones that caused Li Han's heart to sink. She had been counting on his support, for as an Orion he would hardly be concerned with risk to the volunteer crew. "I have studied the data on the Kasssugawwa generator. It is, of necessity, a massive piece of equipment. We must assume that the ship will be built around it—essentially, the generator and a very long-term life-support system with a Desssai Prime drive attached. It could not possibly carry any significant armament."

"No, First Fang," Li Han admitted, knowing what was coming next.

"So if the ship arrives at its destination and finds the enemy in possession of that system, it will be unable to defend itself."

"We have no knowledge that the enemy have, in fact, occupied the Borden System, First Fang." Li Han could hear the lameness in her own voice.

"No. In fact, we have no knowledge whatsoever of what has transpired in the Arm since the initial enemy incursion, do we? So you cannot deny the possibility that the enemy may have picketed the destination system. And if they have, then the expedition will be defenseless prey." The old Orion held her eyes, and she could not look away. "It was you humans, Ahhdmiraaaal Liii, who taught my ancestors—and charged a heavy tuition for the lesson—that the honor of a warrior must be subordinated to the cold logic of military necessity. It is an *absolute* necessity that the Kasssugawwa generator must not fall into the hands of these *chofaki,* who are already very experienced in normal-space interstellar flight. The potential consequences do not bear contemplating." He gave a head shake that was as uncannily human as his nod. "No. This is too risky."

Li Han looked around desperately. She could see—no, feel—the sense of the meeting going Thraaiewlahk's and Tolkaru's way.

Then, just as the general mood was about to congeal into a firm consensus of opposition, Ian Trevayne rose slowly to his feet.

He had been oddly silent for a long time. It had almost been possible to forget that he was there. But now all the hum of negativity ceased, one whispered conversation at a time, until he stood in the midst of dead silence.

How the hell does he do it? she wondered, as she had wondered so many times before, and with the same flare of resentment. Was it the mythic clout he now wielded? But she knew better than that. It was something inherent to the man himself, however youthful the fleshly guise his essence currently wore.

"First Fang"—his deep baritone rolled over the room—"are we agreed that the Borden system is uninhabitable?"

"Of course," said Thraaiewlahk, clearly curious as to what Trevayne was driving at.

"And are we also agreed that it is a cul-de-sac system—a dead end with only one warp point?"

"This is self-evident."

"Very well, then. Even if we assume that the enemy has extended his control that far into the Bellerophon Arm . . . why should he keep any forces whatsoever in such a manifestly worthless system?"

Thraaiewlahk opened his mouth, then closed it again.

"I am in favor of Admiral Li's proposal." Trevayne's voice did not appreciably rise in volume, but in some indefinable way it filled the room to the exclusion of anything else. "She has offered us a way out of this intolerable deadlock. Does anyone have another way to offer? No? Well, I'm sure I bloody well don't! So I say our only honorable course is to support her to the hilt."

"But Admiral Trevayne," said Tolkaru in a kind of stammering rumble, "we cannot ignore the concerns the First Fang has raised, even if—as you have suggested—the probability is extremely low."

"Granted." Trevayne paused a moment. "It has already been established that the crew of this expedition will be volunteers, with a full understanding of what they are risking. I propose that the terms under which they volunteer include an agreement that, if absolutely necessary, they will blow up the ship rather than let it be captured." He gave his trademark crooked grin. "This may make it harder to get volunteers—but we'll still get them."

"We cannot take it upon ourselves to make such a decision," Tolkaru protested—but weakly, for a Gorm. "Our governments—"

"The government of the Terran Republic is already behind it," Li Han stated flatly.

"And I," said Ian Trevayne, "will undertake to assure that the Rim Federation will be." They all stared at him, knowing that he could do precisely that. "So if the Pan-Sentient Union . . ." He looked at Thraaiewlahk and raised one interrogatory eyebrow.

"*Yes!*" The Orion surged to his feet. "If we do not seize this chance, we forfeit the name of warriors! May our claws strike deep!"

You magnificent bastard! thought Li Han, staring at Trevayne. *You knew damned well that with that suicide-pact clause you made this plan the concentrated, purified, and distilled essence of* theernowlus— *literally, "risk bearing." You played Thraaiewlahk like a Stradivarius!*

"I agree," said Zhwaaraa. There wasn't a lot else the avian could have done in the face of the big-power consensus that had emerged. "But I sssuggest that we not ignore contingency planning in event of lack of sssuccesss. There is a human proverb—which we have alwaysss found to be in quessstionable tassste—about putting all of your eggssss in one basssket."

"Of course, Admiral," Trevayne nodded. ""We must not limit ourselves to a single technique. In particular, we should press forward with conventional survey work, in the hope of finding 'natural' warp lines into either or both of the isolated areas via closed warp points." There was a rumble of agreement, as everyone recalled the Bug War and the ultimately successful search for "El Dorado," the closed warp point into the Arachnids' Home Hive systems. "But we must recognize that it is only by statistically improbable chance that this can yield results."

"We must also continue to press conventional offensives along the known lines of approach," Tolkaru cautioned. "If only to keep the enemy's attention focused on the threats of which they are already aware."

"Also," Dr. Kasugawa piped up, "do not overlook the possibility of using other generators within our own existing warp networks, to create new cross-connections—"

"Yes!" Thraaiewlahk exclaimed. "This has the potential to improve our logistics immeasurably."

"And to provide routes around warp nexi that may be cut off in the future by new enemy incursions," added Tolkaru pessimistically.

"These ideas all have distinct possibilities, and will certainly be followed up," said Trevayne firmly. "But the fact remains that Admiral Li's is the only focused, war-winning strategy currently open to us. It is Bellerophon's only hope of liberation within the foreseeable future. It must be the centerpiece of our planning. And we must represent this to our governments in the strongest possible terms. Are we agreed?"

And so it was agreed. The course of the war was set.

As they were departing, Li Han managed to catch Trevayne alone.

"Admiral Trevayne . . . thank you," she said, not without difficulty. Then, with even more difficulty: "I . . . couldn't have done that."

"Oh, tosh!" he said airily. "I have a feeling that what really did it was the sight of the two of us on the same side. I fancy none of them had ever expected to see that."

"Probably not," she agreed with a smile. But beneath her smile, she wondered what it must have been like, seeing two legendary archenemies standing together. "I certainly never did."

"Then," he said, suddenly serious, "perhaps you can imagine what it's like for me. Remember, what . . . occurred between us is a matter of recent memory in my case. I haven't had eight subjective decades for it to fade."

"I hadn't thought of it like that," she admitted. "Yes, I suppose the past was more difficult for you to overcome. Not," she had to add, "that it wasn't difficult for me. But . . . I think we've overcome it."

"I think we may have. Later generations will just have to come up with another pair of names to use as a byword for enmity."

"Their problem," she said shortly. She extended her hand. He took it. A journey ended, and another began. Neither of them knew where it would end. But they both knew it had begun.

Epilogue

This time the weather was terrible as Ankaht stood by her cairn where she had buried her memory box. She realized now why she'd chosen the spot. It reminded her of her father's house.

Who would have guessed, when she and Harrok had stood looking out over the sea and the mountains, and begun the enormous task of evacuating the People to another star, that she would have found *this*. Not just one new planet, but many and all of them with other creatures on them.

What an interesting conversation they would have once he reached rebirth again and grew to the age of reason. It was possible that he would be reborn as her son, though that was unlikely. She missed his support.

I wonder... I suppose he would believe that Illudor would have many more tentacles than just us. And I know he would have probably challenged Torhok before now.

She braced herself as the wind howled from the ocean, up the cliffs. It was such a beautiful planet. The rain would be on her soon, the dark *vrel* and *herrm* and green-gray clouds billowed up over the far shore, bright sparks of distant lightning connecting cloud and sky for microseconds. She told herself that she should go in, but the beauty and violence of the storm suited her mood suddenly and she waited for it.

Too many of the People are dying in this war. We should be bringing more people out of the interlife. I admit to selfishness—if we are not increasing it will put off the time when I will meet my parents in this life, again. Torhok and his Destolfi montu shilkiene *is going to bring us disaster.*

She was training hard, now. Not knowing whether she could challenge the senior admiral yet, but aiming for the day when she needed to. She could see it coming. *That is the* narmata *of another time.*

The sound of the thunder finally reached her hearing, a rumble that she could feel in the pounding sea on the cliffs below, the waves whipped up and running before the storm. She let her *sulhaji* of the situation go, let it get ripped away from her the way the wind whipped the breath away from her.

When I can, I will build a villa here, once we have a peaceful world again. We will stand on my terrace, that soul and I, and contemplate the shining vrel *ocean.*

Appendix: Arduan Glossary

Asth: a continent on Ardu; later, a new star system

at'holodahk: insult to enlightenment

Anaht'doh Kainat: Star Wanderers

crivan: a color invisible to humans in the ultraviolet range

Destolfi montu shilkiene: a philosophical statement; "death is but a tiny thing"

Destoshaz: warrior caste

Fetket: Arduan name for Jason star system

Flixit: a small, songbirdlike creature like a cross between a bird and a lizard

Griarfeksh: a bald, semiaquatic scavenger with nasty habits

herrm: another color humans cannot perceive

holodah: a satorilike state of enlightenment

holodah'kri: high priest

Illudor: the name of God

kreevix fly: an insect like a mayfly

'kri: priest

maatkah: a form of Arduan hand-to-hand combat

matsokah: training of the soul

murn: a color invisible to humans and Orions on the infrared end of the spectrum

Myrtak: the Arduan Einstein

narmata: group harmony or harmonious action

ranarmata: chaos, disharmony in action; willful disarray

Sekahmant: a blue giant star 1.973 parsecs from the Arduan sun

selnarm: the empathetic sense

shaxzhu: one who has past-life memories

shaxzhutok: the state of having past-life memories

shotan: sense/taste

skeerba: a three-bladed knife that sits on the hand like a set of brass knuckles

sokhata: soul building

sulhaji: true vision

vrel: a color invisible to humans

xen-narmatum: forever outside order

yihrt: a larger murn- and black-colored predator on Ardu